ARMOREL OF LYONESSE

Emanuel Rosevean takes the rubies

ARMOREL OF LYONESSE

A ROMANCE OF TODAY

by

WALTER BESANT

A FACSIMILE REPRINT
OF THE 1939, LONDON IMPRESSION
WITH DRAWINGS BY
ANASTASIA KASHIAN
PRINTED IN 1993
BY LLANERCH PUBLISHERS, FELINFACH.
ISBN 1 897853 11 4

CONTENTS

PART I.

PART II.

CONTENTS

ARMOREL OF LYONESSE

PART I

CHAPTER I

THE CHILD OF SAMSON

It was the evening of a fine September day. Through the square window, built out so as to form another room almost as large as that which had been thus enlarged, the autumn sun, now fast declining to the west, poured in warm and strong; but not too warm or too strong for the girl on whose head it fell as she sat leaning back in the low chair, her face turned towards the window. The sun of Scilly is never too fierce or too burning in summer, nor in winter does it ever lose its force; in July, when the people of the adjacent islands of Great Britain and Ireland venture not forth into the glare of the sun, here the soft sea mists and the strong sea air temper the heat; and in December the sun still shines with a lingering warmth, as if he loved the place. This girl lived in the sunshine all the year round; rowed in it; lay in it; basked in it bare-headed, summer and winter; in the winter she would sit sheltered from the wind in some warm corner of the rocks; in summer she would lie on the hillside or stand upon the high headlands and the sea-beat crags, while the breezes, which in the Land of Lyonesse do never cease, played with her long tresses and kept her soft cheek cool.

The window was wide open on all three sides; the girl had been doing some kind of work, but it had dropped from her hands, and now lay unregarded on the floor; she was gazing upon the scene before her, but with the accustomed eyes which looked out upon it every day. A girl who has such a picture continually before her all day long never tires of it, though she may not be always consciously considering it and praising it. The stranger, for his part, cannot choose but cry aloud for admiration; but the native, who knows it as no stranger can, is silent. The house, half-way up the low hill, looked out upon the south—to be exact, its aspect was S.W. by S.—so that from this window the girl saw always, stretched out at her feet, the ocean, now glowing in the golden sunshine of September. Had she been tall enough, she might even have seen the coast of South America, the nearest land in the far distance. Looking S.W., that is, she would have seen the broad mouth of Oroonooque and the shores of El Dorado. This broad sea-scape was broken exactly in the middle by the Bishop's Rock and its stately lighthouse rising tall and straight out of the water; on the left hand the low hill of Annet shut out the sea; and on the right Great Minalto, rugged and black, the white foam always playing round its foot or flying over its great black northern headland, bounded and framed the picture. Almost in the middle of the water, not more than two miles distant, a sailing ship, all sails set, made swift way, bound outward one knows not whither. Lovely at all times is a ship in full sail, but doubly lovely when she is seen from afar, sailing on a smooth sea, under a cloudless sky, the sun of afternoon lighting up her white sails. No other ships were in sight; there was not even the long line of smoke which proclaims the steamer below the horizon; there was not even a Penzance fishing-boat tacking slowly homewards with brown sails and its two masts: in this direction there was no other sign of man.

The girl, I say, saw this sight every day: she never tired of it, partly because no one ever tires of the place in which he was born and has lived—not even an Arab of the Great Sandy Desert; partly because the sea, which has been called, by unobservant poets, unchanging, does in fact change—face, colour, mood, even shape—every day, and is never the same, except, perhaps, when the east wind of March covers the sky with a monotony of grey, and takes the colour out of the face of ocean as it takes the colour from the granite rocks, last year's brown and yellow fern, and the purple heath. To this girl, who lived with the sea around her, it always formed a setting, a background, a frame for her thoughts and dreams. Wherever she went, whatever she said or sang, or thought or did, there was always in her ears the lapping or the lashing of the waves; always before her eyes was the white surge flying over the rocks; always the tumbling waves. But, as for what she actually thought or what she dreamed, seeing how ignorant of the world she was, and how innocent and how young, and as for what was passing in her mind this afternoon as she sat at the window, I know not. On the first consideration of the thing, one would be inclined to ask how, without knowledge, can a girl think, or imagine, or dream anything? On further thought, one understands that knowledge has very little to do with dreams or fancies. Yet, with or without knowledge, no poet, sacred bard, or prophet has ever been able to divine the thoughts of a girl, or to interpret them, or even to set them down in consecutive language. I suppose they are not, in truth, thoughts. Thought implies reasoning and the connection of facts, and the experience of life as far as it has gone. A young maiden's mind is full of dimly seen shadows and pallid ghosts which flit across the brain and disappear. These shadows have the semblance of shape, but it is dim and uncertain: they have the pretence of colour, but it changes every moment: if they seem to show a face, it vanishes immediately and is forgotten. Yet these shadows smile upon the young with kindly eyes; they beckon with their fingers, and point to where, low down on the horizon, with cloudy outline, lies the Purple Island—to such a girl as this the future is always a small island girt by the sea, far off and lonely. The shadows whisper to her; they sing to her; but no girl has ever yet told us—even if she understands—what it is they tell her.

She had been lying there, quiet and motionless, for an hour or more, ever since the tea-things had been taken away—at Holy Hill they have tea at half-past four. The ancient lady who was in the room with her had fallen back again into the slumber which held her nearly all day long as well as all the night. The house seemed thoroughly wrapped and lapped in the softest peace and stillness; in one corner a high clock, wooden-cased, swung its brass pendulum behind a pane of glass with solemn and sonorous chronicle of the moments, so that they seemed to march rather than to fly. A clock ought not to tick as if Father Time were hurried and driven along without dignity and by a scourge. This clock, for one, was not in a hurry. Its tick showed that Time rests not—but hastes not. There is admonition in such a clock. When it has no one to admonish but a girl whose work depends on her own sweet will, its voice might seem thrown away; yet one never knows the worth of an admonition. Besides, the clock suited the place and the room. Where should Time march with solemn step and slow, if not on the quiet island of Samson, in the archipelago of Scilly? On its face was written the name of its maker, plain for all the world to see—'Peter Trevellick, Penzance, A.D. 1741.'

The room was not ceiled, but showed the dark joists and beams above, once painted, but a long time ago. The walls were wainscotted and painted drab, after an old fashion now gone out: within the panels hung coloured prints, which must have been there since the beginning of this century. They represented rural subjects—the farmer sitting before a sirloin of beef, while his wife, a cheerful nymph, brought him 'Brown George,' foaming with her best home-brewed; the children hung about his knees expectant of morsels; or the rustic bade farewell to his sweetheart, the recruiting-sergeant waiting for him, and the villagers, to a woman, bathed in tears. There were half a dozen of those compositions simply coloured. I believe they are now worth much money. But there were many other things in this room worth money. Opposite the fireplace stood a cabinet of carved oak, black with age, precious beyond price. Behind its glass windows one could see a collection of things once strange and rare—things which used to be brought home by sailors long before steamers ploughed every ocean and globe-trotters trotted over every land. There were wonderful things in coral, white and red and pink; Venus's-fingers from the Philippines; fans from the Seychelles; stuffed birds of wondrous hue, daggers and knives, carven tomahawks, ivory toys, and many other wonders from the far East and fabulous Cathay. Beside the cabinet was a wooden desk, carved in mahogany, with a date of 1645, said to have been brought to the islands by one of the Royalist prisoners whom Cromwell hanged upon the highest carn of Hangman's Island. There was no escaping Cromwell—not even in Scilly any more than in Jamaica. In one corner was a cupboard, the door standing open. No collector ever came here to gaze upon the treasures unspeakable of cups and saucers, plates and punchbowls. On the mantelshelf were brass candlesticks and silver candlesticks, side by side with 'ornaments' of china, pink and gold, belonging to the artistic reign of good King George the Fourth. On the hearthrug before the fire, which was always burning in this room all the year round, lay an old dog sleeping.

Everybody knows the feeling of a room or a house belonging to the old. Even if the windows are kept open, the air is always close. Rest, a gentle, elderly angel, sits in the least frequented room with folded wings. Sleep is always coming to the doors at all hours: for the sake of Rest and Sleep the house must be kept very quiet: nobody must ever laugh in the house: there is none of the litter that children make: nothing is out of its place: nothing is disturbed: the furniture is old-fashioned and formal: the curtains are old and faded: the carpets are old, faded, and worn: it is always evening: everything belonging to the house has done its work: all together, like the tenant, are sitting still—solemn, hushed, at rest, waiting for the approaching end.

The only young thing at Holy Hill was the girl at the window. Everything else was old—the servants, the farm labourers, the house and the furniture. In the great hooded arm-chair beside the fire reposed the proprietor, tenant, or owner of all. She was the oldest and most venerable dame ever seen. At this time she was asleep: her head had dropped forward a little, but not much; her eyes were closed; her hands were folded in her lap. She was now so very ancient that she never left her chair except for her bed; also, by reason of her great antiquity, she now passed most of the day in sleep, partly awake in the morning, when she gazed about and asked questions of the day. But sometimes, as you will presently see, she revived again in the evening, became lively and talkative, and suffered her memory to return to the ancient days.

By the assistance of her handmaidens, this venerable lady was enabled to present an appearance both picturesque and pleasing, chiefly because it carried the imagination back to a period so very remote. To begin with, she wore her bonnet all day long. Fifty years ago it was not uncommon in country places to find very old ladies who wore their bonnets all day long. Ursula Rosevean, however, was the last who still preserved that ancient custom. It was a large bonnet that she wore, a kind of bonnet calculated to impress very deeply the imagination of one—whether male or female—who saw it for the first time: it was of bold design, as capacious as a store-ship, as flowing in its lines as an old man-of-war—inspired to a certain extent by the fashions of the Waterloo period—yet, in great part, of independent design. Those few who were permitted to gaze upon the bonnet beheld it reverently. Within the bonnet an adroit arrangement of cap and ribbons concealed whatever of baldness or exiguity as to locks—but what does one know? Venus Calva has never been worshipped by men; and women only pay their tribute at her shrine from fear—never from love. The face of the sleeping lady reminded one—at first, vaguely—of history. Presently one perceived that it was the identical face which that dread occidental star, Queen Elizabeth herself, would have assumed had she lived to the age of ninety-five, which was Ursula's time of life in the year 1884. For it was an aquiline face, thin and sharp; and if her eyes had been open you would have remarked that they were bright and piercing, also like those of the Tudor Queen. Her cheek still preserved something of the colour which had once made it beautiful; but cheek and forehead alike were covered with lines innumerable, and her withered hands seemed to have grown too small for their natural glove. She was dressed in black silk, and wore a gold chain about her neck.

The clock struck half-past five, melodiously. Then the girl started and sat upright—as awakened out of her dream. 'Armorel,' it seemed to say—nay, since it seemed to say, it actually did say—'Child Armorel, I am old and wise. For a hundred and forty-three years, ever since I left the hands of the ingenious Peter Trevellick, of Penzance, in the year 1741, I have been counting the moments, never ceasing save at those periods when surgical operations have been necessary. In each year there are 31,536,000 moments. Judge, therefore, for yourself how many moments in all I have counted. I must, you will own, be very wise indeed. I am older even than your great-great-grandmother. I remember her a baby first, and then a pretty child, and then a beautiful woman, for all she is now so worn and wizened. I remember her father and her grandfather. Also her brothers and her son, and her grandson—and your own father, dear Armorel. The moments pass: they never cease: I tell them as they go. You have but short space to do all you wish to do. You, child, have done nothing at all yet. But the moments pass. Patience. For you, too, work will be found. Youth passes. You can hear it pass. I tell the moments in which it melts away and vanishes. Age itself shall pass. You may listen if you please. I tell the moments in which it slowly passes.'

Armorel looked at the clock with serious eyes during the

delivery of this fine sermon, the whole bearing of which she did not perhaps comprehend. Then she started up suddenly and sprang to her feet, stung by a sudden pang of restlessness, with a quick breath and a sigh. We who have passed the noon of life are apt to forget the disease of restlessness to which youth is prone: it is an affection which greatly troubles that period of life, though it should be the happiest and the most contented; it is a disorder due to anticipation, impatience, and inexperience. The voyage is all before: youth is eager to be sailing on that unknown ocean full of strange islands. Who would not be restless with such a journey before one and such discoveries to make?

Armorel opened the door noiselessly, and slipped out. At the same moment the old dog awoke and crept out with her, going delicately and on tiptoe, lest he should awaken the ancient lady. In the hall outside the girl stood listening. The house was quite silent, save that from the kitchen there was wafted on the air a soft droning—gentle, melodious, and murmurous, like the contented booming of a bumble-bee among the figwort. Armorel laughed gently. 'Oh!' she murmured, 'they are all asleep. Grandmother is asleep in the parlour; Dorcas and Chessun are asleep in the kitchen; Justinian is asleep in the cottage; and I suppose the boy is asleep somewhere in the farmyard.'

The girl led the way, and the dog followed.

She passed through the door into the garden of the front. It was not exactly a well-ordered garden, because everything seemed to grow as it pleased; but then in Samson you have not to coax flowers and plants into growing: they grow because it pleases them to grow: this is the reason why they grow so tall and so fast. The garden faced the south-west, and was protected from the north and east by the house itself and by a high stone wall. There is not anywhere on the island a warmer and sunnier corner than this little front garden of Holy Hill. The geranium clambered up the walls beside and among the branches of the tree-fuchsia, both together covering the front of the house with the rich colouring of their flowers. On either side of the door grew a great tree, with gnarled trunk and twisted branches, of lemon verbena, fragrant and sweet, perfuming the air; the myrtles were like unto trees for size; the very marguerites ran to timber of the smaller kind; the pampas-grass in the warmest corner rose eight feet high, waving its long silver plumes; the tall stalk still stood which had borne the flowers of an aloe that very summer; the leaves of the plant itself were slowly dying away, their life-work, which is nothing at all but the production of that one flowering stem, finished. That done, the world has no more attractions for the aloe: it is content —it slowly dies away. And in the front of the garden was a row of tall dracæna palms. An old ship's figure-head, thrown ashore after a wreck, representing the head and bust of a beautiful maiden, gilded, but with a good deal of the gilt rubbed off, stood on the left hand of the garden, half hidden by another fuchsia-tree in flower: and a huge old-fashioned ship's lantern hung from an iron bar projecting over the door of the house.

The house itself was of stone, with a roof of small slates. Impossible to say how old it was, because in this land stone-work ages rapidly, and soon becomes covered with yellow and orange lichen, while in the interstices there grows the grey sandwort; and in the soft sea air and the damp sea mists the sharp edges even of granite are quickly rounded off and crumbled. But it was a very old house, save for the square projecting window, which had been added recently—say thirty or forty years ago—a long, low house of two storeys, simply built; it stands half-way up the hill which slopes down to the water's edge; it is protected from the north and north-east winds, which are the deadliest enemies to Scilly, partly by the hill behind and partly by a spur of grey rock running like an ancient Cyclopean wall down the whole face of the hill into the sea, where for many a fathom it sticks out black teeth, round which the white surge rises and tumbles, even in the calmest time.

Beyond the garden-wall—why they wanted a garden-wall I know not, except for the pride and dignity of the thing—was a narrow green, with a little, a very little, pond; in the pond there were ducks; and beside the green was a small farmyard, containing everything that a farmyard should contain, except a stable. It had no stable, because there are no horses or carts upon the island. Pigs there are, and cows; fowls there are, and ducks and geese, and a single donkey for the purpose of carrying the flower-baskets from the farm to the landing-place; but neither horse nor cart.

Beyond the farmyard was a cottage, exactly like the house, but smaller. It was thatched, and on the thatch grew clumps of samphire. This was the abode of Justinian Tryeth, bailiff, head man, or foreman, who managed the farm. When you have named Ursula Rosevean, and Armorel, her great-great-granddaughter, and Justinian Tryeth, and Dorcas his wife—she was a native of St. Agnes, and therefore a Hicks by birth—Peter his son, and Chessun his daughter, you have a complete directory of the island, because nobody else now lives on Samson. Formerly, however, and almost within the memory of the oldest inhabitant, according to the computation of antiquaries and the voice of tradition, this island maintained a population of over two score.

The hill which rises behind the house is the southern hill of the two, which, with the broad valley between them, make up the island of Samson. This hill slopes steeply seaward to south and west. It is not a lofty hill, by any means. In Scilly there are no lofty hills. When Nature addressed herself to the construction of this archipelago she brought to the task a light touch: at the moment she happened to be full of feeling for the great and artistic effects which may be produced by small elevations, especially in those places where the material is granite. Therefore, though she raised no Alpine peak in Scilly, she provided great abundance and any variety of bold coast-line with rugged cliffs, lofty carns, and headlands piled with rocks. And her success as an artist in this *genre* has been undoubtedly wonderful. The actual measurement of Holy Hill, Samson—but why should we measure ?—has been taken, for the admiration of the world, by the Ordnance Survey. It is really no more than a hundred and thirty-two feet —not a foot more or less. But then one knows hills ten times that height—the Herefordshire Beacon, for example—which are not half so mountainous in the effect produced. Only a hundred and thirty-two feet—yet on its summit one feels the exhilaration of spirits caused by the air, elsewhere of five thousand feet at least. On its southern and western slopes lie the fields which form the flower-farm of Holy Hill.

Below the farmyard the ground sloped more steeply to the water : the slope was covered with short heather fern, now brown and yellow, and long trailing branches of bramble, now laden with ripe blackberries, the leaves enriched with blazon of gold and purple and crimson.

Armorel ran across the green and plunged among the fern, tossing her arms and singing aloud, the old dog trotting and jumping, but with less elasticity, beside her. She was bare-headed ; the sunshine made her dark cheeks ruddy and caused her black eyes to glow. Hebe, young and strong, loves Phœbus, and fears not any freckles. When she came to the water's edge, where the boulders lie piled in a broken mass among and above the water, she stood still and looked across the sea, silent for a moment. Then she began to sing in a strong contralto ; but no one could hear her, not even the coastguard on Telegraph Hill, or he of the Star Fort : the song she sang was one taught her by the old lady, who had sung it herself in the old, old days, when the road was always filled with merchantmen waiting for convoy up the Channel, and when the islands were rich with the trade of the ships, and their piloting, and their wrecks—to say nothing of the free trade which went on gallantly and without break or stop. As she sang she lifted her arms and swung them in slow cadence, as a Nautch-girl sometimes swings her arms. What she sang was none other than the old song—

Early one morning, just as the sun was rising,
I heard a maid sing in the valley below:
Oh ! don't deceive me. Oh ! never leave me.
How could you use a poor maiden so?

In the year of grace 1884 Armorel was fifteen years of age. But she looked nineteen or twenty, because she was so tall and so well-grown. She was dressed simply in a blue flannel ; the straw hat which she carried in her hand was trimmed with red ribbons ; at her throat she had stuck a red verbena—she naturally took to red, because her complexion was so dark. Black hair; black eyes; a strongly marked brow; a dark cheek of warm and ruddy hue; the lips full, but the mouth finely curved; features large but regular—she was already, though so young, a tall and handsome woman. Those able to understand things would recognise in her dark complexion, in her carriage, in her eyes, and in her upright figure, the true Castilian touch. The gipsy is swarthy; the negro is black; the mulatto is dusky: it is not the colour alone, but the figure and the carriage also, which mark the Spanish blood A noble Spanish lady; yet how could she get to Samson?

She wore no gloves—you cannot buy gloves in Samson—and her hands were brown with exposure to sea and sun, to wind and rain: they were by no means tiny hands, but strong and capable hands; her arms—no one ever saw them, but for shape and whiteness they could not be matched—would have disgraced no young fellow of her own age for strength and muscle. That was fairly to be expected in one who continually sailed and rowed across the inland seas of this archipelago; who went to church by boat and to market by boat; who paid her visits by boat and transacted her business by boat, and went by boat to do her shopping. She who rows every day upon the salt water, and knows how to manage a sail when the breeze is strong and the Atlantic surge rolls over the rocks and roughens the still water of the road, must needs be strong and sound. For my own part, I admire not the fragile maiden so much as her who rejoices in her strength. Youth, in woman as well as in man, should be brave and lusty; clean of limb as well as of heart; strong of arm as well as of will; enduring hardness of voluntary labour as well as hardness of involuntary pain; with feet that can walk, run, and climb, and with hands that can hold on. Such a girl as Armorel—so tall, so strong, so healthy—offers, methinks, a home ready-made for all the virtues, and especially the virtues feminine, to house themselves therein. Here they will remain, growing stronger every day, until at last they have become part and parcel of the very girl herself, and cannot be parted from her. Whereas, when they visit the puny creature, weak, timid, delicate—but no—'tis better to remain silent.

How many times had the girl wandered, morning or afternoon, down the rough face of the hill, and stood looking vaguely out to sea, and presently returned home again? How many such walks had she taken and forgotten? For a hundred times—yea, a thousand times—we do over and over again the old familiar action, the little piece of the day's routine, and forget it when we lie down to sleep. But there comes the thousandth time, when the same thing is done again in the same way, yet is never to be forgotten. For on that day happens the thing which changes and charges a whole life. It is the first of many days. It is the beginning of new days. From it, whatever may have happened before, everything shall now be dated until the end. Mohammed lived many years, but all the things that happened unto him or his successors are dated from the Flight. Is it for nothing that it has been told what things Armorel did and how she looked on this day? Not so, but for the sake of what happened afterwards, and because the history of Armorel begins with this restless fit, which drove her out of the quiet room down the hillside to the sea. Her history begins, like every history of a woman worth relating, with the man cast by the sea upon the shores of her island. The maiden always lives upon an island, and whether the man is cast upon the shore by the sea of Society, or the sea of travel, or the sea of accident, or the sea of adventure, or the sea of briny waves and roaring winds and jagged rocks, matters little. To Armorel it was the last. To you, dear Dorothy or Violet, it will doubtless be by the sea of Society. And the day that casts him before your feet will ever after begin a new period in your reckoning.

Armorel stopped her song as suddenly as she had begun it. She stopped because on the water below her, not far from the shore, she saw a strange thing. She had good sea eyes—an ordinary telescope does not afford a field of vision much larger or clearer across water than Armorel's eyes—but the thing was so strange that she shaded her forehead with her hand, and looked more curiously.

It would be strange on any evening, even after the calmest day of summer, when the sun is setting low, to see a small boat going out beyond Samson towards the Western Islets. There the swell of ocean is always rolling among the rocks and round the crags and headlands of the isles. Only in calm weather and in broad daylight can the boatman who knows the place venture in those waters. Not even the most skilled boatman would steer for the Outer Islands at sunset. For there are hidden rocks, long ridges of teeth that run out from the islands to tear and grind to powder any boat that should be caught in their devouring jaws. There are currents also which run swiftly and unexpectedly between the islands to sweep the boat along with them till it shall strike the rocks and so go down with any who are abroad; and there are strong gusts which sweep round the headlands and blow through the narrow sounds. So that it is only when the day is calm and in the full light of the sun that a boat can sail among these islands.

Yet Armorel saw a boat on the water, not half a mile from Samson, with two men on board. More than this, the boat was apparently without oars or sails, and it was drifting out to sea. What did this mean?

She looked and wondered. She looked again, and she remembered.

The tide was ebbing, the boat was floating out with the tide; the breeze had dropped, but there was still something left—what there was came from the south-east and helped the boat along; there was not much sea, but the feet of Great Minalto were white, and the white foam kept leaping up the sides, and on her right, over the ledges round White Island, the water was tearing and boiling, a white and angry heap. Why, the wind was getting up, and the sun was setting, and if they did not begin to row back as hard as they could, and that soon, they would be out to sea and in the dark.

She looked again, and she thought more. The sinking sun fell upon the boat, and lit it up so plainly that she could now see very well two things. First, that the boat was really without any oars or sails at all; and next, that the two men in her were not natives of Scilly. She could not discern their faces, but she could tell by their appearance and the way they sat in the boat that they were not men of the place. Besides, what would an islander want out in a boat at such a time and in such a place? They were, therefore, visitors; and by the quiet way in which they sat, as if it mattered not at all, it was perfectly plain that they understood little or nothing of their danger.

Again she considered, and now it became certain to her, looking down upon the boat, that the current was not taking her out to sea at all, which would be dangerous enough, but actually straight on the ridge or ledge of rocks lying off the south-west of White Island. Then, seized with sudden terror, she turned and fled back to the farm.

CHAPTER II

PRESENTED BY THE SEA

'PETER!' cried Armorel in the farmyard. 'Peter! Peter! Wake up! Where is the boy? Wake up and come quick!'

The boy was not sleeping, however, and came forth slowly, but obediently, in rustic fashion. He was a little older than most of those who still permit themselves to be called boys: unless his looks deceived one, he was a great deal older, for he was entirely bald, save for a few long, scattered hairs, which were white. His beard and whiskers also consisted of nothing but a few sparse white hairs. He moved heavily, without the spring of boyhood in his feet. Had Peter jumped or run, one might in haste have inferred a condition of drink or mental disorder. As for his shoulders, too, they were rounded, as if by the weight of years—a thing which is rarely seen in boys. Yet Armorel called this antique person 'the boy,' and he answered to the name without remonstrance.

'Quick, Peter!' she cried. 'There's a boat drifting on White Island Ledge, and the tide's running out strong; and there are two men in her, and they've got no oars in the boat. Ignorant trippers, I suppose! They will both be killed to a certainty, unless—— Quick!'

Peter followed her flying footsteps with a show of haste and a movement of the legs approaching alacrity. But then he was always a slow boy, and one who loved to have his work done for him. Therefore, when he reached the landing-place, he found that Armorel was well before him, and that she had already shipped mast and sail and oars, and was waiting for him to shove off.

Samson has two landing beaches, one on the north-east below Bryher Hill, and the other farther south, on the eastern side of the valley. There might be a third, better than either, on Porth Bay, if anyone desired to put off there, on the west side facing the other islands, where nobody has any business at all except to see the rocks or shoot wild birds.

The beach used by the Holy Hill folk was the second of these two; here they kept their boats, and had their old stone boat-house to store the gear; and it was here that Armorel stood waiting for her companion.

Peter was slow on land; at sea, however, he alone is slow who does not know what can be got out of a boat, and how it can be got. Peter did possess this knowledge; all the islanders, in fact, have it. They are born with it. They also know that nothing at sea is gained by hurry. It is a maxim which is said to rule or govern their conduct on land as well as afloat. Peter, therefore, when he had pushed off, sat down and took an oar with no more appearance of hurry than if he were taking a boat-load of boxes filled with flowers across to the port. Armorel took the other oar.

'They are drifting on White Island Ledge,' repeated Armorel; 'and the tide is running out fast.'

Peter made no reply—Armorel expected none—but dipped his oar. They rowed in silence for ten minutes. Then Peter found utterance, and spoke slowly.

'Twenty years ago—I remember it well—a boat went ashore on that very Ledge. The tide was running out—strong, like to-night. There was three men in her—visitors they were, who wanted to save the boatman's pay. Their bodies was never found.'

Then both pulled on in silence, and doggedly.

In ten minutes or more they had rounded the Point at a respectful distance, for reasons well known to the navigator and the nautical surveyor of Scilly. Peter, without a word, shipped his oar. Armorel did likewise. Then Peter stepped the mast and hoisted the sail, keeping the line in his own hand, and looked ahead, while Armorel took the helm.

'It's Jinkins's boat,' said Peter, because they were now in sight of her. 'What'll Jinkins say when he hears that his boat's gone to pieces?'

'And the two men? Who are they? Will Jinkins say nothing about the men?'

'Strangers they are; gentlemen, I suppose. Well, if the breeze doesn't soon—— Ah, here it is!'

The wind suddenly filled the sail. The boat heeled over under the breeze, and a moment after was flying through the water straight up the broad channel between the two Minaltos and Samson.

The sun was very low now. Between them and the west lay the boat they were pursuing—a small black object, with two black silhouettes of figures clear against the crimson sky. And now Armorel perceived that they had by this time gotten an inkling, at least, of their danger, for they no longer sat passive, but had torn up a plank from the bottom, with which one, kneeling in the bows, was working as with a paddle, but without science. The boat yawed this way and that, but still kept on her course drifting to the rocks.

'If she touches the Ledge, Peter,' said Armorel, 'she will be in little bits in five minutes. The water is rushing over it like a mill-stream.'

This she said ignorant of mill-streams, because there are none on Scilly; but the comparison served.

'If she touches,' Peter replied, 'we may just go home again. For we shall be no good to nobody.'

Beyond the boat they could plainly see the waters breaking over the Ledge; the sun lit up the white foam that leaped and flew over the black rocks just showing their teeth above the water as the tide went down.

Here is a problem—you may find plenty like it in every book of algebra. Given a boat drifting upon a ledge of rocks with the current and the tide; given a boat sailing in pursuit with a fair wind aft; given also the velocity of the current and the speed of the boat and the distance of the first boat from the rocks: at what distance must the second boat commence the race in order to catch up the first before it drives upon the rocks?

This second boat, paying close attention to the problem, came up hand over hand, rapidly overtaking the first boat, where the two men not only understood at last the danger they were in, but also that an attempt was being made to save them. In fact, one of them, who had some tincture or flavour of the mathematics left in him from his school days, remembered the problems of this class, and would have given a great deal to have been back again in school working out one of them.

Presently the boats were so near that Peter hailed, 'Boat ahoy! Back her! Back her! or you'll be upon the rocks. Back her all you know!'

'We've broken our oars,' they shouted.

'Keep her off!' Peter bawled again.

Even with a plank taken from the bottom of the boat a practised boatman would have been able to keep her off long enough to clear the rocks; but these two young men were not used to the ways of the sea.

'Put up your hellum,' said Peter, quietly.

'What are you going to do?' The girl obeyed first, as one must do at sea, and asked the question afterwards.

'There's only one chance. We must cut across her bows. Two lubbers! They ought not to be trusted with a boat. There's plenty of room.' He looked at the Ledge ahead and at his own sail. 'Now—steady.' He tightened the rope, the boat changed her course. Then Peter stood up and called again, his hand to his mouth, 'Back her! Back her! Back her all you know!' He sat down and said quietly, 'Now, then—luff it is—luff—all you can.'

The boat turned suddenly. It was high time. Right in front of them—only a few yards in front—the water rushed as if over a cascade, boiling and surging among the rocks. At high tide there would have been the calm, unruffled surface of the ocean swell; now there were roaring floods and swelling whirlpools. The girl looked round, but only for an instant. Then the boat crossed the bows of the other, and Armorel, as they passed, caught the rope that was held out to her.

One moment more and they were off the rocks, in deep water, towing the other boat after them.

Then Peter arose, lowered the sail, and took down his mast.

'Nothing,' he said, 'between us and Mincarlo. Now, gentlemen, if you will step into this boat we can tow yours along with us. So—take care, sir! Sit in the stern beside the young lady. Can you row, either of you?'

They could both row, they said. In these days a man is as much ashamed of not being able to row as, fifty years ago, he was ashamed of not being able to ride. Peter took one oar and gave the other to the stranger nearest. Then, without more words, he dipped his oar and began to row back again. The sun went down, and it suddenly became cold.

Armorel perceived that the man beside her was quite a young man—not more than one- or two-and-twenty. He wore brave attire—even a brown velvet jacket, a white waistcoat, and a crimson necktie; he also had a soft felt hat. Nature had not yet given him much beard, but what there was of it he wore pointed, with a light moustache so arranged as to show how it would be worn when it became of a respectable length. As he sat in the boat he seemed tall; and he did not look at all like one of the bawling and boastful trippers who sometimes come over to the islands for a night and pretend to know how to manage a boat. Yet——

'What do you mean,' asked the girl, severely, 'by going out in a boat, when you ought to have known very well that you could not manage her?'

'We thought we could,' replied this disconcerted pretender, with meekness suitable to the occasion. Indeed, under such humiliating circumstances, Captain Parolles himself would become meek.

If we had not seen you,' she continued, 'you would most certainly have been killed.'

'I begin to think we might. We should certainly have gone on those rocks. But there is an island close by. We could swim.'

'If your boat had touched those rocks you would have been dead in three minutes,' this maid of wisdom continued. 'Nothing could have saved you. No boat could have come near you. And to think of standing or swimming in that current and among those rocks! Oh! but you don't know Scilly.'

'No,' he replied, still with a meekness that disarmed wrath, 'I'm afraid not.'

'Tell me how it happened.'

The other man struck in—he who was wielding the oar. He also was a young man, of shorter and more sturdy build than the other. Had he not, unfortunately, confined his whole attention in youth to football, he might have made a good boatman. Really, a young man whose appearance conveyed no information or suggestion at all about him except that he seemed healthy, active, and vigorous, and that he was presumably short-sighted, or he would not have worn spectacles.

'I will tell you how it came about,' he said. 'This man would go sketching the coast. I told him that the islands are so beautifully and benevolently built that every good bit has got another bit on the next island, or across a cove, or on the other side of a bay, put there on purpose for the finest view of the first bit. You only get that arrangement, you know, in the Isles of Scilly and the Isles of Greece. But he wouldn't be persuaded, and so we took a boat and went to sea, like the three merchants of Bristol city. We saw Jerusalem and Madagascar very well, and if you hadn't turned up in the nick of time I believe we should have seen the river Styx as well, with Cocytus very likely: good old Charon certainly: and Tantalus, too much punished—overdone—up to his neck.'

Armorel heard, wondering what, in the name of goodness, this talker of strange language might mean.

'When his oar broke, you know,' the talker went on, 'I began to laugh, and so I caught a crab; and while I lay in the bottom laughing like Tom of Bedlam, my oar dropped overboard, and there we were. Five mortal hours we drifted; but we had tobacco and a flask, and we didn't mind so very much. Some boat, we thought, might pick us up.'

'Some boat!' echoed Armorel. 'And outside Samson!'

'As for the rocks, we never thought about them. Had we known of the rocks, we should not have laughed——'

'You have saved our lives,' said the young man in the velvet jacket. He had a soft sweet voice, which trembled a little as he spoke. And, indeed, it is a solemn thing to be rescued from certain death.

'Peter did it,' Armorel replied. 'You may thank Peter.'

'Let me thank you,' he said, softly and persuasively. 'The other man may thank Peter.'

'Just as you like. So long, that is, as you remember that it will have to be a lesson to you as long as you live never to go out in a boat without a man.'

'It shall be a lesson. I promise. And the man I go out with, next time, shall not be you, Dick.'

'Never,' she went on, enforcing the lesson, 'never go in a boat alone, unless you know the waters. Are you Plymouth trippers? But then Plymouth people generally know how to handle a boat.'

'We are from London.' In the twilight the blush caused by being taken for a Plymouth tripper was not perceived. 'I am an artist, and I came to sketch.' He said this with some slight emphasis and distinction. There must be no mistaking an artist from London for a Plymouth tripper.

'You must be hungry.'

'We are ravenous, but at this moment one can only feel that it is better to be hungry and alive than to be drowned and dead.'

'Oh!' she said, earnestly, 'you don't know how strong the water is. It would have thrown you down and rolled you over and over among the rocks, your head would have been knocked to pieces, your face would have been crushed out of shape, every bone would have been broken: Peter has seen them so.'

'Ay! ay!' said Peter. 'I've picked 'em up just so. You are well off those rocks, gentlemen.'

Silence fell upon them. The twilight was deepening, the breeze was chill. Armorel felt that the young man beside her was shivering—perhaps with the cold. He looked across the dark water and gasped: 'We are coming up,' he said, 'out of the gates of death and the jaws of hell. Strange! to have been so near unto dying. Five minutes more, and there would have been an end, and two more men would have been created for no other purpose but to be drowned.'

Armorel made no reply. The oars kept dipping, dipping, evenly and steadily. Across the waters on either hand flashed lights: St. Agnes and the Bishop from the south—they are white lights; and from the north the crimson splendour of Round Island: the wind was dropping, and there was a little phosphorescence on the water, which gleamed along the blade of the oar.

In half an hour the boat rounded the new pier, and they were in the harbour of Hugh Town at the foot of the landing-steps.

'Now,' said Armorel, 'you had better get home as fast as you can and have some supper.'

'Why,' cried the artist, realising the fact for the first time, 'you are bare-headed! You will kill yourself.'

'I am used to going about bare-headed. I shall come to no harm. Now go and get some food.'

'And you?' The young man stood on the stepping-stones ready to mount.

'We shall put up the sail and get back to Samson in twenty minutes. There is breeze enough for that.'

'Will you tell us,' said the artist, 'before you go—to whom we are indebted for our very lives?'

'My name is Armorel.'

'May we call upon you? To-night we are too bewildered We cannot say what we ought and must say.'

'I live on Samson. What is your name?'

'My name is Roland Lee. My friend here is called Dick Stephenson.'

'You can come if you wish. I shall be glad to see you,' she corrected herself, thinking she had been inhospitable and ungracious.

'Am I to ask for Miss Armorel?'

She laughed merrily. 'You will find no one to ask, I am afraid. Nobody else, you see, lives on Samson. When you land, just turn to the left, walk over the hill, and you will find the house on the other side. Samson is not so big that you can miss the house. Good-night, Roland Lee! Good-night, Dick Stephenson!'

'She's only a child,' said the young man called Dick, as he climbed painfully and fearfully up the dark and narrow steps, slippery with sea-weed and not even protected by an inner bar. 'I suppose it doesn't much matter since she's only a child. But I merely desire to point out that it's always the way. If there does happen to be an adventure accompanied by a girl—most adventures bring along the girl: nobody cares, in fact, for an adventure without a girl in it—I'm put in the background and made to do the work while you sit down and talk to the girl. Don't tell me it was accidental. It was the accident of design. Hang it all! I'll turn painter myself.'

CHAPTER III

IN THE BAR PARLOUR

At nine o'clock the little bar parlour of Tregarthen's was nearly full. It is a very little room, low as well as little, therefore it is easily filled. And though it is the principal club-room of Hugh Town, where the better sort and the notables meet, it can easily accommodate them all. They do not, however, meet every evening, and they do not all come at once. There is a wooden settle along the wall, beautifully polished by constant use, which holds four: a smaller one beside the fire, where at a pinch two might sit; there is a seat in the window which also might hold two, but is only comfortable for one. A small round table only leaves room for one chair. This makes sitting accommodation for nine, and when all are present, and all nine are smoking tobacco like one, the atmosphere is convivially pungent. This evening there were only seven. They consisted of the two young men whose perils on the deep you have just witnessed; a Justice of the Peace—but his office is a sinecure, because on the Scilly Isles virtue reigns in every heart; a flower-farmer of the highest standing; two other gentlemen weighed down with the mercantile anxieties and interests of the place—they ought to have been in wigs and square brown coats, with silver buckles to their shoes; and one who held office and exercised authority.

The art of conversation cannot be successfully cultivated on a small island, on board ship, or in a small country town. Conversation requires a continual change of company, and a great variety of topics. Your great talker, when he inconsiderately remains too long among the same set, becomes a bore. After a little, unless he goes away, or dies, or becomes silent, they kill him, or lock him up in an asylum. At Tregarthen's he would be made to understand that either he or the rest of the population must leave the archipelago and go elsewhere. In some colonial circles they play whist, which is an excellent method, perhaps the best ever invented, for disguising the poverty or the absence of conversation. At Tregarthen's they do not feel this necessity—they are contented with their conversation; they are so happily contented that they do not repine even though they get no more than an observation dropped every ten minutes or so. They are not anxious to reply hurriedly; they are even contented to sit silently enjoying the proximity of each other—the thing, in fact, which lies at the root of all society. The evening is not felt to be dull, though there are no fireworks of wit and repartee. Indeed, if Douglas Jerrold himself were to appear with a bag full of the most sparkling epigrams and repartees, nobody would laugh, even when he was kicked out into the cold and unappreciative night—the stars have no sense of humour—as a punishment for impudence.

This evening the notables spoke occasionally; they spoke slowly—the Scillonians all talk slowly—they neither attempted nor looked for smartness. They did not tell stories, because all the stories are known, and they can now only be told to strangers. The two young men from London listened without taking any part in the talk: people who have just escaped—and that narrowly—a sharp and painful death by drowning and banging on jagged rocks are expected to be hushed for awhile. But they listened. And they became aware that the talk, in whatever direction it wandered, always came back to the sea. Everything in Scilly belongs to the sea: they may go up country, which is a journey of a mile and a half, or even two miles—and speak for a moment of the crops and the farms; but that leads to the question of import and export, and, therefore, to the vessels lying within the pier, and to the steam service to Penzance and to vessels in other ports, and, generally, to steam service about the world. And again, wherever two or three are gathered together in Scilly, one at least will be found to have ploughed the seas in distant parts. This confers a superiority on the society of the islands which cannot, even in these days, be denied or concealed. In the last century, when a man who was known to have crossed the Pacific entered a coffee-house, the company with one accord gazed upon him with envy and wonder. Even now, familiarity hath not quite bred contempt. We still look with unconcealed respect upon one who can tell of Tahiti and the New Hebrides, and has stood upon the mysterious shores of Papua. And, at Tregarthen's this evening, these two strangers were young; they had not yet made the circuit of the round earth; they had had, as yet, not many opportunities of talking with travellers and sailors. Therefore, they listened, and were silent.

Presently, one after the other, the company got up and went out. There is no sitting late at night in Scilly. There were left of all only the Permanent Official.

'I hear, gentlemen,' he said, 'that you have had rather a nasty time this evening.'

'We should have been lost,' said the artist, 'but for a—young lady, who saw our danger and came out to us.'

'Armorel. I saw her towing in your boat and landing you. Yes, it was a mighty lucky job that she saw you in time. There's a girl! Not yet sixteen years old! Yet I'd rather trust myself with her in a boat, especially if she had the boy Peter with her, than any boatman of the islands. And there's not a rock or an islet, not a bay or a headland in this country of bays and capes and rocks, that she does not know. She could find her way blindfold by the feel of the wind and the force of the current. But it's in her blood. Father to son—father to son and daughter too—the Roseveans are born boatmen.'

'She saved our lives,' repeated the artist. 'That is all we know of her. It is a good deal to know, perhaps, from our own point of view.'

'She belongs to Samson. They've always lived on Samson. Once there were Roseveans, Tryeths, Jenkinses, and Woodcocks on Samson. Now, they are nearly all gone—only one family of Rosevean left, and one of Tryeth.'

'She said that nobody else lived there.'

'Well, it is only her own family. They've started a flower-farm lately on Holy Hill, and I hear it's doing pretty well. It's a likely situation, too, facing south-west and well sheltered. You should go and see the flower-farm. Armorel will be glad to show you the farm, and the island too. Samson has got a good many curious things—more curious, perhaps, than she knows, poor child!'

He paused for a moment, and then continued; 'There's nobody

on the island now but themselves. There's the old woman, first—you should see her too. She's a curiosity by herself—Ursula Rosevean—she was a Traverse, and came from Bryher to be married. She married Methusalem Rosevean, Armorel's great-great-grandfather—that was nigh upon eighty years ago; she's close upon a hundred now; and she's been a widow since—when was it?—I believe she'd only been a wife for twelve months or so. He was drowned on a smuggling run—his brother Emanuel, too. Widow used to look for him from the hill-top every night for a year and more afterwards. A wonderful old woman! Go and look at her. Perhaps she will talk to you. Sometimes, when Armorel plays the fiddle, she will brighten up and talk for an hour. She knows how to cure all diseases, and she can foretell the future. But she's too old now, and mostly she's asleep. Then there's Justinian Tryeth and Dorcas, his wife—they're over seventy, both of them, if they're a day. Dorcas was a St. Agnes girl—that's the reason why her name was Hicks: if she'd come from Bryher she'd have been a Traverse; if from Tresco she'd have been a Jenkins. But she was a Hicks. She's as old as her husband, I should say. As for the boy, Peter——'

'She called him the boy, I remember. But he seemed to me——'

'He's fifty, but he's always been the boy. He never married, because there was nobody left on Samson for him to marry, and he's always been too busy on the farm to come over here after a wife. And he looks more than fifty, because once he fell off the pier, head first, into the stern of a boat, and after he'd been unconscious for three days, all his hair fell off except a few stragglers, and they'd turned white. Looks most as old as his father. Chessun's near fifty-two.'

'Who is Chessun?'

'She's the girl. She's always been the girl. She's never married, just like Peter her brother, because there was no one left on Samson for her. And she never leaves the island except once or twice a year, when she goes to the afternoon service at Bryher. Well, gentlemen, that's all the people left on Samson. There used to be more—a great many more—quite a population, and if all stories are true, they were a lively lot. You'll see their cottages standing in ruins. As for getting drowned, you'd hardly believe! Why, take Armorel alone. Her father, Emanuel—he'd be about fifty-seven now—he was drowned—twelve years ago it must be now—with his wife and his three boys, Emanuel, John, and Andrew, crossing over from a wedding at St. Agnes. He married Rovena Wetherel, from St. Mary's. Then there was her grandfather, he was a pilot—but they were all pilots—and he was cast away taking an East Indiaman up the Channel, cast away on Chesil Bank in a fog—that was in the year 1845—and all hands lost. His father—no, no, that was his uncle—all in the line were drowned;

that one's uncle died in his bed unexpectedly—you can see the bed still—but they do say, just before some officers came over about a little bit of business connected with French brandy. One of the Roseveans went away, and became a purser in the Royal Navy. Those were the days for pursers! Their accounts were never audited, and when they'd squared the captain and paid him the wages and allowances for the dummies and the dead men, they had left as much—ay, as a couple of thousand a year. After this he left the Navy and purveyed for the Fleet, and became so rich that they had to make him a knight.'

'Was there much smuggling here in the old days?'

'Look here, sir; a Scillonian in the old days called himself a pilot, a fisherman, a shopkeeper, or a farmer, just as he pleased. That was his pleasant way. But he was always—mind you—a smuggler. Armorel's great-great-great-grandfather, father of the old lady's husband—him who was never heard of afterwards, but was supposed to have been cast away off the French coast—he was known to have made great sums of money. Never was anyone on the islands in such a big way. Lots of money came to the islands from smuggling. They say that the St. Martin's people have kept theirs, and have got it invested; but, for all the rest, it's gone. And they were wreckers too. Many and many a good ship before the islands were lit up have struck on the rocks and gone to pieces. What do you think became of the cargoes? Where were the Scilly boats when the craft was breaking up? And did you never hear of the ship's lantern tied to the horns of a cow? They've got one on Samson could tell a tale or two; and they've still got a figure-head there which ought to have haunted old Emanuel Rosevean when his boat capsized off the coast of France.'

'An interesting family history.'

'Yes. Until the Preventive Service put an end to the trade, the Roseveans were the most successful and the most daring smugglers in the islands. But an unlucky family. All these drownings make people talk. Old wives' talk, I dare say. But for something one of them did—wrecking a ship, robbing the dead, who knows—they say the bad luck will go on till something is done—I know not what.'

He got up and put on his cap, the blue-cloth cap with a cloth peak, much affected in Scilly, because the wind blows off any other form of hat ever invented.

'It is ten o'clock—I must go. Did you ever hear the story, gentlemen, of the Scillonian sailor?' He sat down again. 'I believe it must have been one of the Roseveans. He was on board a West Indiaman, homeward bound, and the skipper got into a fog and lost his reckoning. Then he asked this man if he knew the Scilly Isles. "Better nor any book," says the sailor. "Then," says the skipper, "take the wheel." In an hour crash went the ship upon the rocks. "Damn your eyes!" says the skipper, "you said you knew the Scilly Isles." "So I do," says the man; "this is one of 'em." The ship went to pieces, and near all the hands were lost. But the people of the islands had a fine time with the flotsam and the jetsam for a good many days afterwards.'

'I believe,' said the young man—he who answered to the name of Dick—'that this patriot is buried in the old churchyard. I saw an inscription to-day which probably marks his tomb. Under the name is written the words "Dulce et decor"—but the rest is obliterated.'

'Very likely—they would bury him in the old churchyard. Good-night, gentlemen!'

'Roland!' The young man called Dick jumped from the settle. 'Roland! Pinch me—shake me—stick a knife into me—but not too far—I feel as if I was going off my head. The fair Armorel's father was a corsair, who was drowned on his way from the coast of France, with his grandfather and his great-grandfather and great-grand-uncles, after having been cast away upon the Chesil Bank, and never heard of again, though he was wanted on account of a keg of French brandy picked up in the Channel. He made an immense pile of money, which has been lost; and there's an old lady at the farm so old—so old—so very, very old—it takes your breath away only to think of it—that she married Methusalem. Her husband was drowned—a new light, this, on history—and of course she escaped on the Ark—as a stowaway or a cabin passenger. Armorel plays the fiddle and makes the old lady jump.'

'We'll go over there to-morrow.'

'We will. It is a Land of Enchantment, this outlying bit of Lyonesse. Meanwhile, just to clear my brain, I think I must have a whisky. The weakness of humanity demands it.

Oh! 'twas in Tregarthen's bar,
Where the pipes and whiskies are——

They are an unlucky family,' he went on, 'because they "did something." Remark, Roland, that here is the very element of romance. My ancestors have "done something" too. I am sure they have, because my grandfather kept a shop, and you can't keep a shop without "doing something." But Fate never persecuted my father, the dean, and I am not in much anxiety that I too shall be shadowed on account of the old man. Yet look at Armorel Rosevean! There's distinction, mind you, in being selected by Fate for vicarious punishment. The old corsair wrecked a ship and robbed the bodies: therefore, all his descendants have got to be drowned. Dear me! If we were all to be drowned because our people had once "done something," the hungry, insatiate sea would be choked, and the world would come to an end. A Scotch whisky, Rebecca, if you please, and a seltzer! To-morrow, Roland, we will once more cross the raging main, but under protection. If you break an oar again, you shall be put overboard. We will visit this fair child of Samson. Child of Samson! The Child of Samson! Was Delilah her mother, or is she the grand daughter of the Timnite? Has she inherited the virtues of her father as well as his strength? Were the latter days of Delilah sanctified and purified? Happily, she is only as yet a child —only a child, Roland'—he emphasised the words—'although a child of Samson.'

. . . . . .

In the night a vision came to Roland Lee. He saw Armorel once more sailing to his rescue. And in his vision he was seized with a mighty terror and a shaking of the limbs, and his heart sank and his cheek blanched; and he cried aloud, as he sank beneath the cold waters: 'Oh, Armorel, you have come too late! Armorel, you cannot save me now.'

CHAPTER IV

THE GOLDEN TORQUE

THE morning was bright, the sky blue, the breeze fresh—so fresh that even in the Road the sea broke over the bows and the boat ran almost gunwale under. This time the two landsmen were not unprotected: they were in charge of two boatmen. Humiliating, perhaps; but your true courage consisteth not in vain boasting and arrogant pretence, and he is safest who doth not ignorantly presume to manage a boat. Therefore, boatmen twain now guided the light bark and held the ropes.

'Dick,' said Roland, presently, looking ahead, 'I see her. There she is—upon the hillside among the brown fern. I can see her, with her blue dress.'

Dick looked, and shook his short-sighted head.

'I only see Samson,' he said. 'He groweth bigger as we approach. That is not uncommon with islands. I perceive that he hath two hills, one on the north and the other on the south; he showeth—perhaps with pride—a narrow plain in the middle. The hills appear to be strewn with boulders, and there are carns, and perhaps Logan stones. There is always a Logan stone, but you can never find it. There are also, I perceive, ruins. Samson looks quite a large island when you come near to it. Life on Samson must be curiously peaceful. No post-office, no telegrams, no telephones, no tennis, no shops, no papers, no people—good heavens! For a whole month one would enjoy Samson.'

'Don't you see her?' repeated Roland. 'She is coming down the hillside.'

'I dare say I do see her if I knew it; but I cannot at this distance, even with assisted eyes——'

'Oh! a blue dress—blue—against the brown and yellow of the fern. Can you not——?'

Dick gazed with the slow, uncertain eyes of short sight, and adjusted his glasses.

'My pal,' he said, 'to please you I would pretend to see anything. In fact, I always do: it saves trouble. I see her plainly—blue dress, you say—certainly—sitting on a rock——'

'Nonsense! She is walking down the hill. You don't see her at all.'

'Quite so. Coming down the hill,' Dick replied, unmoved.

'She has been in my mind all night. I have been thinking all kinds of things—impossible things—about this nymph. She is not in the least common, to begin with. She is——'

'She is only a child, Roland. Don't——'

'A child? Why shouldn't she be a child? I suppose I may admire a beautiful child? Do you insinuate that I am going to make love to her?'

'Well, old man, you mostly do.'

'It was not so dark last night but one could see that she is a very beautiful girl. She looks eighteen, but our friend last night assured us that she is not yet sixteen. A very beautiful girl she is: features regular, and a head that ought to be modelled. She is dark, like a Spaniard.'

'Gipsy, probably. Name of Stanley or Smith—Pharaoh Stanley was, most likely, her papa.'

'Gipsy yourself! Who ever heard of a gipsy on Scilly? You might as well look for an organ-grinder! Spanish blood, I swear! Castilian of the deepest blue. Then her eyes! You didn't observe her eyes?'

'I was too hungry. Besides, as usual, I was doing all the work.'

'They are black eyes——'

'The Romany have black eyes—roving eyes—hard, bold, bad, black eyes.'

'Soft black—not hard black. The dark velvet eyes which hold the light. Dick, I should like to paint those eyes. She is now looking at our boat. I can see her lifting her hand to shade her eyes. I should like to paint those eyes just at the moment when she gives away her heart.'

'You cannot, Childe Roland, because there could only be one other person present on that interesting occasion. And that person must not be you.'

'Dick, too often you are little better than an ass.'

'If you painted those eyes when she was giving away her heart it might lead to another and a later picture when she was giving away her temper. Eyes which hold the light also hold the fire. You might be killed with lightning, or, at least, blinded with excess of light. Take care!'

'Better be blinded with excess of light than pass by insensible. Some men are worse than the fellow with the muck-rake. He was only insensible to a golden crown; they are insensible to Venus. Without loveliness, where is love? Without love, what is life?'

'Yet,' said Dick, drily, 'most of us have got to shape our lives for ourselves before we can afford to think of Venus.'

It will be understood that these two young men represented two large classes of humanity. One would not go so far as to say that mankind may be divided into those two classes only: but, undoubtedly, they are always with us. First, the young man who walketh humbly, doing his appointed task with honesty, and taking with gratitude any good thing that is bestowed upon him by Fate. Next, the young man who believes that the whole round world and all that therein is are created for his own special pleasure and enjoyment; that for him the lovely girls attire themselves, and for his pleasure go forth to dance and ball; for him the actress plays her best; for him the feasts are spread, the corks are popped, the fruits are ripened, the suns shine. To the former class belonged Dick Stephenson: to the latter, Roland Lee. Indeed, the artistic temperament not uncommonly enlists a young man in the latter class.

'Look!' cried the artist. 'She sees us. She is coming down the hill. Even you can see her now. Oh! the light, elastic step! Nothing in the world more beautiful than the light, elastic step of a girl. Somehow, I don't remember it in pictures. Perhaps—some day—I may——' He began to talk in unconnected jerks. 'As for the Greek maiden by the sea-shore playing at ball and showing bony shoulders, and all that—I don't like it. Only very young girls should play at ball and jump about—not women grown and formed. They may walk or spring as much as they like, but they must not jump, and they must not run. They must not laugh loud. Violent emotions are masculine. Figure and dress alike make violence ungraceful: that is why I don't like to see women jump about. If they knew how it uglifies most of them! Armorel is only a child—yes—but how graceful, how complete she is in her movements!'

She was now visible, even to a short-sighted man, tripping lightly through the fern on the slope of the hill. As she ran, she tossed her arms to balance herself from boulder to boulder. She was singing, too, but those in the boat could not hear her; and before the keel touched the sand she was silent.

She stood waiting for them on the beach, her old dog Jack beside her, a smile of welcome in her eyes, and the sunlight on her cheeks. Hebe herself—who remained always fifteen from prehistoric times until the melancholy catastrophe of the fourth century, when, with the other Olympians, she was snuffed out—was not sweeter, more dainty, or stronger, or more vigorous of aspect.

'I thought you would come across this morning,' she said. 'I went to the top of the hill and looked out, and presently I saw your boat. You have not ventured out alone again, I see. Good-morning, Roland Lee! Good-morning, Dick Stephenson!'

She called them thus by their Christian names, not with familiarity, but quite naturally, and because when she went into the world—that is to say, to Bryher Church—on Sunday afternoon, each called unto each by his Christian name. And to each she gave her hand with a smile of welcome. But it seemed to Dick, who was observant rather than jealous, that his companion appropriated to himself and absorbed both smiles.

'Shall I show you Samson? Have you seen the islands yet?'

No; they had only arrived two days before, and were going back the next day.

'Many do that,' said the girl. 'They stay here a day or two: they go across to Tresco and see the gardens: then perhaps they walk over Sallakey Down, and they see Peninnis and Porthellick and the old church, and they think they have seen the islands. You will know nothing whatever about Scilly if you go to-morrow.'

'Why should we go to-morrow?' asked the artist. 'Tell me, that, Dick.'

'I, because my time is up, and Somerset House once more expects me. You, my friend,' Dick replied, with meaning, 'because you have got your work to do and you must not fool around any longer.'

Roland Lee laughed. 'We came first of all,' he said, turning to Armorel, 'in order to thank you for——'

'Oh! you thanked me last night. Besides it was Peter——'

'No, no. I refuse to believe in Peter.'

'Well, do not let us say any more about it. Come with me.'

The landing-place of Samson is a flat beach, covered with a fine white sand and strewn with little shells—yellow and grey, green and blue. Behind the beach is a low bank on which grow the sea-holly, the sea-lavender, the horned poppy, and the spurge, and behind the bank stretches a small plain, low and sandy, raised above the high tide by no more than a foot or two. Armorel led the way across this plain to the foot of the northern hill. It is a rough and rugged hill, wild and uncultivated. The slope facing the south is covered with gorse and fern, the latter brown and yellow in September. Among the fern at this season stood the tall dead stalks of foxglove. Here and there were patches of short turf set about with the withered flowers of the sea-pink, and the long branches of the bramble lay trailing over the ground. The hand of some prehistoric giant has sprinkled the slopes of this hill with boulders of granite: they are piled above each other so as to make carns, headlands, and capes with strange resemblances and odd surprises. Upon the top they found a small plateau sloping gently to the north.

'See!' said Armorel. 'This is the finest thing we have to show on Samson, or on any of the islands. This is the burial-place of the kings. Here are their tombs.'

'What kings?' asked Dick, looking about him. 'Where are the tombs?'

'The kings,' Roland repeated; 'there can be no other kings. These are their tombs. Do not interrupt.'

'The ancient kings,' Armorel replied, with historic precision. 'These mounds are tneir tombs. See—one—two—half a dozen of them are here. Only kings had barrows raised over them. Did you expect graves and headstones, Dick Stephenson?'

'Oh, these are barrows, are they?' he replied, in some confusion. A man of the world does not expect to be caught in ignorance by the solitary inhabitant of a desert island.

'A long time ago,' Armorel went on, 'these islands formed part of the mainland. Bryher and Tresco, St. Helen's, Tean, St. Martin's and St. Mary's, were all joined together, and the road was only a creek of the sea. Then the sea washed away all the land between Scilly and the Land's End. They used to call the place Lyonesse. The kings of Lyonesse were buried on Samson. Their kingdom is gone, but their graves remain. It is said that their ghosts have been seen. Dorcas saw them once.'

'I should like to see them very much,' said Roland.

'If you were here at night, we could go out and look for them. I have been here often after dark looking for them.'

'What did you see?'

She answered like unto the bold Sir Bedivere—who, perhaps, was standing on that occasion not far from this hilltop.

'I saw the moonlight on the rocks, and I heard the beating of the waves.'

Quoth Dick: 'The spook of a king of Lyonesse would be indeed worth coming out to see.'

Armorel led the way to a barrow, the top of which showed signs of the spade.

'See!' she said. 'Here is one that has been opened. It was a long time ago.'

There were the four slabs of stone still in position which formed the sides of the grave, and the slab which had been its cover lying close beside.

Armorel looked into the grave. 'They found,' she whispered, 'the bones of the king lying on the stone. But when someone touched them they turned to dust. There is the dust at your feet in the grave. The wind cannot bear it away. It may blow the sand and earth into it, but the dust remains. The rain can turn it into mud, but it cannot melt it. This is the dust of a king.'

The young men stood beside her silent, awed a little, partly by the serious look in the girl's face, and partly because, though it now lay open to the wind and rain, it was really a grave. One must not laugh beside the grave of a man. The wind lifted Armorel's long locks and blew them off her white forehead: her eyes were sad and even solemn. Even the short-sighted Dick saw that his friend was right: they were soft black eyes, not of the gipsy kind, and he repented him of a hasty inference. To the artist it seemed as if here was a princess of Lyonesse mourning over the grave of her buried king and—what?—father—brother—cousin—lover? Everything, in his imagination, vanished—except that one figure: even her clothes were changed for the raiment—say the court mourning—of that vanished realm. And also, like Sir Bedivere, he heard nothing but the wild water lapping on the crag.

And here followed a thing so strange that the historian hesitates about putting it down.

Let us remember that it is thirty years, or thereabouts, since this barrow was laid open; that we may suppose those who opened it to have had eyes in their heads; that it has been lying open ever since; and that every visitor—to be sure there are not many—who lands on Samson is bound to climb this hill and visit this open barrow with its perfect kistvaen. These things borne in mind, it will seem indeed wonderful that anything in the grave should have escaped discovery.

Roland Lee, leaning over, began idly to poke about the mould and dust of the grave with his stick. He was thinking of the girl and of the romance with which his imagination had already clothed this lonely spot; he was also thinking of a picture which might be made of her; he was wondering what excuse he could make for staying another week at Tregarthen's—when he was startled by striking his stick against metal. He knelt down and felt about with his hands. Then he found something and drew it out, and arose with the triumph that belongs to an archæologist who picks up an ancient thing—say, a rose noble in a newly ploughed field. The thing which he found was a hoop or ring. It was covered and encrusted with mould; he rubbed this off with his fingers. Lo: it was of gold: a hoop of gold as thick as a lady's little finger, twisted spirally, bent into the form of a circle, the two ends not joined, but turned back. Pure gold: yellow, soft gold.

'I believe,' he said, gasping, 'that this must be—it *is*—a torque. I think I have seen something like it in museums. And I've read of them. It was your king's necklace: it was buried with him: it lay around the skeleton neck all these thousand years. Take it, Miss Armorel. It is yours.'

'No! no! Let me look at it. Let me have it in my hands. It is yours'—in ignorance of ancient law and the rights of the lord proprietor—'it is yours because you found it.'

'Then I will give it to you, because you are the Princess of the Island.'

She took it with a blush and placed it round her own neck, bending open the ends and closing them again. It lay there—the red, red gold—as if it belonged to her and had been made for her.

'The buried king is your ancestor,' said Roland. 'It is his legacy to his descendant. Wear the king's necklace.'

'My luck, as usual,' grumbled Dick, aside. 'Why couldn't I find a torque and say pretty things?'

'Come,' said Armorel, 'we have seen the barrows. There are others scattered about—but this is the best place for them. Now I will show you the island.'

The hill slopes gently northward till it reaches a headland or carn of granite boldly projecting. Here it breaks away sharply to the sea. Armorel climbed lightly up the carn and stood upon the highest boulder, a pretty figure against the sky. The young men followed and stood below her.

At their feet the waves broke in white foam (in the calmest weather the Atlantic surge rolling over the rocks is broken into foam), a broad sound or channel lay between Samson and the adjacent island: in the channel half a dozen rocks and islets showed black and threatening.

'The island across the channel,' said Armorel, 'is Bryher. This is Bryher Hill, because it faces Bryher Island. Yonder, on Bryher is Samson Hill, because it faces Samson Island. Bryher is a large place. There are houses and farms on Bryher, and a church where they have service every Sunday afternoon. If you were here on Sunday, you could go in our boat with Peter, Chessun, and me. Justinian and Dorcas mostly stay at home now, because they are old.'

'Can anybody stay on the island, then?' asked Roland, quickly.

'Once the doctor came for Justinian's rheumatism, and bad weather began and he had to stay a week.'

'His other patients meanly took advantage and got well, I suppose,' said Dick.

'I hope so,' Armorel replied simply.

She turned and looked to the north-east, where lie the eastern islands, the group between St. Martin's and St. Mary's, a miniature in little of the greater group. From this point they looked to the eye of ignorance like one island. Armorel distinguished them. There were Great and Little Arthur; Ganilly, with his two hills, like Samson; the Ganninicks and Meneweather, Ragged Island, and Inisvouls.

'They are not inhabited,' said the girl, pointing to them one by one; 'but it is pleasant to row about among them in fine weather. In the old time, when they made kelp, people would go and live there for weeks together. But they are not cultivated.'

Then she turned northwards, and showed them the long island of St. Martin's, with its white houses, its church, its gentle hills, and its white and red daymark on the highest point. Half of St. Martin's was hidden by Tresco, and more than half of Tresco by Bryher. Over the downs of Tresco rose the dome of Round Island, crowned with its white lighthouse. And over Bryher, out at sea, showed the rent and jagged crest of the great rock Menovawr.

'You should land on Tresco,' said Armorel. 'There is the church to see. Oh! it is a most beautiful church. They say that in Cornwall itself there is hardly any church so fine as Tresco Church. And then there are the gardens and the lake. Everybody goes to see the gardens, but they do not walk over the down to Cromwell's Castle. Yet there is nothing in the islands like Cromwell's Castle, standing on the Sound, with Shipman's Head beyond. And you must go out beyond Tresco, to the islands which we cannot see here—Tean and St. Helen's, and the rest.'

Then she turned westward. Lying scattered among the bright waters, whitened by the breeze, there lay before their eyes—dots and specks upon the biggest maps, but here great massive rocks and rugged islets piled with granite, surrounded by ledges and reefs, cut and carved by winds and flying foam into ragged edges, bold peaks, and defiant cliffs—places where all the year round the seals play and the sea-gulls scream, and, in spring, the puffins lay their eggs, with the oyster-catchers and the sherewaters, the shags and the hern. Over all shone the golden sun of September, and round them all the water leaped and sparkled in the light.

'Those are the Outer Islands.' The girl pointed them out, her eyes brightening. 'It is among the Outer Islands that I like best to sail. Look! that great rock with the ledge at foot is Castle Bryher; that noble rock beyond is Maiden Bower; the rock farthest out is Scilly. If you were going to stay, we would sail round Scilly and watch the waves always tearing at his sides. You cannot see from here, but he is divided by a narrow channel; the water always rushes through this channel roaring and tearing. But once we found it calm—and we got through; only Peter would never try again. If you were going to stay—sometimes in September it is very still——'

'I did not know,' said Roland, 'that there was anything near England so wonderful and so lovely.'

'You cannot see the islands in one morning. You cannot see half of them from this hill. You like them more and more as you stay longer, and see them every day with a different light and a different sea.'

'You know them all, I suppose?' Roland asked.

'Oh! every one. If you had sailed among them so often, you would know them too. There are hundreds, and every one has got its name. I think I have stood on all, though there are some on which no one can land, even at low tide and in the calmest weather. And no one knows what beautiful bays and beaches and headlands there are hidden away and never seen by anyone. If you could stay, I would show them to you. But since you cannot——' She sighed. 'Well, you have not even seen the whole of Samson yet—and that is only one of all the rest.'

She leaped lightly from the rocks, and led them southward.

'See!' she said. 'On this hill there are ten great barrows at least, every one the tomb of a king—a king of Lyonesse. And on the sides of the hill—they kept the top for the kings—there are smaller barrows, I suppose of the princes and princesses. I told you that the island was a royal burying-ground. At the foot of the hill—you can see them—are some walls which they say are the ruins of a church; but I suppose that in those days they had no church.'

They left these venerable tombs behind them and descended the hill. At its foot, between the two hills, there lies a pretty little bay, circular and fringed with a beach of white sand. If one wanted a port for Samson, here is the spot, looking straight across the Atlantic, with Mincarlo lying like a lion couchant on the water a mile out.

'This is Porth Bay,' said their guide. 'Out there at the end is Shark Point. There are sharks sometimes, I believe: but I have never seen them. Now we are going up the southern hill.'

It began with a gentle ascent. There were signs of former cultivation; stone walls remained, enclosing spaces which once were fields—nothing in them now but fern and gorse and bramble and wild flowers. Half-way up there stood a ruined cottage. The walls were standing, but the roof was gone and all the woodwork. The garden-wall remained, but the little garden was overrun with fern.

'This was my great-great-grandmother's cottage,' said Armorel. 'It was built by her husband. They lived in it for twelve months after they were married. Then he was drowned, and she came to live at the farm. See!'—she showed them in a corner of the garden a little wizened apple-tree, crouching under the stone wall out of the reach of the north wind—'she planted this tree on her wedding-day. It is too old now to bear fruit; but she is still living, and her husband has been dead for seventy-five years. I often come to look at the place, and to wonder how it looked when it was first inhabited. There were flowers, I suppose, in the garden, when she was young and happy.'

'There are more ruins,' said Roland.

'Yes, there are other ruins. When all the people except ourelves went away, these cottages were deserted, and so they fell into decay. They used to live by smuggling and wrecking, you see, and when they could no longer do either, they had to go away or starve.'

They stood upon the highest point of Holy Hill, some twenty feet above the summit of the northern hill, and looked out upon the Southern Islands.

'There!' said Armorel, with a flush of pride, because the view here is so different and yet so lovely.

'Here you can see the South Islands. Look! there is Minalto, which you drifted past yesterday: those are the ledges of White Island, where you were nearly cast away and lost: there is Annet, where the sea-birds lay their eggs—oh! thousands and thousands of puffins, though now there are not any: you should see them in the spring. That is St. Agnes—a beautiful island. I should like to show you Camberdizl and St. Warna's Cove. And there are the Dogs of Scilly beyond—they look to be black spots from here. You should see them close: then you would understand how big they are and how terrible. There are Gorregan and Daisy, Rosevean and Rosevear, Crebawethan and Pednathias; and there—where you see a little circle of white—that is Retarrier Ledge. Not long ago there was a great ship coming slowly up the Channel in bad weather: she was filled with Germans from New York going home to spend the money they had saved in America: most of them had their money with them tied up in bags. Suddenly the ship struck on Retarrier. It was ten o'clock in the evening and a great sea running. For two hours the ship kept bumping on the rocks: then she began to break up, and they were all drowned—all the women and all the children, and most of the men. Some of them had life-belts on, but they did not know how to tie them, and so the things only slipped down over their legs and helped to drown them. The money was found on them. In the old days the people of the islands would have had it all; but the coastguard took care of it. There, on the right of Retarrier, is the Bishop's Rock and lighthouse. In storms, the lighthouse rocks like a tree in the wind. You ought to sail over to those rocks, if it was only to see the surf dashing up their sides. But, since you cannot stay ——' Again she sighed.

'These are very interesting islands,' said Dick. 'Especially is it interesting to consider the consequences of being a native.'

'I should like to stay and sail among them,' said Roland.

'For instance'—Dick pursued his line of thought—'in the study of geography. We who are from the inland parts of Great Britain must begin by learning the elements, the definitions, the terminology. Now to a Scilly boy——'

'A Scillonian,' the girl corrected him. 'We never speak of Scilly folk.'

'Naturally. To a Scillonian no explanation is needed. He knows, without being told, the meaning of peninsula, island, bay, shore, archipelago, current, tide, cape, headland, ocean, lake, road, harbour, reef, lighthouse, beacon, buoy, sounding—everything. He must know also what is meant by a gale of wind, a stiff breeze, a dead calm. He recognises, by the look of it, a lively sea, a chopping sea, a heavy sea, a roaring sea, a sulky sea. He knows everything except a river. That, I suppose, requires very careful explanation. It was a Scilly youth—I mean a Scillonian—who sat down on the river bank to wait for the water to go by. The history seems to prove the commercial intercourse which in remote antiquity took place between Phœnicia and the Cassiterides or Scilly Islands.'

Armorel looked puzzled. 'I did not know that story of a Scillonian and a river,' she said, coldly.

'Never mind his stories,' said Roland. 'This place is a story in itself: you are a story: we are all in fairyland.'

'No'—she shook her head. 'Bryher is the only island in all Scilly which has any fairies. They call them pixies there. I do not think that fairies would ever like to come and live on Samson: because of the graves, you know.'

She led them down the hill along a path worn by her own feet alone, and brought them out to the level space occupied by the farm-buildings.

'This is where we live,' she said. 'If you could stay here, Roland Lee, we could give you a room. We have many empty rooms'—she sighed—'since my father and mother and my brothers were all drowned. Will you come in?'

She took them into the 'best parlour,' a room which struck a sudden chill to anyone who entered therein. It was the room reserved for days of ceremony—for a wedding, a christening, or a funeral. Between these events the room was never used. The furniture presented the aspect common to 'best parlours,' being formal and awkward. In one corner stood a bookcase with glass doors, filled with books. Armorel showed them into this apartment, drew up the blind, opened the window—there was certainly a stuffiness in the air—and looked about the room with evident pride. Few best parlours, she thought, in the adjacent islands of St. Mary's, Bryher, Tresco, or even Great Britain itself, could beat this.

She left them for a few minutes, and came back bearing a tray on which were a plate of apples, another of biscuits, and a decanter full of a very black liquid. Hospitality has its rules even on Samson, whither come so few visitors.

'Will you taste our Scilly apples?' she said. 'These are from our own orchard, behind the house. You will find them very sweet.'

Roland took one—as a general rule, this young man would rather take a dose of medicine than an apple—and munched it with avidity. 'A delicious fruit!' he cried. But his friend refused the proffered gift.

'Then you will take a biscuit, Dick Stephenson? Nothing? At least, a glass of wine?'

'Never in the morning, thank you.'

'You will, Roland Lee?' She turned, with a look of disappointment, to the other man, who was so easily pleased and who said such beautiful things. 'It is my own wine—I made it myself last year, of ripe blackberries.'

'Indeed I will! Your own wine? Your own making, Miss Armorel? Wine of Samson—the glorious vintage of the blackberry! In pies and in jam-pots I know the blackberry, but not, as yet, in decanters. Thank you, thank you!'

He smiled heroically while he held the glass to the light, smelt it, rolled it gently round. Then he tasted it. 'Sweet,' he said.

critically. 'And strong. Clings to the palate. A liqueur wine—a curious wine.' He drank it up, and smiled again. 'Your own making! It is wonderful! No—not another drop, thank you!'

'Shall I show you?'—the girl asked, timidly—'would you like to see my great-great-grandmother? She is so very old that the people come all the way from St. Agnes only just to look at her. Sometimes she answers questions for them, and they think it is telling their fortunes. She is asleep. But you may talk aloud. You will not awaken her. She is so very, very old, you know. Consider: she has been a widow nearly eighty years.'

She led them into the other room, where, in effect, the ancient dame sat in her hooded chair fast asleep, in cap and bonnet, her hands, in black mittens, crossed.

'Heavens!' Roland murmured. 'What a face! I must draw that face! And'—he looked at the girl bending over the chair placing a pillow in position—'and that other. It is wonderful!' he said aloud. 'This is, indeed, the face of one who has lived a hundred years. Does she sometimes wake up and talk?'

'In the evening she recovers her memory for awhile and talks—sometimes quite nicely, sometimes she rambles.'

'And you have a spinning-wheel in the corner.'

'She likes someone to work at the spinning-wheel while she talks. Then she thinks it is the old time back again.'

'And there is a violin.'

'I play it in the evening. It keeps her awake, and helps her to remember. Justinian taught me. He used to play very well indeed until his fingers grew stiff. I can play a great many tunes, but it is difficult to learn any new ones. Last summer there were some ladies at Tregarthen's—one of them had a most beautiful voice, and she used to sing in the evening with the window open. I used to sail across on purpose to land and listen outside. And I learned a very pretty tune. I would play it to you in the evening if you were not going away.'

'I am not obliged to go away,' the young man said, with strangely flushing cheeks.

'Roland!' That was Dick's voice—but it was unheeded.

'Will you stay here, then?' the girl asked.

'Here in this house? In your house?'

'You can have my brother Emanuel's room. I shall be very glad if you will stay. And I will show you everything.' She did not invite the young man called Dick, but this other, the young man who drank her wine and ate her apple.

'If your—your—your guardian—or your great-great-grandmother approves.'

'Oh! she will approve. Stay, Roland Lee. We will make you very happy here. And you don't know what a lot there is to see.'

'Roland!' Again Dick's warning voice.

'A thousand thanks!' he said. 'I will stay.'

CHAPTER V

THE ENCHANTED ISLAND

THE striking of seven by the most sonorous and musical of clocks ever heard reminded Roland of the dinner-hour. At seven most of us are preparing for this function, which civilisation has converted almost into an act of praise and worship. Some men, he remembered, were now walking in the direction of the club: some were dressing: some were making for restaurants: some had already begun. One naturally associates seven o'clock with the anticipation of dinner. There are men, it is true, who habitually take in food at midday and call it dinner: there are also those who have no dinner at all. He began to realise that he was not, this evening, going to have any dinner at all. For he was now at the farmhouse, sitting in the square window with Armorel: he had gone back to Tregarthen's and returned with his portmanteau and his painting gear: fortunately he had also taken an abundant lunch at that establishment. He had become an inhabitant of Samson. The increased population, therefore, now consisted of seven souls.

In fact, there was no dinner for him. Everybody in Samson dines at half-past twelve: he had tea with Armorel at half-past four: after tea they wandered along the shore and stood upon Shark Point to see the sun set behind Mincarlo, an operation performed with zeal and despatch, and with great breadth and largeness of colouring. When the shades of evening began to prevail they were fain to get home quickly, because there is no path among the boulders, nor have former inhabitants provided hand-rails for visitors on the carns. Therefore they retraced their steps to the farm, and Armorel left him sitting alone in the square window while she went about some household duties. In the quiet room the solemn clock told the moments, and there was light enough left to discern the ghostly figure of the ancient dame sleeping in her chair. The place was so quiet and so strange that the visitor presently felt as if he was sitting among ghosts. It is at twilight, in fact, that the spirits of the past make themselves most readily felt, if not seen. Now, it was exactly as if he had been in the place before. He knew, now, why he had been so suddenly and strangely attracted to Samson. He *had been there before*—when, or under what conditions, he knew not, and did not ask himself. It is a condition of the mind known to everybody. A touch—a word—a look—and we are transported back—how many years ago? The hills, the rocks, the house, Armorel herself—all were familiar to him. The thing was absurd, yet in his mind it was quite clear. It was so absurd that he thought his mind was wandering, and he arose and went out into the garden. There, the figure-head of the woman under the tall fuchsia-tree—the glow from the fire in the sitting-room fell upon the face through the window—seemed to smile upon him as upon an old friend. He went back again and sat down. Where was Armorel?

This strange familiarity with an unknown place quickly passes, though it may return. He now began to feel as if, perhaps, he was making a mistake. He was living on an island, with, practically, no other companion than a girl of fifteen. Dick, who had become suddenly grumpy on learning his resolution to stay, might be right. Well, he would sketch and paint; he would be very careful; not a word should be said that might disturb the child's tranquillity. No—Dick was a fool. He was going to have a day or two—just a day or two—of quiet happiness. The girl was young and beautiful and innocent. She was also made happy—she showed that happiness without an attempt at concealment—because he was going to stay. What would follow?

Well—it was an adventure. One does not ask what is going to follow on first encountering an adventure. What young man, besides, sallying forth upon a simple holiday, looks to find himself upon a desert island with no other companion than a trustful and admiring maiden of fifteen?

Then Armorel returned and took a chair beside him. He was a little surprised—but then, on a desert island nothing happens as on terra firma—that she did not ring for lights, and was still not without some hope of dinner. They took up the thread of talk about the islands, concerning which Roland Lee perceived that he would before long know a good deal. Local knowledge is always interesting; but it does not, except to novelists, possess a marketable value. One cannot, for instance, at a dinner-party, turn the conversation on the respective families of St. Agnes and St. Martin's. He made a mental note that he would presently change the subject to one of deeper personal interest. Perhaps he could get Armorel to talk about herself. That would be very much more interesting than to hear about the three Pipers' Holes of Tresco, White, and St. Mary's Islands. How did she live—this girl—and what did she do—and what did she think?

Meantime, while the girl herself was talking of the rocks and bays, the crags and coves, the white sand and the grey granite, the seals and the shags, the puffins and the dottrells, she was wondering, for her part, what manner of man this was—how he lived, and what he did, and what he thought. For when man and woman meet they are clothed and covered up; they are a mystery each to the other; never, since the Fall, have we been able to read each other's hearts.

But when the clock struck seven Armorel sprang to her feet, as one who hath a serious duty to perform, and preparations to make for it.

First she pulled down the blind, and so shut out what was left of the twilight. The fire had sunk low, but by its light she was dimly visible. She pushed back the table; she placed two chairs opposite the old lady, and another chair before the spinning-wheel.

'Something,' said the young man to himself, 'is certainly going to happen. One can no longer hope for dinner. Family prayers, perhaps; or the worship of the old lady as an ancestor. The descendants of the ancient people of Lyonesse no doubt bow down to the sun and dance to the moon, and pass the children through the holèd stone, and make Baal fires, and worship their grandmothers. It will be an interesting function. But, perhaps, only family prayers.'

Armorel took down the fiddle that hung on the wall and began to tune it, twanging the strings and drawing the bow across in the manner which so pleasantly excites the theatre before the music begins.

'Not family prayers, then,' said the young man, perhaps disappointed.

What did happen, however, was a series of things quite new and wholly unexpected. Never was known such a desert island.

First of all, the lady of many generations moved uneasily in her sleep at the twanging of the strings, and her fingers clutched at her dress as if she was startled by an uneasy dream.

And then the door opened, and a small procession of three came in. At this point, had the young man been a Roman Catholic, he would have crossed himself. As he was not, he only started and murmured, 'As I thought. The worship of the ancestor! These are the ghosts of the grandfather and the grandmother. The old lady is a mummy. They are all ghosts—I shall presently awake and find myself on my back among the barrows.'

First came an ancient dame, but not so ancient as she of the great chair. Grey-headed she was, and equipped in a large cap; wrinkled was her face, and her chin, for lack of teeth, approached her nose, quite in the ancestral manner. She was followed by an old man, also grey-headed and grey-bearded, wrinkled of face, his shoulders bent and twisted with rheumatism, his fingers gnarled and twisted. These two took the chairs set for them by Armorel. The third in the procession was a woman already elderly and with streaks of grey in her hair. She was thin and sharp faced. She sat down before the spinning-wheel and began to work, not as you may now see the amateur, but in the quiet, quick, professional manner which means business.

The stranger was not quite right in his conjecture. They were not ancestors. The old man, who had worked on the farm, man and boy, for nearly seventy years, and now managed it altogether, was Justinian Tryeth. The old woman was Dorcas, his wife. The middle-aged woman was their daughter Chessun, who had been maid on the farm, as her brother Peter had been boy, all her life.

Whatever was intended was clearly a daily function, because each dropped into his own place without hesitation. The old woman had brought some knitting with her, her daughter picked up the thread of the spindle, and the old man, taking the tongs, stimulated the coals into a flame, which he continually nursed and maintained with new fuel. There was neither lamp nor candle in the room; the ruddy firelight, rising and falling, played about the room, warming the drab panels into crimson, sinking into the dark beams of the joists, flashing among the china in the cupboard, painting red the Venus's-fingers in the cabinet, and throwing strange lights and shadows upon the aged lady in the chair. Was she really alive? Was she, after all, only a mummy?

Roland looked on breathless. What was to be done next? Time had gone back eighty years—a hundred and eighty years—any number of years. As they sat here in the fire-light with the spinning-wheel, the old serving-people with their mistress, without lamp or candle, so they sat in the generations long gone by. And again that curious feeling fell upon him that he had seen it all before. Yet he could not remember what was to be done next. Armorel, the tuning complete, turned with a look of inquiry to the old man.

"Singleton's Slip," he commanded with the authority of a professor.

The girl began to play this old tune. Perhaps you remember the style of the fiddler—he is getting scarce now—who used to sit in the corner and play the hornpipe for the sailors in the days when every sailor could dance the hornpipe. Perhaps you do not remember that fiddler and his style. That is your misfortune. For there was a noble freedom in the handling of his bow, and the interpretation of his melodies was bold and original. He poured into the music all the spirit it was capable of containing, and drew out of his hearers every emotion that each particular tune was able to draw. Because you see tunes have their limitations. You cannot strike every chord in the human heart with a simple hornpipe. This sailor's best friend, however, did all that could be done. And always conscientious, if you please, never allowing his playing to become slovenly or to lack spirit.

Armorel played after the manner of this old fiddler, standing up to her work in the middle of the room.

'Singleton's Slip' is a ditty which was formerly much admired by those who danced the hey, the jig, or the simple country dance: it was also much played by the pipe and tabor upon the village green; it accompanied the bear when he carried the pole; it assisted those who danced on stilts; and it lent spirit to those who frolicked in the morrice. Charles II. knew it; Tom D'Urfey wrote words to it, I believe, but I have not yet found them in his collection; Rochester must certainly have danced to it. Armorel played it; first cheerfully and loudly, as if to arouse the spirits of those who listened, to remind them that legs may be shaken to this tune, and that ladies may be, and should be, when this tune begins, taken to their places and presently handed round and down the middle. Then she played it trippingly, as if they were actually all dancing. Then she played it tenderly—there is, if you come to think of it, a good deal of possible tenderness in the air—and, lastly, she played it joyfully, yet softly. How had she learned all these modes and moods?

While she played the old man listened critically, nodding his head and beating the time. Then, fired with memory, he bent his arms and worked his fingers as if they held the fiddle and the bow. And he threw back his head and thrust out his leg and leaned sideways, just like that jolly fiddler of whom we have just been reminded. Such, my friends, is the power of music.

After a little while Justinian stopped this imaginary performance, and sitting forward yielded himself wholly to the influence of the tune, cracking his fingers over his head and beating time with one foot, just as you may see the old villager in the old coloured prints—no villager in these days of bad beer ever cracks his fingers or shows any external signs of joyful emotion. As for the two serving-women, they reminded the spectator of the supers on the stage who march when they are told to march, sit down to feast when they are ordered, and swell a procession for a funeral or a festival, all with unmoved countenance, showing a philosophy so great that the triumph of victory or the disaster of defeat finds them equally calm and self-contained—that is to say, the two women showed no sense at all of being pleased or moved by 'Singleton's Slip.' They went on—one with her knitting and the other with her spinning.

As for the ancient lady, however, when the music began she straightened herself, sat upright, and opened her eyes. Then Chessun hastened to adjust her bonnet: if ladies sleep in their bonnets, these adornments have a tendency to fall out of the perpendicular. Heaven forbid that we should gaze upon Ursula Rosevean with her bonnet tilted, like a lady in a van coming home to Wapping from Fairlop Fair! This done, the venerable dame looked about her with eyes curiously bright and keen. Then she began to beat time with her fingers; and then she began to talk; but—and this added to the strangeness of the whole business—nobody seemed to regard what she said. It was much as if the Oracle of Delphi were pouring out the most valuable prophecies and none of her attendants paid any heed. 'If,' thought the young man, 'I were to take down her words, they would be a Message.' And what with the voice of the Oracle, the spirited fiddling, the firelight dancing about the room, the old man snapping his fingers, and perhaps some physical exhaustion following on the absence of dinner, the young man felt as if the music had got into his head; he wanted to get up and dance with Armorel round and round the room; he would not have marvelled had Dorcas and Justinian bidden him lead out Chessun and so take hands, round twice, down the middle and back again, set and turn single—where had he learnt these phrases and terms of the old country dance? Nowhere; they belonged to the place and to the music and to the time—and that was at least a hundred and eighty years back.

The fiddle stopped. Armorel held it down, and looked again at her master.

''Tis well played,' he said. 'A moving piece. Now, "Prince Rupert's March."'

She nodded, and began another tune. This is a piece which may be played many ways. First, to those who understand it rightly, it indicates the tramp of an army, the riding of the cavalry, the jingling of sabres. Next, it may serve for a battle-piece, and you shall hear between the bars the charge of the horse and the clashing of the steel. Or, it may be played as a triumphal march after victory; or, again, as a country dance, in which a stately dignity takes the place of youthful mirth and merriment. At such a dance, to the tune of 'Prince Rupert's March,' the elders themselves—yea, the Justice of Peace, the Vicar, the Mayor and Aldermen, and the Head-borough himself—may stand up in line.

And now Roland became conscious of the old lady's words; he heard them clear and distinct, and as she talked the fire-light fell upon her eyes, and she seemed to be gazing fixedly upon the stranger.

'When the "Princess Augusta," East Indiaman, struck upon the Castinicks in the middle of the night, she went to pieces in an hour—any vessel would. They said she was wrecked by the people of Samson, who tied a ship's lantern between the horns of a cow. But it was never proved. There are other islands in Scilly, and other islanders, if you talk of wrecking. Some of the dead bodies were washed ashore, and a good part of the cargo, so that there was something for everybody; a finer wreck never came to the islands. What! If a ship is bound to be wrecked, better that she should strike on British rocks and cast her cargo ashore for the king's subjects. Better the rocks of Scilly than the rocks of France. What the sea casts up belongs to the people who find it. That is just. But you must not rob the living. No. That is a great crime. 'Twas in the year '13. When Emanuel Rosevean, my father-in-law, rescued the passenger who was lying senseless lashed to a spar, he should not have taken the bag that was hanging round his neck. That was not well done. He should have given the man his bag again. He stood here before he went away. "You have saved my life," he said. "I had all my treasure in a bag tied about my neck. If I had brought that safe ashore I could have offered you something worth your acceptance. But I have nothing I begin the world again." Emanuel heard him say this, and he let him go. But the bag was in his box. He kept the bag. Very soon the wrath of the Lord fell upon the house, and His Hand has been heavy upon us ever since. No luck for us—nor shall be any till we find the man and give him back his bag of treasure.'

She went on repeating this story with small variations and additions. But Roland was now listening again to the fiddle.

Armorel stopped again.

'"Dissembling Love,"' said her master.

She began that tune obediently.

The stranger within the gates seemed compelled to listen. His brain reeled; the old woman fascinated him. The words which he had heard had been few, but now he seemed to see, standing before the fire, his hair powdered, and in black silk stockings and shoes with steel buckles, the man who had been saved and robbed shaking hands with the man who had saved and robbed him. Oh! it was quite clear: he had seen it all before; he remembered it. This time he heard nothing of the tune.

'My husband, Methusalem, my dear husband, with his only brother, began to pay for that wickedness. They were capsized crossing to St. Mary's, and drowned. If I had thought what was going to happen I would have taken the bag and walked through all England looking for him until I had found him. Yes—if it took me fifty years. But I knew nothing. I thought our happiness would last for ever. Five-and-twenty years after, my son, Emanuel, was cast away in the Bristol Channel piloting a vessel. They struck on Steep Holm in a fog. And your own father, Armorel, was drowned with his wife and three boys on their way home from a wedding-feast at St. Agnes.'

Here her voice dropped, and Roland heard the concluding bars of 'Dissembling Love,' which Armorel was playing with quite uncommon tenderness.

When she stopped, Justinian gave her no rest. '"Blue Petticoats,"' he commanded.

Armorel again obeyed.

Then the old lady went back in memory to the days of her girlhood—now so long ago. Nowhere now can one find an old lady who will tell of her girlish days when the century was not yet arrived at the age of ten.

'We shall dance to-night,' she said, 'on Bryher Green. My boy will be there. We shall dance together. John Tryeth from Samson will play his fiddle. We shall dance "Prince Rupert's March" and "Blue Petticoats" and "Dissembling Love." The Ensign from the garrison is coming and the Deputy Commissary. They will drink my health. But they shall not have me for partner. My boy will be there—my own boy—the handsomest man on all the islands, though he is so black. That's the Spaniard in him. His mother was a Mureno—Honor Mureno, the last of the Murenos. He has got the old Spaniard's sword still. It's the Spanish blood. It gives my boy his black eyes and his black hair;

it makes his cheeks swarthy; and it makes him proud and hot-tempered. I like a man to be quick and proud if he's strong and brave as well. When I have sons, the Lord make them all like their father!'

So she went on talking of her lover.

Armorel stopped and looked again at her master.

'"The Chirping of the Lark,"' he said.

Armorel began this tune. It is of an artificial character, lending itself less readily than the rest to emotion; the composer called it 'The Chirping of the Lark' because he wanted a title: it resembles the song of that warbler in no single particular. But it changed the old lady's current of thought.

'This long war,' she said, looking round cheerfully, 'will be the making of the islands if it lasts. Never was there so much money about: we roll in money: the women have all got silks and satins: the men drink port wine and the finest French brandy, which they run over for themselves: the merchantmen put into the road, and the sailors spend their money at the port. Why shouldn't we go on fighting the French until they haven't a ship left afloat? My man made the run last week, and hid the cargo—I know where. I shall help him to carry the kegs across to the garrison, where they want brandy badly. A fine run and a good day's work!'

She looked around with a jubilant countenance. Then another memory seized her, and the light left her eyes.

'Better be drowned yourself than marry a man who is going to be drowned! Better not marry at all than lose your husband six months afterwards. It is long ago, now, Armorel. Time goes on—one can remember. He would be very old now—yes—very old. Sometimes I see him still. But he has not grown old where he is staying. That is bad for me, because he liked young women, not old women. Men mostly do. They are so made, even the oldest of them. Perhaps the old women, when they rise again, are made young again, so that their lovers may love them still.'

The clock struck half-past eight. Armorel stopped playing and the old lady stopped talking at the same moment. Her eyes closed, her head fell forward, she became comatose.

Then the two serving-women got up and helped her, or carried her, out of the room to her bedroom behind. And the old man arose, and without so much as a good-night hobbled away to his own cottage.

'She will go to bed now,' said Armorel. 'Chessun will take in her broth and her wine, and she will sleep all night.'

'Do you have this performance every night?'

'Yes; the playing seems to put life and heart into her. All the morning she dozes, or if she wakes she is not often able to talk; but in the evening, when we sit around the fire just as they used to sit in the old days, without candles—because my people were poor and candles were dear—and when Chessun spins and I play—she revives and sits up and talks, as you have seen her.'

'Yes. It is rather ghostly.'

'Justinian used to play—oh! he could play very well indeed.'

'Not so well as you.'

'Yes—much better—and he knows hundreds of tunes.' But his fingers became stiff with rheumatism, and, as he had put off teaching Peter until it was too late, he taught me. That is all.'

'I think you play wonderfully well. Do you play nothing but old tunes?'

'I only know what I have learned. There is that song which I heard the lady sing last year—I don't know what it is called. Tell me if you like it.'

She struck the strings again and played a song full of life and spirit, of tenderness and fond memory—a bright, sparkling song—which wanted no words.

'Oh!' cried Roland, 'you are really wonderful. You are playing the "Kerry Dance."'

She laughed and layed down the violin.

'We must not have any more playing to-night. Do you really like to hear me play? You look as if you did.'

'It is wonderful,' he replied. 'I could listen all night. But if there is to be no more music, shall we look outside?'

If there were no light in the house the ship's lantern was hanging up, with one of those big ship's candles in it which are of such noble dimensions, and of generosity so unbounded in the matter of tallow. There was no moon; but the sky was clear and the sea could be seen by the light of the stars, and the revolving lights of Bishop's Rock and St. Agnes flashed across the water.

The young man shivered.

'We are in fairyland,' he said. 'It is a charmed island. Nothing is real. Armorel, your name should be Titania. How have you made me hear and believe all these things? How do you contrive your sorceries? Are you an enchantress? Confess—you cannot, in sober truth, play those tunes; the old lady is in reality only a phantom, called into visible shape by your incantations? But you are a benevolent witch—you will not turn me into a pig?'

'I do not understand. There have been no sorceries. There are no witches left on the Scilly Islands. Formerly there were many. Dorcas knows about them. I do not know what was the good of them.'

'I suppose you are quite real, after all. It is only strange and incomprehensible.'

'It is a fine night. To-morrow it will be a fine day with a gentle breeze. We will go sailing among the Outer Islands.'

'The air is heavy with perfume. What is it? Surely an enchanted land!'

'It is the scent of the lemon-verbena tree—see, here is a sprig. It is very sweet.'

'How silent it is here! Night after night never to hear a sound.'

'Nothing but the sound of the waves. They never cease. Listen—it is a calm night. But you can hear them lapping on the beach.'

Ten minutes later, when they returned to the house, they found candles lighted and supper spread. A substantial supper, such as was owed to a man who had had no dinner. There was cold roast fowl and ham; there was a lettuce-salad and a goodly cheese. And there was the unexpected and grateful sight of a 'Brown George,' with a most delectable ball of white froth at the top. Also, Roland remarked the presence of the decanter containing the blackberry wine.

'Now you shall have some supper.' Armorel assumed the head of the table and took up the carving-knife. 'No, thank you — I can carve very well. Besides, you are our visitor, and it is a pleasure to carve for you. Will you have a wing or a leg? Do you like your ham thin? Not too thin? Oh, how hungry you must be! That is ale—home-brewed ale: will you take some? or would you prefer a glass of the blackberry wine? No?—help yourself.'

'The beer for me,' said Roland. He filled and drank a tumbler of the beverage dear to every right-minded Briton. It was strong and generous, with flakes of hop floating in it like the bee's-wing in port. 'This is splendid beer,' he said. 'I do not remember that I ever tasted such beer as this. It is humming ale—October ale—stingo. No wonder our forefathers fought so well when they had such beer as this to fight upon!'

'Peter is proud of his home-brewed.'

'Do you make everything for yourselves? Is Samson sufficient for all the needs of the islanders? This beer is the beer of Samson —strong and mighty. My hair is growing long already—and curly.'

'We make all we can. There are no shops, you see, on Samson. We bake our own bread: we brew our own beer: we make our own butter: we even spin our own linen.'

'And you make your own wine, Armorel.' He called her naturally by her Christian name. You could not call such a girl 'Miss Armorel' or 'Miss Rosevean.' 'It is a wonderful island!'

After supper they sat by the fireside, and, by permission, he smoked his pipe.

Then, everybody else on the island being in bed and asleep, they talked. The young man had his way. That is to say, he encouraged the girl to talk about herself. He led her on: he had a soft voice, soft eyes, and a general manner of sympathy which surprised confidence.

She began, timidly at first, to talk about herself, yet with feminine reservation. No woman will ever talk about herself in the way which delights young men. But she told him all he asked: her simple lonely life—how she arose early in the morning, how she roamed about the island and sang aloud with none to hear her but the sea-gulls and the shags.

'Do you never draw?' he asked.

She had tried to draw, but there was no one to help her.

'Do you read?'

No, she seldom read. In the best parlour there was a bookcase full of books, but she never looked at them. As for the old lady and Dorcas, they had never learned to read. She had been at school over at St. Mary's, till she was thirteen, but she hardly cared to read.

'And the newspapers—do you ever read them?'

She never read them. She knew nothing that went on.

As for her ambitions and her hopes—if he could get at them. Fond youth!—as if a girl would ever tell her ambitions! But Armorel, apparently, had none to tell. She lived in the present; it was joy enough for her to wander in the soft warm air of her island home, upon the hills and round the coast, to cruise among the rocks while the breeze filled out the sail and the sparkling water leaped above the bow.

So far she told: nay, she hid nothing, because there was nothing to hide. She told no more because, as yet, her ambitions and her dreams of the future had no shape: they were vague and misty—she was only aware of their existence when restlessness seized her and impelled her to get up and run over the hills to Porth Bay and back again.

But at night, when she went to bed, she experienced quite a new and disquieting sensation. It showed at least that she was no longer a child, but already on the threshold of womanhood. With blushing cheek and beating heart she remembered that for an hour and more she had been talking about nothing but herself! What would Mr. Roland Lee think of a girl who could waste his time in talking about nothing but herself?

CHAPTER VI

THE FLOWER-FARM

ROLAND, startled out of sleep by the sudden feeling of danger which always seizes us in a strange bed—except a bed at an inn—sat up and looked around him. His room was small and low and simply furnished. He was lying on a feather bed of the old-fashioned kind; the bedstead was of wood, but without curtains. He presently remembered where he was: on Samson Island—the guest of a child, a girl of fifteen.

He sprang out of bed and threw open the window. His room was over the porch. The fragrance of the lemon-verbena tree arose like steam from a haystack, and filled his chamber. Below him, and beyond the garden, the geese waddled on the green, the ducks splashed in the pond, and in the farmyard Peter walked about slowly, carrying a pitchfork in his hands, but, apparently, for amusement rather than use, as if it had been a court sword.

He looked at his watch. It was half-past seven. At this time in London he would have been still in the first long slumber of the night. Now he was eager to be up and dressed, if only for a better understanding of the situation. To be the guest of a child has the freshness of novelty; but it is a situation which might lead to complications. Suppose a guardian, or a lawyer, or a cousin of some kind were to cross over in a boat and ask what he was doing there. And suppose he had no better reply than the plain truth—that this young lady had been so good as to invite him. Would a man go down to stay at a country house on the simple invitation of a schoolgirl? At the same time, this girl appeared to be the mistress of the establishment. There was an ancient lady—too old for superintendence—and there were servants. Well, if no guardian challenged his presence, why, then, for a single day—he must not stay more—it surely mattered little. The girl was but a child. Yet he must not stay longer. Perhaps they were not too well off: he must not be a burden. And, again, though the girl invited him to stay she named no limit of time. She did not invite him to stay, for a week or for a fortnight. Perhaps she expected him to go away that very morning.

He proceeded—with somewhat thoughtful countenance, considering these things—to dress, paying as much attention to his personal appearance as a young man should, and an old man must. It is the privilege of middle-aged men to go slovenly if they please: no one regardeth him of middle age. While their locks are turning grey and their children are growing up they are in the thick of the day's work, and they may disregard, if they choose, the mysteries of the toilette. Apollo, however, must be as jealous about his apparel and adornment as the Graces themselves, who are always represented at the moment before the choice is made. A velvet jacket and a white waistcoat are trifles in themselves, but they become a youthful figure and a face which has finely-cut features and is decorated with a promising silky beard, pointed withal, and the brown shading of a young moustache. Besides, he who is an artist thinks more than other young men about such things. Dress, to him, as to a woman, becomes costume. Colour has to be considered; such picturesqueness as is possible in modern fashion is aimed at; the artistic craving for fitness and beauty must be satisfied. Roland did what he could: and with his velvet coat, a clean white waistcoat, a crimson scarf, a good figure, and a handsome face, he was as handsome a youth of twenty-one as one is likely to find anywhere.

Again, as he opened his door and began to descend the narrow stairs, there came over him that curious feeling of having been in the place before. He had felt it in the evening when Armorel played 'Dissembling Love.' Now he felt it again. And when he stood in the porch he seemed to remember standing there once—long ago, long ago—but how long he could not tell; nor, as happened to him before, could he remember what had happened on that occasion.

Armorel herself was in the garden looking for some flowers for the breakfast-table. She greeted him with a smile of welcome and a friendly grasp of the hand. There was also a look of kindly solicitude on her face which would have suited a châtelaine of forty years. Had he slept well? Had he really been provided with everything he wanted? Was there anything at all lacking? If so, would he speak to Chessun? Breakfast, she said, leaving him in the garden, would be served in a few minutes.

Would he speak to Chessun? Then, it seemed as if she meant him to stay another night. What should he do?

Then Armorel came back.

'Breakfast is quite ready,' she said. 'Come in, Roland Lee. It is a beautiful morning. There is a fresh breeze and a smooth sea. We can go anywhere this morning. I have spoken to Peter, and he will be ready to go with us in an hour or so. I think we may even get out to Scilly and Maiden Bower.'

Yes; the morning was bright and the sky was clear. In the golden sunshine of September the islets across the water showed like creations of a poet's dream.

Roland drew a deep breath of admiration. 'Everybody,' he said, 'ought to come to Scilly and to stay a long time.'

He turned from the view to the girl beside him. She had changed her blue flannel dress for a daintier and a prettier costume—think not that there are no shops at Hugh Town—of grey nun's cloth, daintily embroidered in front. Still at her throat she wore a red flower, and round her neck clung the golden torque found in the old king's grave. Her dark eyes glowed: her lips were parted in a smile: her cheek showed the dewy bloom that some girls, fortunate above their sisters, can exhibit when they first appear in the morning: her long tresses were now tied up and confined; she looked as if she had just stepped forth from her chamber, fresh from her sleep. No one certainly could have guessed that she had been up since six; nor that the fish which had been hissing in the frying-pan, and were now lying meekly side by side in a dish on the breakfast-table, were of her own catching. An hour's sitting in the boat off Samson Ledge with hook and line had procured this splendid contribution to the morning banquet. Fish fragrant with the salt sea: fish that had not been packed tight in boxes, nor travelled in railway trains, nor been slapped about on counters, nor been packed in ice; fish that can never lie on a London table—these were set out before Roland's hungry gaze.

The ancient dame did not appear. The two breakfasted, as they had supped, together. I do not know how or where Armorel learned the art and practice of hospitality, but certainly she showed a true feeling in the matter of feeding—especially at breakfast. First, the table was decorated with the autumn leaves of the bramble—crimson, yellow, purple—few, indeed, know how beautiful a table may be made when decorated with these leaves. There were also a few late flowers from the garden; but not many. The coffee was strong, the milk hot and thick, the bread and butter home-made, like the beer of yester eve: the ham was cured by Chessun: the eggs were collected by Armorel: she had also with her own hands made the jam and the cake.

Armorel sat behind the cups with as much ease as if she had been accustomed from infancy to entertain young gentlemen at breakfast. She was serious over her task, and poured out the coffee as if it was something precious, not to be wasted or carelessly administered, which is the spirit in which all good food should be approached. She did not ask any questions, nor did she talk much during the banquet. Perhaps she had an instinctive perception of the great truth that breakfast, which is taken at the beginning of the day—the sacred day, with all its possibilities and its chances of what may happen; the fateful day, which alone and unaided may change the whole course and current of a life—should be approached with a becoming gravity. At breakfast the man fortifies himself before he goes forth to work. But he has the work before him. In the evening it is done: he has passed through the dangers of the day: he still lives: he has received no hurt: he has, we hope, prospered in his honest handiwork: he may laugh and rejoice. But at breakfast we should be serious.

'What will you do,' asked Armorel, breakfast completed, 'until Peter is ready? He has got some work, you know, before he can come out.'

'I should like first,' he said, 'to see your flower-farm, if I may.

'If you please. But there is nothing to see at this time of the year. You must not think we grow flowers all the year round. If you were here in February, you would see the fields covered with beautiful flowers—iris, anemone, jonquil, narcissus, and daffodil. They are very pretty then, and the air is sweet with their scent. But now the fields are quite bare.'

'I should like to see them, however.'

'I will show them to you. It is a great happiness to the islands,' said Armorel, gravely, 'that we have found out the flower-farming. Everybody was very poor before. All the old ways of living were gone, you see. A long time ago the people had wrecks every winter—the sea cast up quantities of things which they could sell, or they went out in boats and took the things out of the hold when the ship was on the rocks. And then they were all smugglers: the Scillonians used to run over to France openly, day and night.

with no one to stop them. And they used to carry fruit and vegetables out to the homeward-bound ships in the Channel. And then they were pilots as well. Some of the men used to make as much as two hundred pounds a year as pilots. My grandfathers were all pilots. They were smugglers too; and they had this farm and grew vegetables for the ships. Then the Government built the lighthouses, and there were no more wrecks; and the Preventive Service came and stopped the smuggling; and since the steamers took the place of the sailing-ships no vessels put in here, and there are no more pilots wanted. So, you see, it was as if nothing was left at all.'

'It does seem rough on the people.'

'First they tried kelp-making. They collected the sea-weed and put it in a kiln or furnace, and made a fire under it. I can show you some of the old furnaces still. But that came to an end. Then they tried a fishing company; but I believe it did not pay. And then they began to build ships; but I suppose other people could build them better. So that came to an end too. And for some time I do not know how all the people lived. As for the farms, they could never grow enough for the islands. Then a great many of the people went away. They had to go, or they would have starved. Some went to England, and some to America, and some to Australia. All the families went away from Samson, one by one, until at last there were none left but ourselves and Justinian. On Bryher and St. Martin's they became fishermen, but not here. As for Justinian, he sent away all his boys except Peter. Oh! they have done very well—splendidly. One is a coastguard, and one is bo's'n in the Queen's Navy. One is captain of a steamer trading between Philadelphia and Cuba, and one is actually chief steward on a great Pacific liner! Justinian is very proud of him.'

'Indeed, yes,' said Roland, 'with reason.'

'The Scillonians,' the girl continued, proudly, 'all get on very well wherever they go. They are honest, you see, as well as clever.'

'And the flower-farming?'

'Somebody discovered that the early spring flowers, which begin here in January, could be carried to London and sold quite fresh. And then everybody began to plant bulbs. That is all. We have had a farm of some kind here for I do not know how many generations.'

'Since the time,' Roland suggested, 'when, in consequence of the separation of Scilly from the mainland and the disappearance of Lyonesse, the royal family found themselves left in Samson.'

She laughed. 'Well, all these stone inclosures on the hill belonged to our farm. We grew things and ate them, I suppose. Perhaps we sold them. But we were then poor, I know, and now we have no more trouble.'

Beside and behind the farmhouse on the slope of the hill they came upon a series of little fields following one after the other. They were quite small—some mere patches, none larger than a garden of ordinary size, and they were all enclosed and shut in by high hedges, so that they looked like largish boxes with the lids off. Some of the hedges were of elm, growing thick and close; some of escallonia, with its red flowers; some of veronica, its purple blossom like heads of bulrush; some of the service-tree; and some, but not many, of tamarisk, its pink bunches of blossom all displayed at this time of the year. But the fields were now brown and bare, and had nothing at all growing in them, except a few patches of gladiolus, now dying. Beyond these fields, however, there were others of larger area, with ruder hedges formed by laths, reeds, wooden palings, and stone walls. These were inclosed, and partly sheltered for the growth of vegetables.

'These are our fields,' said Armorel. 'At this time of the year there is nothing to show you. Our harvest begins in January, and lasts till May; but February and March are our best months. See—there is Peter, with a young man from Bryher, planting bulbs for next year: they are taken up every three years and replanted.'

Peter, in fact, was at work. He was superintending—a form of work which he found to suit him best—while the young man from Bryher, who looked more than half sailor, with a broad, long-handled spade, was leisurely turning over the light sandy soil and laying in the bulbs side by side out of a great basket.

'It seems an easy form of agriculture,' said Roland.

'It is not hard. There is nothing to do after this until the flowers are picked. But sometimes a cold wind will come down from the north and will kill a whole field full of blossoms—in spite of all our hedges. That is a terrible loss. When everything goes well, we cut the flowers, pack them in boxes, carry them over to the port, and next morning they are sold in London—oh! and all over the country, in every big town.'

'I shall never again behold a daffodil in February,' said Roland, 'without thinking of Samson. You have lent a new association to the spring flowers. Henceforth they will bring back this glorious view of sea and islands, grey and black rocks, the splendid sunshine and the fresh breeze—and,' he added, with a winning smile and deferential eyes, 'the Lady of Lyonesse.'

Armorel laughed. It was very nice to be called the Lady of Lyonesse—nobody before had ever called her anything except plain Armorel. And it was quite a new experience to have a young gentleman treating her with deference as well as compliment.

At the back of the house was an orchard, through which they presently passed. Like the flower-fields, it was protected by a high hedge. But the apple-trees looked like the olives of Provence: every one seemed in the last decay of age. They were twisted and dwarfish; the branches grew in queer angles and elbows, as if they were crouching down out of reach of the north wind; the trunks were bent, and, which completed their resemblance to the olive, all alike were covered and clothed with a thick grey lichen, clinging to every bough like a glove, and hanging like a fringe. If you tear it off, the tree begins to shiver and shake, though on Samson it is never cold.

'Let us sit down,' said Roland, 'in this secluded spot and talk. Have I your leave, Armorel, to—— Thank you.' He filled and lit his briar-root, and lay back on the warm bank, gazing upwards at the blue sky through the leaves and the twisted branches of an aged apple-tree.

'It is good to be here. Do you know how very, very good it was of you to ask me, Armorel? And do you know how very, very rash it was?'

The girl, who showed her youth and inexperience in many little ways, regarded him with admiration unconcealed. Certainly, he was a personable young man, even picturesque; when his beard should be a little longer, when his moustache should be a little stronger, he might be able to pass for Charles I. idealised, and in early manhood, when as yet he had not begun to dissimulate.

'I was so glad when you promised to stay,' she replied, truthfully.

'Again, it is most good of you to say so. But, Armorel, a dreadful misgiving has possessed me. Does your—does the Ancestress approve of the invitation?'

Armorel laughed. 'Why,' she said, 'we never consult her about anything. She is too old, you know.'

'Was nobody consulted at all? Did you ask me here all out of your own head, as the children say?'

'Why not? There is nobody to consult. Why should I not ask you?'

'It was very good of you—only—well—you are younger than most ladies who invite people to their house.'

'Well—but I asked you,' she replied, with a little irritation, 'and you said you would come. You asked if anybody could stay on the island.'

'Yes, of course.' He did not explain that at first he thought the place was a lodging-house. The mistake was not unnatural; but he could not explain. 'I ought to have known,' he said. 'You are the Queen of Samson, as well as a Princess in Lyonesse. I beg your Majesty to forgive the ignorance of a traveller from foreign parts.'

'Justinian and Peter manage the farm. Dorcas and Chessun manage the house. There is no one to ask,' she added, simply, 'what I am doing.'

She said this with a touch of sadness.

'Have you no relations—cousins—nobody?'

'I have some far-off cousins. They live in London, I believe. One of them went away—a long, long time ago, in the Great War—

and became a purser in the Navy. After that he was purveyor for the Fleet, and was made a knight. He was my grandfather's cousin, so I suppose he is dead by this time, but I dare say he has left children.'

'You are very lonely, Armorel.'

'I had three brothers; but they were all drowned—father, mother, three brothers, all drowned together coming from St. Agnes. That was ten years ago, when I was only a little girl and did not know what it meant. All our misfortunes, my great-great-grandmother says, are due to the wickedness of her husband's father, who took a bag of treasure from the neck of a passenger rescued from a wreck. You heard her last night. Do you think that God would drown my innocent brothers and my innocent father and mother all on the same day, because, eighty years ago, that wicked thing was done?'

'No, Armorel. I can believe a great deal, but that I cannot believe.'

'And so, you see, I am quite alone. Why should I not invite you to stay here?'

'There is not, in reality, Armorel, any reason, except that you did not know anything about me.'

'Oh! but I saw you and talked with you.'

'Yes; but that was not enough. We do not ask people into our houses unless we know something about them.'

'I could see that you were a gentleman.'

'You are very good to think so. Let me try to justify that belief. But, Armorel, seriously, there are thieves and rogues and wicked men in the world. Some of these may come to Scilly. Do not ask another stranger. Believe me, it is dangerous. As for me, you have shown me your flower-farm and have entertained me hospitably: let me thank you and take my departure.'

'Go away? Take your departure? Why?' Armorel looked ready to cry. 'You have only just come. You have seen nothing.'

'Do you wish me to stay another night?'

'Of course I do. What is it, Roland Lee? You have got something on your mind. Why should you not stay?'

'I should like somebody,' he replied, weakly, 'to approve. If the Ancestress, or even Dorcas, or Chessun herself, would approve——'

'Why, of course Dorcas approves. She says it is the best thing in the world for me to have someone here to talk to. She said so yesterday evening, and again this morning.'

'In that case, Armorel, and since it is so delightful here—and so new—and since you are so kind, I will stay one more day.'

He remembered his friend's warning, and the grumpiness which he showed on the way back. His conscience smote him, but not severely. He would be very careful. And, after all, she was but a child. He would just stay the one day and make a sketch or two. Then he would go away.

'That is settled, then. One more day—or, perhaps, one more week, or a month, or a year,' she said, laughing. 'And now, before Peter is ready, I must leave you for ten minutes, because I have to make a cake for your tea this evening. As for dinner, we shall have that in the boat, or on one of the islands. It is my business, you know, to make the puddings and the cakes.'

'Armorel—you shall not. I would rather go without.'

'You shall certainly not go without a cake. Why, I like to make things. It would be dull here indeed if I had not got things to do all day long.'

'Do you not find it dull sometimes, even with things to do?'

'Perhaps. Sometimes. I suppose we are all of us tempted to be discontented at times, even when we have so many blessings as I enjoy.' Armorel was young enough, you see, to talk the language of her nurses and serving-women.

'How do you get through the day?'

'I get up at six o'clock, except in winter, when it is too dark. I have a run with Jack after breakfast; we run up the hill and down the other side—round Porth Bay, just to see the waves beating on White Island Ledge, where you very nearly——'

'Very nearly,' Roland echoed, 'but for you.'

'Then we run up Bryher Hill and stand on the carn just for Jack to bark at the north wind.'

'Sometimes it rains.'

'Oh, yes—and sometimes it blows such a gale of wind that I could not stand on the carn for a moment. Then I stay at home and make or mend something. There are always things to be made or mended. Then we are always wanting stores of some kind or other, and I have to go over to Hugh Town and buy them. At Hugh Town there are shops where they keep beautiful things—you can buy anything you want at Hugh Town. We cannot make pins and needles at home, can we? Then we have dinner, and Granny is brought in. Sometimes she wakes up then, and gets lively, and knows everything that is going on. She will talk quite sensibly for an hour at a time. And I have my fiddle to practise. After tea, when the days are long enough, I go up on the hills again and wander about till dark.'

'And do you never have any companions at all?' he asked with a curious, unreasoning, perfectly inexcusable touch of jealousy, because it could not matter to him even if all the young men of St. Mary's and Bryher and Tresco and St. Martin's came over every Sunday to court this dainty damsel. Yet he did feel the least bit anxious.

'Never any companions. Nobody ever comes here. They used to come, when Granny was still able to talk, in order to ask her advice. She was so wise, you see.'

'And every evening you make music for the Ancestress and the worthy Tryeth family?'

'Yes, and then I have supper and go to bed. Generally by nine o'clock we are all asleep in the house.'

'It would be a monotonous life if you were older. But it is only a preliminary or a preparation to something else. It is the overture, played in soft music, to the happy comedy of your future life, Armorel.'

'You mean to say something kind,' she replied. 'Of course, my life must seem dull to you.'

'One cannot always live on lovely skies and sunlit seas and enchanted islands.'

'Sometimes it seems to me that a little more talk would be pleasant. Justinian talks very well, to be sure; but he is the only one. He knows quantities of wrecks. It would astonish you to hear him tell of the wrecks he has seen. Dorcas talks very little now, because she has lost all her teeth. Chessun is a silent woman, because she's always been kept under by her mother. And Peter's not a talkative boy, because he's always been kept under both by his father and his mother. Besides, he got that nasty fall which made all his hair fall off. You can't wonder if he thinks about that a good deal. And they are all getting old.'

'Yes. They seem to be getting very old indeed. Some day they will follow the example of other old people and vanish. Then, Armorel, you will be like Robinson Crusoe or Alexander Selkirk.'

'I know all about Alexander Selkirk. He lived alone on Juan Fernandez, having been put ashore by Captain Stradling, of the "Cinque Ports." He had been four years and four months on the island when Captain Woodes Rogers found him. He was clothed in goat-skin. He built two huts with pimento-trees, and covered them with long grass and lined them with the skin of goats. He made fire by rubbing two sticks together on his knee. And he lived by catching goats. You mean, Roland Lee,' she said, with great seriousness, 'that some day or other all these old people will die—my great-great-grandmother, Justinian, Dorcas, and even Peter and Chessun, and that then I shall be alone on the island. That would be terrible. But it will not happen in that way. I am sure it will not, because it would be so very terrible. We are in the Lord's hand, and it will not be allowed.'

The young man coloured and dropped his eyes. There certainly was not a single girl of all those whom he knew in London who could have said such a thing so simply and so sincerely. Not the youngest girl fresh from the most religious teaching could say such a thing. Yet they go to church a good deal oftener than Armorel, whose chances were only once a week, and then only when the weather was fine. This it is to be a Scillonian, and to believe what you hear in church. Roland had no reply to make. Even to hint that faith so simple and so complete was rare would have been cruel and wicked.

'You have quoted Woodes Rogers,' he said presently. 'Have you read that good old navigator? It is not often that one finds a girl quoting from Woodes Rogers.'

'Oh! I do not read much. There is a bookcase full of books; but I only read the voyages. There is a whole row of them. Woodes Rogers, Shelvocke, Commodore Anson, Wallis, Carteret, and Cook—and more besides. I like Carteret best, because his ship was so small and so crazy, and his men so few and so weak, and yet he would keep on traversing the ocean as long as he could, and discovered a great deal more than his commander, who cowardly deserted him.'

'There are other things in the world besides voyages—and other books.'

'I learned the other things at school. There was geography—the world is only the Scilly Islands spread out big—and history, too. You would be surprised to find what a lot of English history there is that belongs to Scilly. Queen Elizabeth built the Star Fort—you've seen the Star Fort on the Garrison. There is Charles the First's Castle, on Tresco, all in ruins; and, down below it, Cromwell's Castle, which I will show you. And Charles the Second stayed here. Oh! and there was the Spanish Armada; I must not forget that, because of another great-great-far-off-great-grandfather, three hundred years ago, who was wrecked here.'

'How was that?'

'He was a captain, or officer of some kind, on board one of the Spanish ships; his name was Don Hernando Mureno. After the Armada was defeated and driven away, some of the ships came down the Irish Sea, and among them his ship—and she ran ashore on one of the Outer Islands—I think on Maiden Bower. How many were saved I cannot tell you; but some were, and among them Don Hernando Mureno himself. He stayed here, and never wanted to go away any more; but married a Scillonian, and lived out his life on Bryher, and is buried at the old church at St. Mary's, where I could show you his grave and the headstone—though the letters are all gone by this time. I have his sword still, and I will show it to you. One of my grandfathers married his granddaughter. They say I take after the Spanish side.'

'You are a true Castilian, Armorel; unless, indeed, you happen to be an Andalusian or a Biscayan.'

'Do you think I ought to read the other books?' she asked him, anxiously. 'If you really think so, I will try—I will, really.'

I suppose that no young man—not even the most hardened lecturers at Newnham—ever becomes quite indifferent to the spectacle of Venus entrusting the care of her intellect to a young philosopher. It is a moving spectacle, and still novel. It makes a much more beautiful picture than that of Venus handing over the care of her soul to the Shaven and Shorn. Roland coloured. He felt at once the responsibility and the delicacy of the task thus offered him.

'We will look into the shelves,' he said. 'I suppose that the Ancestress no longer reads?'

'She never learned to read at all. She can neither read nor write: yet there was never anyone who knew so much. She could cure all diseases, and the people came over here from all the islands for her advice. Dorcas knew a great deal, but she does not know the half or the quarter of her mistress's knowledge.'

'Armorel'—Roland knocked out the ashes of his pipe—'I think you want—very badly—someone to advise you.'

'Will you advise me, Roland Lee?'

'Child'—he slowly got up—'all my life, so far, I have been looking for someone to advise and help myself. You must not lean upon a reed. Come—let us seek Peter the boy, and launch the ship and go forth upon our voyage about this sea of many islands. Perchance we may discover Circe upon one of them—unless you are yourself Circe—and I shall presently find myself transformed; but you are too good to turn me into anything except a prince or a poet. And we may light upon St. Brandan's Land; or we may find Judas Iscariot floating on that island of red-hot brass; or we may chance on Andromeda, and witness the battle of Perseus and the dragon; or we may find the weeping Ariadne—everything is possible on an island.'

'Roland Lee,' said the girl, 'you are talking like your friend Dick Stephenson. Why do you say such extravagant things? This is the island of Samson, and I am nothing in the world but Armorel Rosevean.'

CHAPTER VII

A VOYAGE OF DISCOVERY

All day long the boat sailed about among the channels and over the shallow ledges of the Outer or Western Islands, whither no boat may reach save on such a day, so quiet and so calm. The visitor who comes by one boat and goes away by the next thinks he has seen this archipelago. As well stand inside a great cathedral for half an hour and then go away thinking you have seen it all. It takes many days to see these fragments of Lyonesse, and to get a true sense of the place. They sailed round the southern point of Samson, and they steered westward, leaving Great Minalto on the lee, towards Mincarlo, lying, like an old-fashioned sofa, high at the two ends and flat in the middle. They found a landing at the southern point, and clambered up the steep and rocky sides of the low hill. On this island there are four peaks with a down in the middle, all complete. It is like a doll's island.

Everywhere in Scilly there are the same features: here a hill strewn with boulders; here a little down, with fern and gorse and heath; here a bay in which the water, on such days as it can be approached, peacefully laps a smooth white beach; here dark caves and holes in which the water always, even in the calmest day of summer, grumbles and groans, and, when the least sea rises, begins to roar and bellow—in time of storm it shrieks and howls. Those who sail round these rumbling water-dungeons begin to think of sea monsters. Hidden in those recesses the awful calamary lies watching, waiting, his tentacles forty feet long stretching out in the green water, floating innocently till they touch their prey, then seizing and haling it within sight of the baleful, gleaming eyes and within reach of the devouring mouth. In these holes, too, lie the great conger-eels—they fear nothing that swims except that calamary: and in these recesses walk about the huge crabs which devour the dead bodies of shipwrecked sailors. On the sunlit rocks one looks to see a mermaiden, with glittering scales, combing out her long fair tresses: perhaps one may unfortunately miss this beautiful sight, which is rare even in Scilly; but one cannot miss seeing the seals flopping in the water and swimming out to sea, with seeming intent to cross the broad ocean. And in windy weather porpoises blow in the shallow waters of the sounds. All round the rocks at low tide hangs the long sea-weed, undisturbed since the days when they manufactured kelp, like the rank growth of a tropical creeper: at high tide it stands up erect, rocking to and fro in the wash and sway of the water like the tree-tops of the forest in the breeze. Everywhere, except in the rare places where men come and go, the wild sea-birds make their nests; the shags stand on the ledges of the highest rocks in silent rows gazing upon the water below; the sea-gulls fly, shrieking in sea-gullic rapture—there is surely no life quite so joyous as a sea-gull's; the curlews call; the herons sail across the sky; and, in spring, millions of puffins swim and dive and fly about the rocks, and lay their eggs in the hollow places of these wild and lonely islands.

These things, which one presently expects and observes without wonder in all the islands, were new to Roland when he set foot on the rugged rock of Mincarlo. He climbed up the steep sides of the rock and stood upon the top of its highest peak. He made two or three rapid sketches of rock and sea, the girl looking over his shoulder, watching curiously, for the first time in her life, the growth of a picture.

Then he stood and looked around. The great stones were piled about; the brown turf crept up their sides; where there was space to grow, the yellow branches of the fern were spread; and on all four sides lay the shining water.

'All my life,' he said, 'I have dreamed of islands. This is true joy, Armorel For a permanency, Samson is better than Mincarlo, because there is more of it. But to come here sometimes—to sit on this carn while the wind whistles in your ear, and the waves are lapping against the rocks all day long and always——Armorel, is there any other world? Are there men and women living somewhere? Is there anybody but you and me—and Peter?' he added, hastily 'I don't believe in London. It is a dream. Everything is a dream but the islands and the boat and Armorel.'

She was only a child, but she turned a rosy red at the compliment. Nothing but the boat and herself. She was very fond of the boat, you see, and she felt that the words conveyed a high compliment. Then they began to explore the rest of this mountainous island, which has such a variety of scenery all packed away in the small space of twelve acres. When they had walked over the whole of Mincarlo that is accessible, they returned to their landing-place, where Peter sat in the boat keeping her off, with head bent as if he was asleep.

'It must be half-past twelve,' said Armorel. 'I am sure you are hungry. We will have dinner here.'

'No better place for a picnic. Come along, Peter. Bear a hand with the basket. Here, Armorel, is a rock that will do for a table, and here is one on which we two can sit. There is a rock for you, Peter. Now! The opening of a luncheon-basket is always a moment of grave anxiety. What have we got?'

'This is a rabbit-pie,' said Armorel. 'And this is a cake-pudding. I made it yesterday. Do you like cake-pudding? Here are bread and salt and things. Can you make your dinner off a rabbit-pie, Roland Lee?'

'A very good dinner too.' The young man now understood that on Samson one uses the word dinner instead of lunch, and that supper is an excellent cold spread served at eight. 'A very good dinner, Armorel. I mean to carve this. Sit down and let me see you make a good dinner.'

An admirable rabbit-pie, and an excellent cake-pudding. Also, there had not been forgotten a stone jar filled with that home-brewed of which the like can no longer be found in any other spot in the British Islands. I hope one need do no more than indicate the truly appreciative havoc wrought by the young gentleman among all these good gifts and blessings.

After dinner, to lie in the sunshine and have a pipe, looking across the wide stretch of sunny water to the broken line of rocks and the blue horizon beyond, was happiness undeserved. Beside him sat the girl, anxious that he should be happy—thinking of nothing but what might best please her guest.

Then they got into the boat again, and sailed half a mile or so due north by the compass, until they came within another separate archipelago, of which Mincarlo is an outlying companion.

It is the group of rocks, called the Outer or the Western Islands, lying tumbled about in the water west of Bryher and Samson.

Some of them are close together, some are separated by broad channels. Here the sea is never calm: at the foot of the rocks stretch out ledges, some of them bare at low water, revealing their ugly black stone teeth: the swell of the Atlantic on the calmest days rises and falls and makes white eddies, broken water, and flying spray. Among these rocks they rowed: Peter and Roland taking the oars, while Armorel steered. They rowed round Maiden Bower, with its cluster of granite forts defying the whole strength of the Atlantic, which will want another hundred thousand years to grind them down—about and among the Black Rocks and the Seal Rocks, dark and threatening: they landed on Ilyswillig, with his peak of fifty feet, a strange wild island: they stood on the ledge of Castle Bryher and looked up at the tower of granite which rises out of the water like the round keep of a Norman castle: they hoisted sail and stood out to Scilly himself, where his twin rocks command the entrance to the islands. Scilly is of the dual number: he consists of two great mountains rising from the water sheer, precipitous, and threatening: each about eighty feet high, but with the air of eight hundred; each black and square and terrible of aspect: they are separated by a narrow channel hardly broad enough for a boat to pass through.

'One day last year,' said Armorel—'it was in July, after a fortnight of fine weather—we went through this channel, Peter and I—didn't we, Peter? It was a dead calm, and at high tide.'

The boy nodded his head.

The channel was now, the tide being nearly high, like a foaming torrent, through which the water raced and rushed, boiling into whirlpools, foaming and tearing at the sides. The rapids below Niagara are not fiercer than was this channel, though the day was so fair and the sea without so quiet.

'Once,' said Peter, breaking the silence, 'there was a ship cast up by a wave right into the fork of the channel. She went to pieces in ten minutes, for she was held in a vice like, while the waves beat her into sticks. Some of the men got on to the north rock—what they call "Cuckoo"—and there they stuck till the gale abated. Then people saw them from Bryher, and a pilot-boat put off for them.'

'So they were saved?' said Roland.

'No, they were not saved,' Peter replied, slowly. ''Twas this way: the pilot-boat that took them off the rock capsized on the way home. So they was all drowned.'

'Poor beggars! Now, if they had been brought safe ashore we might have been told what these rocks look like in rough weather: and what Scilly is like when you have climbed it: and how a man feels in the middle of a storm on Scilly.'

'You can see very well what it is like from Samson,' said Armorel. 'The waves beat upon the rocks, and the white spray flies over them and hides them.'

'I should like to hear as well as to see,' said Roland. 'Fancy the thunder of the Atlantic waves against this mass of rock, the hissing and boiling in the channel, the roaring of the wind and the dashing of the waves! I wonder if any of these shipwrecked men had a sketch-book in his pocket.

'To be drowned,' he continued, 'just by the upsetting of a boat, and after escaping death in a much more exciting manner! Their companions were torn from the deck and hurled and dashed against the rock, so that in a moment their bones were broken to fragments, and the fragments themselves were thrown against the rocks till there was nothing left of them. And these poor fellows clung to the rock, hiding under a boulder from the driving wind—cold, starving, wet, and miserable. And just as they thought of food and shelter and warmth again, to be taken and plunged into the cold water, there to roll about till they were drowned! A dreadful tragedy!'

Having thus broken the ice, Peter proceeded to relate more stories of shipwreck, taking after his father, Justinian Tryeth, whose conversational powers in this direction were, according to Armorel, unrivalled. There is a shipwreck story belonging to every rock of Scilly, and to many there are several shipwrecks. As there are about as many rocks of Scilly as there are days in the year, the stories would take long in the telling.

Fortunately, Peter did not know all. It is natural, however, that a native of Samson, and the descendant of many generations of wreckers, should love to talk about wrecks. Therefore he proceeded to tell of the French frigate which came over to conquer Scilly in 1798, and was very properly driven ashore by the sea which owns allegiance to Britannia, and all hands lost, so that the Frenchmen captured no more than their graves, which now lie in a triumphant row on St. Agnes. On Maiden Bower he placed, I know not with what truth, the wreck of the Spaniard which gave Armorel an ancestor. On Mincarlo he remembered the loss of an orange-ship on her way from the Azores. On Menovaur he had seen a collier driven in broad daylight and broken all to pieces in half a day, and of her crew not a man saved. Other things, similarly cheerful, he narrated slowly while the sunshine made these grey rocks put on a hospitable look and the boat danced over the rippling waves. With his droning voice, his smooth face with the long white hair upon it, like the last scanty leaves upon a tree, he was like the figure of Death at the Feast, while Armorel—young, beautiful, smiling—reminded her guest of Life, and Love, and Hope.

They sailed round so many of these rocks and islets: they landed on so many: they lingered so long among the reefs, loth to leave the wild, strange place, that the sun was fast going down when they hoisted sail and steered for New Grinsey Sound on their homeward way.

You may enter New Grinsey Sound either from the north or from the south. The disadvantage of attempting it from the former on ordinary days is that those who do so are generally capsized and frequently drowned. On such a day as this, however, the northern passage may be attempted. It is the channel, dangerous and beset with rocks and ledges, between the islands of Bryher and Tresco. As the boat sailed slowly in, losing the breeze as it rounded the point, the channel spread itself out broad and clear. On the right hand rose, precipitous, the cliffs and crags of Shipman's Head, which looks like a continuation of Bryher, but is really separated from the island by a narrow passage—you may work through it in calm weather—running from Hell Bay to the Sound. On the left is Tresco, its downs rising steeply from the water, and making a great pretence of being a very lofty ascent indeed. In the middle of the coast juts out a high promontory, surrounded on all sides but one by the water. On this rock stands Cromwell's Castle, a round tower, older than the Martello Towers. It still possesses a roof, but its interior has been long since gutted. In front of it has been built a square stone platform or bastion, where once, no doubt, they mounted guns for the purpose of defending this channel against an invader, as if Nature had not already defended it by her ledges and shallows and hardly concealed teeth of granite. To protect by a fort a channel when the way is so tortuous and difficult, and where there are so many other ways, is almost as if Warkworth Castle, five miles inland, on the winding Coquet, had been built to protect the shores of Northumberland from the invading Dane: or as if Chepstow above the muddy Wye had been built for the defence of Bristol. There, however, the castle is, and a very noble picture it made as the boat slowly voyaged through the Sound. The declining sun, not yet sunk too low behind Bryher, clothed it with light and splendour, and brought out the rich colour of grey rock and yellow fern upon the steep hillside behind. Beyond the castle, in the midst of the Sound, rose a pyramidal island, a pile of rocks, seventy or eighty feet high, on whose highest carn some of Oliver Cromwell's prisoners were hanged, according to the voice of tradition, which, somehow, always goes dead against that strong person.

Roland, who had exhausted the language of delight among the Outer Islands, contemplated this picture in silence.

'Do you not like it?' asked the girl.

'Like it?' he repeated. 'Armorel! It is splendid.'

'Will you make a sketch of it?'

'I cannot. I must make a picture. I ought to come here day after day. There must be a good place to take it from—over there, I think, on that beach. Armorel! It is splendid. To think that the picture is to be seen so near to London, and that no one comes to see it!'

'If you want to come day after day, Roland,' she said, softly, 'you will not be able to go away to-morrow. You must stay longer with us on Samson.'

'I ought not, child. You should not ask me.'

'Why should you not stay if you are happy with us? We will make you as comfortable as ever we can. You have only to tell us what you want.'

She looked so eagerly and sincerely anxious that he yielded.

'If you are really and truly sure,' he said.

'Of course I am really and truly sure. The weather will be fine, I think, and we will go sailing every day.'

'Then I will stay a day or two longer. I will make a picture of Cromwell's Castle—and the hill at the back of it and the water below it. I will make it for you, Armorel; but I will keep a copy of it for myself. Then we shall each have a memento of this day—something to remember it by.'

'I should like to have the picture. But, oh! Roland!—as if I could ever forget this day!'

She spoke with perfect simplicity, this child of Nature, without the least touch of coquetry. Why should she not speak what was in her heart? Never before had she seen a young man so brave, so gallant, so comely: nor one who spoke so gently: nor one who treated her with so much consideration.

He turned his face: he could not meet those trustful eyes, with the innocence that lay there: he was abashed by reason of this innocence. A child—only a child. Armorel would change. In a year or two this trustfulness would vanish. She would become like all other girls—shy and reserved, self-conscious in intuitive self-defence. But there was no harm as yet. She was a child—only a child.

As the sun went down the bows ran into the fine white sand of the landing-place, and their voyage was ended.

'A perfect day,' he murmured. 'A day to dream of. How shall I thank you enough, Armorel?'

'You can stay and have some more days like it.'

CHAPTER VIII

THE VOYAGERS

This was the first of many such voyages and travels, though not often in the outside waters, for the vexed Bermoothes themselves are not more lashed by breezes from all the quarters of the compass than these isles of Scilly. They sailed from point to point, and from island to island, landing where they listed or where Armorel led, wandering for long hours round the shores or on the hills. All the islands, except the bare rocks, are covered with down and moorland, bounded in every direction by rocky headlands and slopes covered with granite boulders. They were quite alone in their explorations: no native is ever met upon those downs: no visitor, except on St. Mary's, wanders on the beaches and around the bays. They were quite alone all the day long: the sea-breeze whistled in their ears; the gulls flew over their heads—the cormorants hardly stirred from the rocks when they climbed up; the hawk that hung motionless in the air above them changed not his place when they drew near. And always, day after day, they came continually upon unexpected places: strange places, beautiful places: beaches of dazzling white: wildly heaped carns: here a cromlech, a logan stone, a barrow—Samson is not the only island which guards the tombs of the Great Departed—a new view of sea and sky and white-footed rock. I believe that there does not live any single man who has actually explored all the isles of Scilly: stood upon every rock, climbed every hill, and searched on every island for its treasures of ancient barrows, plants, birds, carns, and headlands. Once there was a worthy person who came here as chaplain to St. Martin's. He started with the excellent intention of seeing everything. Alas! he never saw a single island properly: he never walked round one exhaustively. He wrote a book about them, to be sure; but he saw only half. As for Samson, this person of feeble intelligence even declared that the island was not worth a second visit! After that one would shut the book, but is lured on in the hope of finding something new.

One must not ask of the islanders themselves for information about the isles, because few of them ever go outside their own island unless to Hugh Town, where is the Port, and where are the shops. Why should they? On the other islands they have no business. Justinian Tryeth, for instance, was seventy-five years of age; Hugh Town he knew, and had often been there, though now Peter did the business of the farm at the Port: St. Agnes he knew, having wooed and won a wife there: he had been to Bryher Church, which is close to the shore—the rest of Bryher was to him as unknown as Iceland. As for St. Martin's, or Annet, or Great Ganilly, he saw them constantly; they were always within his sight, yet he had never desired to visit them. They were an emblem, a shape, a name to him, and nothing more. It is so always with those who live in strange and beautiful places: the marvels are part of their daily life: they heed them not, unless, like Armorel, they have no work to do and are quick to feel the influences of things around them. Most Swiss people seem to care nothing for their Alps, but here and there is one who would gladly spend all his days high up among the fragrant pines, or climbing the slope of ice with steady step and slow.

But these young people did try to visit all the islands. Upon Roland there fell the insatiate curiosity—the rage—of an explorer and a discoverer. He became like Captain Cook himself: he longed for more islands: every day he found a new island. 'Give,' cries he who sails upon unknown seas and scans the round circle of the horizon for the cloudy peak of some far-distant mountain, 'give—give more islands—still more islands! Let us sail for yonder cloud! Let us sail on until the cloud becomes a hill-top, and the hill another island! Largesse for him who first calls "Land ahead!" There shall we find strange monsters and treasures rare, with friendly natives, and girls more blooming than those of fair Tahiti. Let us sail thither, though it prove no more than a barren rock, the resting-place of the sea-lion; though we can do no more than climb its steep sides and stand upon the top while the spray flies over the rocks and beats upon our faces.' In such a spirit as Captain Carteret (Armorel's favourite) steered his frail bark from shore to shore did Roland sail among those Scilly seas.

Of course they went to Tresco, where there is the finest garden in all the world. But one should not go to see the garden more than once, because its perfumed alleys, its glasshouses, its cultivated and artificial air, are somehow incongruous with the rest of the islands. As well expect to meet a gentleman in a Court dress walking across Fylingdale Moor. Yet it is indeed a very noble and royal garden: other gardens have finer hothouses: none have a better show of flowers and trees of every kind: for variety it is like unto the botanical gardens of a tropical land: you might be standing in one of the alleys of the garden of Mauritius, or of Java, or the Cape. Here everything grows and flourishes that will grow anywhere, except, of course, those plants which carry patriotism to an extreme and refuse absolutely to leave their native soil. You cannot go picking pepper here, nor can you strip the cinnamon-tree of its bark. But here you will see the bamboos cluster, tall and graceful: the eucalyptus here parades his naked trunk and his blue leaves: here the fern-tree lifts its circle of glory of lace and embroidery twenty feet high: the prickly pear nestles in warm corners: the aloe shoots up its tall stalk of flower and of seed: the palms stand in long rows: and every lovely plant, every sweet flower, created for the solace of man, grows abundantly, and hastens with zeal to display its blossoms: the soft air is full of perfumes, strange and familiar: it is as if Kew had taken off her glass roofs and placed all her plants and trees to face the English winter. But, then, the winter of Scilly is not the winter of Great Britain. The botanist may visit this garden many times, and always find something to please him; but the ordinary traveller will go but once, and admire and come away. It is far better outside on the breezy down, where the dry fern and withered bents crack beneath your feet, and the elastic turf springs as you tread upon it. There are other things on Tresco: there is a big fresh-water lake—it would be a respectable lake even in Westmoreland—where the wild birds disport themselves: beside it South American ostriches roam gravely, after the manner of the bird. It is pleasant to see the creatures. There is a great cave, if you like dark damp caves: better than the cave, there is a splendid bold coast sloping steeply from the down all round the northern part of the island.

Then they walked all round St. Mary's. It is nine miles round; but if, as these young people did, you climb every headland and walk round every bay, and descend every possible place where the boulders make a ladder down to the boiling water below, it is nine hundred miles round, and, for its length, the most wonderful walk in all the world. They crossed the broad Sound to St. Agnes, and saw St. Warna's wondrous cove: they stood on the desolate Gugh and the lonely Annet, beloved of puffins: they climbed on every one of the Eastern Islands, and even sailed, when they found a day calm enough to permit the voyage, among the Dogs of Scilly, and clambered up the black boulders of Rosevear and scared the astonished cormorants from wild Goreggan.

One day it rained in the morning. Then they had to stay at home, and Armorel showed the house. She took her guest into the dairy, where Chessun made the butter and scalded the cream—that rich cream which the West-country folk eat with everything. She made him stand by and help make a junket, which Devonshire people believe cannot be made outside the shadow of Dartmoor: she took him into the kitchen—the old room with its old furniture, the candlesticks and snuffers of brass, the bacon hanging to the joists, the blue china, the ancient pewter platters, the long bright spit—a kitchen of the eighteenth century. And then she took him into a room which no longer exists anywhere else save in name. It was the still-room, and on the shelves there stood the elixirs and cordials of ancient time: the currant gin to fortify the stomach on a raw morning before crossing the Road; the cherry brandy for a cold and stormy night; the elderberry wine, good mulled and spiced at Christmas-time; the blackberry wine; the home-made distilled waters—lavender water, Hungary water, Cyprus water, and the Divine Cordial itself, which takes three seasons to complete, and requires all the flowers of spring, summer, and autumn. Then they went into the best parlour, and Armorel, opening a cupboard, took out an old sword of strange shape and with faded scabbard. On the blade there was a graven Latin legend. 'This is my ancestor's sword,' she said. 'He was an officer of the Spanish Armada—Hernando Mureno was his name.'

'You are indeed a Spanish lady, Armorel. Your ancestor is well known to have been the bravest and most honourable gentleman in King Philip's service.'

'He remained here—he would not go home: he married and became a Protestant.'

She put back the sword in its place, and brought forth other things to show him—old-fashioned watches, old compasses, sextants, telescopes, flint-and-steel pistols—all kinds of things belonging to the old days of smuggling and of piloting.

Then she opened the bookcase. It should have been filled with histories of pirates and buccaneers; but it was not: it contained a whole body of theology of the Methodist kind. Roland tossed them over impatiently. 'I don't wonder,' he said, 'at your reading nothing if this is all you have.' But he found one or two books which he set aside.

As they wandered about the islands, of course they talked. It wants but little to make a young man open his heart to a girl; only a pair of soft and sympathetic eyes, a face full of interest and questions of admiration. Whether she tells him anything in return is quite another matter. Most young men, when they review the situation afterwards, discover that they have told everything and learned nothing. Perhaps there is nothing to learn. In a few days Armorel knew everything about her guest. He had come from Australia—from that far-distant land—in search of fortune. He had as yet made but few friends. He was unknown and without patrons. He had no family connections which would help him. The patrimony on which he was to live until he should begin to succeed was but small, and although he held money-making in the customary contempt, it was necessary that he should make a good deal, because—which is often the case—his standard of comfort was pitched rather high: it included, for instance, a good club, good cigars, and good claret. Also, as he said, an artist should be free from sordid anxieties: Art demands an atmosphere of calm: therefore, he must have an income. This, like everything that does not exist, must be created. Man is godlike because he alone of creatures can create: he, and he alone, constantly creates things which previously did not exist—an income, honour, rank, tastes, wants, desires, necessities, habits, rules, and laws.

'How can you bear to sell your pictures?' asked the girl. 'We sell our flowers, but then we grow them by the thousand. You make every picture by itself—how can you sell the beautiful things? You must want to keep them every one to look at all your life. Those that you have given to me I could never part with.'

'One must live, fair friend of mine,' he replied, lightly. 'It is my only way of making money, and without money we can do nothing. It is not the selling of his pictures that the artist dreads—that is the necessity of Art as a profession: it is the danger that no one will care about seeing them or buying them. That is much more terrible, because it means failure. Sometimes I dream that I have become old and grey, and have been working all my life, and have had no success at all, and am still unknown and despised. In Art there are thousands of such failures. I think the artist who fails is despised more than any other man. It is truly miserable to aspire so high and to fall so low. Yet who am I that I should reach the port?'

'All good painters succeed,' said the girl, who had never seen a painter before or any painting save her own coloured engravings. 'You are a good painter, Roland. You must succeed. You will become a great painter in everybody's estimation.'

'I will take your words for an oracle,' he said. 'When I am melancholy, and the future looks dark, I will say, "Thus and thus spoke Armorel."'

The young man who is about to attempt fortune by the pursuit of Art must not consider too long the wrecks that strew the shores and float about the waters, lest he lose self-confidence. Continually these wrecks occur, and there is no insurance against them: yet continually other barques hoist sail and set forth upon their perilous voyage. It may be reckoned as a good point in this aspirant that he was not over-confident.

'Some are wrecked at the outset,' he said. 'Others gain a kind of success. Heavens! what a kind! To struggle all their lives for admission to the galleries, and to rejoice if once in a while a picture is sold.'

'They are not the good painters,' the girl of large experience again reminded him.

'Am I a good painter?' he replied, humbly. 'Well, one can but try to do good work, and leave to the gods the rest. There is luck in things. It is not every good man who succeeds, Armorel. To every man, however, there is allotted the highest stature possible for him to reach. Let me be contented if I grow to my full height.'

'You must, Roland. You could not be contented with anything less.'

'To reach one's full height, one must live for work alone. It is a hard saying, Armorel. It is a great deal harder than you can understand.'

'If you love your work, and if you are happy in it——' said the girl.

'You do not understand, child, Most men never reach their full height. You can see their pictures in the galleries—poor, stunted things. It is because they live for anything rather than their work. They are pictures without a soul in them.'

Now, when a young man holds forth in this strain, one or two things suggest themselves. First, one thinks that he is playing a part, putting on 'side,' affecting depths—in fact, enacting the part of the common Prig, who is now, methinks, less common than he was. If he is not a prig uttering insincere sentimentalities, he may be a young man who has preserved his ideals beyond the usual age by some accident. The ideals and beliefs and aspirations of young men, when they first begin the study of Art in any of its branches, are very beautiful things, and full of truths which can only, somehow, be expressed by very young men. The third explanation is that in certain circumstances, as in the companionship of a girl not belonging to society and the world—a young, innocent, and receptive girl—whose mind is ready for pure ideas, uncontaminated by earthly touch, the old enthusiasms are apt to return and the old beliefs to come back. Then such things may spring in the heart and rise to the lips as one could not think or utter in a London studio.

Sincere or not, this young man pursued his theme, making a kind of confession which Armorel could not, as yet, understand. But she remembered. Women at all ages remember tenaciously, and treasure up in their hearts things which they may at some other time learn to understand.

'There was an old allegory, Armorel,' this young man went on, 'of a young man choosing his way, once for all. It is an absurd story, because every day and all day long we are pulled the other way. Sometimes it makes me tremble all over only to think of the flowery way. I know what the end would be. But yet, Armorel, what can you know or understand about the Way of Pleasure, and how men are drawn into it with ropes? My soul is sometimes sick with yearning when I think of those who run along that Way and sing and feast.'

'What kind of Way is it, Roland?'

'You cannot understand, and I cannot tell you. The Way of Pleasure and the Way of Wealth. These are the two roads by which the artistic life is ruined. Yet we are dragged into them by ropes.'

'You shall keep to the true path, Roland,' the girl said, with glistening eyes. 'Oh! how happy you will be when you have reached your full height—you will be a giant then.'

He laughed and shook his head. 'Again, Armorel, I will take it from your lips—a prophecy. But you do not understand.'

'No,' she said. 'I am very ignorant. Yet if I cannot understand, I can remember. The Way of Pleasure and the Way of Wealth. I shall remember. We are told that we must not set our hearts upon the things of this world. I used to think that it meant being too fond of pretty frocks and ribbons. Dorcas said so once. Since you have come I see that there are many, many things that I know nothing of. If I am to be dragged to them by ropes, I do not want to know them. The Way of Pleasure and the Way of Wealth. They destroy the artistic life,' she repeated, as if learning a lesson. 'These ways must be ways of Sin, don't you think?' she asked, looking up with curious eyes.

Doubtless. Yet this is not quite the modern manner of regarding and speaking of the subject. And considering what an eighteenth-century and bourgeois-like manner it is, and how fond we now are of that remarkable century, one is surprised that the manner has not before now been revived. When we again tie our hair behind and assume silver-buckled shoes and white silk stockings, we shall once more adopt that manner. It was not, however, artificial with Armorel. The words fell naturally from her lips. A thing that was prejudicial to the better nature of a man must, she thought, belong to ways of Sin. Again—doubtless. But Roland did not think of it in that way, and the words startled him.

'Puritan!' he said. 'But you are always right. It is the instinct of your heart always to be right. But we no longer talk that language. It is a hundred years old. In these days there is no more talk about Sin—at least, outside certain circles. There are habits, it is true, which harm an artist's eye and destroy his hand. We say that it is a pity when an artist falls into these habits. We call it a pity, Armorel, not the way of Sin. A pity—that is all. It means the same thing, I dare say, so far as the artist is concerned.'

CHAPTER IX

THE LAST DAY BUT ONE

The last day but one! It always comes at length—it is bound to come—the saddest, the most sentimental of all days. The boy who leaves school—I speak of the old-fashioned boy and the ancient school—where he has been fagged and bullied and flogged, on this last day but one looks round with a choking throat upon the dingy walls and the battered desks. Even the convict who is about to be released after years of prison feels a sentimental melancholy in gazing for the last time upon the whitewashed walls. The world, which misunderstands the power of temptation and is distrustful as to the reality of repentance, will probably prove cold to him. How much more, then, when one looks around on the last day but one of a holiday! To-morrow we part. This is the last day of companionship.

Roland's holiday was to consist of a day or two, or three at the most—yet lo! the evening and the morning were the twenty-first day. There was always something new to be seen, something more to be sketched, some fresh excuse for staying in a house where this young man lived from the first as if he had been there all his life and belonged to the family. Scilly has to be seen in cloud as well as in sunshine: in wind and rain as well as in fair weather: one island had been accidentally overlooked; another must be re-visited.

So the days went on, each one like the days before it, but with a difference. The weather was for the most part fine, so that they could at least sail about the islands of the Road. Every morning the young man got up at six and, after a bathe from Shark Point, walked all round Samson and refreshed his soul by gazing upon the Outer Islands. Breakfast over, he took a pipe in the farmyard with Justinian and Peter, who continually talked of shipwrecks and of things washed ashore. During this interval Armorel made the puddings and the cakes. When she had accomplished this delicate and responsible duty, she came out, prepared for the day. They took their dinner-basket with them, and sallied forth: in the afternoon they returned: in the evening, at seven o'clock, the table was pushed back: the old serving people came in; the fire was stirred into animation; Armorel played the old-fashioned tunes; and the ancient lady rallied, and sat up, and talked, her mind in the past. All the days alike, yet each one differing from its neighbours. There is no monotony, though place and people remain exactly the same, when there is the semblance of variety. For, besides the discovery of so many curious and interesting islands, this fortunate young man, as we have seen, discovered that his daily companion, though so young—'only a child'—was a girl of wonderful quickness and ready sympathy. A young artist wants sympathy—it is necessary for his growth: sympathy, interest, and flattery are necessary for the artistic temperament. All these Armorel offered him in large measure, running over. She kept alive in him that faith in his own star which every artist, as well as every general, must possess. Great is the encouragement of such sympathy to the young man of ambitions. This consideration is, indeed, the principal excuse for early marriages. Three weeks of talk with such a girl—no one else to consider or to interrupt—no permission to be sought—surely these things made up a holiday which quite beat the record! Three whole weeks! Such a holiday should form the foundation of a life-long friendship! Could either of them ever forget such a holiday?

Now it was all over. For very shame Roland could make no longer any excuses for staying. His sketch-book was crammed. There were materials in it for a hundred pictures—most of them might be called Studies of Armorel. She was in the boat holding the tiller, bareheaded, her hair flying in the breeze, the spray dashing into her face, and the clear blue water rushing past the boat: or she was sitting idly in the same boat lying in Grinsey Sound, with Shipman's Head behind her: or she was standing on the sea-weed at low water under the mighty rock of Castle Bryher: or she was standing upright in the low room, violin in hand, her face and figure crimsoned in the red firelight: or she was standing in the porch between the verbena-trees, the golden figure-head smiling benevolently upon her, and the old ship's lanthorn swinging overhead with an innocent air, as if it had never heard of a wreck and knew not how valuable a property may be a cow, judiciously treated—with a lighted lanthorn between its horns—on a stormy night. There were other things: sketches of bays and coves, and headlands and carns, gathered from all the islands—from Porthellick and Peninnis on St. Mary's, which everybody goes to see, to St. Warna's Cove on St. Agnes, whither no traveller ever wendeth.

A very noble time. No letters, no newspapers, no trouble of any kind: yet one cannot remain for ever even in a house where such a permanent guest would be welcomed. Now and then, it is true, one hears how such a one went to a friend's house and stayed there. La Fontaine, Gay, and Coleridge are examples. But I have never heard, before this case, of a young man going to a house where a quite young girl, almost a child, was the mistress, and staying there. Now the end had come: he must go back to London, where all the men and most of the women have their own shows to run, and there is not enough sympathy to go round: back to what the young artist, he who has as yet exhibited little and sold nothing, calls his Work—putting a capital letter to it, like the young clergyman. Perhaps he did not understand that under the eyes of a girl who knew nothing about Art he had done really better and finer work, and had learned more, in those three weeks than in all the time that he had spent in a studio. Well; it was all over. The sketching was ended: there would be no more sailing over the blue waves of the rolling Atlantic outside the islands: no more quiet cruising in the Road: no more fishing: no more clambering among the granite rocks: no more sitting in sunny places looking out to sea, with this bright child at his side.

Alas! And no more talks with Armorel. From the first day the child sat at his feet and became his disciple, Heloïse herself was not an apter pupil. She ardently desired to learn: like a curious child she asked him questions all day long, and received the answers as if they were gospel: but no child that he had ever known betrayed blacker gaps of ignorance than this girl of fifteen. Consider. What could she know? Other girls learn at school Armorel's schooling was over at fourteen, when she came home from St. Mary's to her desert island. Other girls continue their education by reading books: but Armorel never read anything except voyages of the last century, which treat but little of the modern life. Other girls also learn from hearing their elders talk: but Armorel's elders never talked. Other girls, again, learn from conversation with companions: but Armorel had no companions. And they learn from the shops in the street, the people who walk about, from the church, the theatre, the shows: but Armorel had no better street than the main street of Hugh Town. And they learn from society: but this girl had none. And they learn from newspapers, magazines, and novels: but Armorel had none of these. No voice, no sound of the outer world reached Alexandra Selkirk of Samson. Juan Fernandez itself was not more cut off from men and women. Therefore, in her seclusion and her ignorance, this young man came to her like another Apollo or a Vishnu at least—a revelation of the world of which she knew nothing, and to which she never gave a thought. He opened a door and bade her look within. All she saw was a great company painting pictures and talking Art; but that was something. As for what he said, this young man ardent, she remembered and treasured all, even the lightest things, the most trivial opinions. He did not abuse her confidence. Had he been older he might have been cynical: had he not been an artist he might have been flippant:

had he been a City man and a money-grub he might have shown her the sordid side of the world. Being such as he was he showed her the best and most beautiful part—the world of Art. But as for these black gaps of ignorance, most of them remained even after Roland's visit.

'Your best friend, Armorel,' said her guest, 'would not deny that you are ignorant of many things. You have never gone to a dinner-party or sat in a drawing-room: you cannot play lawn-tennis; you know none of the arts feminine: you cannot talk the language of Society: oh! you are a very ignorant person indeed! But then there are compensations.'

'What are compensations? Things that make up? Do you mean the boat and the islands?'

'The boat is certainly something, and the islands give a flavour of their own to life on Samson, don't they? If I were talking the usual cant I should say that the chief compensation is the absence of the hollow world and its insincere society. That is cant and humbug, because society is very pleasant, only, I suppose, one must not expect too much from it. Your real compensations, Armorel, are of another kind. You can fiddle like a jolly sailor, all of the olden time. If you were to carry that fiddle of yours on to the Common Hard at Portsea not a man among them all, even the decayed veteran—if he still lives—who caught Nelson, the Dying Hero, in his arms, but would jump to his feet and shuffle—heel and toe, double-step, back-step, flourish and fling. I believe those terms are correct.'

'I am so glad you think I can fiddle.'

'You want only instruction in style to make you a very fine violinist. Besides, there is nothing more pleasing to look at, just now, than a girl playing a violin. It is partly fashion. Formerly it was thought graceful for a girl to play the guitar, then the harp; now it is the fiddle, when it is not the zither or the banjo. That is one compensation. There is another. I declare that I do not believe there is in all London a girl with such a genius as yours for puddings and pies, cakes and biscuits. I now understand that there is more wanted, in this confection, than industry and application. It is an art. Every art affords scope for genius born not made. The true—the really artistic—administration of spice and sugar, milk, eggs, butter, and flour requires real genius—such as yours, my child. And as to the still-room, there isn't such a thing left, I believe, in the whole world except on Samson, any more than there is a spinning-wheel. Who but yourself, Armorel, possesses the secret, long since supposed to be hopelessly lost, of composing Cyprus water, and the Divine Cordial? In this respect, you belong to a hundred years ago, when the modern ignorance was unknown. And where can I find—I should like to know—a London girl who understands cherry brandy, and can make her own blackberry wine?'

'You want to please me, Roland, because you are going away and I am unhappy.' She hung her head in sadness too deep for tears. 'That is why you say all these fine things. But I know that they mean very little. I am only an ignorant girl.'

'I must always, out of common gratitude, want to please you. But I am only speaking the bare truth. Then there is the delicate question of dress. An ordinary man is not supposed to know anything about dress, but an artist has always to consider it. There are certainly other girls—thousands of other girls—more expensively dressed than you, Armorel; but you have the taste for costume, which is far better than any amount of costly stuff.'

'Chessun taught me how to sew and how to cut out.' But the assurance of this excellence brought her no comfort.

'When I am gone, Armorel, you will go on with your drawing, will you not?' It will be seen that he endeavoured, as an Apostle of Art, to introduce its cult even on remote Samson. That was so, and not without success. The girl, he discovered, had been always making untaught attempts at drawing, and wanted nothing but a little instruction. This was a fresh discovery. 'That you should have the gift of the pencil is delightful to think of. The pencil, you see, is like the Jinn—I fear you have no Jinn on Samson—who could do almost anything for those who knew how to command his obedience, but only made those people ridiculous who ignorantly tried to order him around. If you go on drawing every day I am sure you will learn how to make that Jinn obedient. I will send you, when I get home, some simple books for your guidance. Promise, child, that you will not throw away this gift.'

'I will draw every day,' she replied, obediently, but with profound dejection.

'Then there is your reading. You must read something. I have looked through your shelves, and have picked out some books for you. There is a volume of Cowper and of Pope, and an old copy of the *Spectator*, and there is Goldsmith's "Deserted Village."'

'I will read anything you wish me to read,' she replied.

'I will send you some more books. You ought to know something about the world of to-day. Addison and Goldsmith will not teach you that. But I don't know what to send you. Novels are supposed to represent life; but then they pre-suppose a knowledge of the world, to begin with. You want an account of modern society as it is, and the thing does not exist. I will consider about it.'

'I will read whatever you send me. Roland, when I have read all the books and learned to draw, shall I have grown to my full height? Remember what you said about yourself.'

'I don't know, Armorel. It is not reading. But——' He left the sentence unfinished.

'Who is to tell me—on Samson?' she asked.

In the afternoon of this day Roland planted his easel on the plateau of the northern hill, where the barrows are, and put the last touches to the sketch, which he afterwards made into the first picture which he ever exhibited. It appeared in the Grosvenor of '85: of course everybody remembers the picture, which attracted a very respectable amount of attention. It was called the 'Daughter of Lyonesse.' It represented a maiden in the first blossom of womanhood—tall and shapely. She was dressed in a robe of white wool thrown over her left shoulder and gathered at the waist by a simple belt of brown leather: a white linen vest was seen below the wool: round her neck was a golden torque: behind her was the setting sun: she stood upon the highest of a low pile of granite boulders, round the feet of which were spread the yellow branches of the fern and the faded flowers of the heather: she shaded her eyes from the sun with her left hand, and looked out to sea. She was bareheaded: the strong breeze lifted her long black hair and blew it from her shoulders: her eyes were black and her complexion was dark. Behind her and below her was the splendour of sun and sky and sea, with the Western Islands rising black above the golden waters.

The sketch showed the figure, but the drapery was not complete: as yet it was a study of light and colour and a portrait.

'I don't quite know,' said the painter, thoughtfully, 'whether you ought not to wear a purple chiton: Phœnician trade must have brought Phœnician luxuries to Lyonesse. Your ancestors were tin-men—rich miners—no doubt the ladies of the family went dressed in the very, very best. I wonder whether in those days the King's daughter was barefooted. The *caliga,* I think—the leather sandal—would have been early introduced into the royal family on account of the spikiness of the fern in autumn and the thorns of the gorse all the year round. The slaves and common people, of course, would have to endure the thorns.'

He continued his work while he talked, Armorel making no reply, enacting the model with zeal.

'It is a strange sunset,' he went on, as if talking to himself, 'a day of clouds, but in the west a broad belt of blue low down in the horizon: in the midst of the belt the sun flaming crimson: on either hand the sky aglow, but only in the belt of clear: above is the solid cloud, grey and sulky, receiving none of the colour: below is also the solid, sulky cloud, but under the sun there spreads out a fan of light which strikes the waters and sets them aflame in a long broad road from the heavens to your feet, O child of Lyonesse. Outside this road of light the waters are dull and gloomy: in the sky the coloured belt of light fades gradually into soft yellows, clear greens, and azure blues. A strange sunset! A strange effect of light! Armorel, you see your life: it is prefigured by the light. Overhead the sky is grey and colourless: where the glow of the future does not lie on the waters they are grey and colourless.

Nothing around you but the waste of grey sea: before you black rocks—life is always full of black rocks: and beyond, the splendid sun—soft, warm, and glowing. You shall interpret that in your own way.'

Armorel listened, standing motionless, her left hand shading her eyes.

'If the picture,' he went on, 'comes out as I hope it may, it will be one of those that suggest many things. Every good picture, Armorel, as well as every good poem, suggests. It is like that statue of Christ which is always taller than the tallest man. Nobody can ever get above the thought and soul of a good picture or a good poem. There is always more in it than the wisest man knows. That is the proof of genius. That is why I long all day for the mysterious power of putting into my work the soul of everyone who looks upon it—as well as my own soul. When you come to stand before a great picture, Armorel, perhaps you will understand what I mean. You will find your heart agitated with strange emotions—you will leave it with new thoughts. When you go away from your desert island, remember every day to read a piece of great verse, to look upon a great picture, and to hear a piece of great music. As for these suggested thoughts, you will not perhaps be able to put them into words. But they will be there.'

Still Armorel made no reply. It was as if he were talking to a statue.

'I have painted you,' he said, 'with the golden torque round your neck: the red gold is caught by the sunshine: as for your dress, I think it must be a white woollen robe—perhaps a border of purple—but I don't know—— There are already heaps of colour—colour of sky and of water, of the granite with the yellow lichen, and of brown and yellow fern and of heather faded—— No—you shall be all in white, Armorel. No dress so sweet for a girl as white. A vest of white linen made by yourself from your own spinning-wheel, up to the throat and covering the right shoulder. Are you tired, child?'

'No—I like to hear you talk.'

'I have nearly done—in fact,' he leaned back and contemplated his work with the enthusiasm which is to a painter what the glow of composition is to the writer, 'I have done all I can until I go home. The sun of Scilly hath a more golden glow in September than the sun of St. John's Wood. If I have caught aright—or something like it—the light that is around you and about you, Armorel—— The sun in your left hand is like the red light of the candle through the closed fingers. So—I can do no more—Armorel! you are all glorious within and without. You are indeed the King's Daughter: you are clothed with the sun as with a garment. if the sun were to disappear this moment, you would stand upon the Peak, for all the island to admire—a flaming beacon!'

His voice was jubilant—he had done well. Yet he shaded his eyes and looked at canvas and at model once more with jealousy and suspicion. If he had passed over something! It was an ambitious picture—the most ambitious thing he had yet attempted.

'Armorel!' he cried. 'If I could only paint as well as I can see! Come down, child; you are good indeed to stand so long and so patiently.'

She obeyed and jumped off her eminence, and stood beside him looking at the picture.

'Tell me what you think,' said the painter. 'You see—it is the King's Daughter. She stands on a peak in Lyonesse and looks forth upon the waters. Why? I know not. She seeks the secrets of the future, perhaps. She looks for the coming of the Perfect Knight, perhaps. She expects the Heaven that waits for every maiden—in this world as well as in the next. Everyone may interpret the picture for himself. She is young—everything is possible to the young. Tell me, Armorel, what do you think?'

She drew a long breath. 'A—h!' she murmured. 'I have never seen anything like this before. It is not me you have painted, Roland. You say it is a picture of me—just to please and flatter me. There is my face—yet not my face. All is changed. Roland, when I am grown to my full height, shall I look like this?'

'If you do, when that day comes, I shall be proved to be a painter indeed,' he replied. 'If you had seen nothing but yourself—your own self—and no more, I would have burnt the thing. Now you give me hopes.'

Afterwards, Armorel loved best to remember him as he stood there beside this unfinished picture, glowing with the thought that he had done what he had attempted. The soul was there.

Out of the chatter of the studio, the endless discussions of style and method, he had come down to this simple spot, to live for three weeks, cut off from the world, with a child who knew nothing of these things. He came at a time when his enthusiasm for his work was at its fiercest: that is, when the early studies are beginning to bear fruit, when the hand has acquired command of the pencil and can control the brush, and when the eye is already trained to colour. It was at a time when the young artist refuses to look at any but the greatest work, and refuses to dream of any future except that of the greatest and noblest work. It is a splendid thing to have had, even for a short time, these dreams and these enthusiasms.

'The picture is finished,' said Armorel, 'and to-morrow you will go away and leave me.' The tears welled up in her eyes. Why should not the child cry for the departure of this sweet friend?

'My dear child,' he said, 'I cannot believe that you will stay for ever on this desert island.'

'I do not want to leave the island. I want to keep you here. Why don't you stay altogether, Roland? You can paint here. Have we made you happy? Are you satisfied with our way of living? We will change it for you, if you wish.'

'No—no—it is not that. I must go home. I must go back to my work. But I cannot bear to think of you left alone with these old people, with no companions and no friends. The time will come when you will leave the place and go away somewhere—where people live and talk——'

He reflected that if she went away it might be among people ignorant of Art and void of culture. This beautiful child, who might have been a Princess—she was only a flower-farmer of the Scilly Islands. What could she hope or expect?

'I do not want to go into the world,' she went on. 'I am afraid, because I am so ignorant. People would laugh at me. I would rather stay here always, if you were with me. Then we would do nothing but sail and row and go fishing: and you could paint and sketch all the time.'

'It is impossible, Armorel. You talk like a child. In a year or two you will understand that it is impossible. Besides, we should both grow old. Think of that. Think of two old people going about sailing among the islands for ever: I, like Justinian Tryeth, bald and bowed and wrinkled: you, like Dorcas—no, no; you could never grow like Dorcas: you shall grow serenely, beautifully old.'

'What would that matter?' she replied. 'Some day, even, one of us would die. What would that matter, either, because we should only be parted by a year or two? Oh! whether we are old or young the sea never grows old, nor the hills and rocks—and the sunshine is always the same. And when we die there will be a new heaven and a new earth—you can read it in the Book of Revelation—but no more sea, no more sea. That I cannot understand. How could angels and saints be happy without the sea? If one lives among people in towns, I dare say it may be disagreeable to grow old, and perhaps to look ugly like poor Dorcas; but not, no, not when one lives in such a place as this.'

'Where did you get your wisdom, Armorel?'

'Is that wisdom?'

'When I go away my chief regret will be that I kept talking to you about myself. Men are selfish pigs. We should have talked about nothing but you. Then I should have learned a great deal. See how we miss our opportunities.'

'No, no; I had nothing to tell you. And you had such a great deal to tell me. It was you who taught me that everybody ought to try to grow to his full height.'

'Did I? It was only a passing thought. Such things occur to one sometimes.'

She sat down on a boulder and crossed her hands in her lap, looking at him seriously and gravely with her great black eyes.

'Now,' she said, 'I want to be very serious. It is my last chance. Roland, I am resolved that I will try to grow to my full height. You are going away to-morrow, and I shall have no one to advise me. Give me all the help you can before you go.'

'What help can I give you, Armorel?'

'I have been thinking. You have told me all about yourself. You are going to be a great artist: you will give up all your life to your work: when you have grown as tall as you can, everybody will congratulate you, and you will be proud and happy. But who is to tell me? How shall I know when I am grown to my full height?'

'You have got something more in your mind, Armorel.'

'Give me a model, Roland. You always paint from a model yourself—you told me so. Now, think of the very best actual girl of all the girls you know—the most perfect girl, mind: she must be a girl that I can remember and try to copy. I must have something to think of and go by, you know.'

'The very best actual girl I know?' he laughed, with a touch of the abominable modern cynicism which no longer believes in girls. 'That wouldn't help you much, I am afraid. You see, Armorel, I should not look to the actual girls I know for the best girl at all. There is, however'—he pulled his shadowy moustache, looking very wise—'a most wonderful girl—I confess that I have never met her, but I have heard of her: the poets keep talking about her—and some of the novelists are fond of drawing her; I have heard of her, read of her, and dreamed of her. Shall I tell you about her?'

'If you please—that is, if she can become my model.'

'Perhaps. She is quite a possible girl, Armorel, like yourself. That is to say, a girl who may really develop out of certain qualities. As for actual girls, there are any number whom one knows in a way—one can distinguish them—I mean by their voices, their faces, and their figures and so forth. But as for knowing anything more about them——'

'Tell me, then, about the girl whom you do know, though you have never seen her.'

'I will if I can. As for her face—now——'

'Never mind her face,' she interrupted, impatiently.

'Never mind her face, as you say. Besides, you can look in the glass if you want to know her face.'

'Yes; that will do,' said Armorel, simply. 'Now go on.'

'First of all, then, she is always well dressed—beautifully dressed—and with as much taste as the silly fashion of the day allows. A woman, you know, though she is the most beautiful creature in the whole of animated nature, can never afford to do without the adornments of dress. It does not much matter how a man goes dressed. He only dresses for warmth. In any dress and in any rags a handsome man looks well. But not a woman. Her dress either ruins her beauty or it heightens it. A woman must always, and at all ages, look as beautiful as she can. Therefore, she arranges her clothes so as to set off her beauty when she is young: to make her seem still beautiful when she is past her youth: and to hide the ravages of time when she is old. That is the first thing which I remark about this girl. Of course, she doesn't dress as if her father was a Silver King. Such a simple stuff as your grey nun's cloth, Armorel, is good enough to make the most lovely dress.'

'She is always well dressed,' his pupil repeated. 'That is the first thing.'

'She is accomplished, of course,' Roland added, airily, as if accomplishments were as easy to pick up as the blue and grey shells on Porth Bay. 'She understands music, and plays on some instrument. She knows about art of all kinds—art in painting, sculptures, decorations, poetry, literature, music. She can talk intelligently about art; and she has trained her eye so that she knows good work. She is never carried away by shams and humbug.'

'She has trained her eye, and knows good work,' Armorel repeated.

'Above all, she is sympathetic. She does not talk so as to show how clever she is, but to bring out the best points of the man she is talking with. Yet when men leave her they forget what they have said themselves, and only remember how much this girl seems to know.'

'Seems to know?' Armorel looked up.

'One woman cannot know everything. But a clever woman will know about everything that belongs to her own set. We all belong to our own set, and every set talks its own language—scientific, artistic, whatever it is. This girl does not pretend to enter into the arena; but she knows the rules of the game, and talks accordingly. She is always intelligent, gracious, and sympathetic.'

'She is intelligent, gracious, and sympathetic,' Armorel repeated. 'Is she gracious to everybody—even to people she does not like?'

'In society,' said Roland, 'we like everybody. We are all perfectly well-bred and well-behaved: we always say the kindest things about each other.'

'Now you are saying one thing and meaning another. That is like your friend Dick Stephenson. Don't, Roland.'

'Well, then, I have very little more to say. This girl, however, is always a woman's woman.'

'What is that?'

'Difficult to explain. A wise lady once advised me when I went courting, first to make quite sure that the girl was a woman's woman. I think she meant that other girls should speak and think well of her. I haven't always remembered the advice, it is true.

but——' Here he stopped short and in some confusion, remembering that this was not an occasion for plenary confession.

But Armorel only nodded gravely. 'I shall remember,' she said.

'The rest you know. She loves everything that is beautiful and good. She hates everything that is coarse and ugly. That is all.'

'Thank you—I shall remember,' she repeated. 'Roland, you must have thought a good deal about girls to know so much.'

He blushed: he really did. He blushed a rich and rosy red.

'An artist, you know,' he said, 'has to draw beautiful girls. Naturally he thinks of the lovely soul behind the lovely face. These things are only commonplaces. You yourself, Armorel—you—will shame me, presently—when you have grown to that full height—for drawing a picture so insufficient of the Perfect Woman.'

He stooped slightly, as if he would have kissed her forehead. Why not? She was but a child. But he refrained.

'Let us go home,' he said, with a certain harshness in his voice. 'The sun is down. The clouds have covered up the belt of blue. You have seen your splendid future, Armorel, and you are back in the grey and sunless present. It grows cold. To-morrow, I think, we may have rain. Let us go home, child: let us go home.'

CHAPTER X

MR. FLETCHER RETURNS FOR HIS BAG

HALF an hour later the blinds were down, the fire was brightly burning, the red firelight was merrily dancing about the room, and the table was pushed back. Then Dorcas and Justinian came in—the two old serving-folk, bent with age, grey-headed, toothless—followed by Chessun—thin and tall, silent and subdued. And Armorel, taking her violin, tuned it, and turned to her old master for instructions, just as she had done on the first and every following night of Roland's stay.

'"Barley Break,"' said Justinian.

Armorel struck up that well-known air. Then, as before, the ancient dame started, moved uneasily, sat upright, and opened her eyes and began to talk. But to-night she was not rambling: she did not begin one fragment of reminiscence and break off in the middle. She started with a clear story in her mind, which she began at the beginning and carried on. When Armorel saw her thus disposed, she stopped playing 'Barley Break,' which may amuse the aged mind and recall old merriment, but lacks earnestness.

'"Put on thy smock o' Monday,"' said Justinian.

This ditty lends itself to more sustained thought. Armorel put more seriousness into it than the theme of the music would seem to warrant. The old lady, however, seemed to like it, and continued her narrative without interrupting it at any point. Armorel also observed that, though she addressed the assembled multitude generally, she kept glancing furtively at Roland.

'The night was terrible,' said the ancient dame, speaking distinctly and connectedly; 'never was such a storm known—we could hear the waves beating and dashing about the islands louder than the roaring of the wind, and we heard the minute-gun, so that there was little sleep for anyone. At daybreak we were all on the shore, out on Shark Point. Sure enough, on the Castinicks the ship lay, breaking up fast—a splendid East Indiaman she was. Her masts were gone and her bows were stove in—as soon as the light got strong enough we could see so much—and the shore covered already with wreck. But not a sign of passengers or crew. Then my husband's father, who was always first, saw something, and ran into the water up to his middle and dragged ashore a spar. And, sure enough, a man was lashed to the spar. When father hauled the man up, he was quite senseless, and he seemed dead, so that another quarter of an hour would have finished him, even if his head had not been knocked against a rock, or the spar turned over and drowned him. Just as father was going to call for help to drag him up, he saw a little leather bag hanging from his neck by a leather thong. There were others about, all the people of Samson—fifty of them—men, women, and children—all busy collecting the things that had been washed ashore, and some up to their waists in the water after the things still floating about. But nobody was looking. Therefore, father, thinking it was a dead man, whipped out his knife, cut the leather thong, and slipped the bag into his own pocket, not stopping to look at it. No one saw him, mind—no one—not even your father, Justinian, who was close beside him at the time.'

'Ay, ay,' said Justinian: 'if father had seen it, naturally——' But his voice died away, and Roland was left to wonder what, under such circumstances, a native of Samson would have done.

'No one saw it. Father thought the man was dead. But he wasn't. Presently he moved. Then they carried him up the hill to the farm—this very house—and laid him down before the fire—just at your feet, Armorel—and I was standing by. "Get him a cordial," says father. So we gave him a dram, and he drank it and opened his eyes. He was a gentleman—we could see that—not a common sailor: not a common man.'

Here her head dropped, and she seemed to be losing herself again.

'Try her with a Saraband,' said Justinian, as if a determined effort had to be made. Armorel changed her tune. A Saraband lends itself to a serious and even solemn turn of thought. As a dance it requires the best manners, the bravest dress, and the most dignified air. It will be seen, therefore, that to a mind bent upon a grave narrative of deeds lamentable and fateful, the Saraband, played in a proper frame of mind, may prove sympathetic. The ancient lady lifted her head, strengthened by the opening bars, which, indeed, are very strong, and resumed her story. Armorel, to be sure, and all her hearers, knew the history well, having heard it every night in disjointed bits. The Tale of the Stolen Treasure was familiar to her: it was more than familiar—it was a bore: the Family Doom seemed unjust to her: it disturbed her sense of Providential benevolence: yet she threw all her soul into the Saraband in order to prolong by a few minutes the waking and conscious moments of this remote ancestress. A striking illustration, had the others understood it, of filial piety.

'But I was standing close by father,' she went on—'I was beside him on the beach, and I saw it. I saw him cut the thong and slip the bag into his pocket. When he came to himself, I whispered to father, "There's his bag: you've got his bag in your pocket." "I know," he said, rough. "Hold your tongue, girl." So I said no more, but waited. Then the man opened his eyes and tried to sit up; but he couldn't, being still dizzy with the beating of the waves. But he looked at us, wondering where he was. "You are ashore, Master," said father. "The only one of all the ship's company that is, so far." "Ashore?" he asked. "Ay, ashore: where else would you be? Your ship's in splinters: your captain and your crew are dead men all. But you're ashore." With that the man shut his eyes and lay quiet for a time. Then he opened them again. "Where am I?" he asked. "You are on Samson, in Scilly," I told him. Then he tried to get up again, but he couldn't. And so we carried him upstairs and laid him on the bed.

'He was in bed for nigh upon six weeks. Never was any man so near his latter end. I nursed him all the time. He had a fever, and his head wandered. In his rambling he told me who he was. His name was Robert Fletcher—Robert Fletcher,' she repeated, nodding to Roland with strange significance. 'A brave gentleman, and handsome and well-mannered. He had been in the service of an Indian King; and, though he was only thirty, he had made his fortune and was bringing it home, thinking that he would do nothing more all his life but just sit down and enjoy himself. All his fortune was in the bag. When he recovered he told me that the last thing he remembered, before he was washed off the ship, was feeling for the safety of his bag. And it was gone. And he was a beggar. Poor man! And I knew all the time where the bag was and who had it. But I could not tell him. If father sinned when he kept the bag, I sinned as well, because I knew he kept it. If father was punished when his son was drowned, that son was my husband, and I was punished too.'

She stopped, and it seemed as if for the evening she had run down; but Armorel stimulated her again, and she went on, looking more and more at the face of the stranger that was in their gates.

'While he lay ill and was like to die, father was uneasy—I know why. He wanted him to die, because then he could keep the treasure with a quiet mind. "All's ours that comes ashore," that's what we used to say. He never confessed his thoughts—but I, who knew what was in the bag, guessed them very well.

'The stranger began to recover, and father fell into a gloomy fit, and would go and sit by himself for hours. Nobody dared ask him—for he was a man of short temper and rough in his speech—what was the matter with him, but I knew very well. He was gloomy because he didn't want to lose that bag. But the man got better, and at last quite well, and one morning he came down dressed in clothes that father lent him, because his own were ruined in the washing of him ashore, and he bade us all farewell. "Captain Rosevean," he said, very earnestly, "when I left India I was rich: I was carrying all my fortune home with me in a small compass, for safety, as I thought. I was going to be a rich man, and work no more. Well—I have escaped with my life, and that is all. If I were not a beggar I would offer you half my fortune for saving my life. As it is, I can offer you nothing but my gratitude."

'So he shook hands with father, who stood as white as a sheet, for all he was a ruddy-faced man and inclined to brandy. "And farewell, Mistress Ursula," he said. "Farewell, my kind nurse." So he kissed me, being a courteous gentleman. "I shall come back again to see you," he said; "I shall surely come back. Look to see me some day, when you least expect me." So he went away, and they rowed him over to the Port, and he sailed to Penzance. Father went to his own room, where the treasure was. And my heart sank heavy as lead. The more I thought of the wickedness, the heavier fell my heart. There was father and his son, my husband, and myself and my own son not yet born. The Hand of the Lord would be upon us for that wickedness. I ought to have cried out to the stranger before he went away that his treasure was safe and that we were keeping it for him. But I didn't. Then I tried to comfort myself. I said that when he came again I would give him back the bag, even if I had to steal it from father's chest.

'It was a long time ago—they are all gone, swallowed up by the sea—which was right, because we stole the treasure from the sea. He never came back. I looked for him to come after my husband was drowned, and after my son went too, and my grandson—but he never came again as he promised. And at last, at last'—her voice rose almost to a shriek, and everybody jumped in his chair; but Armorel continued to play the Saraband slowly and with much expression—'at last he has come back, and we are saved. All that are left of us are saved. Armorel, my child, you are saved. Your bones shall not lie rotting among the sea-weed: your flesh shall not be devoured by crabs and conger-eels: you may sail without fear among the islands. For he has kept his promise and has come back.

Then she rose—she, who had not stood upon her feet for three years—actually rose and stood up, or seemed to stand: the red light, playing on her face, made her eyes shine like two balls of fire. 'You,' she cried, pointing her long, skinny, finger at Roland. 'You! oh! you have come at last. You have suffered all that innocent blood to be shed: but you have come at last.' She sank back among her pillows, but her finger still pointed at the stranger. 'Sir,' she said now, with tremulous voice, 'you are welcome. Late though it is, Mr. Fletcher, you are welcome. When you came a day or two ago I wondered, being now very old and foolish, if it was really you. Now I know. I remember, though it is nearly eighty years ago. You are welcome again to Samson, Mr. Fletcher. You find me changed, no doubt. I knew you would keep your promise and come again, some time or other. As for you, I see little change. You are dressed differently, and when you were here last your hair was worn in another fashion. But you are no older to look at. You are not changed at all by time. You would not know me again. How should you? I suppose you knew—somebody told you, perhaps—that the bag was safe after all. That knowledge has kept you young. Nothing short of that knowledge could have kept you young. I assure you, Sir, had I known where to find you I would have taken the bag and its contents to you long, long ago. And now you are come back in search of it.'

'It was eighty years ago!' Dorcas whispered to Chessun, shuddering. 'He must be more than a hundred!'

'A hundred years!' returned her daughter, with pallid cheeks. 'It isn't in nature. He looks no more than twenty. Mother, is he a man and alive?'

'Pretend that you are Mr. Fletcher,' whispered Armorel. 'Do not contradict her. Say something.'

'It is a long time ago,' said Roland. 'I should have kept my promise much sooner. And as for that bag—you saved my life, you know. Pray keep the bag. It has long been forgotten.'

'Keep the bag? Do you know what is in it? Do you know what it is worth? That, Mr. Fletcher, is your politeness. We, who have suffered so much from the possession of the bag, cannot believe that you have forgotten it, because if we have suffered for our guilt you must have suffered through that guilt. Else there would be no justice. No justice at all unless you have suffered too. Else all those lives have been wasted and thrown away.'

The old lady spoke with the voice and firmness of a woman of fifty. She looked strong: she sat up erect. Armorel played on, now softly, now loudly. The serving-folk looked on open-mouthed: the women with terror undisguised. Was this gentleman, so young and so pleasant, none other than the man whose injury had brought all these drownings upon the family? Nearly eighty years ago that happened. Then, he must be a ghost! What else could he be? No human creature could come back after eighty years still so young.

'When I said, Madam,' Roland explained, 'that I had forgotten the bag, what I meant was that after losing it so long I had quite abandoned all hope of finding it again. I assure you that I have not come here in search of it. In fact, I thought it was lying at the bottom of the sea, where so many other treasures lie.'

'It is not at the bottom of the sea, Mr. Fletcher. You shall have it again, to-morrow. You are still so young that you can enjoy your fortune. Make good use of it, Sir, and do not forget the poor. I have counted the contents again and again. They are not things that wear out and rust, are they? No, no. You must often have laughed to think that the moth and the worm cannot destroy that treasure. You will be very pleased to have it back.'

'I shall be very pleased indeed,' he echoed, 'to have my treasure again.'

'Face and voice unchanged.' The old lady shook her head. 'And after eighty years. It is a miracle, yet not a greater miracle than the Vengeance which has pursued this house so long. This single crime has been visited upon the third and fourth generation. 'Tis time that punishment should cease at last—cease at last! I must tell you, Mr. Fletcher,' she went on, 'that when my husband was drowned and my father-in-law died, I took possession of the bag and everything else. I said nothing to my son. Why? Because, until the owner of the stolen bag came back, the curse was on him and his children. No—no; I would not let him know. But I knew very well what would happen to all of them. Oh! yes; I knew, and I waited. But he was happy, and his son and his grandson and his great-grandson, until they were drowned, one after the other. And still you stayed away.'

'Madam, had I known, I would have returned fifty years ago and more, in time to have saved them all.'

'You might have come sooner, Sir, permit me to say, and so have saved some.' It was wonderful how erect the old lady held herself, and with what firmness and precision she spoke.

'There is now only one left—the child Armorel. To-morrow, Sir, you shall have your bag again. Once more you are our guest: this time, I hope you will leave a blessing instead of a curse upon the house.'

At this moment Armorel ceased playing. Then this ancient lady stopped talking. She looked round: her eyes lost their fire: her face its expression: her mouth its firmness: she fell back in her pillows, and her head dropped.

Dorcas and Chessun rose and carried her to her own room. The old man got up, too, and shambled out. Armorel pushed the table into its place, and lit the candles. The incident was closed. In the morning the old lady had forgotten everything.

'Almost,' said Roland, 'she has made me believe that my name is Fletcher. Shall I to-morrow morning ask her for the bag? Where is that bag? Armorel, it is a true story. I am quite certain of it.'

'Oh, yes, it is true. Justinian knows about the wreck, though it happened before he was born. Mr. Fletcher was the only man saved of all the ship and company—captain, officers, crew, and passengers—the only one. He was rescued by Captain Rosevean himself and brought here. He had the bedroom where you sleep—the bedroom which was my brother Emanuel's room. Here he lay ill a long time, but recovered and went away.'

'And the bag?'

'I know nothing about the bag. That has gone long ago, I suppose, with all the money that my people made by smuggling and by piloting. I have seen her watching you for some days past: I thought she would speak to you last night. To-morrow she will have forgotten everything.'

'I suppose I have some kind of resemblance to Mr. Robert Fletcher, presumably deceased. Well—but, Armorel, this is a fortunate evening. The family luck has come back—I have brought it back. The Ancient one said so, and you are saved. She may call me Fletcher—call me Tryeth—call me any name that flyeth—if she only calls me him who arrived in time to save you, Armorel.'

CHAPTER XI

ROLAND'S LETTER

ROLAND went away. Like Mr. Robert Fletcher, he promised to return, and, like her great-great-grandmother, but for other reasons, Armorel treasured this promise. Also like Mr. Robert Fletcher, now presumably deceased, Roland went away with the sense of having left something behind him. Not his heart, dear reader. A young man of twenty-one does not give away his heart in the old-fashioned way any longer: he carries it about with him, carefully kept in its proper place: what Roland had left behind him, for awhile, was a part of himself. It would perhaps come back to him in good time, but for the present it remained on Samson, and discoursed to the rest of him in London whenever he would listen, on the beauties of that archipelago and the graces of the child Armorel. And this part of himself, which haunted Samson, made him sit down and write a letter. It would have been a tender, a sorrowful, an affectionate letter had it not been for that other part of him—the greater part—which went to London. That other part of him remonstrated. 'She is but a simple country girl,' it said. 'Her future will be to marry a simple Scillonian. Why disturb her mind? Why seek to plant the seeds of discontent under the guise of culture? Leave her—leave her to herself. Forget those dark eyes, in whose depths there seemed to lie so sweet, so great a soul. Believe me, there was nothing at all behind those eyes but ignorance and curiosity. How could there be anything? Leave her in peace. Or, since you must write, let it be a cold letter—friendly, but fatherly—and let her understand clearly that the visit can produce no further consequences whatever.' Thus the London half of him—the bigger half. Perhaps his friend Dick Stephenson remonstrated in the same strain. But the lesser half insisted on writing a letter of some kind—and had his way.

He wrote a letter, and sent it off.

It was the very first letter that had ever been sent to Samson. Of that I am quite sure. No letters ever reached that island. If people had business with Samson, they transacted it at the Port with Justinian or Peter. Of course it was the first letter that had ever been received by Armorel. Peter brought it across for her. He had wrapped the unaccustomed thing in brown paper for fear the spray should fall upon it. Armorel drew it forth from its covering and gazed upon it with the wonder of a child who gets an unexpected toy. She read over the address a dozen times: '"Miss Rosevean"—look at it, Dorcas. What a pity you cannot read! "Miss Rosevean"—he might have written "Armorel"—"Island of Samson, Scilly." Of course, it is from Roland. No one else would write to me.' Then she opened it carefully, so as not to injure any part of the writing—indeed, Roland possessed that desirable, but very rare, gift of a very beautiful hand. No Penman of the monastery: no scrivener of a later age: no Arab or Persian scribe, could write a more beautiful hand. It was a hand in which every letter was clearly formed, as if it made a picture of itself, and every word was a Group, like the Eastern Isles of Scilly, to be admired by the whole world.

The letter began—the London portion conceding so much—with a pen-and-ink sketch of the writer's head: if it was just a little idealised, who shall blame the limner? This was delightful. Armorel had no portrait of her friend. What would follow after such a beautiful beginning? Then the writing began, and Armorel addressed herself seriously to the mastering of and the meaning of the letter. I blush to record the fact, but Armorel read handwriting slowly. Consider. Since she left school she had seen none: while at school she had seen little. People easily forget such a simple thing, though we who write all day long cannot understand how a man can forget how to write. Yet there are many working-men who cannot read handwriting, nor can they themselves write. They have had no occasion, all their lives, to use either accomplishment, and so have readily forgotten it—a fact which shows the profound wisdom of the School Boards in teaching spelling. Armorel could read the letter, but she read it slowly.

It seemed, when she read it first, sentence by sentence, a really beautiful letter—regarded as a letter in the abstract. After she had read it two or three times over, and had mastered the whole document, she began to understand that the writer of it was not the man she remembered, not the man whose memory she loved and cherished, not at all her friend Roland Lee. All the old *camaraderie* was gone. It was the letter of another man altogether. It was cold and stiff. The coldness went to the girl's heart. She had never known Roland to be cold. Where was the sympathy which formerly flowed in magnetic currents from one to the other? Where was the brotherly interest?—she called it brotherly. The writer spoke, it is true, with gratitude overwhelming, of his stay on the island, and her hospitality. But, good gracious! Armorel wanted no thanks. His visit had made her happy: he knew that. Why should he take up a page and a half in returning thanks to her, when her own heart was full of gratitude to him? He said that the three weeks he had spent among the islands had been a holiday which he could never forget—this was very good, so far; but then he spoiled all by adding that he should not readily forget—'readily forget' he wrote—his fair companion and guide among those labyrinthine waters. 'Fair companion!' What had fairness to do with it? Armorel had been his pupil: he taught her all day long. She did not want to be called his 'fair companion': that was mockery. She wanted to be called 'his dear friend' or 'his dear sister': that would have gone straight to her heart. She expected at least so much when she opened the letter. But worse—far worse—was to follow. He actually spoke of the possibilities of their never meeting again, the world (outside Scilly) being so very wide. Never to meet again! And he had promised to return: he had faithfully promised. Why, he had only to take the steamer from Penzance: Samson Island would not sail away. Why did he not rather say when he was to be expected? Worst of all, he spoke of her forgetting him. Oh! how could she forget him? As for the rest of the letter, the paternal advice to continue in the path of industry, and so forth, no clergyman in the pulpit could speak more wisely: but these things touched not the girl. Woman wants affection rather than wisdom, even though she understands, or has, at least, been told, that Wisdom delivereth from the way of the Evil Man.

Armorel at length laid the letter down with a sigh and a tear. She kept it in her pocket for some days, and read it every day: but with increasing sadness. Finally, she laid it in a drawer where were all the sketches, fragments of illustration, and outline drawings which Roland had given her. She would read it no longer. She would wait till Roland came back, and she would ask him what it meant. Perhaps it was the way of the world to be so cold and so constrained in letter-writing.

There came a box with the letter. It contained books—quite a large number of books—selected by Roland with the view of suiting the case of one who dwells upon a desert island. It was just as if Captain Woodes Rogers had left Alexander alone upon Juan

Fernandez, and gone home to make up for him a parcel of books intended to show him what went on in the wider world. There were also drawing materials, colours, brushes, pencils, books of instruction, and books of music. Roland the fatherly—the London part of Roland—neglected nothing that might be solidly serviceable to the young Person. Observe, here, one of those black gaps of ignorance already spoken of in this girl of the Lonely Isles. She did not know that an answer to the letter was absolutely necessary. In the London studio the writer sat wondering why no answer came. He had been so careful, too: not a word which could be misunderstood: he had been so truly fatherly. And yet no reply.

Nobody was at hand to tell Armorel that she must sit down and write some kind of an answer. She tried, in fact: she made several attempts. But she could not write anything that satisfied her. The coldness of the letter chilled her. She wanted to write as she had talked with him—all out of the fulness of her heart. How could she write to this frigid creature? The writer of such a letter could not be her dear companion who laughed and made her laugh, sang and made her sing, made pictures for her, told her all about his own private ambitions, and had no secrets from her: it was a strange man who wrote to her and signed the name of Roland Lee. The real Roland would never have hinted at the possibility of her forgetting him, or at the chance of their never meeting again. The real Roland would have written to say when he was coming again. She could not reply to this impostor.

Therefore, she never answered that letter at all; and so she got no more letters. It was a pity, because, had she written what was in her mind, for very pity the real Roland would have returned to her. Once, and once only, the voice of Roland came to her across the sea—and then it was a changed voice. He spoke no more. But he would come again: he said he would come again. Every day she sat on the hill beside the barrow, and gazed across the Road. She could see the pier of Hugh Town and the vessels in the port: perhaps Roland had come over from Penzance by the morning steamer, and would shortly sail across the Road, and leap out upon the beach, and run to meet and greet her, with both hands outstretched, the light of affection in his eyes, and the laugh of welcome in his voice. She was graver and more silent than before: she did not sing so often as she walked among the ferns: she did not prattle to Chessun and Dorcas while she made her cakes and puddings. But nobody noticed any change in her: the serving-women, if they observed any, would have said only that Armorel was growing into a woman already.

The autumn changed to winter. Roland would not come in winter, when the sea is stormy and there is little sunshine. She must wait now until spring. Meantime, on Samson, where are no trees except those wizened and crooked little trees of the orchard, there is not much to mark the winter except the cold wind and the short days. Here there is never frost or snow, hail or ice. The brown turf is much the same in December as in August; the dead fern is not so yellow: the dead and dying leaves of the bramble are not so splendid. The wind is colder, the sky is more grey; otherwise winter makes little difference in the external aspect of this archipelago. When the short days begin, the brown fields of the flower-farms clothe themselves with the verdure of spring: before the New Year has fairly set in, some of the fresh delicate flowers have been already cut and laid in the hothouse to be sent across to Covent Garden. The harvest of the year begins with its first day, and they reap it from January to May.

There are plenty of things on such a farm for a girl to do. Armorel did not, if you please, sit down to weep. But she daily recalled with tender regret every one of the pleasant days of that companionship. She kept her promise, too: she read something every morning in the books which Roland had sent her: every afternoon she attempted to carry on the drawing lesson by herself: she practised her violin diligently: and every evening she played the old tunes to the old lady, and awakened her once more to life and memory. There was no change, except that everything now was coloured by what he had said. She was to grow to her full height—he had told her how—but at present she hardly saw her way to carrying out those instructions. Her full height! Ignorant of the truth—since such a girl grown to her full height would be so tall as to be out of all proportion, not only to Samson, but even to St. Mary's itself.

Sometimes one falls into the habit of associating a single person with an idea, a thought, an anticipation, a place. Whenever the mind turns to this thought, the person is present. For example, there is a street in London which I have learned, from long habit, to associate with a second-hand bookseller. He was a gentle creature, full of reading, who had known many men. I sometimes sat at the back of his shop conversing with him. Sometimes a twelvemonth would pass without my seeing him at all. But always when I think of this street I think of this old gentleman. The other day I passed through it. Alas! the shutters were up: the house was to let: my gentle friend was gone. Armorel associated her future—the unknown future—with Roland. Suppose that when that future should be the present she should find the shutters up, the house deserted, the tenant dead!

The harvest of flowers was well begun: the boxes piled in the hold of the steamer merrily danced in the roll of the Atlantic waves as the *Lady of the Isles* made her way to Penzance: in London the delicate narcissus and the jonquil returned to the dinner-tables, and stood about in glasses. Roland Lee bought them and took them home to his studio, where he sat looking at them, reminded of Armorel—who had never even answered his letter. Perhaps the flowers came from Samson. Why did the girl send him no answer to his letter! Then his memory went back to that little island with its two hills, and its barrows, and the quiet house—and to the girl who lived there. On what rock of Samson was she sitting? Where was she at that moment? Gazing somewhere over the wild waste of waters, the wind blowing about her curls, and the beating of the waves in her ears. She had forgotten him. Why not! He was only a visitor of a week or two. She was nothing but a child—and an ignorant farmer-girl living in a desert island. Ignorant? No; that was not the word. He saw her once more standing in the middle of the room, the ruddy firelight in her eyes and on her cheeks, playing 'Singleton's Slip' and 'Prince Rupert's March,' while the Ancient Lady mopped and mowed and discoursed of other days. And again: he saw her standing on the beach when he said farewell, the tears in her eyes, her voice choked. Then he longed again, as he had longed then, to take her in his arms, even in the presence of Peter the boy, to soothe and kiss her and bid her weep no more, because he would never, never leave her.

So strong was the impression made upon this young man by this child of fifteen, that after six months spent in the society of many other girls, of charms more matured, he still remembered her, and thought of her with that kind of yearning regret which is perilously akin to love. An untaught, ignorant girl—whose charm lay in her innocent confidence, her soft black eyes, and the beauty of the maiden emerging from the child—could hardly make a permanent impression on a man of the world, even a young man of only twenty-one. The time would go on, and the girl would be forgotten, except as a pleasant memory associated with a delightful holiday. An artist is, perhaps, above his fellows, liable to swift and sudden changes; his mind dwells continually on beauty. All lovely girls have not black hair and black eyes. Apollo, himself, the god of artists, loved not only all the nine Muses and all the three Graces, but a good many nymphs and princesses as well—such is the artistic temperament, so catholic is its admiration of beauty.

CHAPTER XII

THE CHANGE

'A CHANGE,' said Roland, 'will surely come, and that before long. I cannot believe'—Armorel remembered the words afterwards—'that you will stay on this island for ever.' It needed no unusual gift of prophecy to foretell impending change when the most important member of the household was nearing her hundredth year.

The change foretold actually came in April, when the flower-fields had lost their beauty and the harvest of Scilly was nearly over. Late blossoms of daffodil still reared their heads among the thick leaves, though their blooming companions had all been cut off to grace London tables; there were broad patches of wallflower little regarded; the leaves of the bulbs were drooping and already turning brown: these were the signs of approaching summer to the Scillonian, who has already had his spring. On the adjacent island of Great Britain the primrose clustered on the banks; the hedges of the West Country were splendid, putting forth tender leaves over a wealth of wild flowers; the chestnut-buds were swollen and sticky, ready to burst. Do we not know the signs and tokens of coming spring? On Scilly, the lengthening day—there are no hedges and no trees to speak of—the completion of the flower harvest, and the drooping of the daffodil-leaves in the fields are the chief signs of spring. Yet there are other signs: if there are no woods to show the tender leaf of spring, there are the green shoots of the fern on the down: and there are the birds. The puffin has already come back; he comes in his thousands: he arrives in April, and he departs in September: whence he cometh and whither he goeth no man hath ever learned nor can naturalist discover. At the same time comes the guillemot, and sometimes the solan-goose: the tern and the sheerwater come too, if they come at all, in spring: but the wild ducks and the wild geese depart before the flower-harvest is finished.

Armorel got up one morning in April a little earlier than usual. It was five o'clock: the sun was rising over Telegraph Hill on St. Mary's. She ran down the stairs, opened the door, and stood in the porch drawing a deep breath. No one was as yet stirring on Samson, though I think Peter was beginning to turn in his bed. Out at sea Armorel saw a great steamer, homeward bound, perhaps an Australian liner: the level rays of the early sun shone on her spars and made them stand out clear and fine against the sky: behind her streamed her long white cloud of smoke and steam, hanging over the water, light and feathery. There were no other ships visible. The air was cold, but the sun of April was already strong. Armorel shivered, caught her hat, and ran over the hill, singing as she went, not knowing that in the night, while she slept, the Angel of Death had visited the house.

About seven o'clock she came back, having completely circumnavigated the island of Samson, and made, as usual, many curious observations and discoveries in the manners and customs of puffins, terns, and shags. She returned in the cheerful mood which belongs to youth, health, and readiness for breakfast. She instantly perceived, however, on arriving, that something had happened—something unusual. For Peter stood in the porch: what was Peter doing in the porch at seven o'clock in the morning, when he ought to have been ministering to the pigs? Further, Peter was standing in the attitude of a boy who waits to be sent on an errand. It is an attitude of expectant readiness—of zeal according to duty—of activity bought and freely rendered. You will observe this attitude in all office boys—except telegraph-boys: they never assume it: they affect no zeal: they betray no eagerness to put in a fair day's work. Such an attitude would lack the dignity due to a Government officer. And at sight of Armorel Peter hung his head as one who sorrows, or is ashamed or repentant. What did he do that for? What had happened? Why should he hang his head?

She asked these questions of Peter, who only shook his head and pointed within. She heard Justinian's voice giving some directions. She also heard Dorcas and Chessun. They were all three speaking in low voices. She hurried in. The door of the old lady's bedroom—that sacred apartment into which no one, except the two handmaidens, had ever ventured—stood wide open; not only that, but Justinian himself was in the room—actually in the room—and beside the bed. Then Armorel understood what had happened. On no other condition would Justinian be admitted to his old mistress's room. On the other side of the bed stood Dorcas and Chessun. Seeing Armorel at the door, these two ladies instantly lifted up their voices and wailed aloud—nay, they shrieked and screamed their lamentations, as if it was the first time in the world's history that death had carried off an aged woman. This they did by a kind of instinct: the thing, though they knew it not, was a survival. In ancient times it was the custom in Lyonesse that the women should all wail and weep and shriek, and beat their breasts and tear their hair, and cut their cheeks with their nails, while the body of the dead king or warrior was carried up the slope of the hill to be laid in its kistvaen and covered with its barrow on Samson island.

They wailed aloud, then, because it had always been the right thing for the women of Samson to do. Otherwise, when one so ancient dies at last, mind and memory gone before, what place is there for wailing and weeping? One natural tear we drop, for all must die; but grief belongs to the death-bed of the young. There needed no shriek of the women nor anyone's speech to tell Armorel that the white face upturned on the bed was not the face of a living woman. They had folded the dead hands across her breast: the eyes were closed: the countless wrinkles of the aged face were smoothed out: the lips were parted with a wan smile. After many, many years, Ursula, the widow, was gone to rejoin her husband. Pray Heaven her desire be granted, and that she rise again young and beautiful—such a woman as that ill-starred sailor, dragged to the bottom of the sea by the weight of Robert Fletcher's bag, had loved in life!

Peter presently sailed across the Road, and returned with the doctor. It is the part of the doctor not only to usher the new-born into life, but to bar or open the gates of the tomb: without him very few of us die, and without him no one can be buried. This man of science graciously expressed his willingness to acknowledge, though he had not been called in, that the deceased died of old age. Then he went back.

In the evening there was no music. The violin remained in its place; the great chair was empty; no one brought out the spinning-wheel; the table was not pushed back. How was the long evening to be got through without the violin? How could those ancient tunes be played any more in the presence of that empty chair? When the serving-folk came in as usual and sat round the fire, and the women sighed and moaned, and Justinian stimulated the coals to a flame, and the ruddy light played upon their faces, Armorel began to think that a continuance of these evenings would be tedious. Then they began to talk, the conversation naturally turning on Death and Judgment, and the prospects of Heaven and the departed.

'She was not one of them,' said Dorcas, 'as would never talk of such things. I've often heard her say she wanted to rise again, young and beautiful, same as she was when her husband was took, so that he should love her again.'

'Nay,' said Justinian; 'that's foolish talk. There's neither marrying nor giving in marriage there. You ought to know so much, Dorcas. Husbands and wives will know each other, I doubt not, if it's only for the man's forgiveness after the many crosses and rubs. 'Twould be a pity, wife, if we didn't know each other, golden crown and all. I'd be sorry to think you were not about somewhere.'

Armorel listened without much interest. She wondered vaguely how Dorcas would look in a golden crown, and hoped that she might not laugh when she should be permitted to gaze upon her thus wonderfully adorned. Then she listened in silence while these thinkers followed up their speculations on the next world and the decrees of Heaven, with the freedom of their kind. A strangely brutal freedom! It consigns, without a thought of pity, the majority of mankind to a doom which they are too ignorant to realise and too stupid to understand. The deceased lady, it was agreed, might, perhaps—though this was by no means certain—have fallen under Conviction of Sin at some remote period, before any of them knew her. Not since, that was certain. And as for her husband, he was cut off in his sins—like all the Roseveans, struck down in his sins, without a warning. So that if the old lady expected to meet him, after their separation of nearly eighty years, on the Shores of Everlasting Praise, she would certainly be disappointed, because he was otherwise situated and disposed of. Therefore she might just as well go up old and wrinkled. This kind of talk was quite familiar to Armorel, and generally meant nothing to her. The right of private judgment is claimed and freely exercised in Scilly, where that branch of the Church Catholic called Bryanite greatly flourishes. Formerly, she would have passed over this talk without heeding. Now, she had begun to think of these as well as of many other things. Roland's words on religious things startled her into thinking. She listened, therefore, wondering what view people like Roland Lee would take of her great-grandfather's present condition, and of the poor old lady's prospects of meeting him again. Then her thoughts wandered from these nebulous speculations, and she heard no more, though the conversation became lurid with the flames of Tartarus, and these old religioners gloated over the hopeless sufferings of the condemned. A sweet and holy thing, indeed, has mankind made of the Gospel of Great Joy!

Before they separated, Chessun rose and left the room noiselessly. Armorel had no experience of the situation, but she knew that something was going to be done, something connected with the impending funeral—something solemn.

In fact, Chessun returned after ten minutes or a quarter of an hour, the others making a pretence of expecting nothing. Doctrinal meditation was written on Justinian's brow: resignation on that of Dorcas. Chessun bore in her hands a tray with glasses and a silver tankard filled with something that steamed. It was a posset, made with biscuits, new milk and sherry, nutmeg and sugar—an emotional drink, strong, sweet, comforting, very good for mournful occasions, but, of late years, unfortunately, gone out of fashion.

They all had a glass, the two women moaning over their glasses, and the old man shaking his head. Then they went to bed.

They had a posset every night until the funeral. They buried the ancient dame on Bryher. A boat carried the coffin across the water to the landing-place in New Grinsey Sound, behind which stands the little old church with its churchyard. Armorel and her household followed in one of the family boats, as in a mourning-carriage. All the people of Tresco and Bryher were present at the funeral; and most of them came across to Samson after the ceremony to drink a glass of wine and eat a slice of cake, the women no longer wailing and the men no longer shaking their heads.

All the Roseveans who have escaped the vengeance of Mr. Fletcher's terrible bag lie in Bryher churchyard. They are mostly widows, poor things! They sleep alone, because their husbands' bones lie about among the tall weeds in the tranquil depths of the ocean.

And Armorel, looking forward, thought with terror of the long, silent evenings, while the old serving-folk would sit round in the firelight, silent, or saying things that might as well have been left unsaid.

CHAPTER XIII

ARMOREL'S INHERITANCE

'You are now the mistress, dearie,' said Dorcas. 'It is time that you should learn what that means.'

It was the morning after the funeral—the Day of Accession—the beginning of the new reign.

'Why, Dorcas, it makes no difference, does it? There are still the flowers and the house and everything.'

'Yes—there's everything.' The old woman nodded her head meaningly. 'Oh! yes—there is everything. Oh! you don't know—you don't suspect—nobody knows—what a surprise is in store for you!'

'What surprise, Dorcas?'

'You've never been into her room except to see her lying dead. It's your room now. You can go in whenever you like. Always the master or the mistress has slept in that room. When her father-in-law died she took the room. And she's slept in it ever since. And no one, except me and Chessun to clean up and sweep and dust, has ever been in that room since. And now it's yours.'

'Well, Dorcas, it may be mine; but I shall go on sleeping in my own room.'

'Then keep it locked—keep it locked up—day and night. There's nobody in Samson to dread—but keep it locked! As for sleeping in it, time enough, perhaps, when you come to marry. But keep it locked——'

'Why, Dorcas, what is in it?'

'I am seventy-five years old and past,' Dorcas went on. 'I was fifteen when I came to the house, and here I've been ever since. Not one of the grandchildren nor the great-grandchildren ever came in here. No one ever knew what is kept here.'

'What is it, then?' Armorel asked again.

'She used to come here alone, by daylight, regularly once a month. She locked the door when she came in. No one ever knew what she was doing, and no one ever asked. One day she forgot to lock the door, and by accident I opened it, and saw what she was doing.'

'What was she doing?'

'She'd opened all the cupboards and boxes, and she'd spread out all the things, and was counting, and—no, no—you may guess, when you have looked for yourself, what she was doing. I shut the door softly, and she never knew that I'd looked in upon her. She might have been overseen from the orchard, but no one ever went in there except to gather the fruit. To make safe, however, I've put up a muslin blind now, because Peter might take it into his head—boys go everywhere peering and prying. Nobody knows what I saw. I never even told Justinian. Men blab, you see: they get together, and they drink—then they blab. You can never trust a man with a secret. How long would it be before Peter would let it out if he knew? Once over at Hugh Town, drinking at a bar, and all the world would know in half an hour. No, no; the secret was hers: it was mine as well—but that was an accident—she never knew that: now it will be yours and mine. And we will tell nobody—nobody at all.'

'Where shall I find this wonderful secret, Dorcas?'

'Wherever you look, dearie. Oh! the room is full of things. There can't be such another room in all the world. It's crammed with things. Look everywhere. If they knew, all the young lords and princes would be at your feet, Armorel, because you are so rich. Best keep it secret, though, and get richer.'

'I so rich? Dorcas, you are joking!'

'No—you shall look and find out. Not that you will understand at first—because, how should you know the value of things? Here's her bunch of keys. She always carried them in her pocket, and at night she kept them under her pillows—and there I found them, sure enough, when she was cold and dead. Take them, child. I never told her secret—no—not even to my own husband. Take the keys, child. They are yours—your own. You can open everything: you can look at everything: you can do what you like with everything. It's your inheritance. But tell no one,' she repeated, earnestly. 'Oh! my dear, let it remain a secret. Don't let anyone see you when you come in here. Lock the door, as she did—and keep it locked.'

The old woman led Armorel by the hand to the door of the room where there was to be found the Great Surprise. She opened it, placed a bunch of keys in her hand, pushed her in and closed it behind her, whispering, 'Lock it, and keep it locked.'

The girl turned the key obediently, wondering what would happen next.

The room was on the ground floor, looking out upon the orchard, with a northern aspect, so that the sun could only shine in for a small portion of the year, during the summer months. The apple-trees were now in blossom, the white pink and flowers bright in the sunshine contrasting with the grey lichen which wrapped every branch and hung down like ribbons. The room was the oldest part of the house, the only remaining portion of an earlier house: it was low and small: the fireplace had never been modernised: it stood wide open, with its dogs and its broad chimney: the window was of three narrow lights, one of which could be opened: all were still provided with the old diamond panes in their leaden setting. Armorel observed the muslin blind put up by Dorcas to keep out prying eyes. In dull and cloudy days the room would be gloomy. As it was, even with the bright sunshine out of doors, the air seemed cold and oppressive—perhaps from the fresh association of Death. Armorel shivered as she looked about her.

The greater part of the room was taken up by a large bed. In the old lady's time it had curtains and a head, and things at the four corners like the plumes of a hearse, but in faded crimson. Then it looked splendid. Now, the bed had been stripped: curtains and plumes and all were gone, and only the skeleton bed left, with its four great solid posts and its upper beams, and its feather bed lying exposed, with the bare pillow-cases upon the mattress. But the bedstead was magnificent without its trappings, because it was made of mahogany black with age: they no longer make such bedsteads. There was also a table—an old black table—with massive legs; but there was nothing on it.

Between door and wall there was a row of pegs, with a chair beneath them. Now, by some freak of chance, when Dorcas and Chessun hung up the ancient dame's things for the last time—her great bonnet, and the cap of many ribbons within it, and her silk dress—they arranged them so as to present a most extraordinary presentment of the venerable lady herself—much elongated and without any face: she seemed to be sitting in the chair below the pegs, dressed as usual, and nodding her great bonnet, but pulled out to eight or ten feet in length. Armorel caught the ghostly similitude and started, trembling. It seemed as if in a moment the wrinkled old face, with the hawk-like nose and the keen eyes, would come back to the bonnet and the cap. She was so much startled that she turned the bonnet round. And then the figure seemed watching with the shoulders. This was uncanny, but it was not so terrible as the faceless form.

Beside the fireplace was a cupboard—one of those huge cupboards which one only finds in the old houses. Armorel tried the door, but it was locked. Against the wall stood a chest of drawers, brass-bound, massive. She tried the handles, but every lock was fast. Under the window stood an old sea-chest. It was a very big sea-chest. One would judge, from its rich carvings and its ornamental ironwork, that it was probably the sea-chest of an admiral at least—perhaps that of Admiral Hernando Mureno, Armorel's ancestor, if such was his rank in the navy of his Catholic Majesty. The sight of this sea-chest caused the girl to shiver with the fear of expectation. Nobody contemplates the absolutely unknown without a certain fear. It contained, she was certain, the things that Dorcas had seen, of which she would not speak. The chest seemed to drag her: it cried, 'Open me. Look inside me—see what I have got to show you.'

Then she remembered, as one in a dream, hearing people talk. Words long forgotten came back to her. 'Twas in Hugh Town, whither she went across to school when she was as yet a little girl. 'What have the Roseveans'—thus and thus said the voice—'done with all their money? They've never spent anything: they've gone on saving and saving. Some day we shall find out what became of it.' Was she going to find out what had become of it?

The old lady, in her most lucid moments, had never dropped the least hint of any inheritance, except that disagreeable necessity of getting drowned on account of the unfortunate Robert Fletcher. And that was not an inheritance to gladden the heart. Yet there was an inheritance. It was here, in this room. And she was locked in alone, in order that she, herself unseen by any, might discover what it was.

Baron Bluebeard's last wife—she who afterwards, as a beautiful, rich, and lively young widow, set so many hearts aflame—was not more curious than Armorel. Nor was she, in the course of her investigations, more afraid than Armorel. The girl looked nervously about the room, so ghostly and so full of shadow. All old rooms have their ghosts, but some of them have so many that one is not afraid of them. There is a sense of companionship in a crowd of ghosts. This room had only one—that of the woman who had grown old in it—who had spent nearly eighty years in it. All the old ghosts had grown tired of this monotonous room, gone away and left the place to her. Armorel not only 'believed in ghosts'—many of us accord to these shadows a shadowy, theoretical belief—she actually knew that ghosts do sometimes appear. Dorcas had seen many—Chessun herself, while not going actually that length, threw out hints. She herself had often, too, gone to look for them. Now she glanced nervously where the 'things' were hanging, expecting to see the ancestral figure reappear, shoulders move, the bonnet and cap turn round, the old, old face within them, ready to warn, to admonish, and to guide. If this had happened, it would have seemed to Armorel nothing but what was natural and in the regular course of things looked for. But, outside, the sun shone on the white apple-blossom. No one is very much afraid of ghosts in the sunshine.

She encouraged herself with this reflection, and began with unlocking the chest of drawers. The lower drawers, when they were opened, contained nothing but the 'things' of her great-great-grandmother. Among them was a box roughly made—a boy's box made with a jack-knife: it contained a gold watch with a French name upon it—a very old watch, with a representation of the Annunciation in low relief on the gold face. There were also in the box two or three gold chains and sundry rings and trinkets. Armorel took them out and laid them on the table. They were, she said to herself, part of her inheritance. Was this the Great Surprise spoken of by Dorcas? She tried the two upper drawers. They were locked, but she easily found the right key, and opened them. She found that they were filled with lace; they were crammed with lace. There were packets of lace tied up tight, rolls of lace, cardboards with lace wound round and round—an immense quantity of lace was lying in these drawers. As for its value, Armorel knew nothing. Nor did she even ask herself what the value might be. She only unrolled one or two packets, and wondered vaguely what in the world she should do with so much lace. And she wished it was not so yellow. Yet the packets she unrolled contained Valenciennes—some of it half a yard wide, precious almost beyond price. Armorel knew, however, very well how it had got there, and what it meant. The descendant of so many brave runners was not ignorant that lace, velvet, silk and satin, brandy and claret, all came from the French coast with which her gallant forefathers were so familiar before the Preventive Service interfered. This, then, was left from the smuggling times. They had not sold all. They had kept enough, in fact, to stock half a dozen West-End shops, to adorn the trousseau of fifty Princesses. And here the stuff had lain undisturbed since—well, perhaps, since the unfortunate visit of Mr. Robert Fletcher.

'My inheritance, so far,' said Armorel, 'is a pile of yellow lace and a gold watch and chain and some trinkets. Is this the Great Surprise?' But she looked at the sea-chest. Something more must be there.

Next she turned to the cupboard. It was locked and double-locked. But she found the key. The cupboard was one of those great receptacles common in the oldest houses, almost rooms in themselves, but dark rooms, where mediæval housekeepers kept their stores. In those days, housekeeping on a respectable scale meant the continual maintenance of immense stores. All the things which now we get from shops as we want them were then laid in store long before they were wanted. Outside the country town there were no shops; and, even in London itself, people did not run to the shop every day. The men had great quantities of shirts—three clean shirts a day was the allowance of a solid city man under good Queen Anne—a city man who respected himself: the women had a corresponding quantity of flowered petticoats. Wine was by no means the only thing laid down for future years. All these accumulations helped to give solidity to the appearance of life. When a woman thought of her cupboards filled with fine linen and a man of his cellars filled with wine, the uncertainty and brevity of life alleged by the Preacher seemed not to concern them. It would be absurd to lay down a great bin of good port if one was not going to live long enough to drink it. The fashion, therefore, has its advantages.

Armorel threw open the door and looked in. The place was so dark that she was obliged to light a candle in order to examine the shelves running round the sides of the cupboard. There was a strange smell in the place, which, perhaps, had not been opened for a long time. Bales of some kind lay upon the upper shelves. Armorel took down two and opened them. They contained silk—strong, rich silk. She rolled them up and put them back. On a lower shelf was a most singular collection. In the front row were one—two—no fewer than six punch-bowls, all of silver except one, and that was of silver gilt. This must be the Great Surprise. Armorel took them all out and placed them on the table. For the most part they showed signs of having been used with freedom—one has heard of an empty punch-bowl being kicked about the place as a conclusion to the feast. But six punch-bowls! 'They came,' said Armorel, 'from the wrecks.' Behind the punch-bowls were silver candlesticks, silver snuffers, silver cups, silver tankards—some with coats-of-arms, some with names engraven. There was also a great silver ship, one of those galleons in silver which formerly adorned Royal banquets. All these Armorel took out and arranged upon the table. Among them was a tall hour-glass mounted in silver. Armorel set the sand running again, after many years. On the floor there were packets and bundles tied up and rolled together. Armorel opened one of them, and, finding that it contained a packet of gold lace and a pair of gold epaulettes, she left them undisturbed. And standing against the wall, stacked behind the bundles of gold lace, were swords—dozens of swords. What could she do with swords? Well, then, now, at last, she had found the Great Surprise. But still the sea-chest seemed to drag her and to call to her: 'Open me! Open me! See what I have got for you!'

'So far, then,' she said, 'I have inherited a pile of lace; a gold watch, rings, and chains; six punch-bowls, twenty-four silver candlesticks, twelve silver cups, four great tankards, a silver ship, I know not how many old swords, and a bundle of gold lace. I wonder if these things make a person rich?'

If so, great wealth does not satisfy the soul. This was certain, because Armorel really felt no richer than before. Yet the array of punch-bowls was truly imposing, and the silver candlesticks, the snuffers, the tankards, the cups, and the ship, though they sadly wanted the brush and the chamois leather, with a pinch of 'whitenin',' were worthy of a College Plate-Room. One might surely feel a little elation at the thought of owning all this silver, even if one did not understand its intrinsic value. But, like the effect of champagne, such elation would quickly wear off.

Next, Armorel remembered the secret cupboard at the head of the bed. Her own bed had its secret recess at the head—every respectable bedstead used formerly to have them. Where else could money be hidden away safely? To be sure, everybody knew this hiding-place, but everybody pretended not to know. It was an open secret, like the concealed drawer in a schoolboy's desk. Our forefathers were full of such secrets that everybody knew. The stocking in the teapot: the receptacle under the hearthstone: the hidden compartment in the cabinet: the secret room: the secret staircase: the recess in the head of the bed—these were all secrets that everybody knew and everybody respected. I think that even the burglar respected these conventions. Armorel knew how to open the panel—she found the spring and it flew open, rustily, as if it had not been opened for a great many years. Behind the panel was a recess eighteen inches long and about nine inches deep. And here stood a Black Jack—nothing less than a Black Jack; a quart Jack, not a Leather Jack, but a tankard made of tin and painted with hunting scenes something like an Etruscan vase, or perhaps more like a Brown George. Why should anyone want to hide away a Black Jack? This quart pot, however, held something better than stingo—even stronger: it was half-filled with foreign money. Here were moidores, doubloons, ducats, pieces-of-eight, Louis d'ors, Spanish pillar dollars, sequins, gold coins from India—nothing at all in the pot less than a hundred years old. Armorel took out a handful and looked at them. Well, gold coins do look like money. She began to feel really rich. She had a quart tankard half-full of gold coins. She added the Black Jack to the other treasures on the table. All this foreign money must have come out of the wrecks. And, since it was all so old, out of wrecks that had happened before the memory even of the Ancient Lady. This, then, was perhaps the Great Surprise.

But there remained the sea-chest under the window, and again, when Armorel looked upon it, the chest continued to call to her, 'Open me! Open me! See what I have for you!'

Armorel found the key which unlocked it, and threw open the lid. Within, there was the deep tray which belongs to every sea-chest. This was filled with a quantity of uninteresting brown canvas bags. She wanted to see what was below, and tried to lift the tray, but it was too heavy. Then, still regarding the bags as of no account, she took one out. It was heavy, and when she lifted it there was a clink as of coin. It was tied tightly at the mouth with a piece of string. She opened it. Within there were gold coins. She took out a handful: they were all sovereigns, some of them worn, some quite new and fresh from the Mint. She poured out the whole contents of the bag on the table. Why, it was actually full of golden sovereigns. Nothing else in the bag. All golden sovereigns! And there were five hundred of them. She counted them. Five hundred pounds! She had never, it is true, thought much about money—but—five hundred pounds! It seemed an amazing sum. Five hundred pounds! And all in a single bag. And such a little bag as this. She put back the money and tied up the bag.

Then she took out another bag. This was as big as the first, and heavier. It was full of guineas—Armorel counted them. There were also five hundred of them. Some of them were so old that they bore the impression of the elephant, and therefore belonged to the seventeenth century. But most of them belonged to the eighteenth century, and bore the heads of the three first Georges. Five hundred guineas—and never before had Armorel seen a guinea! Well, she thought, that made a thousand pounds. She took up another bag and opened it. That, too, weighed as much and was full of gold. And another, and yet another. They were all full of gold. And now she knew what Dorcas meant—this—nothing but this—was the Great Surprise! Not the punch-bowls, or the lace, or the bales of silk, but these bags full of gold constituted her wealth. She understood money, you see: lace and silk were beyond her. This was her inheritance!

Consider: the Roseveans, from father to son, had been from time immemorial wreckers, smugglers, and pilots. They were also farmers. On their little farm they grew nearly enough to support their simple lives. They had pigs and poultry; they had milch cows; they had a few sheep; they kept geese, pigeons, ducks; they made their own beer and their own cordials and strong waters; they made their own linen; they were unto themselves millers, tinkers, carpenters, cabinet-makers, builders, and thatchers. They grew their own salads and vegetables, and if they wanted any fruit they grew that as well. Oats and barley they grew, clover and hay. I believe that on Samson wheat has never been grown—indeed, there are only eighty acres in all. There was left, therefore, little to buy. Coals, wood for fuel and for carpentering, things in iron, crockery, tools, cloth clothes, flannel, flour, and sometimes a little beef—what else did they want? As for fish, they had only to catch as much as they wanted. Tea, coffee, sugar, and so forth came in with later civilisation, when small ale, possets, and hypsy died out.

In order to provide these small deficiencies they were pilots, to begin with. This trade brought in a steady income. They also sent out boats, filled with fresh vegetables, to meet the homeward-bound East Indiamen. And they were also, like the rest of the artless islanders, wreckers and smugglers. In the former capacity they occasionally acquired an extraordinary quantity of odd and valuable things. In the latter profession they made at times, and until the Peace and the Preventive Service put an end to the business, a really fine income.

Then, on Samson, they continued to live after the patriarchal fashion and in the old simplicity. Each Captain Rosevean in turn was the chieftain or sheik. To him his family brought all that they earned or found. The sea-chest took it all. For three hundred years, at least, this sea-chest received everything and gave up nothing. Nobody ever took anything out of it: nobody looked into it: nobody knew, until Ursula counted the money and made bags for it, what there was in the chest. Nobody ever asked if they were rich or how rich they were.

There was no bank on Samson: there is not even now a bank in the Scilly archipelago at all: nobody understood any other way of saving money than the good old fashion of putting it by in a bag. On Samson there never were thieves, even when as many as fifty people lived on the island. Therefore the Captain Rosevean of the time, though he knew not how much was saved, nor did he ever inquire, laid the last additions to the pile in the tray of the old sea-chest with the rest, and, having locked it up, dropped the key in his pocket, and went about his business in perfect confidence, never thinking either that it might be stolen, or that he might count up his hoard, proceed to enjoy it, and alter his simple way of life. Every Captain Rosevean in succession added to that hoard every year; not one among them all thought of spending it or taking anything from it. He added to it. Nobody ever counted it until the reign of Ursula. It was she who made the little brown bags of canvas: she, usurping the place of Family Chief or Sheik, took from her sons and grandsons all the money that they made. They gave it over to her keeping—she was the Family Bank. And, like her predecessors in that room, she told no one of the hoard.

Most of the bags contained guineas of George I., George II., and George III., down to the year 1816, when the Mint left off coining guineas. A few contained sovereigns of later date; but the family savings since that year had been small and uncertain. The really fat time—the prosperous time—when the money poured in, was during the long war which lasted for nearly five-and-twenty years.

There were actually forty of these bags. Armorel laid them out upon the table and counted them. Forty! And each bag to all appearance, for she only counted two, contained five hundred guineas or pounds. Forty times five hundred—that makes twenty thousand pounds, if all were sovereigns! There are, I am told, a few young ladies in this country who have as much as twenty thousand pounds for their dot. There are also a great many young ladies in France, and an amazing multitude, whom no man may number, in the United States of America, who have as much. But I am quite sure that not one of these heiresses, except Armorel herself, has ever actually gazed upon her fortune in a concrete form—tangible—to be counted—to be weighed—to be admired. It is a pity that they cannot do this, if only because they would then see for themselves what a very small pile of gold a fortune of twenty thousand pounds actually makes. This would make them humble. Armorel stood looking at the table thus laden with bewildered eyes.

'I have got,' she murmured, 'twenty thousand sovereigns and guineas at least: I have got a painted pot full of old money. I have got six punch-bowls, a great silver ship, a large number of silver candlesticks and cups: I have got a silver-mounted hour-glass'—its sand was now nearly run—'I have got a great quantity of lace and silk. I suppose all this does make riches. Whatever shall I do with it? Shall I give it to the poor? or shall I put it back into the box and leave it there? But perhaps there is something else in the box.'

The chest, in fact, continued to call aloud to be examined. Even while Armorel looked at her glittering treasures spread out upon the table she felt herself drawn towards the chest. There was more in it. There was another Surprise waiting for her—even a greater Surprise, perhaps, than that of the bags of gold. 'Search me!' cried the chest. 'Search me! Look into the innermost recesses of me: explore my contents to the very bottom: let nothing escape your eyes.'

Armorel knelt down before the chest and took out the tray. It was empty now, and she could lift it easily.

Beneath the tray there was a most miscellaneous collection of things.

They lay in layers, separated and divided—Ursula's hand was here—by silk handkerchiefs of the good old kind—the bandanna, now gone out of fashion.

First Armorel took out and laid on the floor a layer of silver spoons, silver ladles, even silver dishes, all of antique appearance and for the most part stamped with a crest or a coat-of-arms: for in the old days if a man was Armiger he loved to place his shield on everything; to look at it and glory in it: to let others see it and envy it.

Then she found a layer of watches. There were gold watches and silver watches; the latter of all kinds, down to the veritable turnip. The glasses were broken of nearly all, and, if one had examined, the works would have been found rusted with the sea-water which had got in. What were they worth now? Perhaps the value of the cases and of the jewels with which the works were set, and more with one or two, where miniatures adorned the back and jewels were set in the face. Armorel turned with impatience from the watches to the gold chains, which lay beside them. There were yards of gold chain: gold chains of all kinds, from the heavy English make to the dainty interlaced Venetian and thread-like Trichinopoly; there were silver chains also—massive silver chains, made for some extinct office-bearer, perhaps bo's'n on the Admiral's ship of the Great Armada. Armorel drew up some of the chains and played with them, tying them round her wrists and letting them slip through her fingers—the pretty delicate things, which spoke of wealth almost as loudly as the bags of guineas.

She laid them aside, and took up a silk handkerchief containing a small collection of miniatures. They were almost all portraits of women: young and pretty women: ladies on land whose faces warmed the hearts and fired the memories of men at sea. The miniatures had hung round the necks of some and had lain in the sea-chests of others, whose bones had long since melted to nothing in the salt sea depths, while those of their mistresses had turned to dust beneath the aisle of some village church, their memory long since forgotten, and their very name trampled out by the feet of the rustics.

Armorel laid aside these pictures—they were very pretty, but she would look at them again another time.

The next parcel was a much larger one. It consisted of snuff-boxes. There were dozens of snuff-boxes: one or two of gold: one or two silver-gilt: some silver. In the lids of some were pictures, some most beautifully and delicately executed; some of subjects which Armorel did not understand—and why, she thought, should painters draw people without proper clothes? Venus and the Graces and the Nymphs, in whom our eighteenth-century ancestors took such huge delight, were to this young person merely people. The snuff-boxes were very well in their way, but Armorel had no inclination to look at them again.

Then she found in a handkerchief, the four corners of which were loosely tied together, a great quantity of rings. There were rings of every kind—the official ring or the ring of office, the signet-ring, the ring with the shield, the ring with the name of a ship, the ring with the name of a regiment, mourning-rings, wedding-rings, betrothal-rings, rings with posies, cramp-rings with the names of the Magi on them—but their power was gone—gimmal-rings, rings episcopal, rings barbaric, mediæval, and modern, rings set with every kind of precious stone—there were hundreds of rings. All drowned sailors used to have rings on their fingers.

Armorel began to get tired of all these treasures. Beneath them, however, at the bottom of the box, lay piled together a mass of curios. They were stowed away for the most part in small boxes, of foreign make and appearance: ivory boxes: carved wood boxes. They consisted of all kinds of things, such as gold and silver buckles, brooches, painted fans, jewel-hilted daggers, crystal tubes of attar of roses, and knives of curious construction. The girl sighed: she would look over them at another time. They would, perhaps, add something to the inheritance, but for the moment she was satisfied. She had seen enough. She was putting back a dagger whose jewelled handle flashed in the unaccustomed light, when she saw, lying half hidden among this pile of curious things, the corner of a chagreen case. This attracted her curiosity, and she took it out. The chagreen had been green in colour, but was now very much discoloured. It had been fastened by a silver clasp, but this was broken: a small leather strap was attached to two corners. Armorel expected to find another bag of money. But this did not contain gold. It was lighter than the canvas bags. As she took it into her hands she remembered the bag of Robert Fletcher. Yes. The leathern strap of this case had been cut through. She held in her hands—she was certain—the abominable Thing that had brought so much trouble on the family. Again the room felt ghostly: she heard voices whispering: the voices of all those who had been drowned: the voices of the women who had mourned for them: the voice of the old lady who was herself a witness of the crime. They all whispered together in her ears: 'Armorel, you must find him. You must give it back to him.'

What was in it? The clasp acted no longer. Armorel lifted the overlapping leather and looked within. There was a thick roll of silk. She took this out. Wrapped up in the silk, laid in folds, side by side, were a quantity of stones—common-looking stones, such as one may pick up, she thought, on the beach of Porth Bay. There were a couple of hundred or more, mostly small stones, only one or two of them bigger than the top of Armorel's little finger.

'Only stones!' she cried. 'All this trouble about a bag full of red stones!'

Among the stones lay a small folded paper. Armorel opened it. The paper was discoloured by age or by water, and most of the writing was effaced. But she could read some of it.

'. . . from the King of Burmah himself. This ruby I estimate to be worth . . . 000*l*. at the very least. The other . . . Mines. The second largest stone weighs . . . about 2,000*l*. The smaller . . . . rt Fletcher.'

It was a note on the contents of the parcel, written by the owner.

The stones, therefore, were rubies, uncut rubies. Armorel knew little about precious stones and jewels, but she had heard and read of them. The price of a virtuous woman, she knew, was far above rubies. And Solomon's fairest among women was made comely with rows of jewels. Queen Sheba, moreover, brought precious stones among her presents to the Wise King. The girl wondered why such common-looking objects as these should be precious. But she was humbly ignorant, and put that wonder by.

This, then, was nothing less than Robert Fletcher's fortune. He had this round his neck, and he was bringing it home to enjoy. And it was taken from him by her ancestor. A wicked thing indeed! A foul and wicked thing! And the poor man had been sent empty away to begin his life all over again. She shivered as she looked at them. All for the sake of these dull, red bits of stone! How can man so easily fall into temptation? In the empty room, so quiet, so ghostly, she heard again the whispers, 'Armorel, find him—find the man—and give him back his jewels.'

She replied aloud, not daring to look round her lest she should see the pale and eager faces of those who had suffered death by drowning in consequence of this sin, 'Yes—yes, I will find him! I will find him!'

She pushed the chagreen case back into its corner and covered it up. 'I will find him,' she repeated. Then she rose to her feet and looked about the room. Heavens! What a sight! The bags of gold, two of them open, their contents lying piled upon the table—the chains of gold on the floor—the handful of old gold coins lying on the table beside the Black Jack, the snuff-boxes, the miniatures, the punch-bowls, the rings, the silver cups—the low room, dark and quiet, filled with ghosts and voices, the recent occupant wagging her shoulders and shaking the back of her bonnet at her from the opposite wall, and, through the open window, the sight of the sunlight on the apple-blossoms mocking the gold and silver in this gloomy cave. She comprehended, as yet, little of the extent of her good fortune. Lace and silk, rings and miniatures, snuff-boxes: all these things had no value to her—of buying and selling she had no kind of experience. All she understood was that she was the possessor of a vast quantity of things for which she could find no possible use—one jewelled dagger, for instance, might be used for a dinner-knife, or for a paper-knife; but what could she do with a dozen? In addition to this museum of pretty and useless things she had forty bags with five hundred guineas, or pounds, in each—twenty-one thousand pounds, say, in cash. This museum was perfectly unique: no family in Great Britain had such a collection. It had been growing for more than three hundred years: it was begun in the time of the Tudor Kings, at least, perhaps even earlier. Wrecks there were, and Roseveans, on Samson, before the seventh Henry. I doubt if any other family, even the oldest and the noblest, has been collecting so long. Certainly no other family, even in this archipelago of wrecks, can have had such opportunities of collecting with such difficulties in dissipating. For more than three hundred years! And Armorel was sole heiress!

She understood that she had inherited something more than twenty thousand pounds—how much more, she knew not. Now, unless one knows something of the capacities of one single pound, one cannot arrive at the possibilities of twenty thousand pounds. Armorel knew as much as this. Tea at Hugh Town costs two shillings a pound—perhaps two-and-four—sugar threepence a pound: nun's cloth so much a yard—serge and flannel so much: coals, so much a ton: wood for fuel, so much. This was nearly the extent of her knowledge: and it must be confessed that it goes very little way towards a right comprehension of twenty thousand pounds.

Once, again, she had heard Justinian talking of the flower-farm. 'It has made,' he said, 'four hundred pounds this year, clear.' To which Dorcas replied, 'And the housekeeping doesn't come to half that, nor near it.' Whence, by the new light of this Great Surprise, she concluded, first, that the other two hundred, thus made, must have been added to those money-bags, and, next, that two hundred pounds a year would be a liberal allowance for her whole yearly expenditure. Then she made a little calculation. Two hundred pounds a year—two hundred into twenty thousand—twenty thousand—two and four noughts—she put five bags in a row for the number—subtract two—she did so—there remained three—divide by two—she did so—one hundred years was the result of that sum. Her twenty thousand pounds would therefore last her exactly one hundred years. At the expiration of the century all would be gone. For the first time in her life Armorel comprehended the fleeting nature of riches. And, naturally, the discovery, though she shivered at the thought of losing all, made her feel a little proud. A strange result of wealth, to advance the inheritor one more step in the knowledge of possible misery! She was like unto the curious youth who opens a book of medicine, only to learn of new diseases and terrible sufferings and alarming symptoms, and to imagine these in his own body of corruption. In a hundred years there would be no more. She would then be reduced to sell the lace and the other things for what they would then be worth. There would still, however, remain the flower-farm. She would, after all, be no worse off than before the Great Surprise. And then there sprang up in her heart the blossom of another thought, to be developed, later on, into a lovely flower.

She had risen from her knees now, and was standing beside the table, vaguely gazing upon her inheritance. It was all before her. So the Ancient Lady had stood many and many a time counting the money: looking to see if all was safe: content to count it and to know that it was there. The old lady was gone, but from the opposite wall her shoulders and the back of her bonnet were looking on.

Well: Armorel might go on doing exactly the same. She might live as her forefathers had lived: there was the flower-farm to provide all their necessities: if it brought in four hundred pounds a year, she could add two hundred to the heap—in every two years and a half another bag of five hundred sovereigns. All her people had done this—why not she? It seemed expected of her; a plain duty laid upon her shoulders. If she were to live on for eighty years longer—which would bring her to her great-great-grandmother's age—she would save eighty times two hundred—sixteen thousand pounds. The inheritance would then be worth thirty-six thousand pounds—a prodigious sum of money indeed. And, besides, the Black Jack, with its foreign gold, and the rings and lace and things!

A strange room it was this morning. What voice was it that whispered solemnly in her ear, 'Lay not up for yourselves treasures upon earth, where moth and rust doth corrupt, and where thieves break through and steal'?

Never before had this injunction possessed any other significance to her than belongs to one manifestly addressed to other people. The Bible is full of warnings addressed to other people. Armorel was like the Royal Duke who used to murmur during the weekly utterance of the Commandments, 'Never did that. Never did that.' Now, this precept was clearly and from the very first intended to meet her own case. Oh! To live for nothing than to add more bags to that tray in the great sea-chest!

Roland had prophesied that there would be a change. It had come already in part, and more was coming.

What next? As yet the girl did not understand that she was mistress of her own fate. Hitherto things had been done for her. She was now about to act for herself. But how? If Roland were only here! But he had only written once, and he had never kept his promise to write back again to Samson. If he were here he could advise.

She looked around, and saw the heaps of things that were all hers, and she laughed. The girl whom Roland thought to be only an ignorant and poor little country girl, a flower-farmer's girl of Samson Island, living alone with her old grandmother and the serving-folk, was ignorant still, no doubt. But she was not poor: she was rich—she could have all that can be bought with money—she was rich. What would Roland say and think? And she laughed aloud.

She was rich—the last girl in the world to hope, or expect, or desire riches. Thus Fate mocks us, giving to one, who wants it not, wealth: and to another, who knows not how to use it, youth: and to a third, insensible of its power, beauty. The young lady of society, she whom the good old hymns used to call the Worldling—fond and pretty title! there are no Worldlings now—would have had no difficulty in knowing how to use this wonderful windfall. She, indeed, is always longing, perhaps praying, for money: she is always thinking how delightful it would be to be rich, and how there is nothing in the whole world more desirable than much fine gold. But to Lady Worldling, poor thing! such a windfall never happens. Again, there are all the distressed gentlewomen, the unappreciated artists, the authors whose books won't sell, the lawyers who have no clients, the wives whose name is Quiverful, the tradesman who 'scapes the Bankruptcy Court year after year by the skin of his teeth, and the poor dear young man who pines away because he cannot join the rabble rout of Comus—why, why does not such a windfall ever come to any of these? It never does: yet they spend all their spare time—all the time when they ought to be planning and devising ways and means of advancement—in dreaming of the golden days they would enjoy, if only such a windfall fell to them. One such man I knew: he dreamed of wealth all his life: he tried to become rich by taking every year a share in a foreign lottery. Of course, he never won a prize. While he was yet young and even far down the shady or outer slope of middle age he continually built castles in the air, fashioning pleasant ways for himself when he should get that prize. When he grew old, he dreamed of the will he would make and of the envy with which other old men, when he was gone, should regard the memory of one who had cut up so well. So he died poor; but I think he had always, through his dreaming, been as happy as if he had been rich.

Armorel told herself, standing in the midst of this great treasure, that she was rich. Roland had once told her, she remembered, that an artist ought to have money in order to be free: only in freedom, he said, could a man make the best of himself. What was good for an artist might be good for her. At the same time—it is not for nothing that a girl reads and ponders over the Gospels—there were terrible words of warning—there were instances. She shuddered, overwhelmed with the prospects of new dangers.

She knew everything: the room had yielded all its secrets

there were no more cupboards, boxes, or drawers. The sight of the treasures already began to pall upon her. She applied herself to putting everything back. First the chagreen case. This she laid carefully in its corner among the daggers and pistols, remembering that she had promised to find the owner. How should she do that if she remained on Samson? Then she put back the snuff-boxes, the miniatures, and the watches in their silk handkerchiefs: then the box of rings and the silver spoons and dishes. Then she put the tray in its place and laid the bags in the tray, and locked the old sea-chest. This done, she bore back to the shelves in the cupboard the punch-bowls, candlesticks, tankards, and the big silver ship: she locked and double-locked the cupboard-door: she crammed the lace into the drawers, and put back the box of trinkets.

Then she dropped the keys in her pocket. Oh! what a lump to carry about all day long! But the weight of the keys in her pocket was nothing to the weight that was laid upon her shoulders by her great possessions. This, however, she hardly felt at first.

Everything was her own.

When the new King comes to the throne he makes a great clearance of all the personal belongings of the old King. He gives away his cloaks and his uniforms, and all the things belonging to the daily life of his predecessor. That is always done. Therefore, Queen Armorel—Vivat Regina!—at this point gathered together all her predecessor's belongings. She turned them out of the drawers and laid them on the floor—with the great bonnet and the wonderful cap of ribbons. And then she opened the door. She would give these things to Dorcas. Her great-great-grandmother should have no more authority there. Even her clothes must go. If her ghost should remain, it should be without the bonnet and the cap.

She called Dorcas, who came, curious to know how her young mistress took the Great Surprise. Armorel had taken it, apparently, as a matter of course. So the new King stands upon the highest step of the Throne, calm and collected, as if he had been prepared for this event, and was expecting it day after day.

'You know all now, dearie?' she whispered, shutting the door carefully. 'Did you find everything?'

'Yes—I believe I found everything.'

'The silver in the cupboard: the lace: the bags of gold?'

'I think I have found everything, Dorcas.'

'Then you are rich, my dear. No Rosevean before you was ever half so rich. For none of it has been spent. They've all gone on saving and adding—almost to the last she saved and added. Oh! the last thing she lost was the love of saving, and the jealousy of her keys she never lost. Oh! you are very rich—you are the richest girl in the whole of Scilly—not even in St. Mary's is there anyone who can compare with you. Even the Lord Proprietor himself—I hardly know.'

'Yes. I believe I must be very rich,' said Armorel. 'Dorcas, you kept her secret. Keep mine as well. Let no one know.'

'No one shall know, dearie—no one. But lock the door. Keep the door locked always.'

'I will. Now, Dorcas, here are all her dresses and things. You must take them all away and keep them. They are for you.'

'Very well, dearie. Though how I'm to wear black silk—— Oh! Child,' she cried, out of the religious terrors of her soul—'it is written that it is harder for a rich man to enter into heaven than for a camel to pass through the eye of a needle. My dear, if these great riches are to drag your soul down into hell, it would be better if they were all thrown into the sea, the silver punch-bowls and the bags of gold and all. But there's one comfort. It doesn't say, impossible. It only says, harder. So that now and then, perhaps, a rich man may wriggle in—just one—and oh! I wish, seeing the number of rich people there are in the world, that there'd been shown one camel—only a single camel—going through the needle's eye. Think what a miracle! 'T would have brought conviction to all who saw it, and consolation ever afterwards to all who considered it—oh! the many thousands of afflicted souls who are born rich! You are not the only one, child, who is rich through no fault of her own. Often have I told Justinian, thinking of her, and he not knowing or suspecting, but believing I was talking silly, that, considering the warnings and woes pronounced against the rich, we cannot be too thankful. But don't despair, my dear—it is nowhere said to be impossible. And there's the rich young man, to be sure, who was told to sell all that he had and to give to the poor. He went away sorrowful. You can't do that, Armorel, because there are no poor on Samson. And it's said, "Woe unto you that are rich, for you have had your consolation!" Well, but if your money never is your consolation—and I'm sure I don't know what it is going to console you for—that doesn't apply to you, does it? There's the story of the Rich Man, again; and there's texts upon texts, when you come to think of them. You will remember them, child, and they will be your warnings. Besides, you are not going to waste and riot like a Prodigal Son, and where your earthly treasure is there you will not set your heart. You will go on like all the Roseveans before you: and though the treasure is kept locked up, you will add to it every year out of your savings, just as they did.'

'There is another parable, Dorcas. I think I ought to remember that as well. It is that of the Talents. If the man who was rich with Five Talents had locked them up, he would not have been called a good and faithful servant.'

'Yes, dearie, yes. You will find some Scripture to comfort and assure your soul, no doubt. There's a good deal in Scripture. Something for all sorts, as they say. Though, after all, riches is a dangerous thing. Child! if they know it over at St. Mary's, not a young man in the place but would be sailing over to Samson to try his luck. Our secret, child, all to ourselves.'

'Yes; our secret, Dorcas. And now take away all these things, everything that belonged to her: there are her shoes—take them too. I want the room to be all my own. So.'

When all the things were gone, Armorel closed and locked the door. Then she ran out of the house gasping, for she choked. Everything was turned into gold. She gasped and choked and ran out over the hill and down the steps and across the narrow plain, and up the northern hill, hoping to drive some of the ghosts from her brain, and to shake off some of the bewildering caused by the Great Surprise. But a good deal remained, and especially the religious terrors suggested by that pious Bryanite Christian and Divider of the Word, Dorcas Tryeth.

When she sat down in the old place upon the carn, the great gulf between herself and Bryher island reminded her of that great gulf in the parable. How if she should be the Rich Man sitting for ever and for ever on the red-hot rock, tormented with pain and thirst—and how if on Samson Hill beyond she should see Abraham himself, the patriarch, with Lazarus lying at his feet—as yet she had developed no Lazarus—but who knows the future? The Rich Man must have been a thoughtless and selfish person. Until now the parable never interested her at all: why should it? She had no money.

The other passages, those which Dorcas had kindly quoted in this her first hour of wealth, came crowding into her mind, and told her they were come to stay. All these texts she had previously classed with the denunciations of sins the very meaning of which she knew not. She had no concern with such wickedness. Nor could she possibly understand how it was that people, when they actually knew that they must not do such things, still went on doing them. Now, however, having become rich herself, all the warnings of the New Testament seemed directed against herself. Already, the load of wealth was beginning to weigh upon her young shoulders.

She changed the current of her thoughts. Even the richest girl cannot be always thinking about woes and warnings. Else she would do nothing, good or bad. She began to think about the outer world. She had been thinking of it constantly ever since Roland left her. Now, as she looked across the broad Roadstead, and remembered that thirty miles beyond Telegraph Hill rose the cliffs where the outer world begins—they can be seen in a clear day—a longing, passionate and irresistible, seized her. She could go away now, whenever she pleased. She could visit the outer world and make the acquaintance of the people who live in it.

She laughed, thinking how Justinian, who had never been beyond St. Mary's, pictured, as he was fond of doing, the outer world. The Sea of Tiberias was to him the Road: the Jordan was like Grinsey Sound: the steep place down which the swine fell into the sea was like Shipman's Head: the Sermon on the Mount took place on just such a spot as the carn of the North Hill on Samson, with the sun shining on the Western Islands: the New Jerusalem in his mind was a city like Hugh Town, consisting of one long street with stone houses, roofed with slate; each house two storeys high, a door in the middle, and one window on each side. On the north side of the New Jerusalem was the harbour, with the ships, the sea-shore, and the open sea beyond: on the south side was a bay with beeches of white sand and black rocks at the entrance, exactly like Porth Cressa. And it was a quiet town, with seldom any noise of wheels, and always the sound of the sea lapping on either hand, north or south.

Now, there was nothing to keep her: she could go to visit the outer world whenever she pleased—if only she knew how. A girl of sixteen can hardly go forth into the wide, wide world all alone, announcing to the four corners her desire to make the acquaintance of everybody and to understand anything.

And then she began to remember her teacher's last instructions. The perfect girl was one who had trained her eye and her hand: she could play one instrument well: she understood music: she understood art: she was always gracious, sympathetic, and encouraging: she knew how to get their best out of men: she was always beautifully dressed: she had the sweetest and the most beautiful manners.

And here she blushed crimson, and then turned pale, and felt a pang as if a knife had pierced her very heart. For a dreadful thought struck her. She thought she understood at last the true reason why Roland never came back, though he promised, and looked so serious when he promised.

Why? why? Because she was so ill-mannered. Of course that was the reason. Why did Roland speak so strongly about the perfect girl's gracious and sympathetic manners, unless to make her understand, in this kindly and thoughtful way, how much was wanting in herself? Of course, he only looked upon her as a common country girl, who knew nothing, and would never learn anything. He wanted her to understand that—to feel that she would never rise to higher levels. He drew this picture of the perfect girl to make and keep her humble. Nay, but now she had this money—all this wealth—now—now—— She sprang to her feet and threw out her arms, the gesture that she had learned I know not where. 'Oh!' she cried, 'it is the gift of the Five Talents! I am not the rich young man. I have not received these riches for my consolation. They are my Five Talents. I will go away and learn—I will learn. I will become the perfect girl. I will train eye and hand. I will grow—grow—grow—to my full height. That will be true work in the service of the Giver of those Talents. I shall become a good and faithful servant when I have risen to the stature that is possible for me!'

PART II

CHAPTER I

SWEET COZ

'I SUPPOSE,' said Philippa, 'that we were obliged to ask her.'

'Well, my dear,' her mother replied, 'Mr. Jagenal is an old friend, and when——' Her voice dropped, and she did not finish the sentence. It is absurd to finish a sentence which is understood.

'Perhaps she will not do anything very outrageous.'

'Well, my dear, Mr. Jagenal distinctly said that her manner ——' Again she left the sentence unfinished. Perhaps it was her habit.

'As she bears our name and comes from our place we can hardly deny the cousinship. In a few minutes, however, we shall know the worst.'

Philippa, dressed for dinner, was standing before the fire, tapping the fender impatiently with her foot, and playing with her fan. A handsome girl of three- or-four-and-twenty: handsome, not pretty, if you please, nor lovely. By no means. Handsome, with a kind of beauty which no painter or sculptor would assign to Lady Venus, because it lacked softness; nor to Diana, because that huntress, chaste and fair, was country-bred, and Philippa was of the town—urban. The young lady was perfectly well satisfied with her own style of beauty. If she exaggerated a little its power, that is a common feminine mistake. The exaggeration brings to dress a moral responsibility. Philippa was dressed this evening in a creamy white silk, which had the effect of softening a face and manner somewhat cold and even hard. The young men of the period complained that Philippa was stand-offish. Certainly she did not commit the mistake, too common among girls, of plunging straight off into sympathetic interest with every young man. Philippa waited for the young men to interest her, if they could. Generally, they could not. And, while many girls listen with affected deference to the opinions of the young man, Philippa made the young man receive hers with deference. These plain facts show, perhaps, why Philippa, at twenty-four, was still free and unengaged.

In appearance she was tall—all young ladies who respect themselves are tall in these days: her features were clearly cut, if a little pronounced: her hazel eyes were intellectually bright, though cold: her hair, the least-marked feature, was of a common brown colour, but she treated it so as to produce a distinctive effect: her mouth was fine, though her lips were rather thin: her figure was correct, though Venus herself would have preferred more of it, and, perhaps, that more flexible. But it is the commonplace girl, we know, who runs to plumpness.

She was dressed with greater care than usual that evening, because people were coming, but not to dinner. The only guests at dinner were to be one Mr. Jagenal, the well known family solicitor, of Lincoln's Inn, and a certain far-off cousin, named Armorel Rosevean, from the Scilly Isles, and her companion and chaperon, one Mrs. Jerome Elstree—unknown.

'My dear,' her mother began, 'you are too desponding. Mr. Jagenal assured your father——' She dropped her voice again.

'Oh! He is an old bachelor. What does he know? Our cousin comes from Scilly. So did we. It does very well to talk of coming from Scilly, as if it was something grand, but I have been looking into a book about it. Old families of Scilly, we say. Why, they have never been anything but farmers and smugglers. And our cousin, I hear, is actually a small tenant-farmer—a flower-farmer—a kind of market-gardener! She grows daffodils and jonquils and anemones and snowdrops, and sells them. Very likely the daffodils on our table have come from her farm. Perhaps she will tell us about the price they fetch a dozen. And she will inform us at dinner how she counts the stalks and makes out the bills.'

'Absurd! She is an heiress. Mr. Jagenal says——'

'An heiress? How can she be an heiress?' Philippa repeated, with scorn. 'She inherits the lease of a little flower-farm. The people of Scilly are all quite, quite poor. My book says so. Some years ago the Scilly folk were nearly starving.'

'Your book must be wrong, Philippa. Mr. Jagenal says that the girl has a respectable fortune. When a man of his experience says that, he means——' Here her voice dropped again.

'Well; the island heiress will go back, I dare say, to her inheritance.'

At this point Mr. Jagenal himself was announced—elderly, precise, exact in appearance and in language.

'You have not yet seen your cousin?' he asked.

'No. She will be here immediately, I suppose.'

'Your cousin came to our house five years ago. My late partner received her. She brought a letter from a clergyman then at the Scilly Islands. She was sixteen, quite ignorant of the world, and a really interesting girl. She had inherited a very handsome fortune. My late partner found her tutors and guardians, and she has been travelling and learning. Now she has come to London again. She chooses to be her own mistress, and has taken a flat. And I have found a companion for her—widow of an artist—our young friend Alec Feilding knew about her—name of Elstree. I think she will do very well.'

'Alec knew her? He has never told me of any lady of that name.' Philippa looked a little astonished.

Then the girl of whom they were talking, with the companion in question, appeared.

You know how one forms in the mind a whole image, or group of images, preparatory; and how these shadows are all dispelled by the appearance of the reality. At the very first sight of Armorel, Philippa's prejudices and expectations—the vision of the dowdy rustic, the half-bred island savage, the uncouth country maiden—all vanished into thin air. New prejudices might arise—it is a mistake to suppose that because old prejudices have been cleared away there can be no more—but, in this case, the old ones vanished. For while Armorel walked across the room, and while Mrs. Rosevean stepped forward to welcome her, Philippa made the discovery that her cousin knew how to carry herself, how to walk, and how to dress. Girls who have learned these three essentials have generally learned how to talk as well. And a young lady of London understands at the first glance whether a strange young person, her sister in the bonds of humanity, is also a lady. As for the dress, it showed genius either on the part of Armorel herself or of her advisers. There was genius in the devising and invention of it. But genius of this kind one can buy. There was the genius of audacity in the wearing of it, because it was a dress of the kind more generally worn by ladies of forty than of twenty-one. And it required a fine face and a good figure to carry it off. Ladies will quite understand when I explain that Armorel wore a train and bodice of green brocaded velvet: the sleeves and the petticoat trimmed with lace. You may see a good deal of lace —of a sort—on many dresses; but Philippa recognised with astonishment that this was old lace, the finest lace in the world, of greater breadth than it is now made—lace that was priceless—lace that only a rich girl could wear. There were also pearls on the sleeves: she wore mousquetaire gloves—which proved many things: there were bracelets on her wrists, and round her neck she had a circlet of plain red gold—it was the torque found in the kistvaen on Samson, but this Philippa did not know. And she observed, taking in all these details in one comprehensive and catholic glance of mind and eye, that her cousin was a very beautiful girl indeed, with something Castilian in her face and appearance—dark and splendid. For a simple dinner she would have been overdressed; but considering the reception to come afterwards, she was fittingly arrayed. She was accompanied by her companion—Philippa might have remembered that one must be an heiress in order to afford the luxury of such a household official. Mrs. Jerome Elstree was almost young enough to want a chaperon for herself, being certainly a good deal under thirty. She was a graceful woman of fair complexion and blue eyes: if Armorel had desired a contrast to herself she could not have chosen better. She wore a dress in the style which is called, I believe, second mourning. The dress suggested widowhood, but no longer in the first passionate agony—widowhood subdued and resigned.

The hostess rose from her chair and advanced a step to meet her guests. She touched the fingers of Mrs. Elstree. 'Very pleased, indeed,' she murmured, and turned to Armorel. 'My dear cousin'—she seized both her hands, and looked as well as spoke most motherly. 'My dear child, this is, indeed, a pleasure! And to think that we have known nothing about your very existence all the time! This is my daughter—my only daughter, Philippa.' Then she subsided into her chair, leaving Philippa to do the rest. 'We are cousins,' said Philippa, kindly but with cold and curious eyes. 'I hope we shall be friends.' Then she turned to the companion. 'Oh!' she cried, with a start of surprise. 'It is Zoe!'

'Yes,' said Mrs. Elstree, a quick smile on her lips. 'Formerly it was Zoe. How do you do, Philippa?' Her voice was naturally soft and sweet, a caressing voice, a voice of velvet. She glanced at Philippa as she spoke, and her eyes flashed with a light which hardly corresponded with the voice. 'I was wondering, as we came here, whether you would remember me. It is so long since we were at school together. How long, dear? Seven years? Eight years? You remember that summer at the seaside—where was it? One changes a good deal in seven years. Yet I thought, somehow, that you would remember me. You are looking very well, Philippa—still.'

A doubtful compliment, but conveyed in the softest manner, which should have removed any possible doubt. Armorel looked on with some astonishment. On Philippa's face there had risen a flaming spot. Something was going on below the surface. But Philippa laughed.

'Of course, I remember you very well,' she said.

'But, dear Philippa,' Mrs. Elstree went on, softly smiling and gently speaking, 'I am no longer Zoe. I am Mrs. Jerome Elstree—I am La Veuve Elstree. I am Armorel's companion.'

'I am sorry,' Philippa replied coldly. Her eyes belied her words. She was not sorry. She did not care whether good or evil had happened to this woman. She was too good a Christian to desire the latter, and not good enough to wish the former. What she had really hoped—whenever she thought of Zoe—was that she might never, never meet her again. And here she was, a guest in her own home, and companion to her own cousin!

Then Mr. Rosevean appeared, and welcomed the new cousin cordially. He seemed a cheerful, good-tempered kind of man, was sixty years of age, bald on the forehead, and of aspect like the conventional Colonel of *Punch*—in fact, he had been in the Army, and served through the Crimean war, which was quite enough for honour. He passed his time laboriously considering his investments—for he had great possessions—and making small collections which never came to anything. He also wrote letters to the papers, but these seldom appeared.

Then they went in to dinner. The conversation naturally turned at first upon Scilly, their common starting-point, and the illustrious family of the Roseveans.

'As soon as I heard about you, my dear young lady, I set to work to discover our exact relationship. My grandfather, Sir Jacob—you have heard of Sir Jacob Rosevean, Knight of Hanover? Yes; naturally—he was born in the year 1760. He was the younger brother of Captain Emanuel Rosevean, your great-grandfather, I believe.'

'My grandfathers were all named either Emanuel or Methusalem. They took turns.'

'Quite so,' Mr. Rosevean nodded his head in approbation. 'The preservation of the same Christian names gives dignity to the family. Anthony goes with Ashley: Emanuel or Methusalem with Rosevean. The survival of the Scripture name shows how the Puritanic spirit lingers yet in the good old stocks.' Philippa glanced at her mother, mindful of her own remarks on the old families of Scilly. 'We come of a very fine old family, cousin Armorel. I hope you have been brought up in becoming pride of birth. It is a possession which the world cannot give and the world cannot take away. We are a race of Vikings—conquering Vikings. The last of them was, perhaps, my grandfather, Sir Jacob, unless any of the later Roseveans——'

'I am afraid they can hardly be called Vikings,' said Armorel, simply.

'Sir Jacob—my grandfather—was cast, my dear young friend, in the heroic mould—the heroic mould. Nothing short of that. For the services which he rendered to the State at the moment of Britannia's greatest peril, he should have been raised to the House of Lords. But it was a time of giants—and he had to be contented with the simple recognition of a knighthood.'

'Jacob Rosevean'—who was it had told Armorel this—long before? And why did she now remember the words so clearly, 'ran away and went to sea. He could read and write and cipher a little, and so they made him clerk to the purser. Then he rose to be purser himself, and when he had made some money he left the service and became Contractor to the Fleet, and supplied stores of all kinds during the long war, and at last he became so rich that they were obliged to make him a Knight.'

'The simple recognition of a Knighthood,' Mr. Rosevean went on. 'This it is to live in an age of heroes.'

Armorel waited for further details. Later on, perhaps, some of the heroic achievements of the great Sir Jacob would be related.

Meantime, every hero must make a beginning: why should not Jacob Rosevean begin as purser's clerk? It was pleasing to the girl to observe how large and generous a view her cousins took of the family greatness—never before had she known to what an illustrious stock she belonged. The smuggling, the wrecking, the piloting, the farming—these were all forgotten. A whole race of heroic ancestors had taken the place of the plain Roseveans whom Armorel knew. Well: if by the third generation of wealth and position one cannot evolve so simple a thing as an ancient family, what is the use of history, genealogy, heraldry, and imagination? The Roseveans were Vikings: they were the terror of the French coast: they went a-crusading with short-legged Robert: they were rovers of the Spanish Main: the great King of Spain trembled when he heard their name: they were buccaneers. Portraits of some of these ancestors hung on the wall: Sir Jacob himself, of course, was there; and Sir Jacob's great-grandfather, a Cavalier; and his grandfather, an Elizabethan worthy. Presumably, these portraits came from Samson Island. But Armorel had never heard of any family portraits, and she had grown up in shameful ignorance of these heroes. There was a coat-of-arms, too, with which she was not acquainted. Yet there were circumstances connected with the grant of that shield by the Sovereign—King Edward the First—which were highly creditable to the family. Armorel listened and marvelled. But her host evidently believed it all: and, indeed, it was his father, not himself, who had imagined these historic splendours.

'It is pleasing,' he said, 'to revive these memories between members of different branches. You, however, are fresh from the ancestral scenes. You are the heiress of the ancient island home: yours is the Hall of the Vikings: to you have been entrusted the relics of the past. I look upon you and seem to see again the Rovers putting forth to drag down the Spanish pride. There are noble memories, Armorel—I must call you Armorel—associated with that isle of Samson, our ancient family domain. Let us never forget them.'

The dinner came to an end at last, and the ladies went away.

Mrs. Elstree sat down in the most comfortable chair by the fire and was silent, leaning her face upon her hands and looking into the firelight. Mrs. Rosevean took a chair on the other side and fell asleep. Philippa and Armorel talked.

'I cannot understand,' said Philippa, bluntly, 'how such a girl as you could have come from Scilly. I have been reading a book about the place, and it says that the people are all poor, and that Samson, your island—our island—is quite a small place.'

'I will tell you if you like,' said Armorel, 'as much about myself as you please to hear.' The chief advantage of an autobiography—as you shall see, dear reader, if you will oblige me by reading mine, when it comes out—is the right of preserving silence upon certain points. Armorel, for example, said nothing at all about Roland Lee. Nor did she tell of the chagreen case with the rubies. But she did tell how she found the treasure of the sea-chest, and the cupboard, and how she took everything, except the punch-bowls and the silver ship and cups, to London, and how she gave them over to the lawyer to whom she had a letter. And she told how she was resolved to repair the deficiencies of her up-bringing, and how, for five long years, she had worked day and night.

'I think you are a very brave girl,' said Philippa. 'Most girls in your place would have been contented to sit down and enjoy their good fortune.'

'I was so very ignorant when I began. And—and one or two things had happened which made me ashamed of my ignorance.'

'Yet it was brave of you to work so hard.'

'At first,' said Armorel, 'when this good fortune came to me I was afraid, thinking of the Parable of the Rich Man.' Philippa started and looked astonished. In the circle of Dives this Parable is never mentioned. No one regardeth that Parable, which is generally believed to be a late interpolation. 'But when I came to think, I understood that it might be the gift of the Five Talents—a sacred trust.'

Philippa's eyes showed no comprehension of this language. Armorel, indeed, had learned long since that the Bryanite or Early Christian language is no longer used in society. But Philippa was her cousin. Perhaps, in the family, it would still pass current.

'I worked most at music. Shall I play to you?'

'Nothing, dear Philippa,' said Zoe, half-turning round, 'would please you so much as to hear Armorel play. You used to play a little yourself'—Philippa had been the pride and glory of the school for her playing—'A little!' Had she lost her memory?

'Will you play this evening?'

'I brought her violin in the carriage,' said Zoe, softly. 'I wanted to give you as many delightful surprises as possible, Philippa. To find your cousin so beautiful: to hear her play: and to receive me again! This will be, indeed, an evening to remember.'

'I will play if you like,' said Armorel, simply. 'But perhaps you have made other arrangements.'

'No—no—you can play? But of course, you have had good masters. You shall play instead of me.'

Zoe murmured her satisfaction, and turned again her face to the fire.

'Tell me, Armorel,' said Philippa, 'all this about the Vikings—the Hall of the Vikings—the Rovers—and the rest of it. Was it familiar to you?'

'No; I have never heard of any Vikings or Rovers. And there is no Hall.'

'We are, I suppose, really an old family of Scilly?'

'We have lived in the same place for I know not how many

years. One of the outlying rocks of Scilly is called Rosevean. Oh! there is no doubt about our antiquity. About the Crusaders, and all the rest of it, I know nothing. Perhaps because there was nobody to tell me.'

'I see,' said Philippa, thoughtfully. 'Well, it does no harm to believe these things. Perhaps some of them are true. Sir Jacob, certainly, cannot be denied; nor the Roseveans of Samson Island. My dear, I am very glad you came.'

CHAPTER II

THE SONATA

The room was full of people. It was the average sort of reception, where one always expects to meet men and women who have done something: men who write, paint, or compose; women who do the same, but not so well; women who play and sing; women who are æsthetic, and show their appreciation of art by wearing hideous dresses; women who recite: men and women who advocate all kinds of things—mostly cranks and cracks. There are, besides, the people who know the people who do things: and these, who are a talkative and appreciative folk, carry on the conversation. Thirdly, there are the people who do nothing, and know nobody, who go away and talk casually of having met this or that great man last night.

'Armorel,' said Philippa, 'let me introduce Dr. Bovey-Tracy. Perhaps you already know his works.'

'Unfortunately—not yet,' Armorel replied.

The Doctor was quite a young man, not more than two- or three-and-twenty. His degree was German, and his appearance, with long light hair and spectacles, was studiously German. If he could have Germanised his name as well as his appearance he would certainly have done so. As a pianist, a teacher of music, and a composer, the young Doctor is already beginning to be known. When Armorel confessed her ignorance, he gently spread his hands and smiled pity. 'If you will really play, Armorel, Dr. Bovey-Tracy will kindly accompany you.'

Armorel took her violin out of the case and began to tune it.

'What will you play?' asked the musician: 'something serious? So?'

Armorel turned over a pile of music and selected a piece. It was the Sonata by Schumann in D minor for violin and pianoforte. 'Shall we play this?'

Philippa looked a little surprised. The choice was daring. The Herr Doctor smiled graciously: 'This is, indeed, serious,' he said.

I suppose that to begin your musical training with the performance of heys and hornpipes and country dances is not the modern scientific method. But he who learns to fiddle for sailors to dance may acquire a mastery over the instrument which the modern scientific method teaches much more slowly. Armorel began her musical training with a fiddle as obedient to her as the Slave of the Lamp to his master. And for five years she had been under masters playing every day, until——

The pianist sat down, held his outstretched fingers professionally over the keys, and struck a chord. Armorel raised her bow, and the sonata began.

I am told that there is now quite a fair percentage of educated people who really do understand music, can tell good playing from bad, and fine playing from its counterfeit. In the same way, there is a percentage—but not nearly so large—of people who know a good picture when they see it, and can appreciate correct drawing if they cannot understand fine colour. Out of the sixty or seventy people who filled this room, there were certainly twenty—but then it was an exceptionally good collection—who understood that a violinist born and trained was playing to them, in a style not often found outside St. James's Hall. And they marvelled while the music delivered its message—which is different for every soul. They sat or stood in silence, spellbound. Of the remaining fifty, thirty understood that a piece of classical music was going on: it had no voice or message for them: they did not comprehend one single phrase—the sonata might have been a sermon in the Bulgarian tongue: but they knew how to behave in the presence of Music, and they governed themselves accordingly. The Remnant—twenty in number—containing all the young men and most of the girls, understood that here was a really beautiful girl playing the fiddle for them. The young men murmured their admiration, and the girls whispered envious things—not necessarily spiteful, but certainly envious. What girl could resist envy at sight of that dress, with its lace, and that command of the violin, and—which every girl concedes last of all, and grudgingly—that face and figure?

Philippa stood beside the piano, rather pale. She knew, now, why her old schoolfellow had been so anxious that Armorel should play. Kind and thoughtful Zoe!

The playing of the first movement surprised her. Here was one who had, indeed, mastered her instrument. At the playing of the second, which is a scherzo, bright and lively, she acknowledged her mistress—not her rival. At the playing of the third, which contains a lovely, simple, innocent, and happy tune, her heart melted—never, never, could she so pour into her playing the soul of that melody: never could she so rise to the spirit of the musician and put into the music what even he himself had not imagined. But Zoe was wrong. Her soul was not filled with envy. Philippa had a larger soul.

It was finished. The twenty who understood gasped. The thirty who listened murmured thanks, and resumed their talk about something else. The twenty who neither listened nor understood went on talking without any comment at all.

'You have had excellent masters,' said the Doctor. 'You play very well indeed—not like an amateur. It is a pity that you cannot play in public.'

'You have made good use of your opportunities,' said Philippa. 'I have never heard an amateur play better. I play a little myself; but——'

'I said you would be pleased,' Zoe murmured softly at her side. 'I knew you would be pleased when you heard Armorel play.'

'You will play yourself, presently?' said the Herr Doctor.

'No; not this evening,' Philippa replied. 'Impossible—after Armorel.'

'Not this evening!' echoed Zoe, sweetly.

Then there came walking tall and erect through the crowd, which respectfully parted right and left to let him pass, a young man of striking and even distinguished appearance.

'Philippa,' he said, 'will you introduce me to your cousin?'

'Armorel, this is another cousin of mine—unfortunately not of yours—Mr. Alec Feilding.'

'I am very unfortunate, Miss Rosevean. I came too late to hear more than the end of the sonata. Normann-Néruda herself could not interpret that music better.' Then he saw Zoe, and greeted her as an old friend. 'Mrs. Elstree and I,' he said, 'have known each other a long time.'

'Fifty years, at least,' Zoe murmured. 'Is it not so long, Philippa?'

'Will you play something else?' he asked. 'The people are dying to hear you again.'

Armorel looked at Philippa. 'If you will,' she said kindly. 'If you are not tired. Play us, this time, something lighter. We cannot all appreciate Schumann.'

'Shall I give you a memory of Scilly?' she replied. 'That will be light enough.'

She played, in fact, that old ditty—one of those which she had been wont to play for the Ancient Lady—called 'Prince Rupert's March.' She played this with variations which that gallant Cavalier had never heard. It is a fine air, however, and lends itself to the phantasy of a musician. Then those who had understood the sonata laughed with condescension, as a philosopher laughs when he hears a simple story; and those who had pretended to understand pricked up their ears, thinking that this was another piece of classical music, and joyfully perceiving that they would understand it; and those who had made no pretence now listened with open mouths and ears as upright as those of any wild-ass of the desert. Music worth hearing, this. Armorel played for five or six minutes. Then she stopped and laid down her violin.

'I think I have played enough for one evening,' she said.

She left the piano and retired into the throng. A girl took her place. The Herr Doctor placed another piece of music before him, lifted his hands, held them suspended for a moment, and then struck a chord. This girl began to sing.

Mr. Alec Feilding followed Armorel and led her to a seat at the end of the room. Then he sat down beside her and, as soon as the song was finished, began to talk.

He began by talking about music, and the Masters in music. His talk was authoritative : he laid down opinions : he talked as if he was writing a book of instruction : and he talked as if the whole wide world was listening to him. But not quite so loudly as if that had been really the case.

He was a man of thirty or so, his features were perfectly regular, but his expression was rather wooden. His eyes were good, but rather too close together. His mouth was hidden by a huge moustache, curled and twisted and pointed forwards.

Armorel disliked his manner, and for some reason or other distrusted his face.

He left off laying down the law on music, and began to talk about things personal.

'I hope you like your new companion,' he said. 'She is an old friend of mine. I was in hopes of being able to advance her husband in his profession. But he died before I got the chance. Mr. Jagenal told me what was wanted, and I was happy in recommending Zoe—Mrs. Elstree.'

'Thank you,' said Armorel, coldly. 'I dare say we shall get to like each other in time.'

'If so, I shall rejoice in having been of some service to you as well as to her. What is her day at home?'

'I believe we are to be at home on Wednesdays.'

'As for me,' he said lightly, 'I am always at home in my studio. I am a triple slave—Miss Rosevean—as you may have heard. I am a slave of the brush, the pen, and the wastepaper-basket. If you will come with Mrs. Elstree to my studio I can show you one or two things that you might like to see.'

'Thank you,' she replied, without apparent interest in his studio. The young man was not accustomed to girls who showed no interest in him, and retired, chilled. Presently she heard his voice again. This time he was talking with Philippa. They were talking low in the doorway beside her, but she could not choose but hear.

'You recommended her—you?' said Philippa.

'Why not?'

'Do you know how—where—she has been living for the last seven years?'

'Certainly. She married an American. He died a year ago, leaving her rather badly off. Is there any reason, Philippa, why I should not recommend her? If there is I will speak to Mr. Jagenal.

'No—no—no. There is no reason that I know of. Somebody told me she had gone on the stage. Who was it?'

'Gone on the stage? No—no: she was married to this American.'

'You have never spoken to me about her.'

'Reason enough, fair cousin. You do not like her.'

'And—you—do,' she replied slowly.

'I like all pretty women, Philippa. I respect one only.'

Then other people came and were introduced to Armorel. One does not leave in cold neglect a girl who is so beautiful and plays so wonderfully. None of them interested Armorel very much. At the beginning, when a girl first goes into society, she expects to be interested and excited at a general gathering. This expectation disappears, and the current coin of everybody's talk takes the place of interest.

Suddenly she caught a face which she knew. When a girl has been travelling about for five years she sees a great many faces. This was a face which she remembered perfectly well, yet could not at first place it in any scene or assign it to any date. Then she recollected. And she walked boldly across the room and stood before the owner of that face.

'You have forgotten me,' she said abruptly.

'I—I—can I ever have known you?' he asked.

'Will you shake hands, Mr. Stephenson? You were Dick Stephenson five years ago. Have you forgotten Armorel, of Samson Island in Scilly?'

No. He had not forgotten that young lady. But he would never have known her thus changed—thus dressed.

'Where is your friend Roland Lee?'

Dick Stephenson changed colour. 'I have not seen him for a long time. We are no longer—exactly—friends.'

'Why not?' she asked, with severity. 'Have you done anything bad? How have you offended him?'

'No, no; certainly not.' He coloured more deeply. 'I have done nothing bad at all,' he added with much indignation.

'Have you deserted him, then? I thought men never gave up their friends. Come to see me, Mr. Stephenson. You shall tell me where he is and what he is doing.'

In the press of the crowd, as they were going away, she heard Mr. Jagenal's voice.

'You are burning the candle at both ends, Alec,' he was saying. 'You cannot possibly go on painting, writing, editing your paper, riding in the Park, and going out every evening as you do now. No man's constitution can stand it, young gentleman. Curb your activity. Be wise in time.'

CHAPTER III

THE CLEVEREST MAN IN LONDON

ALEC FEILDING—everybody, even those who had never seen him, called him Alec—stood before the fire in his own den. In his hand he held a manuscript, which he was reading with great care, making dabs and dashes on it with a thick red pencil.

Sometimes he called the place his studio, sometimes his study. No other man in London, I believe, has so good a right to call his workshop by either name. No other man in London, certainly, is so well known both for pen and pencil. To be at once a poet, a novelist, an essayist, and a painter, and to do all these things well, if not splendidly, is given to few.

The room was large and lofty, as becomes a studio. A heavy curtain hung across the door: the carpet was thick: there was a great fireplace, as deep and broad as that of an old hall, the fire burning on bricks in the ancient style. Above the fireplace there was no modern overmantel, but dark panels of oak, carved in flowers and grapes, with a coat of arms—his own: he claimed descent from the noble House of Feilding: and in the centre panel his own portrait let into the wall without a frame—the work was executed by the most illustrious portrait-painter of the day—the face full of thought, the eyes charged with feeling, the features clear, regular, and classical. A beautiful portrait, with every point idealised. Three sides of the room were fitted with bookshelves, as becomes a study, and these were filled with books. The fourth side was partly hung with tapestry and partly adorned with armour and weapons. Here were also two small pictures, representing the illustrious Alec in childhood—the light of future genius already in his eyes—and in early manhood.

A large library table, littered with books, manuscripts, and proofs, belonged to the study. An easel before the north light, and another table provided with palettes, brushes, paints, and all the tools of the limning trade, belonged to the studio.

The house, which was in St. John's Wood, stood in an old garden at the end of a cul-de-sac off the main road: it was, therefore, quiet: the house itself was new, built in the style now familiar, and put up for the convenience of those who believe that there is nothing in the world to be considered except Art. Therefore there was a spacious hall: stairs broad enough for an ancient mansion led to the first floor and to the great studio. There were also three or four small cupboards, called bedrooms, dining-room, and anything else you might please. But the studio was the real thing. The house was built for the studio.

The place was charged with an atmosphere of peace. Intellectual calm reigned here. Art of all kinds abhors noise. One could feel here the silence necessary for intellectual efforts of the highest order. Apart from the books and the easel and this silence, the character of the occupant was betrayed—or perhaps proclaimed—by other things. The furniture was massive: the library table of the largest kind: the easy chairs by the fire as solid and comfortable as if they had been designed for a club smoking-room: a cabinet showed a collection of china behind glass: the appointments, down to the inkstand and the paper-knife, were large and solid: all together spoke not only of the artist but of the successful artist: not only of the man who works, but of one who works with success and honour: the man arrived. The things also spoke of the splendid man, the man who knows that success should be followed by the splendid life. Too often the successful man is a poor-spirited creature, who continues in the humble middle-class style to which he was born; is satisfied with his suburban villa, never wants a better house or one more finely appointed, and has no craving for society. What is success worth if one does not live up to it? Success is not an end: it is the means: it brings the power of getting the things that make life—wine—horses—the best cook at the best club—sport—the society, every day, of beautiful and well-bred women—all these things the man who has succeeded can enjoy. Those who have not yet succeeded may envy the favourite of Fortune.

As for his work, this highly successful man owned that he could not desert the Muse of Painting any more than her sister of Belles-Lettres. Happy would he be with either, were t' other dear charmer away! Happier still was he with both! And they were not jealous. They allowed him—these tender creatures—to love them both. He was by nature polygamous, perhaps.

Therefore those who were invited to see his latest picture—the lucky few, because you must not think that his studio was open on Show Sunday for all the world to see—stayed, when they had admired that production, to talk of his latest poem or his latest story.

Over the mantelshelf was quite a stack of invitations. And really one hardly knows whether Alec Feilding was most to be envied for his success as a painter—though he painted little: or for his stories—though these were all short—much too short: or for his verses—certainly written in the most delightful vein of *vers de société*: or for his essays, full of observation: or for his social success, which was undoubted. And there is no doubt that there was not any man in London more envied, or who occupied a more enviable position, than Alec Feilding. To be sure, he deserved it: because, without any exception, he was the cleverest man in town.

He owned and edited a paper of his own—a weekly journal devoted to the higher interests of Art. It was called *The Muses Nine*. It was illustrated especially by blocks from art books noticed in its columns. In this paper his own things first appeared: his verses, his stories, his essays. The columns signed *Editor* were the leading feature of the paper, for which alone many people bought it every week. The contents of these columns were always fresh, epigrammatic, and delightful: in the stories a certain feminine quality lent piquancy—it seemed sometimes as if a man could not have written these stories: the verses always tripped lightly, merrily, and gracefully along. An Abbé de la Cour in the last century might have served up such a weekly dish for the Parisians, had he been the cleverest man in Paris.

Alec Feilding's enemies—every man who is rising or has risen has enemies—consoled themselves for a success which could not be denied by sneering at the ephemeral character of his work. It was for to-day: to-morrow, they said, it would be flat. This was not quite true, but, as it is equally true of nearly every piece of modern work, the successful author could afford to disregard this criticism. Perhaps there may be, here and there, a writer who expects more than a limited immortality: I do not know any, but there may be some. And these will probably be disappointed. The enemies said further that his social success—also undoubted—was due to his unbounded cheek. This, too, was partly true, because, if one would rise at all, one must possess that useful quality: without it one will surely sink. It is not to be denied that this young man walked into drawing-rooms as if his presence was a favour: that he spoke as one who delivers a judgment: and that he professed a profound belief in himself. With such gifts and graces—the gift of painting, the gift of verse, the gift of fiction, a handsome presence, good manners, and unbounded cheek—Alec Feilding had already risen very high indeed for so young a man. His enemies, again, said that he was looking out for an heiress.

His enemies, as sometimes but not often happens, spoke from imperfect knowledge. Every man has his weak points, and should be careful to keep them to himself—friends may become enemies—and to let no one know them or suspect them. As for the weak points of Alec Feilding—had his enemies known them—— But you shall see.

He sat down at his library-table and began to copy the manuscript that he had been reading. It was a laborious task, first because copying work is always tedious, and next because he was making alterations—changing names and places—and leaving out bits. He worked on steadily for about half an hour.

Then there was a gentle tap at the door, and his servant—who looked as solemn and discreet as if he had been Charles the Second's confidential clerk of the Back-stairs—came in noiselessly on tiptoe and whispered a name. Alec placed the manuscript and his copy carefully in a drawer, and nodded his head.

You have already seen the man who came in. Five years older, and a good deal altered—changed, perhaps, for the worse—but then the freshness of twenty-one cannot be expected to last. The man who stayed three weeks in Samson, and promised a girl that he would return. The man who broke that promise, and forgot the girl. He never went back to Scilly. Perhaps he had grown handsomer: his Vandyke beard and moustache were by this time thicker and longer: he was more picturesque in appearance than of old: he still wore a brown velvet coat: he looked still more what he was—an artist. But his cheek was thin and pale, dark rings were round his eyes, his face was gloomy: he wore the look of waste—the waste of energy and of purpose. It is not good to see this look in the eyes of a young man.

'You sent for me,' he said, with no other greeting.

'I did. Come in. Is the door shut? I've got some good news for you. Heavens! you look as if you wanted good news badly! What's the matter, man? More debts and duns? And I want to consult you a little about this picture of yours'—he pointed to the easel.

'Mine? No: yours. You have bought me—pictures and all.'

'Just as you like. What does it matter—here—within these walls?'

'Hush! Even here you should not whisper it. The birds of the air, you know—— Take great care'—— Roland laughed, but not mirthfully. 'Mine?' he repeated; 'mine? Suppose I were to call together the fellows at the club, and suppose I were to tell the story of the last three years?—eh? eh? How a man was fooled on until he sold himself and became a slave—eh?'

'You can't tell that story, Roland, you know.'

'Some day I will—I must.'

Alec Feilding threw himself back in his chair, crossed his legs, and joined his fingers. It is an attitude of judicial remonstrance.

'Come, Roland,' he said, smiling blandly. 'Let us have it out. It galls sometimes, doesn't it? But remember you can't have everything—come, now. If you were to tell the fellows at the club, truthfully, the whole story, they would, I dare say, be glad to get such a beautiful pile of stones to throw at me. One more reputation built on pretence and humbug—eh? Yes: the little edifice which you and I have reared together with so much care would be shattered at a single stroke, wouldn't it? You could do that: you can always do that. But at some little cost to yourself—some little cost, remember.'

Roland remarked that the cost or consequences of that little exploit might be condemned.

'Truly. If you will. But not until you realise what they are. Now my version of the story is this. There was once—three years ago—a fellow who had failed. The Academy wouldn't accept his pictures; no one would buy them. And yet he had some power and true feeling. But he could not succeed: he could not get anybody to buy his pictures. And then he was an extravagant kind of man: he was head over ears in debt: he liked to lead the easy life—dinner and billiards at the club—all the rest of it. Then there was another man—an old schoolfellow of his—a man who wanted, for purposes of his own, a reputation for genius in more than one branch of Art. He wanted to seem a master of painting as well as poetry and fiction. This man addressed the Failure. He said, "Unsuccessful Greatness, I will buy your pictures of you, on the simple condition that I may call them mine." The Failure hesitated at first. Naturally. He was loth to write himself down a Failure. Everybody would be. Then he consented. He promised to paint no more in the style in which he had failed except for this other man. Then the other man, who knew his way about, called his friends together, set up a picture painted by the Failure on an easel, bought the tools, laid them out on the table—there they are—and launched himself upon the world as an artist as well as a poet and author. A Fraud, wasn't he? Yet it paid both men—the Fraud and the Failure. For the Fraud knew how to puff the work and to get it puffed and praised and noticed everywhere; he made people talk about it: he had paragraphs about it: he got critics to treat his—or the Failure's—pictures seriously: in fact, he advertised them as successfully and as systematically as if he had been a soap-man. Is this true, so far?'

'Quite true. Go on—Fraud.'

'I will—Failure. Then the price of the pictures went up. The Fraud was able to sell them at a price continually rising. And the Failure received a price in proportion. He shared in the proceeds. The Fraud gave him two thirds. Is that true? Two thirds. He ran your price, Failure, from nothing at all to four hundred and fifty pounds—your last, and biggest price. And he gave you two thirds. All you had to do was to produce the pictures. What he did was to persuade the world that they were great and valuable pictures. Is that true?'

Roland grunted.

'Three years ago you were at your wits' end for the next day's dinner. You had borrowed of all your friends: you had pawned your watch and chain: you were face to face with poverty—no; starvation. Deny that, if you can.' He turned fiercely on Roland. 'You can't deny it. What are you now? You have a good income: you dine every day on the best of everything: you do yourself well in every respect. Hang it, Roland, you are an ungrateful dog!'

'You have ruined my life. You have robbed me of my name.'

'Let us stop heroics. If you are useful to me, I am ten times as useful to you. Because, my dear boy, without me you cannot live. Without you I can do very well. Indeed, I have only to find another starving genius—there are plenty about—in order to keep up my reputation as a painter. Go to the club. Call the men together. Tell them if you like, and what you like. You have no proofs. I can deny it, and I can give you the sack, and I can get that other starving genius to carry on the work.'

Roland made no reply.

'Why, my dear fellow—why should we quarrel? What does it matter about a little reputation? What is the good of your precious name to you when you are dead? Here you are—painting better and better every day—your price rising—your position more assured—what on earth can any man want more? As for me, you are useful to me. If you were not, I should put an end to the arrangement. That is understood. Very well, then. Enough said. Now, if you please, we will look at the picture.'

He got up and walked across the room to the easel. Roland followed submissively, with hanging head. He staggered as he went: not with strong drink, but with the rage that tore his heart.

'It is really a very beautiful thing,' said the cleverest man in all London, looking at it critically. 'I think that even you have never done anything quite so good.'

The picture showed a great rock rising precipitous from the sea—at its base was a reef or projecting shelf. The shags stood in a line on the top of the rock: the seagulls flew around the rock and sailed merrily before the breeze: there was a little sea on, but not much: a boat with a young man in it lay off the rock, and a girl was on the reef standing among the long yellow seaweed: the spray flew up the sides of the rock: the sun was sinking. What was it but one of Roland's sketches made in the Outer Islands, with Armorel for his companion?

'It is very good, Roland,' Alec repeated. 'If I am not so good a painter myself, I am not envious. I can appreciate and acknowledge good work.' Under the circumstances, rather an extraordinary speech. But Roland's gloomy face softened a little. Even at such a moment the artist feels the power of praise. The other, standing before the picture, watched the softening of the face. 'Good work?' he repeated by way of question. 'Man! it is splendid work! I can feel the breath of the salt breeze: I can see the white spray flying over the rock: the girl stands out real and living. It is a splendid piece of work, Roland.'

'I think it is better than the last,' the unlucky painter replied huskily.

'I should rather think it is. I expect to get a great name for this picture'—the painter winced—'and you—you—the painter, will get a much more solid thing—you will get a big cheque. I've sold it already. No dealers this time. It has been bought by a rich American. Three hundred is the figure I can offer you. And here's your cheque.'

He took it, ready drawn and signed, from his pocket-book. Roland Lee received it, but he let it drop from his fingers: the paper fluttered to the floor. He gazed upon the picture in silence.

'Well? What are you thinking of?'

'I was thinking of the day when I made the sketch for that picture. I remember what the girl said to me.'

'What the devil does it matter what the girl said? All we care about is the picture.'

'I remember her very words. You who have bought the picture can see the girl; but I, who painted it, can hear her voice.'

'You are not going off into heroics again?'

'No, no. Don't be afraid. I am not going to tell you what she said. Only I told her, being pleased with what she told me, that she was a prophotess. Nobody ought ever to prophesy good things about a man, for they never come to pass. Let them prophesy disappointment and ruin and shame, and then they always come true. My God! what a prophecy was hers! And what has come of it? I have sold my genius, which is my soul. I have traded it away. It is the sin unforgiven in this world and in the next.'

'When you give over tragedy and blank verse——'

'Oh! I have done.'

'I should like to ask you a question.'

'Ask it.'

'The foreground—the seaweeds lying over the boulders. Does the light fall quite naturally? I hardly understand—look here. If the sunlight——'

'*You* to pretend to be a painter!' Roland snorted impatiently. '*You* to talk about lights and shadows! Man alive! I wonder you haven't been found out ages ago! The light falls this way—this way—see!'—he turned the painting about to show how it fell.

'Oh! I understand. Yes, yes; I see now.' Alec seemed not to resent this language of contempt.

'Is there anything else you want to know before I go? Perhaps you wish the sea painted black?'

'Cornish coast again, I suppose?'

'Somewhere that way. What does it matter where you put it? Call it a view on Primrose Hill.'

He stooped and picked up the cheque. He looked at it savagely for a moment as if he would like to tear it into a thousand fragments. Then he crammed it into his pocket and turned to go.

'My American,' said Alec, 'who rolls in money, is ready to buy another. I think I can make an advance of fifty. Shall we say three hundred and fifty? And shall we expect the painting in three months or so? Before the summer holidays—say. You will become rich, old man. As for this fellow, he is going to the New Gallery. Go and gaze upon it, and say to yourself, "This was worth, to me, three hundred—three hundred." How many men at the club, Roland, can command three hundred for a picture?

Thirty is nearer their figure; and your own, dear boy, would have continued to stand at double duck's egg if it had not been for me. Trust me for running up your price. Our interests, my dear Roland, are identical and indivisible. I think you are the only painter in history whose name will remain unknown though his works will live as long as the pigments keep their colour. Fortune is yours, and fame is mine. You have got the best of the bargain.'

'Curse you and your bargain!'

'Pleasant words, Roland'—his face darkened. 'Pleasant words, if you please, or perhaps . . . . I know, now, what is the reason of this outbreak. I heard last night a rumour. You've been taking opium again.'

'It isn't true. If it was, what does that matter to you?'

'This, my friend. The partnership exists only so long as the work continues to improve. If bad habits spoil the quality of the work I shall dissolve the partnership, and find that other starving genius—plenty, plenty, plenty about. Nothing shakes the nerves more quickly than opium. Nothing destroys the finer powers of head and hand more surely. Don't let me hear any more about opium. Don't fall into bad habits if you want to go on making an income. And don't let me have to speak of this again. Now, there is no more to be said, I think. Well, we part friends. Ta-ta, dear boy.'

Roland flung himself out of the room with an interjection of great strength not found in the school grammars.

Alec Feilding returned to his table. 'Roland's a great fool,' he murmured. 'Because there isn't a gallery in London that wouldn't jump at his pictures, and he could sell as fast as he could paint. A great fool he is. But it would be very difficult for me to find another man so good and such a fool. On fools and their folly the wise man flourishes.'

CHAPTER IV

MASTER OF ALL THE ARTS

This unreasonable person dispatched, and the illustrious artist's doubts about his lights and shadows dispelled, Alec Feilding resumed his interrupted task. That is to say, he took the manuscript out of the drawer and went on laboriously copying it. So great a writer, whose time was so precious, might surely give out his copying work. Lesser men do this. For half an hour he worked on. Then the servant tapped at the door and came in again, noiselessly as before, to whisper a name.

Alec nodded, and once more put back the manuscript in the drawer.

The visitor was a young lady. She was of slight and slender figure, dressed quite plainly, and even poorly, in a cloth jacket and a stuff frock. Her gloves were shabby. Her features were fine but not beautiful, the eyes bright, and the mouth mobile, but the forehead too large for beauty. She carried a black leather roll such as those who teach music generally carry about with them. She was quite young, certainly not more than two-and-twenty.

'Effie?' He looked round, surprised.

'May I come in for two minutes? I will not stay longer. Indeed, I should be so sorry to waste your time.'

'I am sure you would, Effie.' He gave her his hand, without rising. 'Precious time—my time—there is so little of it. Therefore, child ——'

'I have brought you,' she said, 'another little poem. I think it is the kind of thing you like—in the *vers de société* style. She unrolled her leather case and took out a very neatly written paper.

He read it slowly. Then he nodded his head approvingly and read it aloud.

'How long does it take you to knock off this kind of thing, Effie?'

'It took me the whole of yesterday. This morning I corrected it and copied it out. Do you like it?'

'You are a clever little animal, Effie, and you shall make your fortune. Yes; it is very good, very good indeed: Austin Dobson himself is not better. It is very good: light, tripping, graceful—in good taste. It is very good indeed. Leave it with me, Effie. If I like it as well to-morrow as I do to-day, you may depend upon seeing it in the next number.'

'Oh!' she blushed a rosy red with the pleasure of being praised. Indeed, it is a pleasure which never palls. The old man who has been praised all his life is just as eager for more as the young poet who is only just beginning. 'Oh! you really think it is good?'

'I do indeed. The best proof is that I am going to buy it of you. It shall go into the editor's column—my own column—in the place of honour.'

'Yes,' she replied, but doubtfully—and she reddened again for a different reason. 'Oh, Mr. Feilding,' she said with an effort, 'I am so happy when I see my verses in print—in your paper—even without my name. It makes me so proud that I hardly dare to say what I want.'

'Say it, Effie. Get it off your mind. You will feel better afterwards.'

'Well, then, it cannot be anything to you—so great and high, with your beautiful stories and your splendid pictures. What is a poor little set of verses to you?'

'Go on—go on.' His face clouded and his eyes hardened.

'In the paper it doesn't matter a bit. It is—it is—later—when they come out all together in a little volume—with—with——'

'Go on, I say.' He sat upright, his chair half turned, his hands on the arms, his face severe and judicial.

'With your name on the title-page.'

'Oh! that is troubling your mind, is it?'

'When the critics praise the poems and praise the poet—oh! is it right, Mr. Feilding? Is it right?'

'Upon my word!' He pushed back his chair and rose, a tall man of six feet, frowning angrily—so that the girl trembled and tottered. 'Upon my word! This—from you! This from the girl whom I have literally kept from starvation! Miss Effie Wilmot, perhaps you will tell me what you mean! Haven't I bought your verses? Haven't I polished and corrected them, and made them fit to be seen? Am I not free to do what I please with my own?'

'Yes—yes—you buy them. But I—oh!—I write them!'

'Look here, child; I can have no nonsense. Before I took these verses of you, had you any opening or market for them?'

'No. None at all.'

'Nobody would buy them. They were not even returned by editors. They were thrown into the basket. Very well. I buy them on the condition that I do what I please with them. I give you three pounds—three pounds—for a poem, if it is good enough for me to lick into shape. Then it becomes my own. It is a bargain. When you leave off wanting money you will leave off bringing me verses. Then I shall look for another girl. There are thousands of girls about who can write verses as good as these.'

The girl remained silent. What her employer said was perfectly true. And yet—and yet—it was not right.

'What more do you want?' he asked brutally.

'I am the author of these poems,' she said. 'And you are not.'

'Within these walls I allow you to say so—this once. Take care never to say so again. Outside these walls, if you say so, I will bring an action against you for libel and slander and defamation of character. Remember that. You had better, however, take these verses and go away.' He flung them at her feet. 'We will put an end to the arrangement.'

'No, no—I consent.' She humbly stooped and picked them up. 'Do what you like with them. I am too poor to refuse. Do what you please.'

'It is your interest, certainly, to consent. Why, I paid you last year a hundred pounds. A hundred pounds! There's an income for a girl of twenty! Well, Effie, I forgive you. But no more nonsense. And give over crying.' For now she was sobbing and crying. 'Look here, Effie'—he laid his hand on hers—'some day, before long, I will put your verses in another column, with your name at the end—"Effie Wilmot." Come, will that do?'

'Oh! if you would! If you really would!'

'I really will, child. Don't think I care much about the thing. What does it matter to me whether I am counted a writer of society verses? It pleased me that the world should think me capable of these trifles while I am elaborating a really ambitious poem. One more little volume and I shall have done. Besides, all this time you are improving. When you burst upon the world it will be with wings full-fledged and flight-sustained that you will soar to the stars. Fair poetess, I will make your fame assured. Be comforted.'

She looked up, tearful and happy. 'Oh, forgive me!' she said. 'Yes; I will do everything—exactly—as you want!'

'The world wants another poetess. You shall be that sweet singer. Let me be the first to acknowledge the gift divine.' He bowed and raised her hand and kissed the fingers of her shabby glove.

'Now, child,' he said, 'your visit has gained you another three pounds—here they are.'

She took the money, blushing again. The glowing prospect warmed her heart. But the three golden sovereigns chilled her again. She had parted with her child—her own. It was gone—and he would call it his and pretend to be the father. And yet he was going to make such splendid amends to her.

'How is your brother?'

'He is always the same. He works all day at his play. In the afternoon he creeps out for a little on his crutches. In the future, Mr. Feilding, we are both going to be happy, he with his dramas and I with my poems.'

'Is his drama nearly ready?'

'Very nearly.'

'Tell him to let me read it. I can, at least, advise him.

'If you will! Oh! you are so kind! What we should have done without your help and the money you have given me, I do not know.'

'You are welcome, sweet singer and heavenly poet.' The great man took her hand and pressed it. 'Now be thankful that you came here. You have cleared your mind of doubts, and you know what awaits you in the future. Bring your brother's little play. I should like—yes, I should like to see what sort of a play he has written.'

She went away, happier for the prophecy. In the dead of night she dreamed that she saw Mr. Alec Feilding carried along in a triumphal car to the Temple of Fame. The goddess herself, flying aloft in a white satin robe, blew the trumpet, and a nymph flying lower down—in white linen—put on the laurel crown and held it steady when the chariot bumped over the ruts. It was her crown—her own—that adorned those brows. Is it right? she asked again. Is it right?

Mr. Feilding, when she was gone, proceeded to copy out the poem carefully in his own handwriting, adding a few erasures and corrections so as to give the copy the hall-mark of the poet's study. Then he threw the original upon the fire.

'There!' he said, 'if Miss Effie Wilmot should have the audacity to claim these things as her own, at least I have the originals in my own handwriting—with my own corrections upon them, too, as they were sent to the printer. Yes, Effie, my dear; some day perhaps your verses shall appear with your name to them. Not while they are so good, though. I only wish they were a little more masculine.'

Again he lugged out that manuscript, and resumed his copying, laboriously toiling on. The clock ticked, and the ashes dropped, and the silence was profound while he performed this intellectual feat.

At the stroke of noon the servant disturbed him a third time. He put away his work in the drawer, and went out to meet this visitor.

This time it was none other than a Lady of Quality—a Grande Dame de par le monde. She came in splendid attire, sailing into the studio like some richly adorned pinnace or royal yacht. A lady of a certain age, but still comely in the eyes of man.

'Lady Frances!' cried Alec. 'This is, indeed, unexpected. And you know that it is the greatest honour for me to wait upon you.'

'Yes, yes; I know that. But I thought I should like to see you as you are—in your own studio. So I came. I hope not at an inconvenient time.'

'No time could be inconvenient for a visit from you.'

'I don't know. Your model might be sitting to you. To be sure, you are not a figure-painter. But one always supposes that models are standing to artists all day long. Good-looking women, too, I believe. Perhaps you have got one hidden away behind the screen, just as they do on the stage. I will look.' She put up her glasses and walked across the room to look behind the screen. 'No: she has gone. Oh! is this your new picture?'

He bowed. 'I hope you like it.'

'I do,' she said, looking at it. 'It seems to me the very best thing you have done. Oh! it is really beautiful! Do you know, Mr. Feilding, that you are a very wonderful man?'

Alec laughed pleasantly. Of course he knew. 'If you think so,' he said.

'You write the most beautiful verses and the most charming stories: you paint the most wonderful pictures: you belong to society, and you go everywhere. How do you do it? How do you find time to do it? I suppose you never want any sleep? Poet, painter, novelist, journalist! Are you a sculptor as well, by chance?'

'Not yet. Perhaps——'

'Glutton! Are you a dramatist?'

'Again—not yet. Perhaps, some time——'

'Insatiate! You are a Master of all the Arts. Alec Feilding, M.A.' He laughed pleasantly, again.

'You are the cleverest man in all London. Well; I sent you another story yesterday——'

'You did. I was about to write and thank you for it. Is it a true story?'

'Quite true. It happened in my husband's family, thirty years ago. They are not very proud of it. You can dress it up somehow with new names.'

'Quite so. I shall rewrite the whole.'

'I don't mind. It is a great pleasure to me to see the stories in print. And no one suspects poor little Me. Are they so very badly written?'

'The style is a little—just a little, may I say?—jerky. But the stories are admirable. Do let me have some more, Lady Frances.'

'Remember. No one is to know where you get them.'

'A Masonic secrecy forms part of my character. I even put my own name to them for greater security.'

He did. Every week he put his own name to stories which he got from people like this Lady of Quality.

'That ought to disarm suspicion. On the other hand, everybody must know that you cannot invent these things.'

Alec laughed. 'Most people give me credit for inventing even your stories.'

'By the way,' she said, 'are you coming to my dinner next week?'

'With the greatest pleasure.'

'If you don't come you shall have no more stories drawn from the domestic annals and the early escapades of the British Aristocracy.'

'I assure you, Lady Frances, I look forward with the greatest——'

'Very well, then. I shall expect you. And remember—secrecy.'

She laid her finger on her lips and vanished.

The smile faded out of the young man's face. He sat down again, and once more set himself to work doggedly copying out the manuscript, which was, indeed, none other than the story furnished him by Lady Frances. It was going to appear in the next week's issue of the journal, with his name at the end.

Was not Alec Feilding the cleverest all-round man in the whole of London—*Omnium artium magister!*

CHAPTER V

ONLY A SIMPLE SERVICE

MRS. ELSTREE took the card that the maid brought her. She started up, mechanically touched her hair—which was of the feathery and fluffy kind—and her dress, with the woman's instinct to see that everything was in order: the quick colour rose to her cheek—perhaps from the heat of the fire. 'Yes,' she said, 'I am at home.' She was sitting beside the fire in the drawing-room of Armorel's flat. It was a cold afternoon in March: outside, a black east wind raged through the streets; it was no day for driving or for walking: within, soft carpets, easy-chairs, and bright fires invited one to stay at home. This lady, indeed, was one of those who love warmth and physical ease above all other things. Actually to be warm, lazily warm, without any effort to feel warmth, afforded her a positive and distinct physical pleasure, just as a cat is pleased by being stroked. Therefore, though a book lay in her lap, she had not been reading. It is much pleasanter to lie back and feel warm, with half-closed eyes, in a peaceful room, than to be led away by some impetuous novelist into uncomfortable places, cold places, fatiguing places.

She started, however, and the book fell to the floor, where it remained. And she rose to her feet when the owner of the card came in. The relict of Jerome Elstree was still young, and grief had as yet destroyed none of her beauty. She looked better, perhaps, in the morning—which says a great deal.

'Alec?' she murmured—her eyes as soft as her voice. 'I thought you would come this afternoon.'

'Are you quite alone, Mrs. Elstree?' he asked with a look of warning.

'Quite, Mr. Feilding. And, since the door is shut, and we are quite alone—why—then——' She laughed, held out both her hands, and put up her face like a child.

He took her hands and bent to kiss her lips.

'Zoe,' he said, 'you grow lovelier every day. Last night——' He kissed her again.

'Lovelier than Philippa?'

'What is Philippa beside you? An iceberg beside a—a garden of flowers——'

'There is beauty in icebergs, I have read.'

'Never mind Philippa, dear Zoe. She is nothing to us.'

'I don't mind her a bit, Alec, if you don't. If you begin to mind her—— But we will wait until that happens. Why are you here to-day?'

'I have come to call upon Mrs. Elstree, widow of my poor friend Jerome Elstree.'

'Ce pauvre Jerome! The tears come into my eyes'—in fact, they did at that moment—'look!—when I think of him. So often have I spoken of his virtues and his untimely fate that he has really lived. I never before understood that there are ghosts of men who never lived as well as ghosts of the dead.'

'And I came to call upon your charge, Miss Rosevean.'

'Yes'—she said this dubiously, perhaps jealously—'so I supposed. Why did you send me here, Alec? You have always got some reason for everything. There was no need for my coming—I was doing as well as I expect to do.'

The young man looked about the room without replying to this question.

'Someone,' he said presently, 'has furnished this room who knows furniture.'

'It was Armorel herself. I have no taste—as you know.'

'And how do you get on with her? Are you happy here, Zoe?'

'I am as happy as I ever expect to be—until——'

'Yes, yes,' he interrupted, impatiently. 'You like her, then?'

'I like her as much as I can like any woman. You know, Alec, I am not greatly in love with my own sex. If there were no other women in the world than just enough to dress me, get my dinner, and keep my house clean, I should not murmur. Eve was the happiest of women, in spite of the difficulties she must have had in keeping up with the fashion. Because, you see, she was the only woman.'

'No doubt. And now tell me about this girl.'

'She is rich. To be rich is everything. Money makes an angel of every woman. When I was eighteen, and first met you, Alec, I was rich. Then you saw the wings sticking out visibly one on each shoulder, didn't you? They are gone now—at least,' she looked over her shoulder, 'I see them no longer.'

'I heard she was rich. Where did the money come from?'

'It has been saving up for I don't know how long. The girl is only twenty-one, and she has about thirty thousand pounds, besides all kinds of precious things worth I don't know how much.'

'Jagenal told me she was comfortably off—"comfortably," he said—but—thirty thousand pounds!'

'The mere thought of so much makes your eyes glow quite poetically, Alec. Write a poem on thirty thousand pounds. Well, that is what she has, and all her own, without any drawbacks: no nasty poor relations—no profligate brothers—to nibble and gnaw. She has not either brother or sister—an enviable lot when one has money. When one has no money a brother—a successful brother—might be useful.'

'And how do you get on with her?'

'I think we do pretty well together. But my post is precarious.'

'Why?'

'Because the young woman is pretty, rich, and masterful. It is a curious thing about women that the most masterful soonest find their master.'

'You mean that she will marry.'

'If she gets engaged, being rich, she will certainly marry at once. Until she marries I believe we can get on together, because she is totally independent of me. This afternoon, for example, she has gone out to look at pictures somewhere, with a girl she has picked up somehow—a girl who writes.'

'But, my dear Zoe, you must look after her. Don't let her pick up girls and make friendships. You are here to look after her. I hoped that you would gain her complete confidence—become indispensable to her.'

'Oh! that is why you sent me here? Pray, my dear Alec, what can Armorel be to you?'

'Nothing, dear child,' he replied, patting her soft hand, 'that will bring any discord between you and me. But—make yourself indispensable and necessary to her.'

'You will tell me, I dare say, presently, what you mean. But you don't know this young islander. Necessary to me she is, as you know. Necessary to her I shall never become. We have nothing in common. I can do nothing for her at all, except go out to theatres and concerts and things in the evening. Even then our tastes clash. I like to laugh; she likes to sit solemnly with big eyes staring—so—as if she was receiving inspiration. I like comic operas, she likes serious plays; I like dance music, she likes classical music; I like the fool's paradise, she likes—the other kind, where they all behave so well and are under no illusions. In fact, Armorel takes herself quite seriously all round. Of course, a girl with such a fortune can take herself anyhow she pleases.'

'She knows how to dress, apparently. Most advanced girls disdain dress.'

'But she is not an advanced girl. She is only a girl who knows a great deal. She is not in the least emancipated. Why, she still professes the Christian religion. She is just a girl who has set herself resolutely to learn all she can. She has been about it for five years. When she began, I understand that she knew nothing. What she means to do with her knowledge I have not learned. She talks French and German and Italian. You have heard her play? Very well: you can't beat that. You shall see some of her drawings. They are rather in your style, I think. A highly cultivated girl. That is all.'

'A female prig? A consciously superior person?'

'Not a bit. Rather humble-minded. But masterful and independent. Where she fails is, of course, in ordinary talk. She can't talk—she can only converse. She doesn't know the pictures and painters, and poets and novelists of the day—she doesn't know a single person in society. She doesn't know any personal history at all. And she doesn't care about any. That is Armorel.'

'I see,' he replied thoughtfully. 'Things will be difficult, I am afraid.'

'What things? Oh! there is another point in which she differs from people of society.'

'Yes?'

'When you and I, dear Alec, think and talk of people, we conclude that they are exactly like ourselves—do we not? Quite worldly and selfish, you know. Everyone with his little show to run for himself. Now, Armorel, on the other hand, concludes that everyone is like—not us—but herself. Do you catch the difference? There is a difference, you know.'

'Sometimes, Zoe, I seem not to understand you. But never mind. Under your influence——'

'I have no influence at all with her. I never shall have.'

'But, my dear Zoe, why are you here? I want you—I repeat—to exercise an overwhelming influence.'

'Oh! It is impossible. Consider—you who know me so well—how can I influence a girl who is always seeking after great things? She wants everything noble and lofty and pure. She has what they call a great soul—and I—oh! Alec, you know that I belong to the infinitely little souls. There are a great, great number of us, but we are very contemptible.'

'Let us think,' he replied. 'Let us contrive and devise some way——'

'Enough about Armorel. Tell me now about yourself.'

'I am always the same.'

'You have come, perhaps, this afternoon,' she murmured softly, 'to bring me some new hope—Oh! Alec—at last—some hope?'

'I have no new hope to give you, child.'

Both sat in silence, looking into the firelight.

'It is seven years—seven years,' said Zoe, 'since I had my great quarrel with Philippa. She was eighteen then—and so was I—I charged her with throwing herself at your head, you know. So she did. So she does still. Why, the woman can't conceal, even now, that she loves you. I saw it in her eyes last night, I saw it in her attitude when she was talking to you. She swore after the row we had that she would never speak to me again. But you see she has broken that vow. I was eighteen then, and I was rich, a good deal richer than Philippa ever will be. When you and I became engaged I was twenty-one. That is four years ago, Alec. Yet, a year or two, and the girl you were—engaged to—will be thin and faded. For your sake, my dear boy, I hope that you will not keep her waiting very much longer before you present her to the world.'

'My dear child, could I help the smash that came—the smash and scandal? When the whole town was ringing with your father's smash and his suicide, and the ruin of I don't know how many people, was that the moment for us to step forward and take hands before the world?'

'No; you certainly could not. As a man of the world, you would have been justified in breaking off the thing—especially as it was only a day or two old.'

'I could not let you go, Zoe,' he said, with a touch of real tenderness. 'I was madly in love.'

'I think you were, Alec. I really think that at the time you were truly and madly in love. Else you would never have done a thing of which you repented the next day.'

'I have never repented, dear Zoe—never once.'

'Perhaps you calculated that something would be saved out of the smash. Perhaps, for once in your life, you never calculated at all upon anything. Well—I consented to keep the thing a secret.'

'You know that it was necessary.'

'You said so. I obeyed. But four years—four years—and no prospect of a termination. Consider!' She pleaded as she had spoken before, in the same soft, caressing, murmuring tone.

'I do consider, Zoe. You can have your freedom again. I have no right ——'

'Nonsense! My freedom? It is your own that you want My freedom?' she repeated, but without raising her voice. 'Mine! What could I do with it—now? Whither could I turn? Do not, I advise you, think that I will ever while I live restore your freedom to you.'

'I spoke in your own interest, believe me.'

'I am now what you have made me. You know what that is. You know what I was four years ago.'

'I have advised you, it is true.'

'No; you have led me. At the moment of my greatest trouble you made me break away from my own people, who were sorry for my misfortunes, and would have kept me among them in my own circle. There was no reason for me to leave them. The wreck of my father's fortune was not imputed to me. You persuaded me to assert my own independence, and to go upon the stage, for which I was as well fitted as for the kingdom of heaven.'

'I hoped—I thought—that you would succeed.'

'No; what you hoped and intended was to keep me in your power. You would not let me go, and you could not—or would not——'

'Could not, my child. I could not.'

'For four years I have endured the humiliations of the actress who is a failure and can only take the lowest parts. You know what I have endured, and yet—— Oh! Alec, your love is, indeed, a noble gift! And now, for your sake, I am here, playing a part for you. I am the young widow of the man who never existed. I make up a hundred lies every day to a girl who believes every word—which makes it more disgraceful and more horrible. When one knows that she is disbelieved it is different.'

'Zoe, you know my position.'

'Very well, indeed. You live in a little palace. You keep your man-servant and your two horses. You go every day into some kind of good society ——'

'It is necessary : my position demands it.'

'Your position, my friend, has nothing to do with it. If you stayed at home every evening just as many copies of your paper would be sold. You spend all this money on yourself, Alec, because you are a selfish person and indulgent, and because you like to make a great show of success.'

'You do not understand.'

'Oh, yes, I do! You paint lovely pictures, which you sell: you write admirable stories and excellent verses—at least, I suppose they are admirable and excellent. You put them into a paper which is your own ——'

'Yes—yes. But all these things leave me as poor as I was four years ago.'

He got up and stood before the fire, looking into it. Then he walked across to the window and gazed into the street. Then he returned and looked into the fire again. This restlessness may be a sign that something is on a man's mind.

'Zoe,' he said at length, without looking at her, 'your impatience makes you unjust. You do not understand. Things have come to a crisis.'

'What kind of a crisis?'

'A financial crisis. I must have money'

'Then go and make it. Paint more pictures: write more poetry. Make money, as other men do. It is very noble and grand to pretend that you only work when you please; but it isn't business, and it isn't true.'

'Again—you do not understand. I must have money in a short time, or else——'

'Else—what may happen, Alec?' She leaned forward, losing her murmuring manner for the first time.

'I may—I must—become bankrupt. That to me signifies social ruin.'

'You have something more to say. Won't you say it at once?'

'If I can get over this difficulty it will be all right—my anxieties over. I thought, Zoe, when I sent you here, that, with a girl rich, mistress of her own, of age, it would be easy for you to wind yourself into her confidence and borrow—or beg, or somehow get what I want out of her. To borrow would be best.'

'How much do you want? Tell me exactly.'

'I want, before the end of next month, about 3,000*l*. Say, 3,500*l*.'

'That is a very large sum of money.'

'Not to this girl. Make her lend it to you. Make up some story. Beg it or borrow it—and ——' he laid his hand upon her shoulder, but she made no movement in reply; he stooped and kissed her head, but she did not look up. 'Zoe—I swear—if you will do this for me, our long and weary waiting shall be at an end. I will acknowledge everything. I will give up this extravagant life we will settle down like a couple of honest bourgeois: we will live over the shop if you like—that is, the publishing office of the paper.' He took her hand and raised it to his lips, but she made no response.

'Would she ever get the money back again?'

'Perhaps. How can I tell?'

'Even for the bribe you offer, Alec, I am afraid I cannot do it.'

'We will try together. We will lay ourselves out to attract the girl, to win her confidence. Consider. She is alone. She is in our hands ——'

'Yes, yes. But you do not know her. Alec, if I cannot succeed, what will you do?'

'I must look out for some girl with money and get engaged to her. The mere fact of an engagement would be enough for me.'

'Yes,' she said quickly, 'it would have to be. Will you get engaged to—to Philippa?'

'No; Philippa will only have money at the death of her father and mother—not before. Philippa is out of the question.'

'Is there nobody among all your fine friends who will lend you the money?'

'No one. We do not lend money to each other. We go on as if there were no money difficulties in the world, as well as no diseases, no old age, no dying. We do not speak of money.'

'Friendship in society has its limits. Yes; I see. But can't you borrow it in the usual way of business people?'

'I should have to show books and enter into unpleasant explanations. You see, Zoe, the paper has got a very good name, but rather a small circulation. Everybody sees it, but very few buy it.'

'And so you heard of Armorel, and you thought that here was a chance. You say to me, in plain words: "If you get this money, there shall be an end of the false position." Is that so?'

'That is exactly what I do say and swear, Zoe. It is a very simple thing. You have only to persuade the girl to lend you this money, or to advance it, or to invest it by your agency—or something—a very simple and easy thing. You love me well enough to do me such a simple service.'

'I love you well enough, I suppose,' she replied sadly, 'to do everything you tell me to do. A simple service! Only to deceive and plunder this girl, who believes us all to be honourable and truthful!'

'Oh, we shall find a way—some way—to pay her back. Don't be afraid. And don't go off into platitudes, Zoe—you are much too pretty—and when it is done, and you are openly, before the world ——'

'I know you well enough to know how much happiness to expect. I am a fool. All women are fools. Philippa is a fool. And I've set my foolish heart on—you. If I fail—if I fail'—her words sank to the softest and gentlest murmur—'you are going to cast about for an heiress, and you will get engaged to her, and then—then—we shall see, dear Alec, what will happen then.' She sat up, her cheek fiery, and her eyes flashing, though her voice was so soft. 'Hush!' she whispered. 'I hear Armorel's step!'

They heard her voice as well outside, loud and clear.

'Come to my own room,' she said. 'What you want is there. This way.'

'It is the girl with her—the girl who writes. They have gone into her own room—her boudoir—her study—where she works half the day. The girl lives with her brother, close by.'

They listened, silent, with hushed breath, like conspirators.

'Poor Armorel!' said Zoe. 'If she only knew what we are plotting! She thinks me the most truthful of women! And all I am here for is to cheat her out of her money! Don't you think I had better make a clean breast and ask her to give me the money and let me go?'

'Begin to-day,' said Alec. 'Begin to talk about me. Interest her in me. Let her know how great and good——'

'Hush!'

Then they heard her voice again in the hall.

'No—no—you must come this evening. Bring Archie with you. I will play, and he shall listen. You shall both listen. And then great thoughts will come to you.'

'Always great thoughts—great thoughts—great pictures,' Zoe murmured. 'And we are so infinitely little. Brother worm, shall we crawl into some hole and hide ourselves?'

Then the door opened, and Armorel herself appeared, fresh and rosy in spite of the cold wind.

'My dear child,' said Zoe softly, looking up from her cushions, 'come in and sit down. You must be perishing with the east wind. Do sit down and be comfortable. You met Mr. Feilding last night, I believe.'

The visitor remained for a quarter of an hour. Armorel had been to see a certain picture in the National Gallery. He talked of pictures just as, the night before, he had talked of music: that is to say, as one who knows all the facts about the painters and their works and their schools: their merits and their defects. He knew and could talk fluently the language of the Art Critic, just as he knew and could talk the language of the Musical Critic. Armorel listened. Now and then she made a remark. But her manner lacked the reverence with which most maidens listened to this thrice-gifted darling of the Muses. She actually seemed not to care very much what he said.

Zoe, for her part, lay back in her cushions in silence.

'How do you like him?' she asked, when their visitor left them.

'I don't know; I haven't thought about him. He talks too much, I think. And he talks as if he was teaching.'

'No one has a better right to talk with authority.'

'But we are free to listen or not as we please. Why has he the right to teach everybody?'

'My dear child, Alec Feilding is the cleverest man in all London.'

'He must be very clever then. What does he do?'

'He does everything—poetry, painting, fiction—everything!'

'Oh, you will show me his poetry, perhaps, some time? And his pictures I suppose we shall see in May somewhere. He doesn't look as if he was at all great. But one may be wrong.'

'My dear Armorel, you are a fortunate girl, though you do not understand your good fortune. Alec—I am privileged to call him Alec—has conceived a great interest in you. Oh, not of the common love kind, that you despise so much—nothing to do with your *beaux yeux*—but on account of your genius. He was greatly taken with your playing: if you will show him your pictures he will give you instruction that may be useful to you. He wants to know you, my dear.'

'Well,' said Armorel, not in the least overwhelmed, 'he can if he pleases, I suppose, since he is a friend of yours.'

'That is not all: he wants your friendship as a sister in art. Such a man—such an offer, Armorel, must not be taken lightly.'

'I am not drawn towards him,' said the girl. 'In fact, I think I rather dislike his voice, which is domineering; and his manner, which seems to me self-conscious and rather pompous; and his eyes, which are too close together. Zoe, if he were not the cleverest man in London, I should say that he was the most crafty.'

Zoe laughed. 'What man discovers by experiment and experience,' she murmured, incoherently, 'woman discovers at a glance. And yet they say ——'

CHAPTER VI

THE OTHER STUDIO

THE Failure was at work in his own studio. Not the large and lofty chamber fitted and furnished as if for Michael Angelo himself, which served for the Fraud. Not at all. The Failure did his work in a simple second-floor back, a chamber in a commonplace lodging-house of Keppel Street, Bloomsbury. Nowhere in the realms of Art was there a more dismal studio. The walls were bare, save for one picture which was turned round and showed its artistic back. The floor had no carpet: there was no other furniture than a table, strewn and littered with sketches, paints, palettes, brushes: there were canvases leaning against the wall: there was a portfolio also leaning against the wall: there was an easel and the man standing before it: and there was a single chair.

For three years Roland Lee had withdrawn from his former

haunts and companions. No one knew now where he lived: he had not exhibited: he had resigned his membership at the club: he had gone out of sight. Many London men every year go out of sight. It is quite easy. You have only to leave off going to the well-known places of resort: very soon—so soon that it is humiliating only to think of it—men cease asking where you are: then they cease speaking of you: you are clean gone out of their memory—you and your works—it is as if the sea had closed over you. There is not left a trace or a sign of your existence. Perhaps, now and then, something may revive your name: some little adventure may be remembered: some frolic of youth—for the rest—nothing: Silence: Oblivion It does, indeed, humiliate those who look on. When such an accident revived the memory of Roland Lee, one would ask another what had become of him. And no one knew. But, of course, he had gone down—down—down. When a man disappears it means that he sinks. He had gone out of sight: therefore he had gone under. Yet, when you climb, you can never get so high as to be invisible. Even the President, R.A., is not invisible. Again, the higher that a balloon soars, the smaller does it grow; but the higher a man climbs up the Hill of Fame the bigger does he show. It is quite certain that when a man has disappeared he has sunk. The only question—and this can never be answered—is, what becomes of the men who sink? One man I heard of—also, like Roland, an artist—who has been traced to a certain tavern, where he fuddles himself every evening, and where you may treat with him for the purchase of his pictures at ten shillings—ay, or even five shillings—apiece. And two scholars—scholars gone under—I heard of the other day. They now reside in the same lodging-house. It is close to the Gray's Inn Road. One lives in the garret, and the other occupies the cellar. In the evening they get drunk together and dispute on points of the finer scholarship. But this only accounts for three. And where are all the rest?

Of Roland Lee nobody knew anything. There was no story or scandal attached to him: he was no drinker: he was no gambler: he was no profligate. But he had vanished.

Yet he had not gone far—only to Keppel Street, which is really a central place. Here he occupied a second floor, and lived alone. Nobody ever called upon him: he had no friends. Sometimes he sat all day long in his studio doing nothing: sometimes he went forth, and wandered about the streets: in the evening he dined at restaurants where he was certain to meet none of his old friends. He lived quite alone. As to that rumour concerning opium, it was an invention of his employer and proprietor. He did not take opium. Day after day, however, he grew more moody. What developments might have followed in this lonely life I know not. Opium, perhaps: whisky, perhaps: melancholia, perhaps. And from melancholia—Good Lord deliver us!

One thing saved him. The work which filled his soul with rage also kept his soul from madness. When the spirit of his Art seized him and held him he forgot everything. He worked as if he was a free man: he forgot everything, until the time came when he had to lay down his palette and to come back to the reality of his life. Some men would have accepted the position: there were, as we have seen, compensations of a solid and comfortable kind: had he chosen to work his hardest, these golden compensations might have run into four figures. Some men might have sat and laughed among their friends, forgetting the ignominy of their slavery. Not so Roland. His chains jangled as he walked; they cut his wrists and galled his ankles: they filled him with so much shame that he was fain to go away and hide himself. And in this manner he enjoyed the great success which his employer had achieved for his pictures. To arrive at the success for which you have always longed and prayed—and to enjoy it in such a fashion. Oh! mockery of fate!

This morning he was at work contentedly—with ardour. He was beginning a picture from one of his sketches: it was to be another study of rocks and sea: as yet there was little to show: it was growing in his brain, and he was so fully wrapped in his invention that he did not hear the door open, and was not conscious that for the first time within three years he had a visitor.

She opened the door and stood for a moment looking about her. The bare and dingy walls, the scanty furniture, the meanness of the place, made her very soul sink within her. For they cried aloud the story of the painter.

For five long years she had thought of him. He was successful: he was rising to the top of the tree: he was conquering the world—so brave, so strong, so clever! There was no height to which he could not rise. She should find him splendid, triumphant, and yet modest—her old friend the same, but glorified. And she found him thus, in this dingy den—so low, so shabby! Consider, if she had risen while he was sinking, how great was now the gulf between them! Then she stepped into the room and stood beside the artist at his easel.

'Roland Lee,' she whispered.

He started, looked up, and recognised her. 'Armorel!' he cried.

Then, strange to say, instead of hastening to meet and greet her, and to hold out hands of welcome, he stood gazing at her stupidly, his face changing colour from crimson to white. His hair was unkempt, she saw; his cheeks worn; his eyes haggard, with deep lines round them; and his dress was shabby and uncared for.

'You have not forgotten me, then?' she said.

'Forgotten you? No. How could I forget you?'

'Then are you pleased to see me? Shake hands with me, Roland Lee.'

He complied, but with restraint. 'Have you dropped from the clouds?' he asked. 'How did you find me here?'

'I met your old friend Dick Stephenson. He told me that you lived here. You are no longer friends: but he has seen you going in and coming out. That is how I found you. Are you well, Roland?'

'Yes, I am well.'

'Does all go well with you, my old friend?'

'Why not? You see—I have got a magnificent studio: there is every outward sign of wealth and prosperity: and if you look into any art-criticisms you will find the papers ringing with my name.'

'You are changed.' Armorel passed over the bitterness of this speech. 'You are a little older, perhaps.' She did not tell him how haggard and worn he looked, how unkempt and unhappy.

'Let me see some of your work,' she said. The picture on the easel was only in its very first stage. She looked about the room. Nothing on the walls but one picture with its face turned round. 'May I look at this?' She turned it round. It was the picture of herself, 'The Princess of Lyonesse,' the sketch of which he had finished on the last day of his holiday. 'Oh!' she cried, 'I remember this. And you have kept it, Roland—you have kept it. I am glad.'

'Yes, I have kept the only picture which I can call my own.'

'Was I like that in those days?'

'You are like that now. Only, the little Princess has become a tall Queen.'

'Yes, yes; I remember. You said, then, that if I should ever look like this, you would be proved to be a painter indeed. Roland, you are a painter indeed.'

'No, no,' he said; 'I am nothing—nothing at all.'

'We were talking—when you made this sketch—of how one can grow to his highest and noblest.'

'I have grown to my lowest,' he replied. 'But you—you——'

'What has happened, my friend? You told me so much once about yourself—you taught me so much—you put so many new things into my head—you must tell me more! What has happened?'

'Nothing.'

'Why are you here in this poor room? I have been to studios in Rome and Florence, and Paris and Vienna: they are lovely rooms, fit for a man whose mind is always full of lovely images and sweet thoughts. But this—this room is not a studio. It is an ugly little prison. How can light and colour visit such a place?'

'It explains itself. It proclaims aloud—Failure—Failure—Failure!'

'This picture is not Failure.'

'My name is unknown. I work on like a mole under ground. I am a Failure. You have seen Dick Stephenson. What did he say of me?'

'He said that you must have left off working. But you have not.'

'What does it matter how much or how long a Failure goes on working?'

'Have you lost heart, Roland?'

'Heart, and hope, and faith. Everything is lost, Armorel!'

'You have lost your courage because you have failed. But many men have failed at first—great men. Robert Browning failed for years. You were brave once, Roland. You were able to say that if you knew you were doing good work you cared nothing for the critics.'

'You see, Dick was right. I no longer do any work. I never send anything to the exhibitions.'

'But why—why—why?'

'Ask me no more questions, Armorel. Go away and leave me. How beautiful and glorious you have grown, child! But I knew you would. And I have gone down so low, and—and—well, you see! Yes. I remember how we talked of growing to our full height. We did not think, you see, of the depths to which we might also drop. There are awful depths, which you could never guess.'

He sank into the chair, and his head dropped.

Armorel stood over him, the tears gathering into her eyes.

'Roland,' she laid her hand upon his shoulder—there is no action more sisterly—'since I have found you I shall not let you go again. It is five years since you went away. You will tell me about yourself, when you please. I have a great deal to tell you. Don't you remember how sympathetic you used to be in the old days? I want a great deal more sympathy now, because I am five years older, and I am trying so much. I want you to hear me play—you were the first who ever praised my playing, you know. And you must see my drawings. I have worked every day, as I promised you I would. I have remembered all your instructions. Come and see your pupil's work, my master.'

He made no reply.

'You live too much alone,' she went on. 'Dick Stephenson told me that you have given up your club, and that you go nowhere, and that no one knows how you live. You have dropped quite away from your old friends. Why did you do that? You live in this dismal room by yourself—alone with your thoughts: no wonder you lose courage and faith.' She opened the portfolio and drew out a number of the sketches. 'Why,' she said, 'here are some of those you made with me. Here is Castle Bryher—you in the boat, and I on the ledge among the seaweed under the great rock—and the shags in a row on the top: and here is Porth

Cressa—and here Peninnis—and here Round Island. Oh! we have so many things to talk about. Will you come to see me?'

'You had better leave me alone, Armorel,' he said. 'Even you can do no good to me now.'

'When will you come? See—I will write down my address. I have a flat, and it is ever so much better furnished than this, Sir. Will you come to-night? I shall be at home. There will be no one but Effie Wilmot. Oh! I am not going to talk about you, but about myself. I want your praise, Roland, and your sympathy. Both were so ready—once. Will you come to-night?'

'You will drive me mad, I think, Armorel!'

'Will you come?'

He shook his head.

'I have got to tell you how I became rich, if you will listen. You must come and hear my news. Why, there is no one but you in all London who knew me when I lived on Samson alone with those old people. You will come to-night, Roland?' Again she laid her hand upon his shoulder. 'I will ask no questions about you—none at all. You will tell me what you please about yourself. But you must let me talk to you about myself, as frankly as in the old days. If you have got any kindly memory left of me at all, Roland, you will come.'

He rose and lifted his shameful eyes to hers, so full of pity and of tears.

'Yes,' he said; 'I will do whatever you tell me.'

CHAPTER VII

A CANDID OPINION

YOUTH in the London lodging-house! Youth quite poor—youth ambitious—youth with a possible future—youth meditating great things! Walk along the streets of Lodging-land—there are miles of such streets—and consider with trembling that the dingy houses contain thousands of young people—boys and girls—who have come to the city of golden pavements to make—not a fortune, unless that happens as well—but their name. In the long struggle before the lowest rung of the ladder is reached they endure hardness, but they complain not. Everything is going to be made up to them in the splendid time to come.

Something more than a year ago two such young people came up from the country, and found shelter in a London lodging-house, where they could work and study until success should arrive. They were boy and girl, brother and sister—twins. They had very little money, and could afford no more than one sitting-room. Therefore, one worked in the sitting-room and the other in a bedroom, because their occupations demanded solitude. The one in the sitting-room was the girl. She was engaged in the pursuit of poetry:

she made verses continually, every day. Unless she was reading verse, she was either making, or polishing, or devising verses. Of all pursuits in the world this is at once the most absorbing and the most delightful. It is also, with the greater part of these who follow it, the most useless. Thomas the Rhymer sits down and takes his pen: it is nine of the clock. He considers: he writes: he scratches out: he writes again: he corrects again: after ten minutes or so, he looks up. It is three in the afternoon: the luncheon hour is past: the morning is gone: all he has to show for the six golden hours, when an account of them is demanded, will be a single stanza of a ballade. And perhaps not a single editor will look at it. To Effie Wilmot, the girl-twin, thus engaged morning after morning, the hours become moments and the days minutes. The result and outcome of her labours you have already learned. But she was young, and she lived in hope. A few more weeks, and the great man, her patron, would have satisfied that whim of wishing to be thought a poet of society. Strange that one who painted pictures of such wonderful beauty, who wrote such charming stories in such endless variety—stories quaint and bizarre, stories pathetic, stories humorous—should so condescend! What could a few simple verses—such as hers—do to increase his fame? However, that was nearly over. She felt quite happy and light-hearted: as happy as if, like other poets, she was writing things that would appear with her own name: she pursued the light and airy fancies of her brain, capturing one or two, chaining them in the prison of her rhymes, which, of course, were set to the old-new tunes affected by the little poets of the day. If they have got no message to deliver, they can at least come on the stage and repeat over again the old things clad in dress revived. We can keep on dressing up in the poet's habit until the poet himself shall come along.

Effie worked on, sitting at the window. Poets can work anywhere, though, of course, they ought to sit habitually on the sides of hills, with hanging woods and mountain-streams and waterfalls. But they can work just as well in a mean London lodging, such as this where Effie sat, looking out, if she looked through the curtain, upon a most commonplace street. We can all—common spirits as well as poets—rise above our streets and houses and our dingy setting—otherwise there would be no work done at all. Nay, if we were all cockered up, and daintily surrounded with things æsthetic and artistic and beautiful, I believe we should be so happy that nobody would ever do anything. The poet would murmur his thoughts in indolent rhyme by the fireside: the musician would drop his fingers among the notes, echoing faintly and imperfectly the music in his soul—all for his own enjoyment: the story-teller would tell his stories to his wife: the dramatist would make plots without words for his children to act: the painter would half sketch his visions and leave them unfinished. Art would die.

No such temptations were offered to Effie. The æsthetic movement had not touched that ground-floor front. The shaky round table stood under the flaring gas which every night made her head ache; the chiffonier contained in its recesses the tea and sugar and bread and butter, and, when the money ran to such luxuries, her jam or her honey or her oranges. There was one easy-chair and one arm-chair; and before the window a small square table, which had, at least, the merit of being firm; and at this she wrote. Everybody knows this kind of room perfectly.

The poetic workshop is always kept locked. No poet ever tells of the terrific struggles he has to encounter before he finally subdues his thought and compels it to walk or run in double harness of rhythm and rhyme. No poet ever confesses how he sometimes has to let that thought go because he cannot subdue it—nay, the same discomfiture has been reported of those who, like M. Jourdain, speak in prose. And no poet ever shows, as a painter will readily show us, the first sketch, the first rough draft of a poem, the unfinished lines, the first feeble attempts at the rhythmic expression of a great thought. Let us respect the mystery of the craft—have we not all dabbled in verse and essayed to play upon the scrannel-pipe?

It was towards noon, however, that Effie was disturbed by the arrival of a visitor. The event was so unusual—so unprecedented even—that no instructions had ever been given to the lodging-house servant in the art of introducing callers. She therefore opened the door, and put in her head—'A gentleman, Miss'—and went downstairs, leaving the gentleman to walk in if he pleased.

'You, Mr. Feilding?' Effie cried, springing to her feet. 'Oh! This is, indeed——'

The great man took her hand. 'My dear child,' he said, 'I have been thinking over our conversation of the other day. I am of course, only anxious to be of service to you and to your brother, and so I thought I would call.' He was quite magnificent in his fur-lined coat, and he was very tall and big, so that he seemed to fill up the whole room. But he had an unusual air of hesitation. 'I thought,' he repeated, 'that I would call. Yes——'

The girl sat with her hands in her lap, waiting.

'You remember what I told you about—the—the verses which you sometimes bring me——'

'Oh! Yes. I remember. It is so kind of you, Mr. Feilding, so very kind and noble——' For the moment the dazzling prospect of seeing her verses acknowledged as her own in place of seeing them adopted by the Editor, made her believe that none but a truly noble person could do such a thing.

'I mean to begin even sooner than I had intended. It is true that when I took your verses I made them my own by those little touches and corrections which, as you know very well, distinguish true poetry from its imitation'—It was not until he was gone that Effie remembered that not a single alteration had ever been made. So great is the power of the human voice that for the moment she listened and acquiesced, subdued and ashamed of herself—'At last, my young friend, the time for alteration and improvement is past. You can now stand alone—your verses signed—if, of course, we remain, as I hope, on the same friendly relations.'

'Oh!' she murmured.

'Enough. We understand each other. Your brother, you told me, is at work on a play—a romantic drama.'

'Yes. He has finished it. He has been at work upon it for two years, thinking of nothing else all day.'

Mr. Feilding nodded approval.

'That is the way,' he said heartily, 'to produce good work. Perfect—absolute—devotion—regardless of any earthly consider ation. Art—Art—before all else. And now it is done?'

'Yes; he is copying it out.'

'Effie'—he suddenly changed the subject—'you have never told me of your resources. Tell me! I do not ask out of idle curiosity. That you are not rich I know——'

'No, we are not rich. We have a little—a thousand pounds apiece—and we have resolved to live on that, and on what we can get besides, until we have made our way. We have no rich relations to help us. My father is a country clergyman with a small living. We came to town so that Archie could get treatment for his hip. He is better now, and we shall stay altogether if we can only hold on.'

'A thousand pounds each. That is seventy pounds a year, I suppose?'

'Yes. But during the last twelve months you have given me a hundred pounds for my verses—three pounds for every poem, and there were thirty-three altogether in the volume—"Voices and Echoes," you know.'

The poet who had published these verses did not change colour or show any sign of emotion in the presence of the poet who had written them. He nodded his head. 'Yes,' he said, 'on a hundred and seventy pounds a year you can live—on seventy you would starve. Where is your brother?'

'He works in his bedroom. It is the room behind, on the same floor. My room is upstairs.'

'He requires, I suppose, good food, wine, and certain luxuries?'

'When we can afford them. Since you took my verses we have been able to buy things.'

'Your money is well expended. I should like to see your brother, Effie.'

'I will take you to him,' she said. But she hesitated and blushed. 'Oh! Mr. Feilding, Archie knows nothing about the—

The Ancestor

The Chieftain's Daughter

The Legacy

Armorel's Cottage

the volumes, you know! He sees only the verses in the paper. And he only knows that you have been so kind as to take them. Don't tell him anything else.'

'Your secret, Effie,' he replied generously, 'is safe with me. He shall not know it from my lips.'

She thanked him. Again, it was not until he was gone that Effie remembered that he could not possibly reveal that fact to her brother.

She led him into the room, at the back of which was her brother's study and bedroom as well.

Her brother might have been herself, save for a slight manly growth upon the upper lip, and for the pale cheek of ill health. The same large forehead overhanging the face, eyes sunken but as bright as his sister's, the same sensitive lips were his. A finer face than his sister's, and stronger, but not so sweet. Beside his chair a pair of crutches proclaimed tha the was a cripple. Before him was a table, at which he was writing. There were on the table, besides his writing materials, a number of little dolls, some of which were arranged in groups, while others were lying about unused. He was copying his finished play: as he copied it he played the scenes with the dolls and spoke the dialogue. The dolls were his characters: there was not a single scene or change of the grouping which this conscientious young dramatist had not rehearsed over and over again, until every line of the dialogue had its own stage picture, clear and distinct in his mind.

'You are Mr. Feilding?' he asked, rising with some difficulty. 'I have heard so much of you from Effie. It is a great honour to have a call from you.'

'I take a deep interest,' the great man replied, 'in anything that concerns Miss Effie Wilmot. I have been able—I believe you know—to give her some assistance and advice in her work. Oh!'—he waved his hand to deprecate any expressions of gratitude—'I have done very little—very little indeed. Now, about yourself. I learn from your sister that you have ambitions—you would become a dramatist?'

'I have no other ambition. It is my only dream.'

'A very good dream indeed. And you have made, I am told, a start—a maiden effort—a preliminary flight to try your wings. You have written your first attempt at a play?'

'Yes. It is here. It is finished.'

'Tell me, briefly, the plot.'

Some young dramatists mar their plot in getting it out. This young man had taken the trouble to write out first a rough outline of his piece and next a complete scenario with every situation detailed. These he read to his visitor one after the other.

'Yes,' said Mr. Feilding, when he had finished; 'there is something in the idea of the play. Perhaps not a completely novel motif. A good deal might be said as to the arrangement of the scenes. And one or two of the characters might—but these are details. Remains to find out how the dialogue goes. Will you read me a scene or two?'

The dramatist read. As he read he might have observed in the eyes of his listener a growing eagerness, as of one who vehemently yearns to get possession of something—his neighbour's vineyard, for example, or his solitary ewe lamb. But the reader did not observe this. He was wholly wrapped in his piece: he threw his soul into the reading: he was anxious only that his words and his situations should produce the best effect upon his hearer.

'Yes, yes; your dialogue, unhappily, shows the want of skill common to the beginner,' said Mr. Feilding, when he had finished. 'It will have to be completely rewritten. As it stands now, the play would be simply killed by it, in spite of the situations, which, with some alterations, are really pretty good—pretty good for a first effort.'

'You don't think, then—that——' the dramatist's voice broke down. Consider: for two long years he had done nothing but cast, recast, write, rewrite this play. He had dreamed all this time of success with this play. And now—now—the very first critic—and that the most accomplished man of the day—no less than Mr. Alec Feilding—told him that the play would not be received unless the dialogue was entirely rewritten. He *could* not rewrite the dialogue. It was a part of himself. As well ask him to remake his own face or to reconstruct his legs. His face fell: his cheeks grew pale: his eyes filled with unmanly tears.

'I am truly sorry, believe me,' said the critic, 'to throw cold water on your hopes. I have been myself an aspirant. Yet'—he hesitated in his kindliness—'why encourage illusive expectations? The play as it is—I say, as it is only—must be pronounced totally unfit for the stage. No manager would think of it for a moment.'

'Then I may as well throw it on the fire? And all my work wasted!'

'Nay—not wasted. Good work—true work—is never wasted. You ought to have learned much—very much—from this two years' labour. And, as for putting it into the fire'—he laughed genially—'I believe I can show you a better way than that. Look here, Archie—I call you by your Christian name because I have so often talked about you: we are old friends—I should be really sorry to think that you had actually lost all your time. Give me this play: I will take it—skeleton, scenario, dialogue—all, just as it is—the mere rough, crude, shapeless thing that it is. I will buy it of you—useless as it is. I will give you fifty pounds down for it, and it shall become my property—my own, absolutely. I shall then, perhaps, recast and rewrite the play from beginning to end. When I have made a play out of it worth putting on the stage—when, in short, I have made it my own play—I may possibly bring it out—possibly. Most likely, however, not. There's a chance for you, Archie, such as you will never get again! Fifty pounds down—think of that! Fifty pounds!'

The dramatist laid his hand, for reply, upon his papers.

'If it should ever be brought out,' this good Samaritan went on, 'you will come and see it acted. What a splendid lesson it will be for you in the art of writing drama!'

The dramatist's fingers tightened on his manuscript.

'Of course you must consider your sister,' the considerate critic continued. 'She has been able to make a few pounds of late, having been so fortunate as to attract the interest of . . . one who is not wholly without influence. Should that interest fail or be withdrawn you might have—both of you—to suffer much privation. The luxuries which you now enjoy would be impossible—and——'

'Oh, you kill me!' cried the unfortunate youth.

'Shall I leave you for the present? My offer is always open—on the condition of secrecy—one is bound to keep business transactions secret. I will leave you now. There is no hurry. Think it over carefully and send me an answer.'

He went out and shut the door. The young dramatist, I am ashamed to say, fell to tears and weeping over the destruction of his hopes.

'Effie,' said Mr. Feilding, 'I have talked with your brother. He has read some of the play to me——'

'And you think?' she asked him eagerly.

He shook his head mournfully. 'The boy has much to learn—very much. Meantime, the play itself is worthless—quite worthless.'

'Oh! Poor boy! And he has built so much upon it.'

'Yes—they all do at the outset. Mind, Effie, he is a clever boy: he will do. Meantime, he must study.'

'Oh! Poor Archie! Poor boy!'

'It seems hard, doesn't it, not to succeed all at once? Yet Browning and Tennyson and Thackeray were all well on for forty before they succeeded. Why should he despair? Meantime I have made him a little offer.'

'Oh! Mr. Feilding, you are always so good.

'I have offered to give him fifty pounds—down—and to take this rough unlicked thing he calls a Play. If I find time I shall, perhaps, rewrite the whole, and put it on the stage. It will then, of course, be my own—my own, Effie. Good-bye, child. I have not forgotten our talk—or my promise—if we remain on friendly relations.'

He went away. Effie sank into a chair. What she had done with her own work had never seemed to her half so terrible as what was now proposed to be done with her brother's work.

She crept into his room. He sat with his head in his hands, most mournful of bards since the world began.

'Archie, I know—I know; he has told me. Oh! Archie—do you think it is true?'

'He says so, Effie. He says it is worthless.'

'Yet he will give you fifty pounds.'

'That is to please you—for your sake. The thing is worthless—no manager would look at it.'

'Yet—fifty pounds! Why should Mr. Feilding give fifty pounds—a whole fifty pounds—for a worthless play? Archie, don't do it—don't let him have it; wait a little—we will ask somebody else. Oh! I could tell you something. Wait—tell him, if you must say anything, that you will think it over.'

When Effie turned over the pages of the next number of *The Muses Nine*, she found, first of all, her own verses in the Editor's column with his name at the bottom. This sight, which had formerly made her so proud, now filled her with shame. The generous promise of the future failed to awaken in her any glow of hope. For the very words with which her only editor had beguiled her of her verses—the plea that they were worthless, and must be rewritten—he had used to her brother. And as her poems had never been rewritten, so would Archie's play, she felt sure, be presented without a single alteration, with the name of Mr. Alec Feilding as author. That week she took no verses to the studio-study.

And a certain paragraph in the same columns perused by this suspicious young woman brought rage—nothing short of rage—into her heart. No! not her brother, as well as herself! It ran thus: 'I have always been under the impression that the dearth of good plays is due to nothing else in the world than the fact that the good men who ought to be writing them all run off into the domain of fiction. It is a pleasant country—that of Fable Land. I have been there, and I hope to go there again and make a long stay. But Play Land—that is also a pleasant country. I have been there lately, and I hope to demonstrate that a good play may still be produced in the English tongue—a good and original play. In short, I have written a romantic drama, of which all I can say at present is that it lies finished, in my fireproof safe, and that a certain actor-manager will probably play the title-rôle before many moons have waxed and waned.'

'No,' said Effie, crumpling up the paper. 'You have not got Archie's romantic drama yet.'

CHAPTER VIII

ALL ABOUT MYSELF

'You have kept this promise, then.' Armorel welcomed her old friend with eyes of kindness and lips of smiles. 'Do you ever think of the promise that you broke? Effie, dear'—this young lady was the only other occupant of the room—'this is Mr. Roland Lee—my first friend and my first master. He knew me long ago, in Samson, in the days of which I have told you. We have memories of our own—memories such as make the old friendships impossible to be dissolved—whatever happens. Roland, you first put a pencil into my hand and taught me how to use it. In return, I used to play old-fashioned tunes in the evening. And you first put thoughts into my head. Before you came my head was filled with phantoms, which had neither voice nor shape. What am I to do now in return for such a gift?' She gave him both her hands, and her face was so glowing, her eyes so soft yet serious withal, her voice so full of tenderness—that the luckless painter stood confused and overwhelmed. How had he deserved such a reception?

'This evening,' she went on, 'we are going to talk about nobody but myself, and about nothing but my own affairs. Effie, you will be horribly bored. It is five years since I had such a chance. Because, my dear, though you have the best will in the world, and would talk to me about old times if you could, you did not know me when I lived on Samson in the Scilly Islands—and Roland did. That is, if he still remembers Samson.'

'I remember every day on Samson: every blade of grass on the island: every boulder and every crag.'

'And every talk we had in those days?—all the things you told me?'

'I remember, as well, a girl who has so changed, so grown——'

'So much the better. Then we can talk just as we used to do. I thought you would somehow remember the girl, Roland.' She looked up again, smiling. Then she hesitated, and went on slowly: 'Yet I was afraid, this morning, that you might have forgotten one of the two who wandered about the island together.'

'I could never forget you, Armorel.'

'I meant—the other—Roland.'

He made no reply. In his evening dress—which was full of creases, as if it had not been put on for a very long time—he looked a little less forlorn than in the shabby old brown-velvet jacket; he had brushed his hair—nay, he had even had it cut and trimmed: but there still hung about him the look of waste: his eyes were melancholy: his bearing was dejected: he spoke with hesitation: he was even shy, like a schoolboy. Effie noted these things, and wondered. And she observed, besides, not only that his coat was creased, but that his shirt was frayed at the cuffs, and torn in the front. In fact, the young man, in dropping out of society, had, as a natural consequence, neglected his wardrobe and allowed his linen to run to seed unrebuked. Every man who has been a bachelor—most of us have—remembers how shirts behave when the eye of the master is once taken off them.

He was shy because the atmosphere of the drawing-room, so

dainty, so luxurious, so womanly, was strange to him. Three years and more had passed since he had been in such a room. He was also shy because this splendid creature, this girl dressed in silk and lovely lace, this miracle of girls, called herself Armorel, his once simple rustic maid of Samson Isle. Further, he was ashamed because this girl remembered him as he was in the good old days, when his face was turned to the summit of the mountain and his feet were on the upward slope.

Armorel had placed on the table a portfolio full of drawings.

'Now for myself,' she said, gaily. 'Roland, you are an artist. You must look at my drawings. Here are the best I have done. I have had many masters since you, but none that taught me so much in so short a time. Do you remember when you first found out that I could hold a pencil? You were very patient then, Master. Be lenient now.'

'I had a very apt pupil,' he began, turning over the drawings. 'These need no leniency. These are very good indeed. You have had other and better masters.'

'I have had other masters, it is true. I have done my best Roland—to grow.'

He dropped his eyes. But he continued to turn over the sketches. The drawings showed, at least, that natural aptitude which may be genius and may be that imitation of genius which is difficult to distinguish from the real gift. Many painters with no more natural aptitude than Armorel have risen to be Royal Academicians.

'But these are very good indeed,' Roland repeated, with emphasis. 'You have, indeed, worked well, and you have the true feeling.'

'Do you remember, Roland, that day when we talked about the Perfect Woman? No, I see by your eyes that you have forgotten. But I remember. I will not tell you all. One thing she had done: she had trained her eye and her hand. She knew what was good in Art, and was not carried away by any follies or fashions. I did not understand then what you meant by follies and fashions. But I am wiser now. I have been training eye and hand. I think I know a good picture, or a good statue, or a good work in any Art. Do not think me conceited, Master. I have been obedient to your instructions—that is all.'

'You have the soul of an artist, Armorel,' said her Master. 'But yet—I fear—I think—you have missed the supreme gift. You are not a great artist.'

'No, I can grow no higher in painting. I have learned my own limitations. If it is only to understand and to worship the Great Masters it is worth while to get so far. Are you satisfied with your pupil?'

For a moment the old look came back to Roland's eyes. 'You are the best of pupils,' he said. 'But I might have expected so much. Tell me how you succeeded in getting away from Samson?'

She told him, briefly, how the Ancient Lady died, how she found the family treasure, and how she had resolved to go away and learn: how she found masters and guardians: how she lived in Florence, Dresden, Paris: how she worked unceasingly. 'I remembered, always, Roland, your picture of the Perfect Woman.'

'Could I—I—have told you things that have made you—what you are?' It seemed as if another man had given the girl this excellent advice. Not himself—quite another man.

'Effie, dear,' Armorel turned to her, 'you do not understand. I must tell you. Five years ago, when I lived on Samson, a girl so ignorant that it makes me tremble to think what might have happened—there came to the island a young gentleman who was so kind as to take this ignorant girl—me—in hand, and to fill her empty head with all kinds of great and noble thoughts. He was an artist by profession. Oh! an artist filled with ardour and with ambition. He would be satisfied with nothing short of the best: he taught me that none of us ought to be satisfied till we have attained our full stature, and grown as tall as we possibly can. It made that ignorant girl's heart glow only to hear him talk, because she had never heard such talk before. Then he left her, and came back no more. But presently the chance came to this girl, as you have heard, and she was able to leave the island and go where she could find masters and teachers. It is five years ago. And always, every day, Roland'—her lip quivered—'I have said to myself, "My first master is growing taller—taller—taller—every day—I must grow as tall as I can, or else when I meet him again I shall be too insignificant for him to notice." Always I have thought how I should meet him again. So tall, so great, so wonderful!'

Effie remarked that while Armorel addressed Roland she did not look at him until the last words, when she turned and faced him with eyes running over. The man's head dropped: his fingers played with the drawings: he made no reply.

'In the evening,' Armorel went on, 'we used to have music. I played only the old-fashioned tunes then that Justinian Tryeth taught me—do you remember the tunes, Roland? I will play one for you again.' She took a violin out of the case and began to tune the strings. 'This is my old fiddle. It has been Justinian's—and his father's before him. I have had other instruments since then, but I love the old fiddle best.' She drew her bow across the strings. 'I can play much better now, Roland. And I have much better music; but I will play only the old tunes, because I want you to remember quite clearly those two who walked and talked and sailed together. It is so easy for you to forget that young man. But I remember him very well indeed.' She drew the bow across the strings again. 'Now we are in the old room, while the old people are sitting round the fire. Effie, dear, put the shade over the lamp and turn it low—so—now we are all sitting in the firelight, just as it used to be on Samson—see the red light dancing about the walls. It fills your eyes and makes them glow, Roland. Oh! we are back again. What are you thinking of, artist, while the music falls upon your ears?—while I play—what shall I play? "Dissembling Love," which others call "The Lost Heart"?' She played it with the old spirit, but far more than the old delicacy and feeling. 'You remember that, Roland? Do you hear the lapping of the waves in Porth Bay and the breakers over Shark Point? Or is it too rustic a ditty? I will play you something better, but still the old tunes.' She played first 'Prince Rupert's March,' and then 'The Saraband'—great and lofty airs to one who can play them greatly. While she played Effie watched. In Armorel's eyes she read a purpose. This was no mere play. The man she called her master listened, sitting at the table, the sketches spread out before him, ill at ease, and as one in a troubled dream.

'Do you see him again, that young man?' Armorel asked. 'It makes one happy only to think of such a young man. He knew the dangers before him. "The Way of Wealth," he said once, "and the Way of Pleasure draw men as if with ropes." But he was so strong and steadfast. Nothing would turn him from his way. Not Pleasure, not Wealth, not anything mean or low. There was never any young man so noble. Oh! Do you remember him, Roland? Tell me—tell me—do you remember him?'

Over the pictures on the table he bowed his head. But he made no reply. Then Effie, watching the glittering tears in Armorel's eyes and the bowed head of the man, stole softly out of the room and closed the door.

Armorel put down her fiddle. She drew nearer to the man. His head sank lower. She stood over him, tall and queenly, as the Muse stood over Alfred de Musset. She laid her hand upon his shoulder.

'That old spirit is not dead, but sleeping, Roland. You have not driven it forth. It is your own still. You have only silenced its voice for a while. You think that you have killed it; but you remember it still. Thank God! it has been only sleeping. If it were dead you would not remember. Let it wake again. Oh! Roland—let it wake again—again. Oh! Roland—Roland—my friend and Master——' She could say no more.

The man raised his head. It is a shameful and a terrible thing to see the face of a man who is disgraced and conscious of his shame. Perhaps it is worse to see the face of a man who is disgraced and is unconscious of his shame. He looked round, and saw the tears in the girl's eyes and the quivering of her lips.

'The man you remember,' he said hoarsely, 'is dead and buried. He died three years ago and more. Another man—a poor and mean creature—walks about in his shape. He is unworthy to be in your presence. Suffer him to go, and think of him no longer.'

'Not another man, because you remember the former. Roland, come back, my old friend; come back!'

'It is too late.' But he wavered.

'It is never too late. Oh! I wonder—was it the Way of Pleasure or was it the Way of Wealth?'

'Do I look,' he asked bitterly, 'as if it was the Way of Pleasure?'

'It is not too late, Roland. You have sinned against yourself. If it were too late you would be happy after the kind of those who can live in sin and be happy. Since you are not happy, it is not too late. The doors of heaven stand open night and day for all.'

'You talk the old language, Armorel.'

'It is the language of my soul. I will say the same thing in any tongue you please, so that you understand me.'

'To go back—to begin all over again—to go on as if the last three years had never been——'

'Yes—yes—as if they had never been! That is best. As if they had never been.'

'Armorel, do you know,' he asked her quickly—'do you know the thing—the Awful Thing—that I have done?'

'Do not tell me. Never tell me.'

'Some day, I think I must. What shall I say, now?'

'Say that your footsteps are turned in the old way, Roland.'

'He pushed back the chair and stood up. Now, if they had been measured, he would have proved four inches and a half taller than the girl, for he was half an inch short of six feet, and she was exactly five feet seven. Yet as they stood face to face, it seemed to him—and to her as well—as if she towered over him by as many inches as separate the tallest woman from the smallest man. Nature thus accommodates herself to the mental condition of the moment.

The small man, however, did a very strange thing. He drew forth a pocket-book and took from it what Armorel perceived to be a cheque. This he deliberately tore across twice, and threw the fragments into the fire.

'You do not understand this act, Armorel. It is the turning of the footstep.'

She took his hand and pressed it. 'I pray,' she said, 'that the way may prove less thorny than you think!'

Nature, again accommodating herself, caused the small, mean man to grow suddenly several inches. There was still a goodly difference between the two, but it was lessened. More than that, the man continued to grow; and his face was brighter, and his eyes less haggard.

'I will go now, Armorel,' he said.

'You will come again—soon?'

'Not yet. I will come again, when the shame of the present belongs to the past.'

'No. You shall come often. But of past or present we will speak no more. Tell me, in your own good time, Roland, how you fare. But do not desert your old pupil. Come to see me often.'

He bowed his head and went away.

'Effie,' said Armorel, presently, 'I cannot tell you what all this means.'

'It means a man who has fallen,' said the girl, wise with poetic instinct. 'Anyone could see failure and shame written on his face. It ought to be a noble face, but something has gone out of it. You knew him long ago—when he was different—and you tried to bring him to his old self. Oh! Armorel—you are wonderful—you were his better spirit—you were his muse—calling him back.'

She laid her hand in Armorel's. They stood together in silence. Then Armorel spoke.

'I feared it was quite another man—a new man—a stranger that I had found. But it was not. It was the same man after all.'

Effie stooped and picked up a fragment of paper lying on the hearth. 'Mr. Feilding's signature,' she said, unthinking. At times, when one is moved, trifles sometimes seem to acquire importance.

'That? It is a part of a cheque which he tore up. Effie, dear—it was good of you to go away and leave us when you did. Perhaps he would not have spoken so freely if you had been here. Oh! he is the same man, after all. He has come back to me. Effie, tell me; but you know no more than I. If you once loved a man, and if you suffered the thought of him to lie in your heart for years, and if you filled him with all the virtues that there are, and if he grew in your heart to be a knight perfect at all points——'

'Well, Armorel?' For she stopped, and Effie took her hand.

'Oh! Effie,' she replied, with glowing cheeks; 'could you ever afterwards love another man? Could you ever cease to love that man of your imagination? Could any meaner man content you? For my part—never!—never!—never!'

CHAPTER IX

TO MAKE HIM HAPPY

'Shall we discuss Mr. Feilding any longer?' Armorel asked, with a little impatience. 'It really seems as if we had nothing to talk about but the perfections of this incomparable person.' It was in the evening. Armorel had discovered, already, that the evenings spent at home in the society of her companion were both long and dull; that they had nothing to talk about; that Zoe regarded every single subject from a point of view which was not her own; and that both in conversation and in personal intercourse she was having a great deal more than she desired of Mr. Alec Feilding. Therefore, she was naturally a little impatient. One cannot every evening go and sit alone in the study: one cannot play the violin all the evening: and one cannot reduce a companion to absolute silence.

Zoe, who had been talking into the fire from her cushions, turned her fluffy head, opened her blue eyes wide, and looked, not reproachfully but sorrowfully and with wonder, at a girl who could hear too much about Alec Feilding.

'Let me talk—just a little—sometimes—of my best friend, Armorel, dear. If you only knew what Alec has been to me and to my lost lover—my Jerome!'

'Forgive me, Zoe. Go on talking about him.'

'How quiet and cosy,' she murmured, in reply, 'this room is in the evening! It makes one feel virtuous only to think of the cold wind and the cold people outside. This heaven is surely a reward for the righteous. It is enough only to lie in the warmth without talking. But the time and the place invite confidences. Armorel, I am going to repose a great confidence in you—a secret plan of my own. And you are so very, very sympathetic when you please, dear child—especially when Effie is here—I wonder if she is worth it?—that you might spare me a little of your sympathy.'

'My dear Zoe'—Armorel felt a touch of remorse—she had been unsympathetic—'you shall have all there is to spare. But what kind of sympathy do you want? You were talking of Mr. Feilding—not of yourself.'

'Yes—and that is of myself in a way. I know you will not misunderstand me, dear. You will not imagine that I am—well, in love with Alec, when I confess to you that I think a very great deal about him.'

'I never thought so, at all,' said Armorel.

Zoe's eyes opened for a moment and gleamed. It was a doubtful saying. Why should not she be in love with Alec, or Alec with her? But Armorel knew nothing about love.

'When a woman has loved once, dear,' she murmured, 'her heart is gone. My love-passages,' she put her handkerchief to her eyes—to some women the drawing-room is the stage—'my love-story, dear, is finished and done. My heart is in the grave with Jerome. But this you cannot understand. I think so much of Alec—first, because he has been all goodness to me; and, next, because he is so wonderfully clever.'

'Talk about him, Zoe, as long as you please.'

'If he had been an ordinary man,' she went on, 'I should have been equally grateful, I suppose. But there it would have ended. To be under a debt of gratitude to such a man as Alec makes one long to do something in return. And, besides, there are so very,

very few good men in the world that it does one good only to talk about them.'

'I suppose that Mr. Feilding is really a man of great genius,' said Armorel. 'I confess he seems to me rather ponderous in his talk—may I say, dull? From genius one expects the unexpected.'

'Dull? Oh, no! A little constrained in his manner. That comes from his excessive sensibility. But dull?—oh, no!'

'He seemed dull at the theatre last night.'

'It was a curious coincidence meeting him there, was it not?'

'I thought you must have told him that you were going.'

'No, no; quite a coincidence. And he so seldom goes to a theatre. The badness of the acting, he says, irritates his nerves to such a degree that it sometimes spoils his work for a week. And yet he is actually going to bring out a play himself. There is a paragraph in the paper about it—his own paper. Give it to me, dear; it is on the sofa. Thank you.' She read the paragraph, which we already know. 'What do you think of that, Armorel?'

'Isn't it rather arrogant—about good men turning out good work?'

'My dear, genius can afford to be arrogant. True genius is always impatient of small people and of stupidities. It suffers its contempt to be seen, and that makes the stupidities cry out about arrogance. Even the most stupid can cry out, you see. But think. He is going to add a new wreath to his brow. He is already known as a poet, a novelist, a painter, an essayist, and now he is to become a dramatist. He really is the cleverest man in the whole world.'

Armorel expressed none of the admiration that was expected. She was wondering whether, if Mr. Feilding had not been quite so clever, he might not have been quite so heavy and didactic in conversation. Less clever people, perhaps, are more prodigal of their cleverness, and give away some of it in conversation. Perhaps the very clever want it all for their books.

'I said I would give you his poems,' Zoe continued. 'I bought the book for you—the second series, which is better than the first. It is on the piano, dear; that little parcel, thank you.' She opened the parcel and disclosed a dainty little volume in white and gold. It was illustrated by a small etching of the poet's head for a frontispiece. It was printed in beautiful new type on thick paper—the kind called hand-made—the edges left ragged. There were about a hundred and twenty pages, and on every two pages there was a single poem. These were not arranged in any order or sequence of thought. They were all separate. The poet showed knowledge of contemporary manners in serving up so small a dish of verse. Fifty or sixty short poems is quite as much as the reader of poetry will stand in these days.

Armorel turned over the pages and began to read them. Strange! How could a man so ponderous, so pompous in his conceit, so dogmatic, so self-conscious, write such pretty, easy-flowing numbers? The metres fitted the subject; the rhymes were apt, the cadence true, the verses tripped light and graceful like a maiden dancing.

'How could such a man,' she cried, 'get a touch so light? It is truly wonderful.'

'I told you so, dear. He is altogether wonderful.'

She went on reading. Presently she cried out, 'Why! he writes like a woman. Only a woman could have written these lines.' She read them out. 'It is a woman's hand, and a woman's way of thinking.'

'That shows his genius. No one except Alec—or a woman—could have said just that thing in just that manner.'

Armorel closed the volume. 'I think,' she said, 'that I like a man to write like a man and a woman like a woman.'

'Then,' said Zoe, 'how is a novelist to make a woman talk?'

'He makes his women talk like women if he can. But when he speaks himself it must be with the voice of a man. In these poems it is the poet who speaks, not any character, man or woman.'

'You will like the poems better as you read them. They will grow upon you. And you will find the poet himself—not a woman, but a man—in his verses. It helps one so much to understand the verses when you know the poet. I think I could almost understand Browning if I had ever known him. Think of Alec when you read his verses.'

'Yes,' said Armorel, still without enthusiasm.

'You said we were talking about nothing else, dear,' Zoe went on. 'I talk so much of him because I respect and revere him so much. I have known Alec a long time'—she lay back with her head turned from her companion, talking softly into the fire, as if she was communing with herself. 'He is, though you do not understand it yet, a man of the most highly strung and sensitive nature. The true reason why he talks ponderously—as you call it, Armorel—is that he is conscious of the traps into which this very sensitiveness of his may lead him: for instance, he may say, before persons unworthy of his confidence, things which they would most likely misunderstand. It is simply wicked to cast pearls before swine. A poet, more than any other man, must be quite sure of his audience before he gives himself away. I assure you, when Alec feels himself alone with his intimates—a very little circle—his talk is brilliant.'

'We are unlucky, then,' said Armorel, still without enthusiasm.

'Another thing may make him seem dull. He is always preoccupied, always thinking about his work: his mind is overcharged.'

'I thought he was always in society—a great diner-out?'

'He is. Society brings him relief. The inanities of social

intercourse rest his brain. Without this rest he would be crushed.'

'I see,' said Armorel, coldly.

'Then there is that other side of him—of which you know nothing. My dear, he is constantly thinking of others. His private life—but I must not tell too much. Not only the cleverest man in London, but the best.'

Armorel felt guilty. She had not, hitherto, looked upon this phœnix with the reverence which was due to so great a creature. Nay, she did not like him. She was repelled rather than attracted by him. She liked him less every time she met him. And this was oftener than she desired. Somehow or other, they were always meeting. On some pretext or other he was always calling. And certainly for the last few days Zoe was unable to talk about anything else. The genius, the greatness of this man seemed to overwhelm her.

'And now, my dear,' she went on, still talking about him, 'for my little confidences. I have a great scheme in my head. Oh! a very great scheme indeed.' She turned round and sat up, looking Armorel full in the face. Her eyes under her fluffy hair were large and luminous, when she lifted them. Oftener, they were large but sleepy eyes. Now they were quite bright. She was wide awake and she was in earnest. 'I have spoken to no one but you about it as yet. Perhaps you and I can manage it all by ourselves.'

'What is it?'

'You and I, dear, you and I, we two—we can be so associated and bound up in the life of the poet-painter as to be for ever joined with his name. Petrarch and Laura are not more closely connected than we may be with Alec Feilding, if you only join with me.'

'First tell me what it is—this plan of yours.'

'It is nothing less than just to relieve him, once for all, from his business cares.'

'Has he business cares?'

'They take up his precious time. They weigh upon his mind. Why should such a man have any business at all to look after?'

'Well, but,' said Armorel, refusing to rise to this tempting bait, 'why does such a man allow himself to have business cares, if they worry him?'

'It is the conduct of his journal, my dear.'

'But other authors and painters do not conduct journals. Why should he? I believe that successful writers and artists make very large incomes. If he is so successful, why does he trouble about managing a paper? That is certainly work that can be done by a man of inferior brain.'

'You are so matter-of-fact, dear. The paper is his own, and he thinks, I suppose, that nobody but himself could edit the thing.

Leave poor Alec one or two human weaknesses. He may think this, and yet make no allowance for his own shrinking and sensitive nature.'

Certainly Armorel had seen no indications in this poet-painter of the shrinking nature. It was very carefully concealed.

'Of course,' Zoe continued, 'you hardly know him. But his genius you do know. And the business worries that are inseparable from a journal are a serious hindrance to his higher work. Believe me, dear, even if you do not understand why it should be so.'

'I can very well believe it—I only ask why Mr. Feilding alone, among authors and painters, should hamper himself with such worries.'

'Well, dear—there they are. And I have formed a plan—Oh!'—she clasped her hands and opened her eyes wide—'such a plan! The best and the cleverest plan in the world for the best and the cleverest man in the world! But I want your help.'

'What can I do?'

'I will tell you. First of all. You must remember that Alec is the sole proprietor, as well as the editor of this journal—*The Muses Nine*. It is his property. He created it. But the business management of the paper worries him. My plan, Armorel—my plan'—she spoke and looked most impressive—'will relieve him altogether of the work.'

'Yes—and how do I come into your plan?'

'This way. I have found out, through a person of business, that if he would sell a share—say a quarter, or an eighth—of his paper he would be able to put the business part of it into paid hands—the people who do nothing else. Now, Armorel, we will buy that share—you and I between us will buy it. You shall advance the whole of the money, and I will pay you back half. The price will be nothing to you. That is, it will be a great deal, because the investment will be such a splendid thing, and the returns will be so brilliant. You will increase your income enormously, and you will have the satisfaction'—she paused, because, though she was herself more animated, earnest, and eloquent with voice and eyes, and though she threw so much persuasion into her manner, the tell-tale face of the girl showed no kindling light of response at all—'the satisfaction,' she continued, 'of feeling that such a help to Literature and Art will make us both immortal.'

Armorel made no reply. She was considering the proposition coldly, and it was one of those things which must be considered without enthusiasm.

'As for money,' Zoe continued, with one more attempt to awaken a responsive fire, 'I have found out what will be wanted. For three thousand five hundred pounds we can get this share in the paper. Only three thousand five hundred pounds! That is no more than one thousand seven hundred and fifty pounds apiece! I shall insist upon having my share in the investment, because I should grudge you the whole of the work. As for the returns, I have been well advised of that. Of course, Alec is beyond all paltry desire for gain, and he might ask a great deal more. But he leaves everything to his advisers—and oh! my dear, he must on no account know—yet—who is doing this for him. Afterwards, we will break it to him gradually, perhaps, when he has quite recovered from the worries and is rested. If we think of returns, ten, twenty, even fifty per cent. may be expected as the paper gets on. Think of fifty per cent.!'

'No,' said Armorel. 'Let us, too, be above paltry desire for gain. Let those who do want more money go in for this business. If your advice is correct, Mr. Feilding can have no difficulty at all in selling a share of the paper. People who want more money will be only too eager to buy it.'

'My dear child, everybody wants more money.'

'I have quite enough. But why do you ask me to join you, Zoe? I do not know Mr. Feilding, except as an acquaintance. He is, I dare say, all that you think. But I do not find him personally interesting. And there is no reason why I should pretend to be one of the train who follow him and admire him.'

'But I want you—I want you, Armorel.' Zoe clasped her hands and lifted her eyes, humid now. But a woman's eyes move a girl less than a man. 'I want you, and none but you, to join me in this. We two alone will do it. It will be such a splendid thing to do! Nothing short of the rescue of the finest and most poetic mind of the day from sordid cares and worries. Think of what future ages will say of you!'

Armorel laughed. 'Indeed!' she said. 'This kind of immortality does not tempt me very much. But, Zoe, it is really useless to urge me. I could not do this, if I would. And truly I would not if I could; for I made a promise to Mr. Jagenal, when I came of age the other day, that I would not lend or part with any money without taking his advice; and that I would not change any of his investments without consulting him. I seem to know, beforehand, what he would say if I consulted him about this proposal.'

'Then, my dear,' said Zoe, lying back in her cushions and turning her face to the fire, 'let us talk about the matter no more.'

She had failed. From the outset she felt that she was going to fail. The man had had every chance. He had met the girl constantly: she had left him alone with her: but he had not attracted her in the least. Well: she confessed, in spite of his cleverness, Alec had somewhat of a wooden manner: he was too authoritative; and Armorel was too independent. She had failed.

Armorel, for her part, remembered how her lawyer had warned her on the day when she became twenty-one and of age to manage her own affairs : all kinds of traps, he told her, are set to catch women who have got money in order to rob them of their money : they are besieged on every side, especially on the sides presumably the weakest : she must put on the armour of suspicion : she must never—never—never—here he held up a terrifying forefinger—enter into any engagement or promise, verbal or in writing, without consulting him. The memory of this warning made her uneasy—because it was her own companion, the lady appointed by her lawyer himself, who had made the first attempt upon her money. True, the attempt was entirely disinterested. There would be no gain to Zoe even if she were to accede : the proposal was prompted by the purest friendship. And yet she felt uneasy.

As for the disinterested companion, she wrote a letter that very night. She said : 'I have made an attempt to get this money for you. It has failed. It was hopeless from the first. You have had your chance : you have been with the girl often enough to attract and interest her : yet she is neither attracted nor interested. I have given her your poems : she says they ought to be the work of a woman : she likes the verse, but she cares nothing about the poet. Strange ! For my own part, I have been foolish enough to love the man, and to care not one brass farthing about his work. Your poems—your pictures—they all seem to me outside yourself, and not a part of you at all. Why it is so I cannot explain. Well, Alec, you planted me here, and I remain till you tell me I may go. It is not very lively : the girl and I have nothing in common : but it is restful and cosy, and I always did like comfort and warmth. And Armorel pays all the bills. What next, however ? Is there any other way ? What are my lord's commands ?'

CHAPTER X

THE SECRET OF THE TWO PICTURES

A GOOD many things troubled Armorel—the companion with whom she could not talk : her persistent praises of Mr Feilding : the constant attendance of that illustrious genius—and she wanted advice. Generally, she was a self-reliant person, but these were new experiences. Effie, she knew, could not advise her. She might go to Mr. Jagenal ; but, then, elderly lawyers are not always ready to receive confidences from young ladies. Then she thought of her cousin Philippa, whom she had not seen since that first evening. Philippa looked trustworthy and judicious. She went to see her in the morning, when she would be alone. Philippa received her with the greatest friendliness.

'If you really would like a talk about everything,' she said, 'come to my own room.' She led the way. 'Here we shall be quiet and undisturbed. It is the place where I practise every day. But I shall never be able to play like you, dear. Now, take that chair and let us begin. First, why do you come so seldom?'

'Frankly and truly, do you wish me to come often?'

'Frankly and truly, fair cousin, yes. But come alone. Mrs. Elstree and I were at school together, and we were not friends. That is all. I hope you like her for a companion.'

'The first of my difficulties,' said Armorel, 'is that I do not. I imagined when she came that it mattered nothing about her. You see, I have been for five years under masters and teachers, and I never thought anything about them outside the lesson. I thought my companion would be only another master. But she isn't. I have her company at breakfast, lunch, and dinner. And all the evening. I think I am wrong not to like her, because she is always good-tempered. Somehow, she jars upon me. She likes everything I do not care about—comic operas, dance music, French novels. She has no feeling for pictures, and her taste in literature is . . . not mine. Oh, I am talking scandal. And she is so perfectly inoffensive. Mostly she lies by the fire and either dozes or reads her French novels. All day long, I go about my devices. But there is the evening.'

'This is rather unfortunate, Armorel, is it not?'

'If it were only for a month or two, one would not mind. Tell me, Philippa, how long must I have a companion?'

Philippa laughed. 'I dare say the question may solve itself before long. Women generally achieve independence—with the wedding ring—unless that brings worse slavery.'

'No,' said Armorel, gravely, 'I shall not achieve independence that way.'

'Not that way?'

'Not by marrying!'

'Why not, Armorel?'

'You will not laugh at me, Philippa? I learned a long time ago that I could only marry one kind of man. And now I cannot find him.'

'You did know such a man formerly? My dear, you are not going to let a childish passion ruin your own life.'

'I knew a man who was, in my mind, this kind of man. He came across my life for two or three weeks. When he went away I kept his image in my mind, and it gradually grew as I grew—always larger and more beautiful. The more I learned—the more splendid grew this image. It was an Idol that I set up and worshipped for five long years.'

'And now your Idol is shattered?'

'No; the Idol remains. It is the man, who no longer corresponds to the Idol. The man who might have become this wonderful Image is gone—and I can never love any other man. He must be my Idol in the body.

'But, Armorel, this is unreal. We are not angels. Men and women must take each other with their imperfections.'

'My Idol may have had his imperfections, too. Well, the man has gone. I am punished, perhaps, for setting up an Idol.'

She was silent for awhile, and Philippa had nothing to say.

'But about my companion?' Armorel went on. 'When can I do without one?'

'There is nothing but opinion to consider. Opinion says that a young lady must not live alone.'

'If one never hears what opinion says, one need not consider opinion perhaps.'

'Well, but you could not go into society alone.'

'That matters nothing, because I never go into society at all.'

'Never go into society at all? What do you mean?'

'I mean that we go nowhere.'

'Well, what are people about? They call upon you, I suppose?'

'No; nobody ever calls.'

'But where are Mrs. Elstree's friends?'

'She has no friends.'

'Oh! She has—or had—an immense circle of friends.'

'That was before her father lost everything and killed himself. They were fair-weather friends.'

'Yes, but one's own people don't run away because of misfortune.' Philippa looked dissatisfied with the explanation. 'My dear cousin, this must be inquired into. Your lawyer told me that Mrs. Elstree's large circle of friends would be of such service to you. Do you really mean that you go nowhere? And your wonderful playing absolutely wasted? And your face seen nowhere? Oh! it is intolerable that such a girl as you should be so neglected.'

'I have other friends. There is Effie Wilmot and her brother who wants to become a dramatist. And I have found an old friend, an artist. I am not at all lonely. But in the evening, I confess, it is dull. I am not afraid of being alone. I have always been alone. But now I am not alone. I have to talk.'

'And uncongenial talk.'

'Now advise me, Philippa. Her talk is always on one subject—always the wonderful virtues of Mr. Feilding.'

'My cousin Alec? Yes'—Philippa changed colour, and shaded her face with a hand-screen. 'I believe she knows him.'

'Your cousin? Oh! I had forgotten. But it is all the better, because you know him. Philippa, I am troubled about him. For not only does Zoe talk about him perpetually, but he is always calling on one pretext or other. If I go to a picture-gallery, he is there: if I walk in the park, I meet him: if I go to church—Zoe does not go—he meets me in the porch: if we go to the theatre, he is there.'

'I did not think that Alec was that kind of man,' said Philippa, still keeping the hand-screen before her face. 'Are you mistaken, perhaps? Has he said anything?'

'No: he has said nothing. But it annoys me to have this man following me about—and—and—Philippa—he is your cousin—I know—but I detest him.'

'Can you not show that you dislike his attentions? If he will not understand that you dislike him—wait—perhaps he will speak—though I hardly think—you may be mistaken, dear. If he speaks, let your answer be quite unmistakable.'

'Then I hope that he will speak to-morrow. Zoe wanted me to find some money in order to help him in some way—out of some worries.'

'My dear child—I implore you—do not be drawn into any money entanglements. What does Zoe mean? What does it all mean? My dear, there is something here that I cannot understand. What can it mean? Zoe to help my cousin out of worries about money? Zoe? What has Zoe to do with him and his worries?'

'He has been very kind to her and to her husband.'

'There is something we do not understand,' Philippa repeated.

'You are not angry with me for not liking your cousin?'

'Angry? No, indeed. He has been so spoiled with his success that I don't wonder at your not liking him. As for me, you know, it is different. I knew Alec before his greatness became visible. No one, in the old days, ever suspected the wonderful powers he has developed. When he was a boy, no one knew that he could even hold a pencil, nobody suspected him of making rhymes—and now see what he has done. Yet, after all, his achievements seem to me only like incongruous additions stuck on to a central house. Alec and painting don't go together, in my mind. Nor Alec and *vers de société*. Nor Alec and story-telling. In his youth he passed for a practical lad, full of common-sense and without imagination.'

'Was he of a sensitive, highly nervous temperament?'

'Not to my knowledge. He has been always, and is still, I think, a man of a singularly calm and even cold temper—not in the least nervous nor particularly sensitive.'

Armorel compared this estimate with that of her companion. Strange that two persons should disagree so widely in their estimate of a man.

'Then, three or four years ago, he suddenly blossomed out into a painter. He invited his friends to his chambers. He told us that he had a little surprise for us. And then he drew aside a curtain and disclosed the first picture he thought worthy of exhibition. It hangs on the wall above your head, Armorel, with its companion of the following year. My father bought them and gave them to me.'

Armorel got up to look at them.

'Oh!' she cried. 'These are copies!'

'Copies? No. They are Alec's own original pictures. What makes you think they are copies?'

What made her think that they were copies was the very remarkable fact that both pictures represented scenes among the Scilly Isles: that in each of them was represented—herself—as a girl of fifteen or sixteen: that the sketches for both these pictures had been made in her own presence by the artist: that he was none other than Roland Lee: and that the picture she had seen in his studio was done by the same hand and in the same style as the two pictures before her. Of that she had no doubt. She had so trained her eye and hand that there could be no doubt at all of that fact.

She stared, bewildered. Philippa, who was beside her looking at the pictures, went on talking without observing the sheer amazement in Armorel's eyes.

'That was his first picture,' she continued; 'and this was the second. I remember very well the little speech he made while we were all crowding round the picture. "I am going," he said, "to make a new departure. You all thought I was just following the beaten road at the Bar. Well, I am trying a new and a shorter way to success. You see my first effort." It was difficult to believe our eyes. Alec a painter? One might as well have expected to find Alec a poet: and in a few months he was a poet: and then a story-teller. And his poetry is as good as it is made in these days; and his short stories are as good as any of those by the French writers.'

'What is the subject of this picture?' Armorel asked with an effort.

'The place is somewhere on the Cornish coast, I believe. He always paints the same kind of picture—always a rocky coast—a tossing sea—perhaps a boat—spray flying over the rocks—and always a girl, the same girl. There she is in both pictures—a handsome black-haired girl, quite young—it might be almost a portrait of yourself when you were younger, Armorel.'

'Almost,' said Armorel.

'This girl is now as well known to Alec's friends as Wouvermann's white horse. But no one knows the model.'

Armorel's memory went back to the day when Roland made that sketch. She stood—so—just as the painter had drawn her, on a round boulder, the water boiling and surging at her feet and the white foam running up. Behind her the granite rock, grey and black. How could she ever forget that sketch?

'Alec is wonderful in his seas,' Philippa went on. 'Look at the bright colour and the clear transparency of the water. You can feel it rolling at your feet. Upon my word, Armorel, the girl is really like you.'

'A little, perhaps. Yes; they are good pictures, Philippa. The man who painted them is a painter indeed.'

She sat down again, still bewildered.

Presently she heard Philippa's voice. 'What is it?' she asked. 'You have become deaf and dumb. Are you ill?'

'No—I am not ill. The sight of those pictures set me thinking. I will go now, Philippa. If he speaks to me I will reply so that there can be no mistake. But if he persists in following me about, I will ask you to interfere.'

'If necessary,' Philippa promised her. 'I will interfere for you. But there is something in all this which I do not understand. Come again soon, dear, and tell me everything.'

When they began this talk, one girl was a little troubled, but not much. The other was free from any trouble. When they parted, both girls were troubled.

One felt, vaguely, that danger was in the air. Zoe meant something by constantly talking about her cousin Alec. What understanding was there between him and that woman—that detestable woman?

The other walked home in a doubt and perplexity that drove everything else out of her head. What did those pictures mean? Had Roland given away his sketches? Was there another painter who had the very touch of Roland as well as his sketches? No, no; it was impossible.

Suddenly she remembered something on the fragment of paper that Effie picked up. The corner of the torn cheque—even the signature of Alec Feilding. What did that mean? Why had Roland torn up a cheque signed by Mr. Feilding? Why had he called that act the turning of the footstep?

CHAPTER XI

A CRITIC ON TRUTH

One painter may make use of another man's sketches for his own pictures. The thing is conceivable, though one cannot recall, and there is no record of, any such case. It is, perhaps, possible. Portrait-painters have employed other men to paint backgrounds and even hands and drapery. Now, the two pictures hanging in Philippa's room were most certainly painted from Roland's sketches. If there were any room for doubt the figure of Armorel herself in the foreground removed that doubt. Therefore, Roland must have lent his sketches to Mr. Feilding. What else did he lend? Can one man lend another his eye, his hand, his sense of colour, his touch, his style? There was once, I seem to have read, a man who sold his soul to the only Functionary who buys such things, and keeps a stock of them second-hand, on the condition that he should be able to paint as well as the immortal Raffaello. He obtained his wish, because the Devil always keeps his bargain to the letter, with the result that, instead of winning the imperishable wreath for himself that he expected, he was never known at all, and his pictures are now sold as those of the master whose works they so miraculously resemble. Armorel had perhaps heard this story somewhere. Could the cleverest man in all London have made a similar transaction, taking Roland Lee for his model? If so, the Devil had not cheated him at all, and he got out of the bargain all he expected, because he not only painted quite as well as his master, and in exactly the same style, so that it was impossible to distinguish between them, but, which the other unfortunate did not get, all the credit was given to him, while the original model or master languished in obscurity.

It was obvious to a trained eye, at very first sight, that the style of the pictures was that of Roland Lee. He had a style of his own. The first mark of genius in any art is individuality. His style was no more to be imitated in painting than the style of Robert Browning can be followed in poetry. Painters there are who have been imitated and have created a school of imitators: even these can always be distinguished from their copyists. The subtle touch of the master, the personal presence of his hand, cannot be copied or imitated. In these two pictures the hand of Roland was clearly, unmistakably visible. The light thrown over them, the atmosphere with which they were charged—everything was his. He had caught the September sunshine as it lies over and enfolds the Scilly Islands—who should know that soft and golden light better than Armorel?—he had caught the transparencies of the seas, the shining yellows of the sea-weed, the browns and purples of bramble and fern, the greyness and the blackness of the rock: you could hear the rush of the water eddying among the boulders; you could see the rapid movement of the sea-gulls' wings as they swept along with the wind. Could another, even with the original sketches lying before him, even with skill and feeling of his own, reproduce these things in Roland's own individual style?

'No,' she cried, but not aloud; 'I know these pictures. They are not his at all. They are Roland's.'

Every line of thought that she followed—to write these down would be to produce another 'Ring and Book'—in her troubled meditations after the discovery led her to the same conclusion. It was that at which she had arrived in a single moment of time, without argument or reasoning, and at the very first sight of the pictures. The first thought is always right. 'They are Roland's pictures'—that was the first thought. The second thought brings along the doubts, suggests objections, endeavours to be judicial, deprecates haste, and calls for the scales. 'They cannot,' said the second thought, 'be Roland's paintings, because Mr. Feilding says they are his.' The third thought, which is the first strengthened by evidence, declared emphatically that they were Roland's.

whatever Mr. Feilding might say, and could be the work of none other.

Therefore, the cleverest man in all London, according to everybody, the best and most generous and most honourable, according to Armorel's companion, was an impostor and a Liar. Never before had she ever heard of such a Liar.

Armorel, it is true, knew but little of the crooked paths by which many men perform this earthly pilgrimage from the world which is to the world which is to come. Children born on Samson —nay, even those also of St. Mary's—have few opportunities of observing these ways. That is why all Scillonians are perfectly honest: they do not know how to cheat—even those who might wish to become dishonest, if they knew. In her five years' apprenticeship the tree of knowledge had dropped some of its baleful fruit at Armorel's feet: that cannot be avoided even in a convent garden. Yet she had not eaten largely of the fruit, nor with the voracity that distinguishes many young people of both sexes when they get hold of these apples. In other words, she only knew of craft and falsehood in general terms, as they are set forth in the Gospels and by the Apostles, and especially in the Book of Revelation, which expressly states the portion of liars. Yet, even with this slight foundation to build upon, Armorel was well aware that here was a fraud of a most monstrous character. Surely, there never was, before this man, any man in the world who dared to present to the world another man's paintings, and to call them his own? Men and women have claimed books which they never wrote —witness the leading case of the false George Eliot and the story told by Anthony Trollope; men have pretended to be well-known writers—did I not myself once meet a man in an hotel pretending to be one of our most genial of story-tellers? Men have written things and pretended that they were the work of famous hands. Literature—alas!—hath many impostors. But in Art the record is clean. There are a few ghosts, to be sure, here and there—sporadic spectres!—but they are obscure and mostly unknown. Armorel had never heard or seen any of them. Surely there never before was any man like unto this man!

And, apart from the colossal impudence of the thing, she began to consider the profound difficulties in carrying it out. Because, you see, no one man, unaided, could carry it through. It requires the consent, the silence, and the active—nay, the zealous—co-operation of another man. And how are you to get that man?

In order to get this other man—this active and zealous fellow-conspirator—you must find means to persuade him to sacrifice every single thing that men care for—honour, reputation, success. He must be satisfied to pursue Art, actually and literally, for Art's own sake. This is, I know, a rule of conduct preached by every art critic, every æsthete, every lecturer or writer on Art. Yet observe what it may lead to. Was there, for instance, an unknown genius who gave his work to Giotto, with permission to call it his own? And was that obscure genius content to sit and watch that work in the crowd, unseen and unsuspected, while he murmured praises and thanksgiving for the skill of hand and eye which had been given to him, but claimed by that other young man, Messer Giotto? Did Turner have his ghost? Sublime sacrifice of self! So to pursue Art for Art's sake as to give your pictures to another man by which he may rise to honour—even, it may be, to the Presidency of the Royal Academy, contented only with the consciousness of good and sincere work, and with the possession of mastery! It is beyond us: we cannot achieve this greatness—we cannot rise to this devotion. Art hath no such votaries. By what persuasions, then—by what bribes—was Roland induced to consent to his own suicide—ignoble, secret, and shameful suicide?

He must have consented; in no other way could the thing be done. He must have agreed to efface himself—but not out of pure devotion to Art. Not so. The Roland of the past survived still. The burning desire for distinction and recognition still flamed in his soul. The bitterness and shame with which he spoke of himself proved that his consent had been wrung from him. He was ashamed. Why? Because another bore the honours that should be his. Because he was a bondman of the impostor. Of this Armorel was certain. Roland Lee—the man whom for five long years she had imagined to be marching from triumph to triumph—conqueror of the world—had sold himself—for what consideration she knew not—hand and eye, genius and brain, heart and soul—had sold himself into slavery. He had consented to a monstrous and most impudent fraud! And the man who stood before the canvas in public, writing his name in the corner, was—the noun appellative, the proper noun—belonging to such an act. And her own friend—her gallant hero of Art—what else was he in this conspiracy of two? You cannot persuade a woman—such is the poverty of the feminine imagination—to call a thing like this by any other name than its plain, simple, and natural one. A man may explain away, find excuses, make suggestions, point out extenuating circumstances, show how the force of events destroys free will, and propose a surplice and a golden crown for the unfortunate victim of fate, instead of bare shoulders and the nine-clawed cat. But a woman—never. If the thing done is a Lie, the man who did it is a ——

'Armorel,' said her companion—it was in the afternoon, and she had been dozing after her lunch—'what is the matter? You have been sitting in the window, which has a detestable view of a dismal street, for two long hours without talking. At lunch you sat as if in a dream. Are you ill? Has anything happened? Has the respectable Mr. Jagenal robbed you of your money? Has Philippa been saying amiable things about me?'

'I have found out something which has disquieted me beyond expression,' said Armorel, gravely.

Zoe changed colour. 'Heavens!'—she laughed curiously. 'What has come out now? Anything about me? One never knows what may come out next. It is very odd what a lot of things may be said about everybody.'

'My discovery has nothing to do with you, at least—no, nothing at all.'

'That is reassuring.' It certainly was, as everybody knows who does not wish the curtain to draw up once again on the earlier and half-forgotten scenes of the play. 'Perhaps it might relieve you, dear, if you were to tell me. But do not think I am curious. Besides, I dare say I could tell you more than you could tell me. Is it about Philippa's hopeless attachment for the man who will never marry her, and her cruelty to the reverend gentleman who will?'

'No—no: it is nothing about Philippa. I know nothing about any attachments.'

'Well, you will tell me when you please.' Zoe relapsed into warmth and silence. But she watched the girl from under her heavy eyelids. Something had happened—something serious. Armorel pursued her meditations, but in a different line. She now remembered that the leader in this Fraud was the man whom Zoe professed to honour above all other living men: could she tell this disciple what she had discovered? One might as well inform Kadysha that her prophet Mohammed was an epileptic impostor. And, again, he was Philippa's first cousin, and she regarded him with pride, if not—as Zoe suggested—with a warmer feeling still. How could she bring this trouble upon Philippa?

And, again, it was Roland's secret. How could she reveal a thing which would cover him with ridicule and discredit for the rest of his life? She must be silent for the sake of everybody.

'Zoe,' she sprang to her feet, 'don't ask me anything more. Forget what I said. It is not my own secret.'

'My dear child,' Zoe murmured, 'if nobody has run away with your money, and if you have found out no mares' nests about me, I don't mind anything. I have already quite forgotten. Why should I remember?'

'Of course,' Armorel repeated impatiently—this companion of hers often made her impatient—'there is nothing about you. It concerns——'

'Mr. Feilding.'

It was only an innocent maid who opened the door to announce an afternoon caller; but Armorel started, for really it was the right completion to her sentence, though not the completion she meant to make.

He came in—the man of whom her mind was full—tall, handsome, calm, and self-possessed. Authority sat, visible to all, upon his brow. His dress, his manner, his voice, proclaimed the man who had succeeded—who deserved to succeed. Oh! how could it be possible?

Armorel mechanically gave him her hand, wondering. Then, quite in the old style, and as a survival of Samson Island, there passed rapidly through her mind the whole procession of those texts which refer to liars. For the moment she felt curious and nervously excited, as one who should talk with a man condemned. Then she came back to London and to the exigencies of the situation. Yet it was really quite wonderful. For he sat down and began to talk for all the world as if he was a perfectly truthful person: and she rang the bell for tea, and poured it out for him, as if she knew nothing to the contrary. That he, being what he was, should so carry himself; that she, who knew everything, should sit down calmly and put milk and sugar in his tea, were two facts so extraordinary that her head reeled.

Presently, however, she began to feel amused. It was like knowing beforehand, so that the mind is free to think of other things, the story and the plot of a comedy. She considered the acting and the make-up. And both were admirable. The part of successful genius could not be better played. One has known genius too modest to accept the position, happiest while sitting in a dark corner. Here, however, was genius stepping to the front and standing there boldly in sight of all, as if the place was his by the double right of birth and of conquest.

He sat down and began to talk of Art. He seldom, indeed, talked about anything else. But Art has many branches, and he talked about them all. To-day, however, he discoursed on drawing and painting. He was accustomed to patient listeners, and therefore he assumed that his discourse was received with respect, and did not observe the preoccupied look on the face of the girl to whom he discoursed—for Zoe made no pretence of listening, except when the conversation seemed likely to take a personal turn. Nor did he observe how from time to time Armorel turned her eyes upon him—eyes full of astonishment—eyes struck with amazement.

Presently he descended for awhile from the heights of principle to the lower level of personal topic. 'Mrs. Elstree tells me,' he said, smiling with some condescension, 'that you paint—of course as an amateur—as well as play. If you can draw as well as you can play you are indeed to be envied. But that is, perhaps, too much to be expected. Will you show me some of your work? And will you—without being offended—suffer me to be a candid critic?'

Armorel went gravely to her own room and returned with a small portfolio full of drawings which she placed before him, still with the wonder in her eyes. What would he say—this man who passed off another man's pictures for his own? She stood at the table over him, looking down upon him, waiting to see him betray himself—the first criminal person—the first really wicked man—she had ever encountered in the flesh.

'You are not afraid of the truth?' he asked, turning over the sketches. 'In Art—truth—truth is everything. Without truth there is no Art. Truth and sincerity should be our aim in criticism as well as in Art itself.'

Oh! what kind of conscience could this man have who was able so to talk about Art, seeing what manner of man he was? Armorel glanced at Zoe, half afraid that he would convict himself in her presence. But she seemed asleep, lying back in her cushions.

His remarks were judgments. Once pronounced, there was no appeal. Yet his judgments produced no effect upon the girl, not the least. She listened, she heard, she acquiesced in silence.

Perhaps because he was struck with her coldness he left off examining the sketches, and began a learned little discourse about composition and harmony, selection and grouping. He illustrated these remarks, not obtrusively, but quite naturally, by referring to his own pictures, appealing to Zoe, who lazily raised her head and murmured response, as one who knew it all beforehand. Now, as to the discourse itself, Armorel recognised every word of it already: she had read and had been taught these very things. It showed, she thought, what a pretender the man must be not to understand work that had been done by one who had studied seriously, and already knew all that he was laboriously enforcing. But she said nothing. It was, moreover, the lesson of a professor, not of an artist. Between the professional critic who can neither paint nor draw and the smallest of the men who can paint and draw there is, if you please, a gulf fixed that cannot be passed over.

'This drawing, for instance,' he concluded, taking up one from the table, 'betrays exactly the weakness of which I have been speaking. It has some merit. There is a desire for truth—without truth what are we? The lights are managed with some dexterity, the colour has real feeling. But consider this figure. From sheer ignorance of the elementary considerations which I have been laying down, you have placed it exactly in front. Had it been here, at the right, the effect of the figure in bringing up the whole of the picture would have been heightened tenfold. For my own part, I always like a figure in a painting—a single figure for choice—a girl, because the treatment of the hair and the dress lends itself to effect.'

'His famous girl!' echoed Zoe. 'That model whom nobody is allowed to see!'

Now, the figure was placed in the middle for very excellent reasons, and in full consideration of those very principles which this expounder had been setting forth. But what yesterday would have puzzled her, now amused her one moment and irritated her the next.

He took up a crayon. 'Shall I show you,' he asked, 'exactly what I mean?'

'If you please. Here is a piece of paper which will do.'

He spoke in the style which Matthew Arnold so much admired—

the Grand Style—the words clear and articulate, the emphasis just, the manner authoritative. 'I will just indicate your background,' he said, poising the pencil professionally—he looked as if the Grand Style really belonged to him—'in two or three strokes, and then I will sketch in your figure in the place—here—where it properly belongs. You will see immediately, though, of course—your eye—cannot——' He played with the chalk as one considering where to begin—but he did not begin. Armorel remembered a certain day when Roland gave her his first lesson, pencil in hand. Never was that pencil idle: it moved about of its own accord: it was drawing all the time: it seemed to be drawing out of its own head. Mr. Feilding, on the other hand, never touched the paper at all. His pencil was dumb and lifeless. But Armorel waited anxiously for him to begin. Now, at any rate, she should see if he could draw. She was disappointed. The clock on the overmantel suddenly struck six. Mr. Feilding dropped the crayon. 'Good heavens!' he cried. 'You make one forget everything, Miss Rosevean. We must put off the rest of this talk for another day. But you will persevere, dear young lady, will you not? Promise me that you will persevere. Even if the highest peak cannot be attained—we may not all reach that height—it is something to stand upon the lower slope, if it is only to recognise the greatness of those who are above and the depths below—how deep they are!—of the world which knows no art. Persevere—persevere! I will call again and help you, if I may.' He pressed her hand warmly, and departed.

'I really think,' said Zoe, 'that he believes you worth teaching, Armorel. I have never known him give so much time to any one girl before. And if you only knew how they flock about him!'

'Zoe,' said Armerel, without answering this remark, 'you have seen all Mr. Feilding's pictures, have you not?'

'I believe, all.'

'Do they all treat the same subject?'

'Up to the present, he has exhibited nothing but sea and coast pieces, headlands, low tide on the rocks, and so forth. Always with this black-haired girl—something like you, but not much more than a child.'

'Did you ever see him actually at work?'

'You mean working at an unfinished thing? No; never. He cannot endure anyone in his studio while he is at work.'

'Did he ever draw anything for you—any pen-and-ink sketch—pencil sketch? Have you got any of his sketches—rough things?'

'No. Alec has a secretive side to his character. It comes out in odd ways. No one suspected that he could paint, or even draw, until, three or four years ago, he suddenly burst upon us with a finished picture; and then it came out that he had been secretly drawing all his life, and studying seriously for years. Where he will break out next, I don't know.'

'He may break out anywhere,' said Armorel, 'except upon the fiddle. I think that he will never play the fiddle. Yes, Zoe, he really is a very, very clever man. He is certainly the very cleverest man in all London.'

CHAPTER XII

TO MAKE THAT PROMISE SURE

THERE are few instincts and impulses of imperfect human nature more deeply rooted or more certain to act upon us than the desire to 'have it out' with some other human creature. Women are especially led or driven by this impulse, even among the less highly civilised to the tearing out of nose- and ear-rings. You may hear every day at all hours in every back street of every city the ladies having it out with each other. In fact there is a perpetual court of Common Pleas being held in these streets, without respite of holiday or truce, in which the folk have it out with each other, while friends—sympathetic friends—stand by and act as judges, jury, arbitrators, lawyers, and all. Things are reported, things are said, things are done, a personal explanation is absolutely necessary, before peace of mind can be restored, or the way to future action become clearly visible. The two parties must have it out.

In Armorel's case she found that before doing anything she must see that member of the conspiracy—if, indeed, there was a conspiracy—who was her own friend: she must see Roland. She must know exactly what it meant, if only to find out how it could be stopped. In plain words, she must have it out. Those who obey a natural impulse generally believe that they are acting by deliberate choice. Thus the doctrine of free will came to be invented: and thus Armorel, when she took a cab to the other studio, had no idea but that she was acting the most original part ever devised for any comedy.

As before, she found the artist in his dingy back room, alone. But the picture was advancing. When she saw it, a fortnight before, it was little more than the ghost of a rock with a spectral sea and a shadowy girl beside the sea. Now, it was advanced so far that one could see the beginnings of a fine painting in it.

Roland stepped forward and greeted his old friend. Why—he was already transformed. What had he done to himself? The black bar was gone from his forehead: his eyes were bright: his cheeks had got something of their old colour: his hair was trimmed, and his dress, as well as his manner, showed a return to self-respect.

'What happy thought brings you here again, Armorel?' he asked, with the familiarity of an old friend.

'I came to see you at work. Last time I came only to see you. Is it permitted?'

'Behold me! I am at work. See my picture—all there is of it.'

Armorel looked at it long and carefully. Then she murmured unintelligibly, 'Yes, of course. But there never could have been any doubt.' She turned to the artist a face full of encouragement. 'What did I prophesy for you, Roland? That you should be a great painter? Well, my prophecy will come true.'

'I hope, but I fear. I am beginning the world again.'

'Not quite. Because you have never ceased to work. Your hand is firmer and your eye is truer now than it was four years ago, when you—ceased to exhibit. But you have never ceased to work. So that you go back to the world with better things.'

'They refused to buy my things before.'

'They will not refuse now. Nay, I am certain. Don't think of money, my old friend: you must not—you shall not think of money. Think of nothing but your work—and your name. What ought to be done to a man who should forget his name? He deserves to be deprived of his genius, and to be cast out among the stupid. But you, Roland, you were always keen for distinction—were you not?'

He made no reply.

'How well I know the place,' she said, standing before the picture. 'It is the narrow channel between Round Island and Camber Rock. Oh! the dear, terrible place. When you and I were there, you remember, Roland, the water was smooth and the sea-birds were flying quietly. I have seen them driven by the wind off the island and beating up against it like a sailing ship. But in September there are no puffins. And I have seen the water racing and roaring through the channel, dashing up the black sides of the rocks—while we lay off, afraid to venture near. It was low tide when you made your sketch. I remember the long, yellow fringing sea-weed hanging from the rock six feet deep. And there is your girl sitting in the boat. Oh! I remember her very well. What a happy time she had while you were with her, Roland! You were the very first person to show her something of the outer world. It seemed, when you were gone, as if you had taken that girl and planted her on a high rock so that she could see right across the water to the world of men and Art. You always keep this girl in your pictures?'

'Always in these pictures of coast and rock.'

'Roland, I want you to make a change. Do not paint the girl of sixteen in this picture. Let me be your model instead. Put me into the picture. It is my fancy. Will you let me sit for you again?'

'Surely, Armorel, if I may. It will be—oh, but you cannot—you must not come to this den of a place.'

'Indeed, I think it is not a nice place at all. But I shall stipulate that you take another and a more decent studio immediately. Will you do this?'

'I will do anything—anything—that you command.'

'You know what I want. The return of my old friend. He is on his way back already.'

'I know—I know. But whether he ever can come back again I know not. A shade or spectre of him, perhaps, or himself, besmirched and smudged, Armorel—dragged through the mud.'

'No. He shall come back—himself—in spotless robes. Now you shall take a studio, and I will come and sit to you. I may bring my little friend, Effie Wilmot, with me? That is agreed, then. You will go, Sir, this very morning and find a studio. Have you gone back to your old friends?'

'Not yet. I had very few friends. I shall go back to them when I have got work to show. Not before.'

'I think you should go back as soon as you have taken your new studio. It will be safer and better. You have been too much alone. And there is another thing—a very important thing—the other night you made me a promise. You tore up something that looked like a cheque. And you assured me that this meant nothing less than a return to the old paths.'

'When I tore up that accursed cheque, Armorel, I became a free man.'

'So I understood. But when one talks of free men one implies the existence of the master or owner of men who are not free. Have you signified to that master or owner your intention to be his bondman no longer?'

'No. I have not.'

'This man, Roland,' she laid her hand on his, 'tell me frankly, has he any hold upon you?'

'None.'

'Can he injure you in any way? Can he revenge himself upon you? Is there any old folly or past wickedness that he can bring up against you?'

'None. I have to begin the world again: that is the outside mischief.'

'All your pictures you have sold to this man, Roland, with me in every one?'

'Yes, all. Spare me, Armorel! With you in every one. Forgive me if you can!'

'I understand now, my poor friend, why you were so cast down and ashamed. What? You sold your genius—your holy, sacred genius—the spirit that is within you! You flung yourself away—your name, which is yourself—you became nothing, while this man pretends that the pictures—yours—were his! He puts his name to them, not your own—he shows them to his friends in the room that he calls his studio—he sends them to the exhibition as his own—and yet you have been able to live! Oh, how could you?—how could you? Oh! it was shameful—shameful—shameful! How could you, Roland? Oh, my master!—I have loaded you with honour—oh, how could you?—how could you?'

The vehemence of her indignation soon revived the old shame. Roland hung his head.

'How could I?' he repeated. 'Yes, say it again—ask the question a thousand times—how could I?'

'Forgive me, Roland! I have been thinking about it continually. It is a thing so dreadful, and yesterday something—an unexpected something—brought it back to my mind—and—and—made me understand more what it meant. And oh, Roland, how could you? I thought, before, that you had only idled and trifled away your time; but now I know. And again—again—again—how could you?'

'It is no excuse—but it is an explanation—I do not defend myself. Not the least in the world—but . . . Armorel, I was starving.'

'Starving?'

'I could not sell my pictures. No one wanted them. The dealers would give me nothing but a few shillings apiece for them. I was penniless, and I was in debt. A man who drops into London out of Australia has no circle of friends and cousins who will stand by him. I was alone. Perhaps I loved too well the luxurious life. I tried for employment on the magazines and papers, but without success. In truth, I knew not where to look for the next week's rent and the next week's meals. I was a Failure, and I was penniless. Do you ask more?'

'Then the man came——'

'He came—my name was worth nothing—he asked me to suppress it. My work—which no one would buy—he offered to buy for what seemed, in my poverty, substantial prices if I would let him call it his own. What was the bargain? A life of ease against the bare chance of a name with the certainty of hard times. I was so desperate that I accepted.'

'You accepted. Yes . . . But you might have given it up at any moment.'

'To be plunged back again into the penniless state. For the life of ease, mark you, brought no ease but a bare subsistence. Only quite lately, terrified by the success of the last picture, my employer has offered to give me two thirds of all he gets. The cheque you saw me tear up and burn was the first considerable sum I have ever received. It is gone, and I am penniless again——'

'And now that you are penniless?

'Now I shall pawn my watch and chain and everything else that I possess. I shall finish this picture, and I will sell it for what the dealers will give me for it. Too late, this year, for exhibition. And so . . . we shall see. If the worst comes I can carry a pair of boards up and down Piccadilly, opposite to the Royal Academy, and dream of the artistic life that once I hoped would be my own.'

'You will do better than that, Roland,' said Armorel, moved to tears. 'Oh! you will make a great name yet. But this man—don't tell me his name. Roland, promise me, please, not to tell me his name. I want you—just now—to think that it is your own secret—to yourself. If I should find it out, by accident, that would be—just now—my secret—to myself. This man—you have not yet broken with him?'

'Not yet.'

'Will you go to him and tell him that it is all over? Or will you write to him?'

'I thought that I would wait, and let him come to me.'

'I would not, if I were you. I would write and tell him at once, and plainly. Sit down, Roland, and write now—at once—without delay. Then you will feel happier.'

'I will do what you command me,' he replied meekly. He had, indeed, resolved with all his might and main that the rupture should be made; but, as yet, he had not made it.

'Get paper, then, and write.'

He obeyed, and sat down. 'What shall I say?' he asked.

'Write: "After four years of slavery, I mean to become a man once more. Our compact is over. You shall no longer put your name to my works; and I will no longer share in the infamy of this fraud. Find, if you can, some other starving painter, and buy him. I have torn up your cheque, and I am now at work on a picture which will be my own. If there is any awkwardness about the subject and the style, in connection with the name upon it, that awkwardness will be yours, not mine." So—will you read it aloud? I think,' said Armorel, 'that it will do. He will probably come here and bluster a little. He may even threaten. He may weep. You will—Roland—are you sure—you will be adamant?'

'I swear, Armorel! I will be true to my promise.'

Armorel heaved a sigh. Would he stand steadfast? He might have much to endure. Would he be able to endure hardness? It is only the very young man who can be happy in a garret and live contentedly on a crust. At twenty-six or twenty-seven, the age at which Roland had now arrived, one is no longer quite so young. The garret is dismal: the crust is insipid, unless there are solid grounds for hope. Yet he had the solid grounds of improved work—good work.

'Should you be afraid of him?' she asked.

'Afraid of him?' Roland laughed. 'Why, I never meet him but I curse him aloud. Afraid of him? No. I have never been afraid of anything but of becoming penniless. Poverty—destitution—is an awful spectre. And not only poverty but—I confess, with shame——'

'Oh! man of little faith'—she did not want to hear the end

of that confession—'you could not endure a single hour. You did this awful thing for want of money.'

'I did,' said Roland, meekly.

'The Way of Pleasure and the Way of Wealth. I remember—you told me long ago—they draw the young man by ropes. But not the girl. Why not the girl? I have never felt this strange yearning for riot and excess. In all the poetry, the novels, the pictures, and the plays the young men are always being dragged by ropes to the Way of Pleasure. Are men so different from women? What does it mean—this yearning? I cannot understand it. What is your Way of Pleasure that it should attract you so? Your poetry and your novels cannot explain it. I see feasting in the Way of Pleasure, drinking, singing, dancing, gambling, sitting up all night, and love-making. As for work, there is none. Why should the young man want to feast? It is like a City Alderman to be always thinking of banquets. Why should you want to drink wine perpetually? I suppose you do not actually get tipsy. If you can sing and like singing, you can sing over your work, I suppose. As for love-making'—she paused. The subject, where a young man and a maiden discuss it, has to be treated delicately.

'I have always supposed'—she added, with hesitation, for experience was lacking—'that two people fall in love when they are fitted for each other. But in this, your wonderful Way of Pleasure, the poets write as if every man was always wanting to make love to every woman if she is pleasant to look at, and without troubling whether she is good or bad, wise or silly. Oh! every woman! any woman! there is neither dignity of manhood nor self-respect nor respect to woman in this folly.'

'You cannot understand any of it, Armorel,' said Roland. 'We ought all of us to be flogged from Newgate to Tyburn.'

'That would not make me understand. Flora, Chloe, Daphne, Amaryllis—they are all the same to the poet. A pretty girl seems all that he cares for. Can that be love?'

'—And back again,' said Roland.

'Still I should not understand. In the poetry I think that love-making comes first, and eating and drinking afterwards. As for, love-making,' she spoke philosophically, as one in search of truth, 'as for love-making, I believe I could wait contentedly without it until I found exactly the one man I could love. But that I should take a delight in writing or singing songs about making love to every man who was a handsome fellow—any man—every man—oh! can one conceive such a thing? There is but one Way of Pleasure to such as you, Roland. If I could paint so good a picture as this is going to be, it would be a lifelong joy. I should never, never, never tire of it. I should want no other pleasure—nothing better—than to work day after day, to work and study, to watch and observe, to feel the mastery of hand and eye. Oh! Roland—with this before you—with this'—she pointed to the picture—'you sold your soul—you—you—you!—for feasting and drinking and—and—perhaps——'

'No, Armorel: no. Everything else if you like, but not love-making.'

CHAPTER XIII

THE DRAMATIST

If Mrs. Elstree was Armorel's official and authorised companion, her private unpaid companion was Effie Wilmot. The official companion was resident in the chambers, and was seen with her charge at the theatres and concerts. The private unpaid companion went about with her all day long, sat with her in her own room, knew what she thought, and talked with her of the things she loved to discuss. So that, though the representative of Order and Propriety had less to do, the unpaid attachée had a much more lively time. Fortunately, the official companion was best pleased when there was nothing to do. In those days, when London was as yet an unknown land to both of them, the girls went together to see things. Nobody knows what a great quantity of things there are to see in London when you once set yourself seriously to explore this great unknown continent. Captain Magalhaens himself, crossing the Pacific Ocean for the first time, did not experience a more interesting and exciting time than these two girls in their walks in and about the great town, new to both. They were as ravenous as American tourists beginning their European round. And, like them, they consulted their Baedeker, their Hare, and their Peter Cunningham. Pictures there are, all in the West-End; museums, with every kind of treasure; historic houses—alas! not many; libraries; art galleries of all kinds; cathedrals, churches, ancient and modern; old streets, whose paving-stones are inscribed in the closest print with the most wonderful recollections; old sites, broken fragments, even. Every morning the two girls wandered forth, sometimes not coming home until late in the afternoon. Then Effie went back to her lodging, and spent the evening working at her verses; while Armorel practised her violin, or read and dreamed away the time opposite her companion, who sat for the most part in silence, gazing into the firelight, lying back in her easy-chair beside the fire.

These ramblings belong to another book—the Book of the Things Left Out. I could show you, dear reader, many curious and interesting places visited by these two pilgrims, but one must not in this place write these down, because Armorel's story is not Armorel's history. Let us always be careful to distinguish. Besides, the events which have to be related destroyed, as you will see, the calm and tranquillity necessary for the proper enjoyment of such ramblings. First, this discovery concerning the pictures.

Who can visit old churches and museums with a mind full of wrath and bitterness? So wrathful was Armorel in considering the impudence of the fraud she had discovered: so bitter was she in considering the cowardice of her old hero: that she even failed to observe the unmistakable signs of trouble which at this time showed themselves in her friend's face. If not a beautiful face, it was expressive. When the projecting forehead showed a thick black line: when the deep-set eyes were ringed with dark circles: when the pale cheeks grew paler and more hollow: and when the girl, who was generally so bright and animated, became silent and *distraite*, something was wrong.

'What is it, Effie?' Armorel asked, waking up. 'I have asked you three questions, and have received no answer. And you are looking ill. Has anything gone wrong?'

'Oh!' cried Effie, 'it is horrid! You are in troubles of your own, and you want me to add to them by telling you about mine.'

'I am in trouble, dear. And it makes me selfish and blind. You know partly what it is about. It is about the Life that has gone wrong. I have found out why and how. But I can never tell you or anybody. Never mind. Tell me about yourself.'

'It is more about my brother than myself. You know that Archie has been writing a play?'

'Yes. You write verses which you have never shown me; and your brother writes plays. I shall see both some day, perhaps.'

'Whenever you like. But Archie has now finished his play.'

'Yes?'

'That means to him more than I can possibly tell you. He has been living for that play, and for nothing else. It has filled his brain day and night. Never was so much trouble given to a play before, I am sure. It is himself.'

'I understand.'

'Well—then—you will understand also what he feels when he has been told that his play is utterly worthless.'

'Who told him that?'

'A great authority—a writer of great reputation—the only living writer whom we have ever known.'

'Well—but—Effie, if a great authority says this, it is frightful.'

'It would be, but for one thing, which you shall hear afterwards. However, he did confess that some of the situations were fine. But the dialogue, he said, was unfitted for the stage, and no manager would so much as look at the play.'

'Poor Archie! What a dreadful blow! What does he say?'

'He is utterly cast down. He sits at home and broods. Sometimes he swears that he will tear up the thing and throw it into the fire; sometimes he recovers a little of his old confidence in it. He will not eat anything, and he does not sleep; and I can find nothing to say that will comfort him. If I knew anyone who would give him another opinion—the play cannot be so bad. Armorel, will you read the play?'

'But, my dear, I am no critic. What would be the good of my reading it?'

'I would rather have your criticism than'—she hesitated—'than anybody's. Because you can feel—and you have the artist's soul; and everybody has not——though he may paint such beautiful pictures,' she added rather obscurely.

'Well, I will read the play, or hear him read it, if you think it will do him any good, Effie. I will go with you at once.'

'Oh! will you, really? Archie will be shy at first. The last criticism caused him so much agony that he dreads another. But yours will be sympathetic, at least. You will understand what he meant, even if he has not succeeded—poor boy!—in putting on the stage what was in his heart. When he sees that you do feel for him, it will be different. Oh! Armorel!'—the tears rose to her eyes—'you cannot know what that play has been to both of us. We have talked over every situation: we have rehearsed all the dialogue. I know it by heart, I think. I could recite the whole of it, straight through. We have cried over it, and laughed over it. I have dressed dolls for all the parts, and one of us made them act while the other read the play. And, after all, to be told that it is worthless! Oh! It is a shame! It is a shame! And it isn't worthless. It is a great, a beautiful play. It is full of tenderness, and of strength as well.'

'Let us go at once, Effie.'

'What a good thing it was for me that the Head of the Reading Room sent me to you! I little thought I was going to make such a friend'—she took Armorel's hand—'We had no friends—yes, there was one, but he is no true friend. We have had no friends at all, and we thought to make our way without any.'

'You came to London to conquer the world—such a great giant of a world—you and your brother, Jack the Giant Killer.'

'Ah! But we had read, somewhere, that the world is a good-natured giant. He only asks to be amused. If you make him laugh or cry, and forget, somehow, his own troubles—the world is full of troubles—he will give in at once. Archie was going to make him laugh and cry; I was going to tickle him with pretty rhymes. But you may play for him, act for him, dance for him, paint for him, sing for him, make stories for him—anything that you will, and he will be subdued. That is what we read, and we kept on repeating this assurance to each other, but as yet we have not got very far. The great difficulty seems to make him look at you and listen to you.'

'My dear, you shall succeed.'

The young dramatist was sitting at his table, as melancholy as Keats might have been after the *Quarterly Review's* belabouring.

He looked wretched : there was no pretence at anything else : it was unmitigated wretchedness. Despair sat upon his countenance, visible for all to see : his hair had not apparently been brushed, nor his collar changed, since the misery began : he seemed to have gone to bed in his clothes. Trouble does thus affect many men. It attacks even their clothes as well as their hair and their minds. The manuscript was lying on the table before him, but the pen was dry : he had no longer any heart to correct the worthless thing. It was the hour of his deepest dejection. The day before he had plucked up a little courage : perhaps the critic was wrong : to-day all was blackness.

'Here is Armorel, Archie!' cried Effie, with the assumption of cheerfulness.

'I have come to ask a favour,' said Armorel, taking the hand that was mechanically extended. 'I hear that your play is finished, and I am told that it is a beautiful play.'

'No—it isn't,' said the author.

'And that an unkind critic has said horrid and unkind things about it. And I want to read it, if I may. Oh! I am not a great critic, but, indeed, Archie, I have some feeling for Art and for things beautiful. May I read it?'

'The play is perfectly worthless,' he replied sternly, but with signs of softening. 'It is only waste of time to read it. Better throw it behind the fire!' He seized the manuscript as he spoke, but he did not throw it behind the fire.

'Is your critic a dramatist?'

'No. He has never written a play that I know of. But he is a great authority. Everybody would acknowledge that.'

'A critic who has never written a play may very easily make mistakes,' said Armorel. 'You have only to read the critiques of pictures in the papers written by men who cannot paint. They are full of mistakes.'

'This man would not make a mistake, would he, Effie?'

'Well, dear, I think he might, and besides, remember what he said at the conclusion.' Armorel sat down. 'Now,' she said, 'tell me first what the play is about, and then read it, or let Effie read it. I am sure she will read it a great deal better than you.'

He hesitated. He was ashamed to show his miserable work to a second critic. And yet he longed to have another opinion, because, when he came to think about it, he could not understand why the thing could be called worthless.

He yielded. He read, with faltering accents, the scenario which he had prepared with so much pride. Now it was like unrolling a canvas daubed for the scenery of Richardson's Show. He took no more pride in it.

'Oh!' cried Armorel, interrupting. 'This seems to me a very fine situation.'

'My critic said that some of the situations were fine.'

He went on to the end without further interruption.

'Now, Effie,' said Armorel, 'you will read it aloud while your brother plays it with his dolls. Then I am sure to catch the points.'

Archie sat up, and began to place his dolls while Effie read. He was so expert in manipulating his puppets that he made them actually represent the piece, changing the groups every moment, while Effie, dropping the manuscript, folded her arms and recited the play, watching Armorel's face.

This was quite another kind of critic. It was such a critic as the playwright loves when he sits in his box and watches the people in the house—a face which is easily moved to laughter or to tears, which catches the points and feels the story. There are thousands of such faces in every theatre every night. It is for them that the play is written, and not for the critic, who comes to show his superiority by picking out faults and watching for slips. For two hours, not pausing for the division of the acts, Effie went on, her soft voice rising and falling, the passion indicated but repressed; and Archie watched, and moved his groups, and the audience of one sat motionless but not unmoved.

'What?' she cried, springing to her feet and clasping her hands. It is easy for this fine gesture to become theatrical and unreal, but Armorel was never unreal. 'He dared to call this splendid play—this glorious play—oh, this beautiful, sweet, and noble play!'—here Archie's eyes began to fill, and his lips to quiver: he was but a young dramatist, and of praise he had as yet had none—'he dared to call this worthless?'

'He said it was utterly worthless,' said Effie.

'He said,' Archie added, 'that the language was wholly unfitted for the stage. And then—then—after he'd said that, he offered to give me fifty pounds for it.'

'Fifty pounds for a play quite worthless?'

'On the condition that he was to bring it out himself if he pleased, under his own name.'

'Oh! but this is monstrous! Can there be,' asked Armorel, thinking of the pictures, 'two such men in London?'

'If I would let him call it his own! He wants to take my play—mine—to do what he likes with it—to bring it out as if it was his own! Never! Never! I would rather starve first.'

'What did you tell him?'

'He said that he would wait for an answer. I have sent him none as yet.'

'When you do,' said Armorel, 'let there be no hesitation or possibility of mistaking. Oh! If I could tell you a thing that I know!'

'I will put it quite plainly. Effie, am I the same man? I feel transformed. What a difference it makes only to think that, perhaps, after all one is not such a dreadful failure!' In fact, he looked transformed. The trouble had gone out of him—out of his face—out of his hair—out of his clothes—out of his attitude. Armorel even fancied that his limp, day-before-yesterday's collar had become white and starched again. That may have been mere fancy, but joy certainly produces very strange effects.

'I would have sent an answer before,' he said, 'but it is so unlucky for Effie. This great man—this critic—is the only editor who would ever take her verses. And now, of course, he will be offended, and will never take any more.'

'He shall not have any more,' said Effie, with red cheeks.

'Oh! But that would be horribly mean. Well, Archie, I will begin by taking advice. I know a dramatic critic—his name is Stephenson. I will ask him what you should do next, and I will ask him about your verses, Effie, too—those verses which you are always going to show me.'

'I tell her,' said her brother, 'that she will easily find another editor. You would say so too, if you were to see her verses. I am always telling her she ought to show them to you.'

The poet blushed. 'Some day, perhaps, when I am very courageous.'

'No—to-day.' Archie opened a drawer and took out a manuscript book bound in limp brown leather. 'I will read you one,' he said.

'Of course, you will say kind things,' said the poet. 'But you cannot deceive me, Armorel. I shall tell by your eyes and by your face if you really like my rhymes.'

'Well, I will read one, and I will lend you the volume, and then you will see whether Effie hasn't got her gifts as well as anybody else.'

He turned over the pages, selected a poem, and read it. The lines showed, first of all, the command that comes of long and constant practice; and next, they were sweet, simple, and pure in tone.

'Strange!' said Armorel. 'I seem to have heard something like them before—a phrase, perhaps. Where did I read only the other day? . . . Never mind. But, Effie, this is not ordinary girl's verse.'

'Oh! you really like it?'

'Of course I like it. But it is so strange—I seemed to know the style. May I borrow the whole volume? I will be very careful with it. Thank you. I will carry it home with me. And now—I have thought of a plan. Listen, Archie. You know that many young dramatists bring out their pieces first at a matinée. Now, suppose that you read your piece, Archie, in my rooms in the evening. Should you like to do so?'

'I read badly,' he said. 'Could Effie read or recite it?'

'The very thing. Bring your dolls along and arrange your groups, while Effie recites. You will do that, Effie?'

'I will do anything that will help Archie.'

'Very well, then. We will get an evening fixed as soon as possible. I fear we shall have to wait a week at least. I will get my dramatic critic and a few more people, and we will have a private performance of our own. And then we shall defy this critic who said the piece was worthless—and then wanted to buy it and to bring it out as his own. I could not have believed,' she added, 'that there were two such impudent pretenders and liars to be found in the whole of London.'

'Two?' asked Effie, changing colour. 'There can be only one.'

CHAPTER XIV

AN HONOURABLE PROPOSAL

At the same time Mr. Alec Feilding, whose ears ought to have been burning, was engaged in a serious conversation in his own studio with Armorel's companion. The conversation took the form of reproach. 'I expected,' he said—'I had a right to expect—greater devotion—more attention to business. It was not for play that you undertook the charge of this girl. How long have you been with her? Three months? And no more influence with her than when you began.'

'Not a bit more,' Mrs. Elstree replied. She had of course taken the most comfortable chair by the fire. 'Not a bit, my dear Alec. What is more, I never shall have any influence over her. A society girl I could manage. I know what she wants, and how she looks at things. With such a girl as Armorel I am powerless.'

'She is a woman, I suppose.' He occupied a commanding position on his own hearthrug, towering above his visitor, but yet he did not command her.

'Therefore, you think, open to flattery and artful wiles. She is a woman, and yet, strange to say, not open to flattery.'

'Rubbish! It is because you are too stupid or too careless to find out the weak point.'

'To return, Alec: I have failed. I have no influence at all upon this girl. I have spent hours and hours in singing your praise. I have enlarged upon the absolute necessity of giving you a rest from business cares. I have proposed that she and I together—that was the way I put it—should buy a share in the paper, and that she should advance my half. Oh! I grew eloquent on the glory that two women thus coming to the relief of a man like yourself would achieve in after years. I tried to speak from my heart, Alec.' The woman caught his hand, but he drew it away. 'Oh! you deserve no help. You are hard-hearted, and you are selfish: you have broken every promise you ever made me: you spend all that you have in selfish pleasures: you leave me almost without assistance——'

'When I have got you into the easiest and most luxurious berth that can be imagined; when I have asked you for nothing but a simple——'

'Yes, dear Alec, but you see that an honest acknowledgment would be worth all this goodness. Well, I say that I spoke from my heart, because in spite of all I was proud of my man—mine, yes, though Philippa still imagines, poor wretch!'

'Do leave my cousin's name out of it, will you, Zoe?' he said, a little less roughly.

'I am proud of the man who is acknowledged to be the cleverest man in London.' She got up and began to walk about the studio. She stopped before the picture. 'Do you know, Alec—I am not a critic, but I can feel a thing—that this is quite the best work you have ever done. Oh! Those waves, they live and dance; and those birds, they fly; and the air is so warm and soft!—you are a great painter. Odd! your girl is curiously like Armorel. One would fancy your model was Armorel at sixteen or so—a lovely girl she must have been then, and a lovely woman she is now.' Zoe left the picture and began to look at the papers on the table. 'What is this—the new story? Is it good?'

'To you, Zoe, I may confess that it is as good as anything I have ever done.'

'You are really splendid, Alec! What is this?' She took up a very neatly written page in his handwriting. 'Poetry?'

'Those are some verses for next week's journal. I think there is no falling off there, Zoe.'

'Have you got another copy?'

'There is the copy that has gone to the printers'.'

'Then I will take this. It will do for a present—the autograph original draft of the poem—or I may keep it.'

'Zoe, come back and sit down. We must talk seriously.'

She returned and took up her old position by the fire. 'As seriously as you please. It means something disagreeable—something to do with money. Let us get it over. To go back to what we were saying, therefore. I cannot get you that money from Armorel. And at the very word of money she refers one to her lawyer. No confidence at all, as between friends who love each other. That is the position, Alec.' She sat with her hands clasped over her right knee.

'I must have some money,' he said.

'Then, as I have before remarked, Alec—make it.'

'If one cannot have money, Zoe, one may get credit, which is sometimes just as good.'

'I cannot help you in getting credit.'

'Perhaps you can. You can help me, Zoe, by keeping quite quiet.'

'Oh! I am always quiet. I have remained quiet for three years and more, while you flirt with countesses and cousins. How much more quiet do you wish me to remain? While you marry them?'

'Not quite that, my child. But next door to it. While I get engaged to one of them—to one who has money.'

'Not—Philippa.'

'No—I told you before. What the devil is the good of harping on Philippa? You see, if I can let it be understood that I am going to marry an heiress, the difficulties will be tided over. Therefore I shall get engaged to your charge—Armorel Rosevean.'

'Oh!' Zoe received this proposition with coldness. 'This is a charming thing for me to sanction, isn't it?'

'It will do you no harm.'

'I have certainly endured things as bad.'

'You see, Zoe, one could always break off the thing when the time came.'

'Certainly.'

'And you would know all the time that it was a mere pretence.'

'I should certainly know that.'

'Well; is there any other observation?'

'You would make it an open engagement—go about with her—have it publicly known?'

'Of course. The whole point is publicity. I must be known to be engaged to an heiress.'

'And it would last ——'

'As long as might prove necessary. One could find an excuse at any time for breaking it off.'

'Or I could.'

'Just so. It really amounts to nothing at all.'

'To nothing at all!' Zoe neither raised her voice nor her eyes. 'Here is a man who proposes to pretend love and to win a girl's affections, when he can never marry her. He also proposes to throw her over, as soon as she has served his purpose. It is nothing at all, of course! Alec, you are really a wonderful man!'

'Nonsense! The thing is done every day.'

'No—not every day. If you are the cleverest man in London, you are also the most heartless.'

'You know that you can say what you please,' he replied, without any outward sign of annoyance. 'Even heroics.'

'But,' she said, nursing her knee and swinging backwards and forwards, 'we have forgotten one thing—the most important thing of all, in fact. My poor boy, there is no more chance of your being engaged to Armorel than of your entering into the Kingdom of Heaven.'

'Why?'

'Other girls you might catch: you are tall and big and handsome; and you have the reputation of being so very, very clever.

Most girls would be carried away. But not Armorel. She is not subdued by bigness in men, and she doesn't especially care for a clever man. She is actually so old-fashioned—think of it!—that she wants—character.'

'Well! What objection would that raise, I should like to know?'

Zoe laughed softly and sweetly.

'Don't you see, dear Alec? Oh! But you must let Armorel explain to you.'

CHAPTER XV

NOT TWO MEN, BUT ONE

GREAT is the power of coincidence. Things have got a habit of happening just when they are most likely to be useful. It is not on the stage alone that the long-lost uncle turns up, or the long-missing will is found in the cupboard. And you cannot invent for fiction anything half so strange as the daily coincidence of common life. A tolerably long experience of the common life has convinced me of this great truth. Therefore, the coincidence which happened to Armorel on the very day when the young dramatist unfolded his griefs will not, by wise men, be thought at all strange.

It was in the evening. She was sitting with her companion, thinking over Archie and his play. Was it really good? Was it good enough to hold the stage, and to command the attention of the audience? To her it seemed a singularly beautiful, poetical, and romantic piece. But Armorel was of a lowly and humble mind. She knew that she had no experience in things dramatic. Had it been a picture, now——

'Oh!' cried her companion, suddenly starting upright in the cushioned chair where she was lying apparently asleep, 'I had almost forgotten. My dear, I have got a present for you.'

'From yourself, Zoe?'

'Yes; from myself. It is a present which cost me nothing, but is worth a good deal. The making of it cost nobody anything. Yet it is a very precious thing. The material of which it is made is worth nothing. Yet the thing is worth anything you please.'

'It must be a picture, then.'

'It is a Work of Art, but not a picture. Guess again.

'No; I will not guess any more. May I have it without guessing?'

Zoe held in her hands a small roll of blue paper. This she now opened, and gazed at the writing upon it with idolatry: but it hardly carried conviction with it—perhaps it was a little overdone.

'Least imaginative of girls,' she said. It pleased her to consider Armorel's refusal to join in that little scheme of hers as proving a lack of imagination. 'I have brought you, though you do not deserve it, what any other girl in London would give—would give—a dance, perhaps, to obtain, and you shall have it for nothing.'

'I want to hear what it is.'

'It is nothing less, Armorel, nothing less—I got it to-day from the table in his studio—than an autograph: it is the copy used by the printers—an autograph poem of Alec's! An autograph poem, as yet unpublished.'

'Is that all?' replied the least imaginative of girls. 'You must not give it to me, really. You will value it far more than I shall. Besides, I suppose it is to be published some day.'

'But the original manuscript—the autograph poem, dear child! Don't you know the value of such a thing? Take it. You shall be enriched in spite of yourself. Take it and put it aside somewhere in your desk, in some safe place. Heavens! if one had the autograph of a poem of Byron, for example!'

'Mr. Feilding is not Byron,' said Armorel, coldly. 'He may write pretty feminine verses, but he is not Byron. Thank you, however. I will take it, and I will keep it and value it because you think it valuable. I do not suppose the autograph verses of small poets are worth keeping; but still—as you value it' . . .

This was very ungracious and ungrateful. But she was really tired of Mr. Feilding's praises, and after the discovery of the pictures, and after the strange story she had heard only that morning—no; she wanted to hear no more, for the present, of the praises of this man—the cleverest man in London!

However, she unrolled the paper, and began to read the contents, at first carelessly. Then, 'Oh! what is this?' she cried.

'What is what?' asked Mrs. Elstree.

'This is a copy.'

They were the same words as she had used concerning the pictures. She remembered this, and a strange suspicion seized her. 'A copy,' she repeated, wondering.

'A copy? Not at all. They are the verses which are to appear in the next number of the journal—or the number after next. Alec's own verses, of course. Sweetly pretty, I think: what makes you say that they are copied?'

'I thought that I had seen them—something like them—somewhere before.' She went on reading. As she read she remembered the lines more clearly.

'What is the matter, Armorel?' asked Zoe. 'What makes you look so fierce? Heaven help your husband when you look like that!'

'Did I look fierce? It must have been something that I remembered. Yes—that was it.'

'May I read the verses again?' Zoe read them, suspiciously. There was something in them which had startled Armorel. What was it? She could see nothing to account for this emotion. Certainly she was not fond of poetry, and failed to appreciate the fine turns and subtle tones, the felicitous phrase and the unexpected thought with which the poet delights his readers. In this little poem she could find nothing but a few jingling rhymes. Why should Armorel behave so strangely?

'What is it, my dear?' she asked again.

'Something I remembered—nothing of any importance.'

'Armorel, has Alec said anything to you? Has he—has he wanted to make love to you? Has he offended you by speaking?'

'No. There has been no question of love-making between us, and there never will be.'

'One cannot say.' Zoe looked at the matter from experience. 'One can never say. Men are strange creatures; and Alec certainly thinks a great deal of you.'

'I cannot imagine his making love—any more than I can imagine his painting a picture or writing a poem. Perhaps he would make love as he paints.'

'Well, he paints very well.'

'Very well indeed, I dare say.' She got up. 'I am going to leave you to-night, Zoe. I want to go to my own room. I have things to write. You don't mind?'

'My dear child, mind! Of course, one would rather have your company. But since you must leave me'—she sank back in her chair with a sigh. 'Give me that book, dear—if you please—the French novel. When one has been married one can read French novels without trying to conceal the fact. They are mostly wicked, and sometimes witty. Not always. Good-night, dear. I shall not expect you back this evening.'

Armorel, in her own room, opened the manuscript book of poems which Archie had given her, and found—the very last of all—the lines which she had remembered. She laid the precious autograph beside Effie's poem. Word for word—comma for comma—they were exactly the same. There was not the slightest difference. And again Armorel thought of the two pictures.

Then she thought of the little dainty volume in white parchment containing the Second Series of 'Voice and Echo, by Alec Feilding.' She had tossed it aside, impatient with the man, when Zoe gave it to her. Now she looked for it, and found it after a little search. She opened it side by side with Effie's manuscript book. Presently she found the page in Effie's book which corresponded with the first page of the printed volume. There were about thirty or forty poems in the little book: in the manuscript book there were double that number; but the same poems followed each other one after the other in the same order, and without the difference of a single word, both in book and manuscript.

This discovery justifies my remarks about the common coincidences of daily life.

Again Armorel remembered that Zoe possessed another volume—the First Series of 'Voice and Echo, by Alec Feilding.' It was lying—she had seen it in the afternoon—in the drawing-room. She went in search of it, and returned without waking her companion, who had apparently fallen asleep over her novel.

As a matter of fact, Mrs. Elstree was not sleeping. She was broad awake, but she was curious. She desired to know what it all meant: why Armorel was suddenly struck with hardness, why her cheek burned, and her eyes flashed; and what she wanted in the drawing-room. She perceived that Armorel had come in search of Alec's first volume of verse. Oh! Alec's first volume of verse. Now—what might Armorel want with that book?

At the end of March it is light at about half-past five. Everybody is then in their soundest sleep. But at that hour Mrs. Elstree came softly out of her bedroom, wrapped in a dressing-gown, her feet in soft slippers of white wool, and looked at the books and papers on the table in Armorel's room. There was a manuscript volume of verse, professing to be by one Effie Wilmot. There were also two printed little volumes, bound in white-and-gold, containing verses by one Alec Feilding. Strange and wonderful! The verses in both books were exactly the same! Mrs. Elstree returned to bed, thoughtful.

Armorel, for her part, when she returned to her own room, compared the first series of poems, as she had compared the second, with the manuscript book. And the first series, too, word for word, was the same as the earlier poems in the book.

'Good heavens!' cried Armorel. 'The man steals his verses, as he steals his pictures! Poor Effie! She is as bad as Roland!'

This was Thought the First. One has already seen how the three Thoughts treated her before. This time it was just the same. Thought the Second came next, and began to argue. A very capable logician is Thought the Second, once distinguished for what Oxford men call Science. If, said Thought the Second, the manuscript and the volumes agree, it seems to show that Effie has copied the latter into her own book, and now tries to pass the poems off as her own. Such things have been done. If this was the case—and why not?—Effie would be, indeed, a girl full of deceit and desperately wicked. But then, how came Effie to have in her volume a poem hitherto unpublished, which was lying on Mr. Feilding's table? Yet, surely, it was quite as probable that the girl should deceive her as that the man should deceive the world.

Next. Thought the Third. This sage remarked calmly, 'The man is full of villany. He has deceived the world in the matter of the pictures. Why not also in the matter of the poems? But let us consider the character of the verses. Take internal evidence.' Then Armorel read the whole series right through in the two little printed volumes. Oh! They were feminine. Only a woman could write these lines. Womanhood breathed in every one. 'Now that the key was supplied, she understood. She recognised the voice, eager, passionate, of her friend.

'They are all Effie's!' she cried again; 'all—all. The man has stolen his verses as well as his pictures.'

This discovery, when she had quite made up her mind that it was as true as the former, entirely fell in with all that Effie had told her concerning herself. She had sold her poems all to one editor—he was the only editor who would ever take them—and now she was afraid that he would take no more. Why?—why?—because—oh, now she understood all—because he wanted to be a dramatist in the same way that he was a painter and a poet, and neither Archie nor his sister would consent! 'Yes,' she said, 'he is, indeed, the cleverest man in London.'

Before she went to bed that night she had devised a little plan—quite an ingenious clever little plan. You shall hear what it was, and how it came off.

CHAPTER XVI

THE PLAY AND THE COMEDY

ARMOREL arranged for the reading of the play one evening four or five days later. It was a short notice, but she secured the people whom she wanted most, and trusted to chance for the others. She occupied herself in the interval in arranging the details and leading situations for a little comedy drama of her own—a play of some melodramatic force, in which, as in 'Hamlet,' a certain guilty person was to discover by a kind of dumb show that his guilt was known to her. It was to be a comedy which no one, except herself, was to understand. You shall see, directly, what an extremely clever little comedy it was, and how effective to the person principally concerned. She said nothing at all about this comedy even to Effie. As for words, there were none. They were left to the principal character. This is, indeed, the ancient and original drama. The situations were, at the outset, devised beforehand. The actors filled in the dialogue. This form of drama is still kept up, and with vigour. When the schoolboy sets the booby-trap, or sews up the shirt-sleeves, or greases the side-walk—if that old situation is still remembered—or practises any other kindly and mirthful sally, the victim supplies the words. The confidence trick in all its branches is another form of the primitive drama, and this evening's performance with reference to a certain person was only another example. You will hear, presently, what admirable dialogue was elicited by Armorel's situations.

By half-past eight she had completed the mounting of her piece. First, for the reading of the play she placed a table at the side of the room, with a space at the back sufficient for a chair, or for a person to sit. A reading-lamp, with one of those silver cowls that throw the whole light upon the table, stood at either end, illuminating a small space in the middle. This was for the manipulation of the dolls. For, though the people had been asked to come for a reading, Armorel had determined to try the experiment of a recitation, accompanied by the presentment of those puppets which Effie had dressed with such care, and her brother manipulated so deftly. Needless to say that more than one rehearsal had been held. In front of the table she placed a semicircle of chairs for some of her audience. At one side of the table was the piano: a music-stand, with a violin case, gave promise of an overture. Between the music-stand and the table was room for a person to stand, and on the table a water-decanter and a glass showed that this was the place for the reciter. On the other side of the table, in the corner of the room, stood an easel, and on it a picture, with curtains arranged so that they could fall over and cover it up. The picture was lighted up by two lamps. The room had no other lights in it at all, so that, if these two lamps were lowered or extinguished, the only light would be that thrown by the reading-lamps upon the table. As for the picture, it was as yet unfinished, but nearly finished. Of course it was Roland Lee's new picture. This evening, indeed, which professed to be the simple reading of a new play by a new writer, included a great deal more: it included, in fact, Roland's return to the arena he had deserted, and, as you shall see, the stepping upon the stage of both the twins, brother and sister. When one adds that Mr. Alec Feilding would be one of the company, you understand, dear reader, the nature of Armorel's comedy, and the kind of situation devised and prepared by that artful and vindictive young lady.

'How long will it take, dear?' asked Mrs. Elstree, wearily contemplating these preparations

'I should say that the play will take an hour and a half or two hours to recite. Then there will be a little music between the acts. I dare say it will last two hours and a half.'

'Oh, that will bring us to half-past eleven at least! And then it will be too late for anything else.'

'We don't want anything else to-night.'

'No, dear. The play will be quite enough for us. I wish it was over. I am so constituted, Armorel, that I cannot see the least use in going out of my way to help anybody. If you succeed in helping people to climb up, they only trample on you as soon as they get the chance. If you fail, they are a burden upon you for life. These two Wilmot people, for instance: what are you going to do with them when you have read their play and stuff? You can't get a manager to play it any the more for having it read. The two are no further advanced.'

'Yes; I shall have made the young man known. He will be introduced. Mr. Stephenson promised to bring some critics with him, and you have asked Mr. Feilding to do the same. An introduction—perhaps the creation of some personal interest—may be to Archie of the greatest advantage.'

'Then he will rise by your help, and he will proceed to trample upon you. That is, if the brother is like the sister. If ever I saw "trampler" written plain on any woman's face, it is written on the great square block of bone that Effie Wilmot calls a forehead.'

'They may trample on me if they please,' Armorel replied, smiling.

The tramplers were naturally the first to arrive. They were both pale, and they trembled, especially the one who was not going to speak. He came in, limping on his crutches, and looked around with terror at the preparations. One does not realise before the night comes what a serious thing is a first appearance in public. Besides, the strong light on the table, the expectant chairs, the arrangement of everything, presented an aspect at once critical and threatening. The manuscript play and the box of puppets were in readiness.

'Now, Archie,' said Armorel, 'it is not yet nine o'clock. You shall have a cup of coffee to steady your nerves. So shall you, Effie. After that we will settle ourselves.' She talked about other things to distract their thoughts. 'See, Effie, that is Roland Lee's new picture. It is not yet finished. The central figure is myself. You see, it is as yet only sketched in. I am going to sit for him, but he has caught a good likeness, has he not? It will be a lovely picture when it is completed, and I am going to give him permission to flatter me as much as ever he pleases. The scene is among the outer rocks of Scilly. We will go there some day and sail about the Western Islands, and I will show you Camber Rock and the Channel, and Castle Bryher and Menovawr and Maiden Bower, and all the lovely places where I lived till I was sixteen years of age. Are you in good voice to-night, Effie?'

'I don't know. I hope so.'

'She has eaten nothing all day,' said Archie.

'You are not really frightened, are you, Effie?' The girl was white with nervousness. 'A little excited and anxious. Will you have another cup of coffee? A little jelly? Remember I shall be close beside you, with the play in my hand, to prompt. I like your dress. You look very well in white, dear.'

'Oh! Armorel, I am horribly frightened. If I should break down, Archie's chance will be ruined. And if I recite it badly I shall spoil the play.'

'You will not break down, dear; you will think of nothing but the play. You will forget the people. Besides, it will be so dark that you will hardly see them.'

'I will try my best. Perhaps when I begin—Oh! for Archie's sake, I would stand up on the stage at the theatre and speak before all the people! And yet——'

'She had no sleep last night,' said her brother. 'I think, after all, I had better read it. Only I read so badly.'

Armorel's face fell. She had thought so much of the reciting. Then Mrs. Elstree came to the rescue.

'Nonsense,' she said. 'You three people are making yourselves so nervous that you will most certainly break down. Now, Mr. Wilmot, go into your own place. Set out your dolls. Here's your cardboard back scene.' She arranged it while Archie got himself and his crutches into the chair behind, and began to take the dolls out of their box. 'So. Now don't speak to your sister. You will only make her worse. And as for you, Effie, if you break down now you will be a most disgraceful coward. With your brother's future, perhaps, dependent on your courage. For shame! Pull yourself together!' Effie, thus rudely stimulated, and by a person she disliked greatly, lost her limpness and stood upright. Her face also put on a little colour, and her lips stiffened. The tonic worked, in fact. Then Zoe went on. 'Now,' she said, 'take up your position here. How are you going to stand? Fold your hands so. That is a very good attitude to begin with. Of course, you understand nothing of gesture. Don't try it. Change your hands a little—so—front—right—left—like that. And don't—don't—don't hold your head like that, facing the crowd. Hold it up—like this. Look at the corner of that cornice—straight up. Oh! you will lower your head as you go on. But, to begin with, and at the opening of each act, look up to that corner. Remember, if you break down——' She held up a forefinger, threatening, admonitory, and left her standing in position. 'You will do now,' she said.

'Besides,' said Armorel, 'no one will look at you. They will all be looking at Archie's actors.'

The dramatist, relegated to the humble position of fantoccini-man, would be also in complete shade behind the table. He would not be seen, whatever emotion of anxiety he should feel. And for dexterity of manipulation with his puppets he could vie even with the firm of Codlin and Short.

The noise of cups and saucers in the dining-room proclaimed the arrival of guests. The first to come was Roland Lee, still a little shy, as Alexander Selkirk might have been, or Philip Quarles, or Mr. Penrose, on his return to civilised society. He looked about the room. Mrs. Elstree—looking resigned—and Armorel, standing by the fire, and the two performers. Nobody else. And, in a place of honour, his unfinished picture.

'It looks very well, doesn't it?' said Armorel. 'I wish it was a little more complete. But it will do to show.'

'Are you quite sure it is wise?'

'Quite sure. The sooner you show everybody what you can do the better.'

'I have found a new studio,' he told her in low tones. 'I have moved in to-day. It is among the old lot of men that I used to know a little. I have gone back to them just as if I had only been gone for a day. I don't find that they have got on very much. Perhaps they spend too much time smoking pipes and cigarettes and talking. They chaff me, but with respect, because, I believe, they think I have been staying in a lunatic asylum. Respect, you know, is due to madmen and to old men.'

'I hope it is the kind of studio you want.'

'It will do. I am anxious to begin your sittings. When can you come?'

'Any day you please. To-morrow. The next day. I can begin at once.'

Then came a small party of men—journalists and critics—captured by Dick Stephenson at the club, and bribed to come by the promise of an introduction to the beautiful Miss Armorel Rosevean. I do not think they expected much joy from the amateur reading of an unacted piece. It is melancholy, indeed, to consider that though the preliminary and tentative performance of the unacted play—long prayed for—has been at last established, the promised appearance of the great dramatist has not yet come off—nay, the theatrical critic weeps, swears, and growls at the mention of a matinée, and when he is requested to attend one passes it on if he can to his younger brother in the calling. And yet such great treasures were expected of the matinée! However, they agreed to come and listen on this occasion. It shall be put down to their credit as a Samaritan deed.

'Dick Stephenson,' said Armorel, with an assumption of old friendship which filled him with pride, 'I hope you are come here to-night in a really serious frame of mind—you and your friends.'

'We are always serious.'

'I mean that you are going to hear an ambitious piece of work. All I ask of you is to listen seriously, and to remember that it is really the work of a man who aims at the very highest.'

'Will he reach the very highest?'

'I do not know. But I am quite certain that there are very few artists, in any branch, who dare to aim high. Listen, and try to understand what the poet has attempted—what has been in his mind. Promise me this.'

'Certainly, I will promise you so much.'

'Thank you. It was for this that I asked you to-night. And see—here is your old friend Roland Lee.' The two young men shook hands rather sheepishly—the one because he had been an Ass—a long-eared Ass; and the other, because he was not guiltless of letting his friend slip out of his hands without a remonstrance and so away into paths unknown. 'I hear,' said Armorel, with her beautiful seriousness, 'that you two have suffered yourselves to drift apart of late. I hope that will be all over now. Oh! you must never give up the early friendships. Have you seen Roland's new picture? He has lent it to me for this evening. Come and look at it.'

'Why,' cried one of the men, 'it is an unfinished picture of Alec Feilding's!'

Roland turned hot and red.

'Not at all,' said Armorel. 'This is a sketch made in the isles of Scilly and in my presence, five years ago. As for the figure, you see it is not yet completed. I am the model. You remember Scilly, Dick Stephenson? To be sure, you were not with us when we used to go sailing about among the rocks.'

'I have reason to remember Scilly, seeing that you saved my life there, and Roland's too. But the picture is curiously in Feilding's style. Only it seems to me better than any of his. Old man'—he laid his hand on Roland's shoulder: it was the renewal of the ancient friendship—'old man, you've done the trick at last.'

Philippa came next, with her father and two or three girls. They, in their turn, called out upon the striking similarity in style. A few more people came, and it was a quarter past nine. But the man for whom Armorel had especially arranged her little comedy did not come. He was late. Perhaps he would not come at all.

'We must wait no longer,' said Armorel. 'Will everybody please to sit down?'

Philippa placed herself at the piano. Armorel took out her violin and tuned it. First, however, she made a little speech.

'I have asked you,' she said, 'to come this evening in order to hear a play read. It is a play written by a young gentleman in whom some of us take the deepest interest. I hope greatly that it will succeed. But we want your judgment and opinion as well as our own. The play belongs to all time and to no time. The scene is laid in Italy, and in the sixteenth century; but it might as well have been laid in London and in the nineteenth—only that we are more self-governed than a dramatist likes, and we conceal our emotions. It is a play of romance and of human passion. I entreat you to consider it seriously—as seriously as the author himself considers it. We have arranged for you a list of the dramatis personæ, with a little scenario of each act—there are three—and we think that if, instead of hearing it read, we have it recited, while the author himself plays the piece before us by puppets on this little stage, we shall get a clearer idea of the dramatic merits of the piece.'

This speech done, everybody took up the little book of the play and began to read the scenario, while Armorel played an overture with Philippa.

She played a Hungarian piece, one of the things that are now played everywhere—a quite short piece.

When it was finished, Roland lowered the lamps beside his

picture, and covered them with crimson shades. Then there was no other light in the room but that from the two reading-lamps on the table. Just before the lamps were lowered Mr. Alec Feilding arrived, with half a dozen men whom he had brought with him. She saw his startled face as he caught sight of the picture as the lights were lowered. In the twilight she could still distinguish his face among the men who stood behind the chairs. And she watched him. Then Effie, who had not seen the latest arrival, took her place, and the play began.

The effect was new and very curious. The people saw a girl standing up beside the table—only the shadow of a girl—a ghostly figure in white—the spectre of a white face—two bright eyes flashing in the dim light. And they heard her voice, a rich, low contralto, beginning to recite the play.

It is not the nervous creature who breaks down. He may generally be trusted. He lies awake for whole nights before the time arrives: he reaches the spot weak-kneed, trembling, and pale; but when the hour strikes he braces himself, stands up, and goes through with it. Effie had been partly pulled together, it is true, by the rough exhortation of Mrs. Elstree, but some credit must be given to her own resolution. She began with a little hesitation, fearing that she should forget the words. Then they came back to her: she saw them written plainly before her eyes in that friendly corner of the cornice: she hesitated no longer: in full and flowing flood she poured forth the dialogue, helped to right modulation by the strength of her own feeling and her belief in the beauty and the splendour of the drama. Armorel meantime watched her man. He had seen the picture. Now he recognised the play, and he knew the reciter. As he stood at the back, tall above the rest, she saw his face change from astonishment gradually to dismay. It was rather a wooden face, but it passed plainly and successively through the phases of doubt and certainty to that of dismay. Yes; dismay was written on that face, with discomfiture and suspicion. In a more demonstrative age he would have sat gnawing his nails: every wicked man, overtaken by the consequence of his own wickedness, used formerly to gnaw his nails. On the stage of the last century he would have turned upon his persecutors with a 'Death and confusion!' before he banged off the scene. We no longer use those fine old phrases. On the modern stage he would stand with straightened arms and bowed head, while the rest of the company pointed fingers of scorn at him, crushed but defiant. In Armorel's drawing-room he stood quiet and motionless, trying to collect himself. He saw, first of all, Roland Lee's new picture in the corner; he saw Roland Lee himself, no longer the negligent, despairing sloven, but once more a gentleman to outer view, and in his right mind. Next, he observed that Effie, his own poet, was reciting the play; and, thirdly, that the play was that for which he had himself made a bid. Thus all three—painter, poet, and dramatist—were friends of this girl Armorel; and they had all three, he knew quite well, slipped clean out of his hands for ever, and were lost to him; and all three, he suspected, had already related to each other the history of his doings and dealings with themselves. Therefore, while the play proceeded, his heart sank low—lower—lower.

There were three acts. When the first was finished Armorel stood up again and, with Philippa, played another little piece, but not long. And so between the second and the third.

Watching the people, Armorel became aware that the play had gripped them, and held them fast. No one moved. The little space upon the table between the two lamps, where the puppets stood before the painted screen of cardboard, became a scene richly mounted: it was a garden, or a dancing-hall, or an arbour, or a library, just as those little books told them, and the puppets were men and women. We want so little of mounting to fire the imagination, if only the poet has the strength to seize it and to hold it by his words. Nothing, in this case, but a modulated voice reciting a dramatic poem, and, to help it out, a dozen dressed dolls, six or seven inches high, standing stiffly on a little stage. Yet, even when passion was at its highest, in the great scene of the third act, they were not ridiculous. Nobody laughed at the dolls. That was because the showman knew their capabilities. When they stood in their place, they indicated the nature of the situation and explained the words. Had he tried to make them act, he would have spoiled the whole. They made a series of groups—*tableaux vivants*, *poses plastiques*—constantly changed by the deft hands of the showman, finding relief in this occupation for the anxiety in his soul. For he, less fortunate than Effie, who had grasped the cheering truth, could not read in the circle of still faces before him their rapt and magnetised condition.

And now the end of the third act was neared. The reciter rose to the concluding situation. Her voice, firm and clear, rang out in the dim light. The younger girls in the audience caught each other's hands. The 'lines' were good lines, strong and nervous, rapid and yet intense, equal to the strength and intensity of the situation.

At last the play was finished.

'Effie!' Armorel caught her in her arms, 'you have done splendidly!'

But the girl drew back. The honours of the evening were not for her, but for her brother: she stood aside.

Armorel took the cowls from the reading-lamps, and the room returned to light. Then the people began all to press round the dramatist and to shake hands solemnly with him, to murmur, to assure, to congratulate, and to prophesy. And the loud voice of

Mr. Alec Feilding arose as he stepped forward among the first and grasped the young man's hand.

'Archie!' he said with astounding friendliness, 'this is better than I expected. Let me congratulate you! I have had the privilege,' he explained to the multitude, 'of hearing this play—at least, a part of it—already. I told you, my dear boy, that your situations were splendid, but your dialogue wanted pulling together in parts. You have attended to my advice. I am glad of it. The result promises to be a splendid success. What say you?' He turned to a very well-known dramatic critic whom he had brought with him.

'If you can get the proper man to play the leading part,' he replied more quietly, 'the play seems to me full of promise. Frankly, Mr. Wilmot, I think you have written a most poetical and most romantic piece. It is valuable, not only for itself, but for the promise it contains.'

'For its promise,' repeated Alec Feilding blandly, 'as I told you, my dear boy, for its promise—its admirable promise. I shall not rest now until this play is produced—either at the Lyceum or at the Haymarket. Once more.' Again he grasped Archie by the hand. Then another and another followed. It was not until the next day the dramatist recovered presence of mind enough to remember that Mr. Feilding had not given him any advice: that he had not said it was a work of promise: that he had offered to buy it for fifty pounds and bring it out as his own, with his own name put to it: and that no alteration of any kind had been made in it.

When Mr. Alec Feilding stepped back, he perceived that some one had turned up the lamps beside the picture. He was a man of great presence of mind and resource. He instantly stepped over to the picture and began to examine it curiously. Armorel followed him.

'This is by my old friend Mr. Roland Lee,' she said. 'Do you know him? Let me introduce him to you.' The men bowed distantly as those who, having met for the first time in a crowd, see no reason for desiring to meet each other again. That they should so meet, with such an assumption of never having met before, struck Armorel with admiration.

'The picture is a good deal in your own style, Feilding,' said one of the critics.

'Perhaps,' replied the successful painter in that style, briefly.

'It is taken from a sketch,' Armorel explained, 'made by Mr. Lee while he was staying at the same spot as myself. He made a great number at the time—which is now five years ago.'

Mr. Alec Feilding heard this statement with outward composure. Inwardly he was raging.

'It is, in fact, exactly in your style,' said the same critic. 'One would say that it was a copy of one of your pictures.'

'Perhaps,' he replied again.

'If,' said Roland, 'Mr. Feilding sends another picture in the same style for exhibition this year, I hope that the similarity of style may be tested by their hanging side by side.'

'Shall you send anything this year—in the same style?' asked Armorel.

'I hardly know. I have not decided.'

The critic looked at the picture more closely. 'Strange!' he murmured. 'One would swear . . . the same style—so individual—and belonging to two different men!'

Then Roland covered his picture over with the curtain. There had been enough said.

'Now,' said Armorel, 'after our emotions and our fatigues of the play, we are exhausted. There is supper in the next room. Before we go in I want to sing you a song. I am not a singer, you know, and you must only expect simple warbling. But I want you to like the song.'

She sat down to the piano and played a few bars of introduction. Then she sang the first verse—it was Effie's latest song, that which Mr. Feilding had accepted but not yet published.

He heard and recognised. This third blow finished him. He sat down on the nearest chair, speechless. Mrs. Elstree watched him, wondering what was the matter with him. For he was in a speechless rage. Lucky for him that it was speechless, because for the moment he was beside himself, and might have said anything.

'That is the first verse,' said Armorel. 'I have set it to an old French air which I found in a book. The words seem written for the music. There are two more verses.'

She sang them through. Her voice was pleasing though not strong: she sang sweetly and with feeling, just as she had sung in the old days on the shores of Samson, to the accompaniment of the waves lapping along the white sands, and she watched the man whom she had been torturing the whole evening through. Would not even this rouse him to some word or deed which might proclaim him a pretender and an impostor discovered? She knew, you see, that the lines were actually in type ready to appear as another poem by the Editor. She finished and rose. 'Do you like the song, Philippa?' she said. 'I have even had it printed and set to music. Anybody that pleases may carry away a copy. I hope everybody will, and keep it in remembrance of this evening. For the words are written by Miss Effie Wilmot, who has recited so beautifully her brother's play. We will share the honours of the evening between them. Archie, will you give me your arm? Roland'—in her excitement she called him by his Christian name, which caused a little surprise—'will you take Effie? Do you like the words, Mr. Feilding?'

'Very much indeed. I had seen them before you, I think.'

'Yes? Then you recognised them. You have seen other poems by the same hand, I believe?'

'Good-night, Miss Rosevean. I have had a delightful evening.' He retired without any supper. On his way out, he passed Effie. 'You should have trusted me,' he whispered hoarsely. 'I expected, at least, common confidence. You will find that I have kept my promise—and you have broken yours.' He passed on, and disappeared. Then they trooped in to the dining-room, where they found spread that kind of midnight refection which is dear to the hearts of those who are yet young enough to love champagne and chicken. And after supper they went back to the drawing-room and danced. Mrs. Elstree played to them—nobody could play a waltz better. Roland danced with Armorel. 'You make me believe,' he said, at the end of the waltz, 'that I am really back again.'

'Of course you are back again.'

Then Armorel danced with the critics, and talked about the play; and they all promised to go to great actors and speak about this wonderful drama. And so all went away at last, and all to bed, well content.

'But,' said Zoe, when the last was gone, 'what was the matter with Alec? Why did he look so glum? What made him in such an awful rage? He can get into a blind rage, Armorel—blind and speechless. As for that, I would not give a button for a man who could not. But what was the matter with him?'

'Was he in a rage? Perhaps he wished that he had written the play himself. Such a clever man as that would be sorry, perhaps, that anything good was written, except by himself.'

Mr. Alec Feilding rushed down the stairs and into the street. He hailed a cab, and jumped into it.

'Fleet Street! Quick!'

His printers, he knew, had work which kept them at work on Thursday nights till long past midnight. It was not too late to make a correction. His paper would be printed in the morning, and ready for issue by five o'clock in the afternoon. In fact, Effie received a note from him on Saturday morning:—

'My dear Effie,' he wrote, 'I send you a copy of my new number. You will find, on looking into the editorial columns, that I have performed what I promised. Not only have I accepted and published your very charming verses, but I have added a brief note introducing the writer as a débutante of promise. So much I am very pleased to have been able to do for you. Now, as one writer introducing another, I leave you with your public. Give them of your best. Let your first set of published verses prove your worst. Aim at the best and highest; write in a spirit of truth; let your Art be sincere and self-respectful.

'I am sorry that this note, written on Tuesday, could not contain what I should much have wished to add, had I known it: that your verses have been adapted to an old air by Miss Armorel Rosevean. You did not, however, think fit to take me into your confidence.

'I cannot hope to give you more than an occasional appearance in my columns. I should advise you, with this introduction of mine and the credentials of being published in my paper, to send verses to the magazines. I think you will have little difficulty with the help of my name in gaining admission.

'Allow me to add my congratulations on your brother's undoubted success. His play is admirable as a chamber play. It may also succeed on the stage, but of this it is impossible to be certain. Meantime, it is very cheering to find that he listens to the advice of those who have a right to speak, and that he follows that advice. It is both cheering to his friends and promising as regards his own future. I do not regret the time that I spent in advising upon that play.

'I remain, my dear Effie, very sincerely yours,

'Alec Feilding.'

The paper which contained the verses contained also the following paragraph:—

'In place of the usual editorial verses—my editorial duties do not always give me leisure for the service of the Muse—I have great pleasure in inserting a set of verses from the pen of a young lady whose name is new to my readers. She makes her bow to my readers in this column. I venture, however, to prophesy that she will not long remain unknown. Wherever the English language is spoken, before many years the name of Effie Wilmot shall be known and loved. This is the prophecy of one who at least can recognise good work when he sees it.'

Effie read both letter and paragraph to her brother, who raged and stormed about the alleged advice and assistance. She also read them both to Armorel, who only laughed a little.

'But,' said Effie, 'he never helped Archie at all! He gave him no advice!'

'My dear, if he chooses to say that he did, what does it matter? Time goes on, and every day will make your brother rise higher and Mr. Feilding sink lower. And as to the verses, Effie, and your—your first appearance'—Effie turned away her shamefaced cheek—'why, we will take his advice and try other editors. Mr. Feilding is, indeed, the cleverest man in London!'

CHAPTER XVII

THE NATIONAL GALLERY

CONTRARY to all reasonable expectation, Alec Feilding called at Armorel's rooms the very next morning—and quite early in the morning, when it was not yet eleven. Armorel, however, had already gone out. He was received by Mrs. Elstree, who was, as usual, sitting, apparently asleep, by the fire.

'You have come in the hope of seeing Armorel alone, I suppose?' she said.

'Yes. You remember, Zoe,' he replied quickly—she observed that he was pale, and that he fidgeted nervously, and that his eyes, restless and scared, looked as if somebody was hunting him—'that we had a talk about it. You said you wouldn't make a row. You know you did. You consented.'

'Oh, yes! I remember. I am to play another part, and quite a new one. You too are about to play a new part—one not generally desired—quite the stage villain.' He made a gesture of impatience. 'Consider, however,' she went on quickly, before he could speak. 'Do you think this morning—the day after yesterday—quite propitious for your purpose?'

'What do you mean?' he asked quickly. 'Why not the day after yesterday?'

'Nothing. Still, if I might advise——'

'Zoe, you know nothing at all. And time presses. If there was reason, a week ago, for me to be the reputed and accepted lover of this girl, there is tenfold more reason now. You don't know, I say. For Heaven's sake don't spoil things now by any interference.'

He was at least in earnest. Mrs. Elstree contemplated him with curiosity. It seemed as if she had never seen him really in earnest before. But now she understood. He knew by this time that Armorel had discovered the source, the origins, of his greatness. She might destroy him by a word. This knowledge would pierce the hide of the most pachydermatous: his strength, you see, was like that of Samson—it depended on a secret: it also now resembled that of Samson in that it lay at the mercy of a woman.

'Alec,' said Mrs. Elstree, softly, 'you were greatly moved last night by several things—by the play, by the picture, by the song. I watched you. While the rest were listening to the play, I watched you. The room was dark, and you thought no one could see you. But I could make out your features. Armorel watched you, too, but for other motives. I was wondering. She was triumphant. You know why?'

'What do you know?'

'Your face, which is generally so well under command, expressed surprise, rage, disgust, and terror—all these passions, dear Alec. On the stage we study how to express them. We represent an exaggeration so that the gallery shall understand, and we call it Art. But I know the symptoms.'

'What else do you know, I ask?'

'This morning you are nervous and agitated. You are afraid of something. Alec, you know what I think of the cruelty and hardheartedness of this project of yours—to sustain your credit on an engagement which will certainly not last a month—I could not possibly suffer the girl to be entangled longer than that—now give it over.'

'I cannot give it over: it is my only chance. Zoe, you don't know the mischief she has done me, and will do me again. It is ruin—ruin!'

'Well then, Alec, don't go after her to-day. Indeed, I advise you not. You are not in a condition to approach the subject, and she is not in a condition to be approached. I do not ask your reasons, or the kind of mischief you mean. I sit here and watch. In the course of time I find out all things.'

'How much do you know, Zoe? What have you found out?'

'Knowledge, Alec, is power. Should I part in a moment, and for nothing, with what I have acquired at the expense of a great deal of contriving and putting together? Certainly not. You can go and find Armorel, if you persist in choosing such a day for such a purpose. She has gone, I believe, to the National Gallery.'

'I must find her to-day. I must bring things to a head. Good Heavens! I don't know what new mischief they may be designing.'

'Go home and wait, Alec. No one will do anything to you to-day. You are nervous and excited.'

'You don't understand, I say. Tell me, did the men talk last night—about me—in your hearing?'

'Not in my hearing, certainly. Go home and rest, Alec.'

'I cannot rest. I must find the girl.'

'Well, if you want her—go and find her. Alec, remember, if you stood the faintest chance of success with her, I think I should have to get up and warn her. Even for your sake I do not think I could suffer this wickedness to be done. But you have no chance—none—not on any day, particularly on this day—and after last night. Go, however—go.'

When things have gone so far that assignations and appointments are made and places of secret meeting agreed upon, there is hardly any place in the whole of London more central, more convenient, or safer than the National Gallery. Here the young lady of society may be perfectly certain of remaining undiscovered. At the South Kensington no one is quite safe, because in the modern enthusiasm for art all kinds of people—even people in society—sometimes go there to see embroideries and hangings, and handiwork of every sort. The India Museum is perhaps safer even than the National Gallery—safer, for such a purpose, than any other spot in the world. But there is a loneliness in its galleries which strikes a chill to the most ardent heart, and damps the spirit of the most resolute lover.

In the National Gallery there are plenty of people: but they are all country visitors, or Americans, or copyists: never any people of the young lady's own set: and there is never any crowd. One can sit and talk undisturbed and quiet: the copyists chatter or go on with their work regardless of anything: the attendants slumber: the visitors pass round room after room, looking for pictures which have a story to tell—and a story which they can read. That, you see, is the only kind of picture—unless it be a picture of a pretty face—which the ordinary visitor commonly understands. Not many young people know of this place, and those who do keep the knowledge to themselves. The upper rooms of the British Museum are also commended by some for the same reason, but the approaches are difficult.

This use of the National Gallery once understood, the thing which happened here the day after the reading of the play will not seem incredible, though it certainly was not intended by the architect when he designed the building. Otherwise there might have been convenient arbours.

Armorel went often to the Gallery: the English girl reserves, as a rule, her study of pictures, and art generally, till she gets to Florence. Armorel, who had also studied art in Florence, found much to learn in our own neglected Gallery. Sometimes she went alone: sometimes she went with Effie, and then, being quite a learned person in the matter of pictures and their makers, she would discourse from room to room, till the day was all too short. The country visitors streamed past her in languid procession: the lovers met by appointment at her very elbow: the copyists flirted, talked scandal, wasted time, and sighed for commissions: but Armorel had not learned to watch people: she came to see the pictures: she had not begun to detach an individual from the crowd as a representative: in other words, she was not a novelist.

This morning she was alone. She carried a notebook and pencil, and was standing before a picture making notes. It was a wet morning: the rooms were nearly empty, and the galleries were very quiet.

She heard a manly step striding across the floor. She half turned as it approached her. Mr. Alec Feilding took off his hat.

'Mrs. Elstree told me you were here,' he said. 'I ventured to follow.'

'Yes?'

'You—you—come often, I believe?' He looked pale, and, for the first time in Armorel's recollection of him, he was nervous. 'There is, I believe, a good deal to be learned here.'

'There is, especially by those who want to paint—of course, I mean—who want to do their own paintings by themselves. Mr. Feilding, frankly, what do you want? Why do you come here in search of me?' Her face hardened: her eyes were cold and resolved. But the man was full of himself; he noted not these symptoms.

'I came because I have something to say.'

'Of importance?'

'Of great importance.'

'Not, I hope, connected with Art. Do not talk to me about Art, if you please, Mr. Feilding—not about any kind of Art.'

He bowed gravely. 'One cannot always listen to conversation involving canons and first principles,' he said, with much condescension. 'Let me, however, congratulate you on the promise of your protégés, Archie and Effie Wilmot.'

'They are clever.'

'They are distinctly clever,' he repeated, recovering his usual self-possession. 'Effie, as perhaps she has told you, has been my pupil for a long time.'

'She has told me, in fact, something about her relations to you.'

'Yes.' The man was preoccupied and rather dense by nature. Therefore he caught only imperfectly these side meanings in Armorel's replies. 'Yes—quite so—I have been able to be useful to her, and to her brother also—very useful, indeed, happily.'

'And to—to others—as well—very useful, indeed,' Armorel echoed.

He understood that there was some kind of menace in these words. But the very air, this morning, was full of menace. He passed them by.

'It is a curious coincidence that you should also have taken up this interesting pair. It ought to bring us closer.'

'Quite the contrary, Mr. Feilding. It puts us far more widely apart.'

'I do not understand that. We have a common interest. For instance, only the other day I accepted a poem of Effie's ——'

'Only the other day, Mr. Feilding?'

'Yes, the day before yesterday. I had it set up, and I added a few words introducing the writer. That was the day before yesterday. Judge of my astonishment when, only yesterday, you sang that very song, and handed it round printed with the accompaniment. I have made no alteration. The verses will appear to-night, with my laudatory introduction. Some men might complain that they had not been taken into confidence. But I do not. Effie is a little genius in her way. She is not practical: she does not understand that having disposed of her verses to one editor she is not free to give them to another. But I do not complain, if your action in her cause brings her into notice.'

Here was a turning of tables! Now, some men overdo a thing. They smile too much: they rub their hands nervously: they show a nervous anxiety to be believed. Not so this man. He spoke naturally—he had now recovered his usual equanimity: he looked blankly unconscious that any doubt could possibly be thrown upon his word. Since he said it, the thing must be so. Men of honour have always claimed and exacted this concession. Therefore, the following syllogism:—

Mr. Alec Feilding is a man of honour:
Everybody must acknowledge so much.
A man of honour cannot lie:
Else—what becomes of his honour?
Therefore:
Any statement made by Mr. Alec Feilding is literally true.

Armorel showed no doubt in her face. Why should she? There was no doubt in her mind. The man was a Liar.

'The Wilmots will get on,' she said coldly, 'without any help from anybody. Now, Mr. Feilding, you came to say something important to me. Shall we go on to that important communication?' She took a seat on the divan in the middle of the room. He stood over her. 'There is no one here this morning,' she said. 'You can speak as freely as in your own study.'

'Among your many fine qualities, Miss Rosevean,' he began floridly, but with heightened colour, 'a certain artistic reserve is reckoned by your friends, perhaps, the highest. It makes you queenly.'

'Mr. Feilding, I cannot possibly discuss my own qualities with any but my friends.'

'Your friends! Surely, I also——'

'My friends, Mr. Feilding,' Armorel repeated, bristling like the fretful porcupine. But the man, preoccupied and thick of skin, and full of vainglory and conceit, actually did not perceive these quills erect. Armorel's pointed remarks did not prick his hide: her coldness he took for her customary reserve. Therefore he hurried to his doom.

'Give me,' he said, 'the right to speak to you as your dearest friend. You cannot possibly mistake the attentions that I have paid to you for the last few weeks. They must have indicated to you—they were, indeed, deliberately designed to indicate—a preference—deepening into a passion——'

'I think you had better stop at once, Mr. Feilding.'

There are many men who honestly believe that they are irresistible. It seems incredible, but it is really true. It is the consciousness of masculine superiority carried to an extreme. They think that they have only to repeat the conventional words in the conventional manner for the woman to be subjugated. They come: they conquer. Now, this man, who plainly saw that he was to a certain extent—he did not know how far—detected, actually imagined that the woman who had detected him in a gigantic fraud one day would accept his proffered hand and heart the very next day! There are no bounds, you see, to personal vanity. Besides, for this man, if it was necessary that he should appear as the accepted suitor of a rich girl, it was doubly necessary that the girl should be the one woman in the world who could do mischief. He was anxious to discover how much she knew. But of his wooing he had no anxiety at all. He should speak: she would yield: she could do nothing else.

'Permit me,' he replied blandly, 'to go on. I am, as you know, a leader in the world of Art. I am known as a painter, a poet, and a writer of fiction. I have other ambitions still.'

'Doubtless you will succeed in these as you have succeeded in those three Arts.'

'Thank you.' He really did not see the meaning of her words. 'I take your words as of happy augury. Armorel——'

'No, Sir! Not my Christian name, if you please.'

'Give me the right to call you by your Christian name.'

'You are asking me to marry you. Is that what you mean?'

'It is nothing less.'

'Really! When I tell you, Mr. Feilding, that I know you—that I know you—it will be plain to you that the thing is absolutely impossible.

'To know me,' he replied, showing no outward emotion, 'should make it more than possible. What could I wish better than to be known to you?'

She looked him full in the face. He neither dropped his eyes nor changed colour.

'What could be better for me?' he repeated. 'What could I hope for better than to be known?'

'Oh! This man is truly wonderful!' she cried. 'Must I tell you what I know?'

'It would be better, perhaps. You look as if you knew something to my—actually—if I may say so—actually to my discredit!'

Armorel gasped. His impudence was colossal.

'To your discredit! Oh! Actually to your discredit! Sir, I know the whole of your disgraceful history—the history of the past three or four years. I know by what frauds you have passed yourself off as a painter and as a poet. I know by what pretences you thought to lay the foundation for a reputation as a dramatist. I know that your talk is borrowed—that you do not know art when you see it: that you could never write a single line of verse—and that of all the humbugs and quacks that ever imposed themselves upon the credulity of people you are the worst and biggest.'

He stared with a wonder which was, at least, admirably acted.

'Good Heavens!' he said. 'These words—these accusations—from you? From Armorel Rosevean—cousin of my cousin—whom I had believed to be a friend? Can this be possible? Who has put this wonderful array of charges into your head?'

'That matters nothing. They are true, and you know it.'

'They are so true,' he replied sternly, 'that if anyone were to dare to repeat these things before a third person, I should instantly—instantly—instruct my solicitors to bring an action for libel. Remember: youth and sex would not avail to protect that libeller. If anyone—anyone—dares, I say——'

'Oh! say no more. Go, and do not speak to me again! What will be done with this knowledge, I cannot say. Perhaps it will be used for the exposure which will drive you from the houses of honest people. Go, I say!'

She stamped her foot and raised her voice, insomuch that two drowsy attendants woke up and looked round, thinking they had dreamed something unusual.

The injured man of Art and Letters obeyed. He strode away. He, who had come pale and hesitating, now, on learning the truth which he had suspected and on receiving this unmistakable rejection, walked away with head erect and lofty mien. He showed, at least by outward bearing, the courage which is awakened by a declaration of war.

CHAPTER XVIII

CONGRATULATIONS

In the afternoon of the same day Armorel received a visit from a certain Lady Frances, of whom mention has already been made. She was sitting in her own room, alone. The excitements of the last night and of the morning were succeeded by a gentle melancholy. These things had not been expected when she took her rooms and plunged into London life. Besides, after these excitements the afternoon was flat.

Lady Frances came in, dressed beautifully, gracious and cordial; she took both Armorel's hands in her own, and looked as if she would have kissed her but for conscientious scruples: she was five-and-forty, or perhaps fifty, fat, comfortable, and rosy-cheeked. And she began to talk volubly. Not in the common and breathless way of volubility which leaves out the stops; but steadily and irresistibly, so that her companion should not be able to get in one single word. Well-bred persons do not leave out their commas and their full stops: but they do sometimes talk continuously, like a cataract or a Westmoreland Force, at least.

'My dear,' she said, 'I told your maid that I wanted to see you alone, and in your own room. She said Mrs. Elstree was out.

So I came in. It is a very pretty little room. They tell me you play wonderfully. This is where you practise, I suppose.' She put up her glasses and looked round, as if to see what impression had been produced on the walls by the music. 'And I hear also that you paint and draw. My dear, you are the very person for him.' Again she looked round. 'A very pretty room, really—wonderful to observe how the taste for decoration and domestic art has spread of late years!' A doubtful compliment, when you consider it. 'Well, my dear, as an old friend of his—at all events a very useful friend of his—I am come to congratulate you.'

'To congratulate me?'

'Yes. I thought I would be one of the first. I asked him two or three days ago if it was settled, and he confessed the truth, but begged me not to spread it abroad, because there were lawyers and people to see. Of course, his secrets are mine. And, except my own very intimate friends and one or two who can be perfectly trusted, I don't think I have mentioned the thing to a soul. I dare say, however, the news is all over the town by this time. Wonderful how things get carried—a bird of the air—the flying thistledown——'

'I do not understand, Lady Frances.'

'My dear, you need not pretend, because he confessed. And I think you are a very lucky girl to catch the cleverest man in all London, and he certainly is a lucky man to catch such a pretty girl as you. They say that he has got through all his money—men of genius are always bad men of business—but your own fortune will set him up again—a hundred thousand, I am told—mind you have it all settled on yourself. No one knows what may happen. I could tell you a heartrending story of a girl who trusted her lover with her money. But your lawyers will, of course, look after that.'

'I assure you——'

'He tells me,' the lady went on, without taking any notice of the interruption, 'that the thing will not come off for some time yet. I wouldn't keep it waiting too long, if I were you. Engagements easily get stale. Like buns. Well, I suppose you have learned all his secrets by this time: of course he is madly in love, and can keep nothing from you.'

'Indeed——'

'Has he told you yet who writes his stories for him? Eh? Has he told you that?' The lady bent forward and lowered her voice, and spoke earnestly. 'Has he told you?'

'I assure you that he has told me nothing—and——'

'That is in reality what I came about. Because, my dear, there must be a little plain speaking.'

'Oh! but let me speak—I——'

'When I have said what I came to say'—Lady Frances motioned with her hand gently but with authority—'then you shall have your turn. Men are so foolish that they tell their sweethearts everything. The chief reason why they fall in love, I believe, is a burning desire to have somebody to whom they can tell everything. I know a man who drove his wife mad by constantly telling her all his difficulties. He was always swimming in difficulties. Well, Alec is bound to tell you before long, even if he has not told you yet, which I can hardly believe. Now, my dear child, it matters very little to him if all the world knew the truth. All the world, to be sure, credits him with those stories, though he has been very careful not to claim them. He knows better. I say to such a clever man as Alec a few stories, more or less, matter nothing. But it matters a great deal to me'—what was this person talking about?—'because, you see, if it were to come out that I had been putting together old family scandals and forgotten stories, and sending them to the papers—there would be—there would be—Heaven knows what there would be! Yes, my dear—you can tell Alec that you know—I am the person who has written those stories. I wrote them, every one. They are all family stories—every good old family has got thousands of stories, and I have been collecting them—some of my own people, some of my husband's, and some of other people—and writing them down, changing names, and scenes, and dates, so that they should not be identified except by the few who knew them.'

Armorel made no further attempt to stem the tide of communication.

'I have come to make you understand clearly, young lady, that it is not his secret alone, but mine. You would do him a little harm, perhaps—I don't know—by letting it out, but you would do me an infinity of harm. I write them down, you see, and I take them to Alec, and he alters them—puts the style right—or says he does—though I never see any difference in them when they come out in the paper. And everybody who knows the story asks how in the name of wonder he got it.'

'Oh! But I do assure you that I know nothing at all of this.'

'Don't you? Well, never mind. Now you do know. And you know also that you can't talk about it, because it is his secret as well as mine. Why, you don't suppose that the man really does all he says he does, do you? Nobody could. It isn't in nature. Everybody who knows anything at all agrees that there must be a ghost—perhaps more than one. I'm the story ghost. I dare say there's a picture ghost, and a poetry ghost. He's a wonderful clever man, no doubt—it's the cleverest thing in the world to make other people work for you; but don't imagine, pray, that he can write stories of society. Bourgeois stories—about the middle class—his own class—perhaps; but not stories about Us. My stories belong to quite another level. Well, my dear, that is off my mind. Remember that this secret would do a great deal of harm to him as well as to me if it were to get about.'

'Oh! You are altogether—wholly—wrong——'

'My dear, I really do not care if I am wrong. You will not, however, damage his reputation by letting out his secrets? A wife can help her husband in a thousand ways, and especially in keeping up the little deceptions. Thousands of wives, I am told, pass their whole lives in the pretence that they and their husbands are gentlefolk. Alec has been received into a few good houses; and though it is, of course, more difficult to get a woman in than a man, I will really do what I can for you. With a good face, good eyes, a good figure, and a little addition of style, you ought to get on very well by degrees. Or you might take the town by storm, and become a professional beauty.'

'Thank you—but ——'

'And there's another thing. As an old friend of Alec's, I feel that I can give advice to you. Let me advise you earnestly, my dear, to make all the haste you can, to get rid of your companion. I know all about it. She was sent to your lawyer's by Alec himself. Why? Well, it is an old story, and I suppose he wanted to place her comfortably—or he had some other reason. He's always been a crafty man. You can see that in his eyes.'

'Oh! But I cannot listen to this!' cried Armorel.

'Nonsense, my dear. You do not expect your husband to be an angel, I suppose. Only silly middle-class girls who read novels do that. It will do you no harm to know that the man is no better than his neighbours. And I am sure he is no worse. I am speaking, in fact, for your own good. My dear child, Alec ran after the woman years ago. She was rich then, and used to go about. Certain houses do not mind who enter within their gates. They lived in Palace Gardens, and Monsieur le Papa was rich—oh! rich à *millions*—and the daughter was sugar-sweet and as innocent as an angel—fluffy hair, all tangled and rebellious—you know the kind—and large blue, wondering eyes, generally lowered until the time came for lifting them in the faces of young men. It was deadly, my dear. I believe she might have married anybody she pleased. There was the young Earl of Silchester—he wanted her. What a fool she was not to take him! No; she was spoony on Alec Feilding——'

'Oh! I must not!' cried Armorel again.

'My dear, I'm telling you. Her papa went smash—poor thing!—a grand, awful, impossible smash; other people's money mixed up in it. A dozen workhouses were filled with the victims, I believe. That kind of smash out of which it is impossible to pull yourself anyhow. Killed himself, therefore. Went out of the world without invitation by means of a coarse, vulgar, common piece of twopenny rope, tied round his great fat neck. I remember him. What did the girl do? Ran away from society: went on the stage as one of a travelling company. Why, I saw her myself three years ago at Leamington. I knew her instantly. "Aha!" I said, "there's Miss Fluffy, with the appealing, wondering eyes. Poor thing! Here is a come down in the world!" Now I find her here—your companion—a widow—widow of one Jerome Elstree deceased—artist, I am told. I never heard of the gentleman, and I confess I have my doubts as to his existence at all.'

Armorel ceased to offer any further opposition to the stream.

'The innocent, appealing blue eyes: the childish face: oh! I remember. My dear, I hope you will not have any reason to be jealous of Mrs. Elstree. But take care. There were other girls, too, now I come to think about it. There was his cousin, Philippa Rosevean. Everybody knows that he went as far with her as a man can go, short of an actual engagement. Canon Langley, of St. Paul's, wants to marry her. She's an admirable person for an ecclesiastical dignitary's wife—beautiful, cold, and dignified. But, as yet, she has not accepted him. They say he will be a bishop. And they say she loves her cousin Alec still. Women are generally dreadful fools about men. But I don't know. I don't think, if I were you, I should be jealous of Philippa. There's another little girl, too, I have seen coming out of his studio. But she's only a model, or something. If you begin to be jealous about the models, there will be no end. Then, there are hundreds of girls about town—especially those who can draw and paint a little, or write a silly little song—who think they are greatly endowed with genius, and would give their heads to get your chance. You are a lucky girl, Miss Armorel Rosevean; but I would advise you, in order to make the most of your good fortune, to change your companion quickly. Persuade her to try the climate of Australia. Else, there may be family jars.'

Here she stopped. She had said what was in her mind. Whether she came to say this out of the goodness of her heart; or whether she intended to make a little mischief between the girl and her lover; or whether she supposed Armorel to be a young lady who accepts a lover with no illusions as to imaginary perfections, so that a new weakness discovered here and there would not lower him in her opinion, I cannot say. Lady Frances was generally considered a good-natured kind of person, and certainly she had no illusions about perfection in any man.

'May I speak now?' asked Armorel.

'Certainly, my dear. It was very good of you to hear me patiently. And I've said all I wanted to. Keep my secret, and get rid of your companion, and I'll take you in hand.'

'Thank you. But you would not suffer me to explain that you are entirely mistaken. I am not engaged to Mr. Feilding at all.'

'But he told me that you were.'

'Yes; but he also tells the world, or allows the world to believe, that he writes your stories. I am not engaged to Mr.

Feilding, Lady Frances, and, what is more, I never shall be engaged to that man—never!'

'Have you quarrelled already?'

'We have not quarrelled, because before people quarrel they must be on terms of some intimacy. We have never been more than acquaintances.'

'Well—but—child—he has been seen with you constantly. At theatres, at concerts, in the park, in galleries—everywhere, he has been walking with you as if he had the right.'

'I could not help that. Besides, I never thought ——'

'Never thought? Why, where were you brought up? Never thought? Good gracious! what do young ladies go into society for?'

'I am not a young lady of society, I am afraid.'

'Well—but—what was your companion about, to allow—— Oh!'—Lady Frances nodded her head—'oh! now I understand. Now one can understand why he got her placed here. Now one understands her business. My dear, you have been placed in a very dangerous position—most dangerous. Your guardians or lawyers are very much to blame. And you really never suspected anything?'

'How should I suspect? I was always told that Mr. Feilding was not the man to begin that kind of thing.'

'Were you? Your companion told you that, I suppose?'

'Oh! I suppose so. There seems a horrid network of deception all about me, Lady Frances.' Armorel rose, and her visitor followed her example. 'You have put a secret into my hands. I shall respect it. Henceforth, I desire but one more interview with this man. Oh! he is all lies—through and through. There is no part of him that is true.'

'Nonsense, my dear; you take things too seriously. We all have our little reservations, and some deceptions are necessary. When you get to my age you will understand. Why won't you marry the man? He is young: his manners are pretty good: he is a man of the world: he is really clever: he is quite sure to get on, particularly if his wife help him. He means to get on. He is the kind of man to get on. You see he is clever enough to take the credit of other people's work: to make others work for you is the first rule in the art of getting on. Oh! he will do. I shall live to see him made a baronet, and in the next generation his son will marry money, and go up into the Lords. That is the way. My dear, you had better take him. You will never get a more promising offer. You seem to me rather an unworldly kind of girl. You should really take advice of those who know the world.'

'I could never—never—marry Mr. Feilding.

'Wealth, position, society, rank, consideration—these are the only things in life worth having, and you are going to throw them away! My dear, is there actually nothing between you at all? Was it all a fib?'

'Actually nothing at all, except that he offered himself to me this very morning, and he received an answer which was, I hope, plain enough.'

'Ah! now I see.' Lady Frances laughed. 'Now I understand, my dear, the vanity of the man! The creature, when he told me that fib, thought it was the truth because he had made up his mind to ask you, and, of course, he concluded that no one could say "No" to him. Now I understand. You need not fall into a rage about it, my dear. It was only his vanity. Poor dear Alec! Well, he'll get another pretty girl, I dare say; but, my dear, I doubt whether—— Rising men are scarce, you know. Good-bye, child! Keep that little secret, and don't bear malice. The vanity—the vanity of the men! Wonderful! wonderful!'

'And now,' cried Armorel, alone—'now there is nothing left. Everything has been torn from him. He can do nothing—nothing. The cleverest man—the very cleverest man in all London!'

CHAPTER XIX

WHAT NEXT?

ROLAND had moved into his new studio before Armorel became, as she had promised, his model in the new picture. She began to go there nearly every morning, accompanied by Effie, and faithfully sat for two or three hours while the painting went on. It was the picture which he had begun under the old conditions, her own figure being substituted for that of the girl which the artist originally designed. The studio was one of a nest of such offices crowded together under a great roof and lying on many floors. The others were, I dare say, prettily furnished and decorated with the customary furniture of a studio, with pictures, sketches, screens, and pretty things of all kinds. This studio was nothing but a great gaunt room, with a big window, and no furniture in it except an easel, a table, and two or three chairs. There was simply nothing else. Under the pressure of want and failure the unfortunate artist had long ago parted with all the pretty things with which he had begun his career, and the present was no time to replace them.

'I have got the studio,' he said, 'for the remainder of a lease, pretty cheap. Unfortunately, I cannot furnish it yet. Wait until the tide turns. I am full of hope. Then this arid wall and this great staring Sahara of a floor shall blossom with all manner of lovely things—armour and weapons, bits of carving and tapestry, drawings. You shall see how jolly it will be.'

Next to the studio there were two rooms. In one of these, his bedroom, he had placed the barest necessaries; the other was empty and unfurnished, so that he had no place to sit in during the evening but his gaunt and ghostly studio. However, the tide had turned in one respect. He was now full of hope.

There is no better time for conversation than when one is sitting for a portrait or standing for a model. The subject has to remain motionless. This would be irksome if silence were imposed as well as inaction. Happily, the painter finds that his sitter only exhibits a natural expression when he or she is talking and thinking about something else. And, which is certainly a Providential arrangement, the painter alone among mortals, if we except the cobbler, can talk and work at the same time. I do not mean that he can talk about the Differential Calculus, or about the relations of Capital and Labour, or about a hot corner in politics · but he can talk of things light, pleasant, and on the surface.

'I feel myself back in Scilly,' said Armorel. 'Whenever I come here and think of what you are painting, I am in the boat, watching the race of the tide through the channel. The puffins are swarming on Camber Rock, and swimming in the smooth water outside: there is the head of a seal, black above the water, shining in the sunlight—how he flounders in the current! The seagulls are flying and crying overhead: the shags stand in rows upon the farthest rocks: the sea-breeze blows upon my cheek. I suppose I have changed so much that when I go back I shall have lost the old feeling. But it was joy enough in those days only to sit in the boat and watch it all. Do you remember, Roland?'

'I remember very well. You are not changed a bit, Armorel: you have only grown larger and ——' 'More beautiful,' he would have added, but refrained. 'You will find that the old joy will return again—*la joie de vivre*—only to breathe and feel and look around. But it will be then ten times as joyous. If you loved Scilly when you were a child and had seen nothing else, how much more will you love the place now that you have travelled and seen strange lands and other coasts and the islands of the Mediterranean!'

'I fear that I shall find the place small: the house will have shrunk—children's houses always shrink. I hope that Holy Farm will not have become mean.'

'Mean? with the verbena-trees, the fuchsias, the tall pampas-grass, and the palms! Mean? with the old ship's lanthorn and the gilded figure-head? Mean, Armorel? with the old orchard behind and the twisted trees with their fringe of grey moss? You talk rank blasphemy! Something dreadful will happen to you.'

'Perhaps it will be I myself, then, that will have grown mean enough to think the old house mean. But Samson is a very little place, isn't it? One cannot make out Samson to be a big place. I could no longer live there always. We will go there for three or four months every year; just for refreshment of the soul, and then return here among men and women or travel abroad together, Effie

We could be happy for a time there: we could sail and row about the rocks in calm weather: and in stormy weather we should watch the waves breaking over the headlands, and in the evening I would play "The Chirping of the Lark."'

'I am ready to go to-morrow, if you will take me with you,' said Effie.

Then they were silent again. Roland walked backwards and forwards, brush and palette in hand, looking at his model and at his canvas. Effie stood beside the picture, watching it grow. To one who cannot paint, the growth of a portrait on the canvas is a kind of magic. The bare outline and shape of head and face, the colour of the eyes, the curve of the neck, the lines of the lips—anyone might draw these. But to transfer to the canvas the very soul that lies beneath the features—that, if you please, is different. Oh! How does the painter catch the soul of the man and show it in his face? One must be oneself an artist of some kind even to appreciate the greatness of the portrait painter.

'When this picture is finished,' said Armorel, 'there will be nothing to keep me in London; and we will go then.'

'At the very beginning of the season?'

'The season is nothing to me. My companion, Mrs. Elstree, who was to have launched me so beautifully into the very best society, turns out not to have any friends; so that there is no society for me, after all. Perhaps it is as well.'

'Will Mrs. Elstree go to Scilly with you?' asked Roland.

'No,' said Armorel, with decision. 'On Samson, at least, one needs no companion.'

Again they relapsed into silence for a space. Conversation in the studio is fitful.

'I have a thing to talk over with you two,' she said. 'First, I thought it would be best to talk about it to you singly; but now I think that you should both hear the whole story, and so we can all three take counsel as to what is best.'

'Your head a little more—so.' Roland indicated the movement with his forefinger. 'That will do. Now pray go on, Armorel.'

'Once there was a man,' she began, as if she was telling a story to children—and, indeed, there is no better way ever found out of beginning a story—'a man who was, in no sense at all, and could never become, try as much as he could, an artist. He was, in fact, entirely devoid of the artistic faculty: he had no ear for music or for poetry, no eye for beauty of form or for colour, no hand for drawing, no brain to conceive: he was quite a prosaic person. Whether he was clever in things that do not require the artistic faculty, I do not know. I should hardly think he could be clever in anything. Perhaps he might be good at buying cheap and selling dear.'

'Won't you take five minutes' rest?' asked the painter; hardly listening at all to the beginning, which, as you see, promised very little in the way of amusement. There are, however, many ways by which the story-teller gets a grip of his hearer, and a dull beginning is not always the least effective. He put down his palette. 'You must be tired,' he said. 'Come and tell me what you think.' He looked thoughtfully at his picture. Armorel's poor little beginning of a story was slighted.

'You are satisfied, so far?' she asked.

'I will tell you when it is finished. Is the water quite right?'

'We are in shoal, close behind us are the broad Black Rock Ledges. The water might be even more transparent still. It is the dark water racing through the narrow ravine that I think of most. It will be a great picture, Roland. Now I will take my place again.' She did so. 'And, with your permission, I will go on with my story: you heard the beginning, Roland?'

'Oh! Yes! Unfortunate man with no eyes and no ears,' he replied, unsuspecting. 'Worse than a one-eyed Calender.'

'This preposterous person, then, with neither eye, nor ear, nor hand, nor understanding, had the absurd ambition to succeed. This you will hardly believe. But he did. And, what is more, he had no patience, but wanted to succeed all at once. I am told that lots of young men, nowadays, are consumed with that yearning to succeed all at once. It seems such a pity, when they should be happily dancing and singing and playing at the time when they were not working. I think they would succeed so very much better afterwards. Well, this person very soon found that in the law—did I say he was a barrister?—he had no chance of success except after long years. Then he looked round the fields of art and literature. Mind, he could neither write nor practise any art. What was he to do? Every day the ambition to seem great filled his soul more and more, and every day the thing appeared to him more hopeless: because, you see, he had no imagination, and therefore could not send his soul to sleep with illusions. I wonder he did not go mad. Perhaps he did, for he resolved to pretend. First, he thought he would pretend to be a painter'—here Roland, who had been listening languidly, started, and became attentive. 'He could neither paint nor draw, remember. He began, I think, by learning the language of Art. He frequented studios, heard the talk and read the books. It must have been weary work for him. But, of course, he was no nearer his object than before; and then a great chance came to him. He found a young artist full of promise—a real artist—one filled with the whole spirit of Art: but he was starving. He was actually penniless, and he had no friends who could help him, because he was an Australian by birth. This young man was not only penniless, but in despair. He was ready to do anything. I suppose, when one is actually starving and sees no prospect of success or any hope, ambition dies away and even self-respect may seem a foolish thing.' Roland listened now, his picture forgotten. What was Armorel intending? 'It must be a most dreadful kind of temptation. There can be nothing like it in the world. That is why we pray for our daily bread. Oh! a terrible temptation. I never understood before how great and terrible a temptation it is. Then the man without eye, or hand, or brain saw a chance for himself. He would profit by his brother's weakness. He proposed to buy the work of this painter and to call it his own.'

'Armorel, must you tell this story?'

'Patience, Roland. In his despair the artist gave way. He consented. For three years and more he received the wages of—of sin. But his food was like ashes in his mouth, and his front was stamped—yes, stamped—by the curse of those who sin against their own soul.'

'Armorel——' But she went on, ruthless.

'The pictures were very good: they were exhibited, praised, and sold. And the man grew quickly in reputation. But he wasn't satisfied. He thought that as it was so easy to be a painter, it would be equally easy to become a poet. All the Arts are allied: many painters have been also poets. He had never written a single line of poetry. I do not know that he had ever read any He found a girl who was struggling, working, and hoping.' Effie started and turned roseate red. 'He took her poems—bought them—and, on the pretence of having improved them and so made them his own, he published them in his own name. They were pretty, bright verses, and presently people began to look for them and to like them. So he got a double reputation. But the poor girl remained unknown. At first she was so pleased at seeing her verses in print—it looked so much like success—that she hardly minded seeing his name at the end. But presently he brought out a little volume of them with his name on the title-page, and then a second volume—also with his name——'

'The scoundrel!' cried Roland. 'He cribbed his poetry too?'

Effie bowed her face, ashamed.

'And then the girl grew unhappy. For she perceived that she was in a bondage from which there was no escape except by sacrificing the money which he gave her, and that was necessary for her brother's sake. So she became very unhappy.'

'Very unhappy,' echoed Effie. Both painter and poet stood confused and ashamed.

'Then this clever man—the cleverest man in London—began to go about in society a good deal, because he was so great a genius. There he met a lady who was full of stories.'

'Oh!' said Roland. 'Is there nothing in him at all?'

'Nothing at all. There is really nothing at all. This man persuaded the lady to write down these stories, which were all based on old family scandals and episodes unknown or forgotten by the world. They form a most charming series of stories. I believe they are written in a most sparkling style—full of wit and life. Well, he did not put his name to them, but he allowed the whole world to believe that they were his own.'

'Good Heavens!' cried Roland.

'And still he was not satisfied. He found a young dramatist who had written a most charming play. He tried to persuade the poor lad that his play was worthless, and he offered to take it himself, alter it—but there needed no alteration—and convert it into a play that could be acted. He would give fifty pounds for the play, but it was to be his own.'

'Yes,' said Effie, savagely. 'He made that offer, but he will not get the play.'

'You have heard, now, what manner of man he was. Very well. I tell you two the story because I want to consult you. The other day I arranged a little play of my own. That is, I invited people to hear the reciting of that drama: I invited the pretender himself among the rest, but he did not know or guess what the play was going to be. And at the same time I invited the painter and the poet. The former brought his unfinished picture—the latter brought her latest poem, which the pretender was going that very week to bring out in his own name. I had set it to music, and I sang it. I meant that he should learn in this way, without being told, that everything was discovered. I watched his face during the recital of the play, and I saw the dismay of the discovery creeping gradually over him as he realised that he had lost his painter, his poet, and his dramatist. There remained nothing more but to discover the author of the stories—and that, too, I have found out. And I think he will lose his story-teller as well. He will be deprived of all his borrowed plumes. At one blow he saw himself ruined.'

Neither of the two made answer for a space. Then spoke Roland: 'Dux femina facti! A woman hath done this.'

'He is ruined unless he can find others to take your places. The question I want you to consider is—What shall be done next? Roland, it is your name and fame that he has stolen—your pictures that he has called his own. Effie, they are your poems that he has published under his name. What will you do? Will you demand your own again? Think.'

'He must exhibit no more pictures of mine,' said Roland. 'He has one in his studio that he has already sold. That one must not go to any gallery. That is all I have to say.'

'He cannot publish any more poems of mine,' said Effie, 'because he hasn't got any, and I shall give him no more.'

'What about the past?'

'Are we so proud of the past and of the part we have played in it'—asked Roland—'that we should desire its story published to all the world?'

Effie shook her head, approvingly.

'As for me,' he continued, 'I wish never to hear of it again.

It makes me sick and ashamed even to think of it. Let it be forgotten. I was an unknown artist—I had few friends—I had exhibited one picture only—so that my work was unknown—I had painted for him six or seven pictures which are mostly bought by an American. As for the resemblance of style, that may make a few men talk for a season. Then it will be forgotten. I shall remain—he will have disappeared. I am content to take my chance with future work, even if at first I may appear to be a mere copyist of Mr. Alec Feilding.'

'And you, Effie?'

'I agree with Mr. Lee,' she replied briefly. 'Let the past alone. I shall write more verses, and, perhaps, better verses.'

'Then I will go to him and tell him that he need fear nothing. We shall hold our tongues. But he is not to exhibit the picture that is in his studio. I will tell him that.'

'You will not actually go to him yourself, Armorel—alone—after what has passed?' asked Effie.

'Why not? He can do me no harm. He knows that he has been found out, and he is tormented by the fear of what we shall do next. I bring him relief. His reputation is secured—that is to say, it will be the reputation of a man who stopped at thirty, in the fulness of his first promise and his best powers, and did no more work.'

'Oh!' cried Effie. 'I thought he was so clever! I thought that his desire to be thought a poet was only a little infirmity of temper, which would pass. And, after all, to think that——' Here the poet looked at the painter, and the painter looked at the poet—but neither spoke the thought: 'How could you—you, with your pencil: how could you—you, with your pen—consent to the iniquity of so great a fraud?'

CHAPTER XX

A RECOVERY AND A FLIGHT

Amid all these excitements Armorel became aware that something —something of a painful and disagreeable character, was going on with her companion. They were at this time very little together. Mrs. Elstree took her breakfast in bed; at luncheon she was, just now, nearly always out; at dinner she sat silent, pale, and anxious; in the evening she lay back in her chair as if she was asleep. One night Armorel heard her weeping and sobbing in her room. She knocked at the door with intent to offer her help if she was ill. 'No, no,' cried Mrs. Elstree; 'you need not come in. I have nothing but a headache.'

This thing as well disquieted her. She remembered what Lady Frances had suggested—it is always the suggestion rather than the bare fact which sticks and pricks like a thorn, and will not come out or suffer itself to be removed. Armorel thought nothing of the allegation concerning the stage—why should not a girl go upon the stage if she wished? The suggestion which pricked was that Mrs. Elstree had been sent to her by the man whom she now knew to be fraudulent through and through, in order to carry out some underhand and secret design. There is nothing more horrid than the suspicion that the people about one are treacherous. It reduces one to the condition of primitive man, for whom every grassy glade concealed a snake and every bush a wild beast. She tried to shake off the suspicion, yet a hundred things confirmed it. Her constant praise of this child of genius, his persistence in meeting them wherever they went, the attempt to make her find money for his schemes. The girl, thus irritated, began to have uneasy dreams; she was as one caught in the meshes; she was lured into a garden whence there was no escape; she was hunted by a cunning and relentless creature; she was in a prison, and could not get out. Always in her dreams Zoe stood on one side of her, crying, 'Oh, the great and glorious creature!—oh, the cleverness of the man!—oh, the wonder and the marvel of him!' And on the other side stood Lady Frances, saying, 'Why don't you take him? He is a liar, it is true, but he is no worse than his neighbours—all men are liars! You can't get a man made on purpose for you. What is your business in life at all but to find a husband? Why are girls in Society at all except to catch husbands? And they are scarce, I assure you. Why don't you take the man? You will never again have such a chance—a rising man—a man who can make other people work for him—a clever man. Besides, you are as good as engaged to him: you have made people talk: you have been seen with him everywhere. If you are not engaged to him you ought to be.'

It was about a week after the reading of the play when this condition of suspicion and unquiet was brought to an end in a very unexpected manner.

Mr. Jagenal called at the rooms in the morning about ten o'clock. Mrs. Elstree was taking breakfast in bed, as usual. Armorel was alone, painting.

'My dear young lady,' said her kindly adviser, 'I would not have disturbed you at this early hour but for a very important matter. You are well and happy, I trust? No, you are not well and happy. You look pale.'

'I have been a little worried lately,' Armorel replied. 'But never mind now.'

'Are you quite alone here? Your companion, Mrs. Elstree?'

'She has not yet left her room. We are quite alone.'

'Very well, then.' The lawyer sat down and began nursing his right knee. 'Very well. You remember, I dare say, making a certain communication to me touching a collection of precious stones in your possession? You made that communication to me five years ago, when first you came from Scilly. You returned to it again when you arrived at your twenty-first birthday, and I handed over to your own keeping all your portable property.'

'Of course I remember perfectly well.'

'Then does your purpose still hold?'

'It is still, and always, my duty to hand over those rubies to their rightful owner—the heir of Robert Fletcher, as soon as he can be found.'

'It is also my duty to warn you again, as I have done already, that there is no reason at all why you should do so. You are the sole heiress of your great-great-grandmother's estate. She died worth a great sum of money in gold, besides treasures in plate, works of art, lace, and jewels cut and uncut. The rambling story of an aged woman cannot be received as evidence on the strength of which you should hand over valuable property to persons unknown, who do not even claim it, and know nothing about it.'

'I must hand over those rubies,' Armorel repeated, 'to the person to whom they belong.'

'It is a very valuable property. If the estimate which was made for me was correct—I see no reason to doubt it—those jewels could be sold, separately, or in small parcels, for nearly thirty-five thousand pounds—a fortune larger than all the rest of your property put together—thirty-five thousand pounds!'

'That has nothing to do with the question, has it? I have got to restore those jewels, you see, to their rightful owner, as soon as he can be discovered.'

'Well—but—consider again. What have you got to go upon? The story about Robert Fletcher may or may not be true. No one can tell after this lapse of time. The things were found by you lying in the old sea-chest with other things—all your own. Who was this Robert Fletcher? Where are his heirs? If they claim the property, and can prove their claim, give it up at once. If not, keep your own. The jewels are undoubtedly your own as much as the lace and the silks and the silver cups, which were all, I take it, recovered from wrecks.'

'Do you disbelieve my great-great-grandmother's story, then?'

'I have neither to believe nor to disbelieve. I say it isn't evidence. Your report of what she said, being then in her dotage, amounts to just nothing, considered as evidence.'

'I am perfectly certain that the story is true. The leathern thong by which the case hung round the man's neck has been cut by a knife, just as granny described it in her story. And there is the writing in the case itself. Nothing will persuade me that the story is anything but true in every particular.'

'It may be true. I cannot say. At the same time, the property is your own, and you would be perfectly justified in keeping it.'

'Mr. Jagenal'—Armorel turned upon him sharply—'you have

found out Robert Fletcher's heir! I am certain you have. That is the reason why you are here this morning.'

Mr. Jagenal laid upon the table a pocket-book full of papers.

'I will tell you what I have discovered. That is why I came here. There has been, unfortunately, a good deal of trouble in discovering this Robert Fletcher and in identifying one of the Robert Fletchers we did discover with your man. We discovered, in fact, ten Robert Fletchers before we came to the man who may reasonably be supposed—— But you shall see.'

He opened the pocket-book, and found a paper of memoranda from which he read his narrative:—

'There was one Robert Fletcher, the eleventh whom we unearthed. This man promised nothing at first. He became a broker in the City in the year 1810. In the same year he married a cousin, daughter of another broker, with whom he entered into partnership. He did so well that when he died, in the year 1846, then aged sixty-nine, his will was proved under 80,000*l.* He left three daughters, among whom the estate was divided, in equal shares. The eldest of the daughters, Eleanor, remained unmarried, and died two years ago, at the age of seventy-seven, leaving the whole of her fortune—greatly increased by accumulations—to hospitals and charities. I believe she was, in early life, alienated from her family, on account of some real or fancied slight. However, she died: and her papers came into the hands of my friends Denham, Mansfield, Westbury, and Co., of New Square, Lincoln's Inn, solicitors. Her second sister, Frances, born in the year 1813, married in 1834, had one son, Francis Alexander, who was born in 1835, and married in 1857. Both Frances and her son are now dead; but one son remained, Frederick Alexander, born in the year 1859. The third daughter, Catharine, born in the year 1815, married in 1835, and emigrated to Australia with her husband, a man named Temple. I have no knowledge of this branch of the family.'

'Then,' said Armorel, 'I suppose the eldest son or grandson of the second sister must have the rubies?'

'You are really in a mighty hurry to get rid of your property. The next question—it should have come earlier—is—How do I connect this Robert Fletcher with your Robert Fletcher? How do we know that Robert Fletcher the broker was Robert Fletcher the shipwrecked passenger? Well; Eleanor, the eldest, left a bundle of family papers and letters behind her. Among them is a packet endorsed "From my son Robert in India." Those letters, signed "Robert Fletcher," are partly dated from Burmah, whither the writer had gone on business. He gives his observations on the manners and customs of the country, then little known or visited. He says that he is doing very well, indeed: so well, he says presently, that, thanks to a gift made to him by the King, he is able to think about returning home with the means of staying at home and doing no more work for the end of his natural days.'

'Of course, he had those jewels.'

'Then he writes from Calcutta. He has returned in safety from Burmah and the King, whose capricious temper had made him tremble for his life. He is putting his affairs in order: he has brought his property from Burmah in a portable form which he can best realise in London: lastly, he is going to sail in a few weeks. This is in the year 1808. According to your story it was somewhere about that date that the wreck took place on the Scilly Isles, and he was washed ashore, saved——'

'And robbed,' said Armorel.

'As we have no evidence of the fact,' answered the man of law, 'I prefer to say that the real story ends with the last of the letters. It remained, however, to compare the handwriting of the letters with that of the fragment of writing in your leather case. I took the liberty to have a photograph made of that fragment while it was in my possession, and I now ask you to compare the handwriting.' He drew out of his pocket-book a letter—one of the good old kind, on large paper, brown with age, and unprovided with any envelope—and the photograph of which he was speaking. 'There,' he said, 'judge for yourself.'

'Why!' cried Armorel. 'The writing corresponds exactly!'

'It certainly does, letter for letter. Well; the conclusion of the whole matter is that I believe the story of the old lady to be correct in the main. On the other hand, there is nothing in the papers to show the existence in the family of any recollection of so great a loss. One would imagine that a man who had dropped—or thought he had dropped—a bag, full of rubies, worth thirty-five thousand pounds, into the sea would have told his children about it, and bemoaned the loss all his life. Perhaps, however, he was so philosophic as to grieve no more after what was hopelessly gone. He was still in the years of hope when the misfortune befell him. Possibly his children knew in general terms that the shipwreck had caused a destruction of property. Again, a man of the City, with the instincts of the City, would not like it to be known that he had returned to his native country a pauper, while it would help him in his business to be considered somewhat of a Nabob. Of this I cannot speak from any knowledge I have, or from any discovery that I have made.'

'Oh!' cried Armorel, 'I cannot tell you what a weight has been lifted from me. I have never ceased to long for the restoration of those jewels ever since I found them in the sea-chest.'

'There is—as I said—only one descendant of the second sister—a man—a man still young. You will give me your instructions in writing. I am to hand over to this young man—this fortunate young man—already trebly fortunate in another sense—this precious packet of jewels. It is still, I suppose, in the bank?'

'It is where you placed it for me when I came of age.'

'Very well. I have brought you an order for its delivery to me. Will you sign it?'

Armorel heaved a great sigh. 'With what relief!' she said. 'Have you got it here?'

Mr. Jagenal gave her the order on the bank for the delivery of sealed packet, numbered III., to himself. She signed it.

'To think,' she said, 'that by a simple stroke of the pen I can remove the curse of those ill-gotten rubies! It is like getting rid of all your sins at once. It is like Christian dropping his bundle.'

'I hope the rubies will not carry on this supposed curse of yours.'

'Oh!' cried Armorel, with a profound sigh, 'I feel as if the poor old lady was present listening. Since I could understand anything, I have understood that the possession of those rubies brought disaster upon my people. From generation to generation they have been drowned one after the other—my father—my grandfather—my great-grandfather—my mother—my brothers—all—all drowned. Can you wonder if I rejoice that the things will threaten me no longer?'

'This is sheer superstition.'

'Oh! yes: I know, and yet I cannot choose but to believe it, I have heard the story so often, and always with the same ending. Now, they are gone.'

'Not quite gone. Nearly. As good as gone, however. Dismiss this superstitious dread from your mind, my dear young lady.'

'The rubies are gone. There will be no more of us swallowed up in the cruel sea.'

'No more of you,' repeated Mr. Jagenal, with the incredulous smile of one who has never had in his family a ghost, or a legend, or a curse, or a doom, or a banshee, or anything at all distinguished. 'And now you will be happy. You don't ask me the name of the fortunate young man.'

'No; I do not want to know anything more about the horrid things.'

'What am I to say to him?'

'Tell him the truth.'

'I shall tell him that you discovered the rubies in an old sea-chest with other property accumulated during a great many years: that a scrap of paper with writing on it gave a clue to the owner: and that, by means of other investigation, he has been discovered: that it was next to impossible for your great-grandfather, Captain Rosevean, to have purchased these jewels: and that the presumption is that he recovered them from the wreck, and laid them in the chest, saying nothing, and that the chest was never opened until your succession to the property. That, my dear young lady, is all the story that I have to tell. And now I will go away, with congratulations to Donna Quixote in getting rid of thirty-five thousand pounds.'

An hour or two afterwards, Mrs. Elstree appeared. She glided into the room and threw herself into her chair, as if she desired to sleep again. She looked harassed and anxious.

'Zoe,' cried Armorel, 'you are surely ill. What is it? Can I do nothing for you?'

'Nothing. I only wish it was all over, or that I could go to sleep for fifty years, and wake up an old woman—in an almshouse or somewhere—all the troubles over. What a beautiful thing it must be to be old and past work, with fifteen shillings a week, say, and nothing to think about all day except to try and forget the black box! If it wasn't for the black box—I know I should see them always coming along the road with it—it must be the loveliest time.'

'Well—but—what makes you look so ill?'

'Nothing. I am not ill. I am never ill. I would rather be ill than—what I am. A tearing, rending neuralgia would be a welcome change. Don't ask me any more questions, Armorel. You look radiant, for your part. Has anything happened to you? —anything good? You are one of those happy girls to whom only good things come.'

'Do you remember the story I told you—about the rubies?'

'Yes.' She turned her face to the fire. 'I remember very well.'

'I have at last—congratulate me, Zoe—I have got rid of them.'

'You have got rid of them?' Mrs. Elstree started up. 'Where are they, then?'

'Mr. Jagenal has been here. He has found a great-grandson of Robert Fletcher, who is entitled to have them. I have never been so relieved! The dreadful things are out of my hands now, and in Mr. Jagenal's. He will give them to this grandson Zoe, what is the matter?'

Mrs. Elstree rose to her feet, and stood facing Armorel, with eyes in which wild terror was the only passion visible, and white cheeks. And, as Armorel was still speaking, she staggered, reeled, and fell forwards in a faint. Armorel caught her, and bore her to the sofa, when she presently came to herself again. But the fainting fit was followed by hysterical weeping and laughing. She knew not what she said. She raved about somebody who had bought something. Armorel paid no heed to what she said. She lamented the hour of her birth: she had been pursued by evil all her life: she lamented the hour when she met a certain man, unnamed, who had dragged her down to his own level: and so on.

When she had calmed a little, Armorel persuaded her to lie down. It is a woman's chief medicine. It is better than all the drugs in the museum of the College of Physicians. Mrs. Elstree pale and trembling, tearful and agitated, lay down. Armorel covered her with a warm wrapper, and left her.

A little while afterwards she looked in. The patient was quite calm now, apparently asleep, and breathing gently. Armorel, satisfied with the result of her medicine, left her in charge of her maid, and went out for an hour. She went out, in fact, to tell Effie Wilmot the joyful news concerning those abominable rubies. When she came back, in time for luncheon, she was met by her maid, who gave her a letter, and told her a strange thing. Mrs. Elstree had gone away! The sick woman, who had been raving in hysterics, hardly able to support herself to her bed, had got up the moment after Armorel left the house, packed all her boxes hurriedly, sent her for a cab, and had driven away. But she had left this note for Armorel. It was brief.

'I am obliged to go away unexpectedly. In order to avoid explanations and questions and farewells, I have thought it best to go away quietly. I could not choose but go. For certain reasons I must leave you. For the same reasons I hope that we may never meet again. I ought never to have come here. Forgive me and forget me. I will write to Mr. Jagenal to-day.

'ZOE.'

There was no reason given. She had gone. Nor, if one may anticipate, has Armorel yet discovered the reasons for this sudden flight. Nor, as you will presently discover, will Armorel ever be able to discover those reasons.

CHAPTER XXI

ALL LOST BUT——

MR. ALEC FEILDING paced the thick carpet of his studio with a restless step and an unquiet mind. Never before had he faced a more gloomy outlook. Black clouds, storm and rain, everywhere. Bad, indeed, is it for the honest tradesman when there is no money left, and no credit. But a man can always begin the world again if he has a trade. The devil of it is when a man has no trade at all, except that of lying and cheating in the abstract. Many men, it is true, combine cheatery and falsehood with their trade. Few are so unfortunate as to have no trade on which to base their frauds and adulterations.

Everything threatened, and all at once. Nay, it seemed as if everything was actually taken from him and all at once. Not something here, which might be repaired, and something there, a little later on, but all at once—everything. Nothing at all left. Even his furniture and his books might be seized. He would be stripped of his house, his journal, his name, his credit, his position

—even his genius! Therefore his face—that face which Armorel found so wooden—was now full of expression, but of the terror-stricken, hunted kind: that of the man who has been found out and is going to be exposed.

On the table lay three or four letters. They had arrived that morning. He took them up and read them one after the other. It was line upon line, blow upon blow.

The first was from Roland Lee.

'I see no object,' he said, 'in granting you the interview which you propose. There is not really anything that requires discussion. As to our interests being identical, as you say—if they have been so hitherto they will remain so no longer. As to the market price of the pictures, which you claim to have raised by your judicious management, I am satisfied to see my work rise to its own level by its own worth. As to your threat that the influence which has been exerted for an artist may be also exerted against him—you will do what you please. Your last demand, for gratitude, needs no reply. I start again, exactly where I was when you found me. I am still as poor and as little known. The half-dozen pictures which you have sold as your own will not help me in any way. Your assertion that I am about to reap the harvest of your labours is absurd. I begin the world over again. The last picture—the one now in your studio—you will be good enough not to exhibit'—'Won't I, though?' asked the owner—'at the penalty of certain inconveniences which you will learn immediately. I have torn up and burned your cheque.'—'So much the better for me,' said the purchaser.—'You say that you will not let me go without a personal interview. If you insist upon one, you must have it. You will find me here any morning. But, as you can only want an interview in the hope of renewing the old arrangement, I am bound to warn you that it is hopeless and impossible, and to beg that you will not trouble yourself to come here at all. Understand that no earthly consideration will induce me to bear any further share in the deception in which I have been too long a confederate. The guilty knowledge of the past should separate us as wide apart as the poles. To see you will be to revive a guilty memory. Since we must meet, perhaps, from time to time, let us meet as a pair of criminals who avoid each other's conversation for fear of stirring up the noisome past. What has been resolved upon, so far as I—and another—are concerned, Miss Armorel Rosevean has undertaken to inform you.—R. L.'

'Deception! Criminals!' I suppose there is no depth of wickedness into which men may not descend, step by step, getting daily deeper in the mire of falsehood and crime, yet walking always with head erect, and meeting the world with the front of rectitude. Had anyone told Mr. Alec Feilding, years before, what he would do in the future, he would have kicked that foul and obscene prophet. Well: he had done these things, and deliberately: he had posed before the world as painter, poet, and writer of fiction. As time went on, and the world accepted his pretensions, they became a part of himself. Nay: he even excused himself. Everybody does the same thing: or, just the same, everybody would do it, given the chance: it is a world of pretension, make-believe, and seeming. Besides, he was no highwayman, he bought the things: he paid for them: they were his property. And yet—'Deception! Criminals!' The words astonished and pained him.

And the base ingratitude of the man. He was starving: no one would buy his things: nobody knew his work, when he stepped in. Then, by dexterity in the art of Puff, which the moderns call *réclame*—he actually believed this, being so ignorant of Art—he had forced these pictures into notice: he had run up their price, until for that picture on the easel he had been offered, and had taken, 450*l.*! Ungrateful!

'Deception! Criminals!'

Why, the man had actually received a cheque for 300*l.* for that very picture. What more could he want or expect? True, he had refused to cash the cheque. More fool he!

And now he was going absolutely to withdraw from the partnership, and work for himself. Well—poor devil! He would starve!

He stood in front of the picture and looked at it mournfully. The beautiful thing—far more beautiful than any he had exhibited before. It cut him to the heart to think—not that he had been such a fraud, but—that he could have no more from the same source. His career was cut short at the outset, his ambitions blasted, by this unlucky accident. Yet a year or two and the Academy would have made him an Associate: a few more years and he would have become R.A. Perhaps, in the end, President. And now it was all over. No Royal Academy for him, unless—a thing almost desperate—he could find some other Roland Lee—some genius as poor, as reckless of himself. And it might be years—years—before he could find such a one. Meantime, what was he to show? What was he to say? 'Deception! Criminals!' Confound the fellow! The words banged about his head and boxed his ears.

The second letter was from Effie—the girl to whom he had paid such vast sums of money, whom he had surrounded with luxuries—on whom he had bestowed the precious gift of his personal friendship. This girl also wrote without the least sense of gratitude. She said, in fact, writing straight to the point, 'I beg to inform you that I shall not, in future, be able to continue those contributions to your paper which you have thought fit to publish in two volumes with your own name attached. I have submitted my original manuscript of those verses to a friend, who has compared them with your published volume, and has ascertained that there is not the alteration of a single word. So that your pretence of having altered and improved them, until they became your own, is absurd. My brother begs me to add that your statement made before all the people at the reading was false. You made no suggestions. You offered no advice. You said that the play was worthless. My brother has made no alterations. You offered to give him fifty pounds for the whole rights in the play, with the right of bringing it out under your own name. This offer he refuses absolutely.

'I sincerely wish I could restore the money you have given me. I now understand that it was the price of my silence—the Wages of Sin.

'E. W.'

No more verses from that quarter. Poets, however, there are in plenty, writers of glib and flowing rhymes. To be sure, they are as a race consumed by vanity, and want to have their absurd names stuck to everything they do. Very well, henceforth he would have anonymous verses, and engage a small army of poets. The letter moved him little, except that it came by the same post as the other. It proved, taken with the evening of the play, concerted action. As for comparing the girl's manuscript verses with the volume, how was she to prove that the manuscript verses were not copied out of the volume?

Then there was a third letter, a very angry letter, from Lady Frances, his story-teller.

'I learn,' she said, 'that you have chosen me as the fittest person upon whom to practise your deceptions. You assured me that you were engaged to Miss Armorel Rosevean. I learn from the young lady herself that this is entirely false: you did offer yourself, it is true, a week after you had assured me of the engagement. You were promptly and decidedly refused. And you had no reason whatever for believing that you would be accepted.

'I should like you to consider that you owe your introduction into society to me. You also owe to me whatever name you have acquired as a story-teller. Every one of the society stories told in your paper has been communicated to you by me. And this is the way in which you repay my kindness to you.

'Under the circumstances, I think you cannot complain if I request that in future we cease to meet even as acquaintances. Of course, my contributions to your paper will be discontinued. And if you venture to state anywhere that they are your own work, I will publicly contradict the statement.

'F. H.'

He stood irresolute. What was to be done? For the moment he could think of nothing. 'It is that cursed girl!' he cried. 'Why did she ever come here? By what unlucky accident did she meet these two—Roland Lee and Effie? Why was I such a fool as to ask Lady Frances to call upon her? Why did I send Zoe to her? It is all folly together. If it had not been for her we should have been all going on as before. I am certain we should—and going on comfortably. I should have made Roland's fortune as well as my own name—and his hand was getting stronger and better every day. And I should have kept that girl in comfort, and made a very pretty little name for myself that way. She was improving, too—a bright and clever girl—a real treasure in proper hands. And I had the boy as well, or should have had. Good Heavens! what losses! What a splendid possession to have destroyed! No man ever before had such a chance—to say nothing of Lady Frances!'

It was maddening. We use the word lightly, and for small cause. But it really was maddening. 'What will they say? What are they going to do? What can they say? If it comes to a question of affirmation I can swear as well as anyone, I suppose. If Roland pretends that he painted my pictures—if Effie says she wrote my poems—how will they prove it? What can they do?

'But things stick. If it is whispered about that there will be no more pictures and no more poems—oh! it is the hardest luck.'

One more letter reached him by that morning's post:—

'Dearest Alec,—I have left Armorel, and am no longer a Companion. The gilt could not disguise the pill. I have, however, a communication to make of a more comfortable character than this. It is true that I am like a housemaid out of a situation. But I think you will change the natural irritation caused by this announcement for a more joyful countenance when you see me. I shall arrive with my communication about noon to-morrow. Be at home, and be alone.—Your affectionate 'Zoe.'

What had she got to say? At the present crisis what could it matter what she had to say? If she had only got that money out of Armorel, or succeeded in making the girl his servant. But she could not do the only really useful thing he ever asked of her.

He laid down the letter on the table, beside one from his printers—three days old. In this communication the printers pointed out that his account was very large; that no satisfactory arrangement had been proposed; that they were going to discontinue printing his paper unless something practical was effected; and that they hoped to hear from him without delay.

There was a knock at the door: the discreet man-servant brought a card, with the silence and confidential manner of one who announces a secret emissary—say a hired assassin.

The visitor was Mr. Jagenal. He came in friendly and expansive.

'My dear boy!' he said with a warm grasp. 'Always at work—always at work?'

Alec dexterously swept the letters into an open drawer. 'Always at work,' he said. 'But I must be hard pressed when I cannot give you five minutes. What is it?'

'I will come to the point at once. You know Mrs. Elstree very well, I believe?'

'Very well indeed—I knew her before her father's failure. Before her marriage.'

'Quite so. Then what do you make of this?' He handed over a note, which the other man read: 'Dear Sir,—Unexpected circumstances have made it necessary for me to give up my charge of Armorel Rosevean at once. I have not even been able to wait a single day. I have been compelled to leave her without even wishing her farewell.—Very truly yours, Zoe Elstree.'

'It is very odd,' he said truthfully. 'I know nothing of these circumstances. I cannot tell you why she has resigned.'

'Oh! I thought I would ask you! Well, she has actually gone: she has vanished: she has left the girl quite alone. This is all very irregular, isn't it? Not quite what one expects of a lady, is it?'

'Very irregular indeed. Well, I am responsible for her introduction to you, and I will find out, if I can, what it means. She is coming here to-day, she writes: no doubt to give me her reasons. What will Miss Rosevean do?'

'Oh! she is an independent girl. She tells me that she has found a young lady about her own age, and they are going to live together. Alec, I don't quite understand why you thought Mrs. Elstree so likely a person for companion. Philippa tells me that she has no friends, and we appointed her because we thought she had so many.'

'Pleasing—attractive—accomplished—what more did you want? And as for friends, she must have had plenty.'

'But it seems she had none. Nobody has ever called upon her. And she never went into any society. Are you sure that you were not misled about her, my dear boy? I have heard, for instance, rumours about her and the provincial stage.'

'Oh! rumours are nothing. I don't think I could have been mistaken in her. However, she has gone. I will find out why. As for Armorel Rosevean——'

'Alec—what a splendid girl! Was there no chance there for you? Are you so critical that even Armorel is not good enough for you?'

'Not my style,' he said shortly. 'Never mind the girl.'

'Well—there is one more thing, Alec—and a more pleasant subject—about yourself. I want to ask you one or two questions—family questions.'

'I thought you knew all about my family.'

'So I do, pretty well. However—this is really important—most important. I wouldn't waste your time if it was not important. Do you remember your great-aunt Eleanor Fletcher?'

'Very well. She left all her money to charities—Cat!'

'And your grandmother, Mrs. Needham?'

'Quite well. What is in the wind now? Has Aunt Eleanor been proved to have made a later will in my favour?'

'You will find out in a day or two. Eh! Alec, you are a lucky dog. Painter—poet—nothing in which you do not command success. And now—now——'

'Now—what?'

'That I will tell you, my dear boy, in two or three days. There's many a slip, we know, but this time the cup will reach your lips.'

'What do you mean?' cried the young man, startled. 'Cup? Do you mean to tell me that you have something—something unexpected—coming to me? Something considerable?'

'If it comes—oh! yes, it is quite certain to come—very considerable. You are your mother's only son, and she was an only child, and her grandfather was one Robert Fletcher, wasn't he?'

'I believe he was. There's a family Bible on the shelves that can tell us.'

'Did you ever hear anything about the early life and adventures of this Robert Fletcher?'

'No: he was in the City, I believe, and he left a good large fortune. That is all.'

'That is all. That is all. Well, my dear boy, the strangest things happen: we must never be surprised at anything. But be prepared to-morrow—or next day—or the day after—to be agreeably—most agreeably—surprised.'

'To the tune of—what? A thousand pounds, say?'

'Perhaps. It may amount very nearly to as much—very nearly—Ha! ha!—to nearly as much as that, I dare say—Ho! ho!' He chuckled, and wagged his white head. 'Very nearly a thousand pounds, I dare say.' He walked over to look at the picture.

'Really, Alec,' he said, 'you deserve all the luck you get. Nobody can possibly grudge it to you. This picture is charming. I don't know when I have seen a sweeter thing. You have the finest feeling for rock and seashore and water. Well, my dear boy, I am very sorry that you haven't as fine a feeling for Armorel Rosevean—the sweetest girl and the best, I believe, in the world. Good-bye!—good-bye! till the day after to-morrow—the day after to-morrow! It will certainly reach to a thousand—or very near. Ho! ho! Lucky dog!'

Mr. Jagenal went away nodding and smiling. There are moments when it is very good to be a solicitor: they are moments rich in blessing: they compensate, in some measure, for those other moments when the guilty are brought to bay and the thriftless are made to tremble: they are the moments when the solicitor announces a windfall—the return of the long-lost Nabob—the discovery of a will—the favourable decision of the Court.

Alec sat down and seized a pen. He wrote hurriedly to his printers: 'Let the present arrangements,' he said, continue unchanged. I shall be in a position in two or three days to make a very considerable payment, and, after that, we will start on a more regular understanding.'

Another knock, and again the discreet man-servant came in on tiptoe. 'Lady refused her card,' he whispered.

The lady was none other than Armorel herself—in morning dress, wearing a hat.

He bowed coldly. There was a light in her eyes, and a heightened colour on her cheek, which hardly looked like a friendly call. But that, of course, one could not expect.

'After our recent interview,' he said, 'and after the very remarkable string of accusations which fell from your lips, I could hardly expect to see you in my studio, Miss Rosevean.'

'I came only to communicate a resolution arrived at by my friends Mr. Roland Lee and Miss Effie Wilmot.'

'From your friends Mr. Roland Lee and Miss Effie Wilmot? May I offer you a chair?'

'Thank you. No. My message is only to tell you this. They have resolved to let the past remain unknown.'

'To let the past remain unknown.' He tried to appear careless, but the girl watched the sudden light of satisfaction in his eyes and the sudden expression of relief in his face. 'The past remain unknown,' he repeated. 'Yes—certainly. Am I—may I ask—interested in this decision?'

'That you know best, Mr. Feilding. It seems hardly necessary to try to carry it off with me—I know everything. But—as you please. They agree that they have been themselves deeply to blame: they cannot acquit themselves. Certainly it is a pitiful thing for an artist to own that he has sold his name and fame in a moment of despair.'

'It would be indeed a pitiful thing if it were ever done.'

'Nothing more, therefore, will be said by either of them as to the pictures or poems.'

'Indeed? From what you have already told me: from the gracious freedom of your utterances at the National Gallery, I seem to connect those two names with the charges you then brought. They refuse to bring forward, or to endorse, those charges, then? Do you withdraw them?'

'They do not refuse to bring forward the charges. They have never made those charges. I made them, and I, Mr. Feilding'—she raised her voice a little—'I do not withdraw them.'

'Oh! you do not withdraw them? May I ask what your word in the matter is worth unsupported by their evidence—even if their evidence were worth anything?'

'You shall hear what my word is worth. This picture'—she placed herself before it—'is painted by Mr. Roland Lee. Perhaps he will not say so. Oh! It is a beautiful picture—it is quite the best he has ever painted—yet. It is a true picture: you cannot understand either its beauty or its truth. You have never been to the place: you do not even know where it is: why, Sir, it is my birthplace. I lived there until I was sixteen years of age: the scene, like all the scenes in those pictures you call your own, was taken in the Scilly archipelago.' He started. 'You do not even know the girl who stands in the foreground—your own model. Why—it is my portrait—mine—look at me, Sir—it is my portrait. Now you know what my word is worth. I have only to stand before this picture and tell the world that this is my portrait.'

He started and changed colour. This was unexpected. If the girl was to go on talking in this way outside, it would be difficult to reply. What was he to say if the words were reported to him? Because, you see, once pointed out, there could be no doubt at all about the portrait.

'A portrait of myself,' she repeated.

'Permit me to observe,' he said, with some assumption of dignity, 'that you will find it very difficult to prove these statements—most difficult—and at the same time highly dangerous, because libellous.'

'No, not dangerous, Mr. Feilding. Would you dare to go into a Court of Justice and swear that these pictures are yours? When did you go to Scilly? Where did you stay? Under what circumstances did you have me for a model? On what island did you find this view?'

He was silent.

'Will you dare to paint anything—the merest sketch—to show that this picture is in your own style? You cannot.'

'Anyone,' he said, 'may bring charges—the most reckless charges. But I think you would hardly dare——'

'I will do this, then. If you dare to exhibit this picture as your own, I will, most assuredly, take all my friends and stand in front of it, and tell them when and where it was painted, and by whom, and show them my own portrait.'

The resolution of this threat quelled him. 'I have no intention,' he said, 'of exhibiting this picture. It is sold to an American, and will go to New York immediately. Next year, perhaps, I may take up your challenge.'

She laughed scornfully. 'I promised Roland,' she said, 'that you should not show this picture. That is settled, then. You shall not, you dare not.'

She left the picture reluctantly. It was dreadful to her to think that it must go, with his name upon it.

On a side-table lay, among a pile of books, the dainty white-and-gold volume of poems bearing the name of this great genius. She took it up, and laughed.

'Oh!' she said. 'Was there ever greater impudence? Every line in this volume was written by Effie Wilmot—every line!'

'Indeed? Who says so?'

'I say so. I have compared the manuscript with the volume. There is not the difference of a word.'

'If Miss Effie Wilmot, for purposes of her own, and for base purposes of deception, has copied out my verses in her own handwriting, probably a wonderful agreement may be found.'

'Shame!' cried Armorel.

'You see the force of that remark. It is a great shame. Some girls take to lying naturally. Others acquire proficiency in the art. Effie, I suppose, took to it naturally. I am sorry for Effie. I used to think better of her.'

'Oh! He tries, even now! How can you pretend—you—to have written this sweet and dainty verse? Oh! You dare to put your signature to these poems!'

'Of course,' said the divine Maker, with brazen front and calmly dignified speech, 'if these things are said in public or outside the studio, I shall be compelled to bring an action for libel. I have warned you already. Before repeating what you have said here you had better make quite sure that you can prove your words. Ask Miss Effie Wilmot what proofs she has of her assertion, if it is hers, and not an invention of your own!'

Armorel threw down the volume. 'Poor Effie!' she said. 'She has been robbed of the first-fruits of her genius. How dare you talk of proofs?' She took up the current number of the journal. 'That is not all,' she said. 'Lóok here! This is one of your stories, is it not? I read in a paper yesterday that no Frenchman ever had so light a touch: that there are no modern stories anywhere so artistic in treatment and in construction as your own—your own—your very own, Mr. Feilding. Yet they are written for you, every one of them: they are written by Lady Frances Hollington. You are a Triple Impostor. I believe that you really are the very greatest Pretender—the most gigantic Pretender in the whole world.'

'Of course,' he went on, a little abashed by her impetuosity. 'I cannot stop your tongue. You may say what you please.'

'We shall say nothing more. That is what I came to say on behalf of my friends. I wished to spare them the pain of further communication with you.'

'Kind and thoughtful!'

'I have one more question to ask you, Mr. Feilding. Pray, why did you tell people that I was engaged to you?'

'Probably,' he replied, unabashed, 'because I wished it to be believed.'

'Why did you wish it to be believed?'

'Probably for private reasons.'

'It was a vile and horrible falsehood!'

'Come, Miss Rosevean, we will not call each other names. Otherwise I might ask you what the world calls a girl who encourages a man to dangle after her for weeks, till everybody talks about her, and then throws him over.'

'Oh! You cannot mean——' Before those flashing eyes his own dropped.

'I mean that this is exactly what you have done,' he said, but without looking up.

'Is it possible that a man can be so base? What encouragement did I ever give you?'

'You surely are not going to deny the thing, after all. Why, it has been patent for all the world to see you. I have been with you everywhere, in all public places. What hint did you ever give me that my addresses were disagreeable to you?'

'How can one reply to such insinuations?' asked Armorel, with flaming face. 'And so you followed me about in order to be able to say that I encouraged you! What a man! What a man! You have taught me to understand, now, why one man may sometimes take a stick and beat another. If I were a man, at this moment, I would beat you with a stick. No other treatment is fit for such a man. I to encourage you!—when for a month and more I have known what an Impostor and Pretender you are! You dare to say that I have encouraged you!—you—the robber of other men's name and fame!'

'Well, if you come to that, I do dare to say as much. Come, Miss Armorel Rosevean. I certainly do dare to say as much.'

She turned with a gesture of impatience.

'I have said what I came to say. I will go.'

'Stop a moment!' said Alec Feilding. 'Is it not rather a bold proceeding for a beautiful girl like you, a day or two after you have refused a man, to visit him alone at his studio? Is it altogether the way to let the world distinctly understand that there never has been anything between us, and that it is all over?'

'I am less afraid of the world than you think. My world is my very little circle of friends. I am very much afraid of what they think. But it is on their account, and with their knowledge, that I am here.'

'Alone and unprotected?'

'Alone, it is true. I can always protect myself.'

'Indeed!' He turned an ugly—a villanous—face towards her. 'We shall see! You come here with your charges and your fine phrases. We shall see!'

He had been standing all this time before his study table. He now stepped quickly to the door. The key was in the lock. He turned it, drew it out, and dropped it in his pocket.

'Now, my lovely lady,' he said, grinning, 'you have had your innings, and I am going to have mine. You have come to this studio in order to have a row with me. You have had that row. You can use your tongue in a manner that does credit to your early education. As for your nonsense about Roland Lee and Effie and Lady Frances, no one is going to believe that stuff, you know. As for your question, I did tell Lady Frances that you were engaged to me. And I told others. Because, of course, you were—or ought to have been. It was only by some kind of accident that I did not speak before. As I intended to speak the next day, I anticipated the thing by twelve hours or so. What of that? Well, I shall now have to explain that you seem not to know your own mind. It will be awkward for you—not for me. You have thrown me over. And all you have got to say in explanation is a long rigmarole of abuse. This not my own painting? These not my own poems? These, again, not my own stories? Really, Miss Armorel Rosevean, you know so very little of the world—you are so inexperienced—you are so easily imposed upon—that I am inclined to pity rather than to blame you. Of course, you have tried to do me harm, and I ought to be angry with you. But I cannot. You are much too beautiful. To a lovely woman everything, even mischief, is forgiven.'

'Will you open the door and let me go?'

'All in good time. When I please. It will do you no harm to be caught alone in my studio—alone with me. It will look so like returning to the lover whom, in a moment of temper, you threw over. I will take care that it shall bear that interpretation, if necessary. You have changed your mind, sweet Armorel, have you not? You have repented of that cruel decision?'

He advanced a little nearer. I really believe that he was still confident in his own power of subjugating the sex feminine—Heaven knows why some men always retain this confidence.

Armorel looked round the room: the window was high, too high for her to reach: there was no way of escape except through the door. Then she saw something hanging on the wall within her reach, and she took courage.

He drew still nearer: he held out his hands, and laughed.

'You are a really lovely girl,' he said. 'I believe there is not a more beautiful girl in the whole world. Before you go let us make friends and forgive. It is not too late to change your mind. I will forget all you have said and all the mischief you have done me. My man is very discreet. He will say nothing about your visit here, unless I give him permission to speak. This I will never allow unless I am compelled. Come, Armorel, once more let me be your lover—once more. Give me your hands.'

He bowed suppliant. He looked in her face with baleful eyes. He tried to take her hands. Armorel sprang from him and darted to the other end of the room.

The thing she had observed was hanging up among the weapons and armour and tapestry which decorated this wall of the studio. It was an axe from foreign parts, I think, from Indian parts, with a stout wooden handle and a boss of steel at the upper part. Armorel seized this lethal weapon. It was so heavy that no ordinary girl could have lifted it. But her arm, strengthened by a thousand days upon the water, tugging at the oar, wielded it easily.

'Open the door!' she cried. 'Open the door this moment!'

Her wooer made no reply. He shrank back before the girl who

handled this heavy axe as lightly as a paper-knife. But he did not open the door.

'Open it, I say!'

He only shrank back farther. He was cowed before the wrath in her face. He did not know what she would do next. I think he even forgot that the key was in his pocket. The door a dainty piece of furniture, was not one of the common machine-made things which the competitive German—or is it the thrifty Swede?—is so good as to send over to us. It was a planned and fitted door, the panels painted with reeds and grasses, the gift of some admirer of genius. Armorel raised the axe—and looked at him. He did not move.

Crash! It went through the panel. Crash! again and again. The upper part of the door was a gaping wreck of splinters. Outside, the discreet man-servant waited in silence and expectation. Often ladies had held interviews alone with his master. But this was the first time that an interview had ended with such a crash.

'Will you open the door?' she asked again.

The man replied by a curse.

The lock—a piece of imitation mediævalism in iron—was fitted on to the inner part of the door, a very pretty ornament. Armorel raised her axe again, and brought the square boss at the top of it down upon the dainty fragile lock, breaking it and tearing it from the wood. There was no more difficulty in opening the door. She did so. She threw the hatchet on the carpet and walked away, the discreet man-servant opening the door for her with unchanged countenance, as if the deplorable incident had not happened at all.

CHAPTER XXII

THE END OF WORLDLY TROUBLES

Not more than five minutes afterwards, Mrs. Elstree arrived upon this scene of wreck. The splintered panels, the broken lock, the axe lying on the floor, proclaimed aloud that there had been an Incident of some gravity—certainly what we have called a Deplorable Incident.

Such a thing as a Deplorable Incident in such a place and with such a man was, indeed, remarkable. Mrs. Elstree gazed upon the wreck with astonishment unfeigned: she turned to the tenant of the studio, who stood exactly where Armorel had left him. As the sea when the storm has ceased continues to heave in sullen anger, so that majestic spirit still heaved with wrath as yet unappeased.

In answer to the mute question of her eyes, he growled, and threw himself into his study-chair. When she picked up the axe and bore it back to its place, he growled. When she pointed to the door, he growled again.

She looked at his angry face, and she laughed gently. The last time we saw her she was pale and hysterical. She was now smiling, apparently in perfect health of body and ease of mind. Perhaps she was a very good actress—off the stage: perhaps she shook off things easily. Otherwise one does not always step from a highly nervous and hysterical condition to one of happiness and cheerfulness.

'There appears to have been a little unpleasantness,' she said softly. 'Something, apparently an axe—something hard and sharp—has been brought into contact with the door. It has been awkward for the door. There has been, I suppose, an earthquake.'

He said nothing, but drummed the table with his fingers—a sign of impatient and enforced listening.

'Earthquakes are dangerous things, sometimes. Meanwhile, Alec, if I were you I would have the broken bits taken away.' She touched the bell on the table. 'Ford'—this was the name of the discreet man-servant—'will you kindly take the door, which you see is broken, off its hinges and send it away to be mended. We will manage with the curtain.'

'What do you want, Zoe?'—when this operation had been effected—'what is the important news you have to bring me? And why have you given up your berth? I suppose you think I am able to find you a place just by lifting up my little finger? And I hear you have gone without a moment's notice, just as if you had run away?'

'I did run away, Alec,' she replied. 'After what has—been done'—she caught her breath—'I was obliged to run away. I could no longer stay.'

'What has been done, then? Did Armorel tell you? No—she couldn't.'

'She has told me nothing. I have hardly seen her at all during the last few days. Of course, I know that you proposed to her—because you went off with that purpose; and that she refused you—because that was certain. And, now, don't begin scolding and questioning, because we have got something much more important to discuss. I have given up my charge of Armorel, and I have come here. If you possibly can, Alec, clear up your face a little, forget the earthquake, and behave with some attempt at politeness. I insist,' she added sharply, 'upon being treated with some pretence at politeness.'

'Mind, I am in no mood to listen to a pack of complaints and squabbles and jealousies.'

'Whatever mind you are in, my dear Alec, it wants the sweetening. You shall have no squabbles or jealousies. I will not even ask who brought along the earthquake—though, of course, it was an Angel in the House. They are generally the cause of all the earthquakes. Fortunately for you, I am not jealous. The important thing about which I want to talk to you is money, Alec—money.'

Something in her manner seemed to hold out promise. A drowning man catches at a straw. Alec lifted his gloomy face.

'What's the use?' he said. 'You have failed to get money in the way I suggested. I haven't got any left at all. And we are now at the very end. All is over and done, Zoe. The game is ended. We must throw up the sponge.'

'Not just yet, dear Alec,' she said softly.

'Look here, Zoe'—he softened a little. 'I have thought over things. I shall have to disappear for a while, I believe, till things blow over. Now, here's just a gleam of luck. Jagenal the lawyer has been here to-day. He came to tell me that he has discovered, somehow, something belonging to me. He says it will run up to nearly a thousand pounds. It isn't much, but it is something. Now, Zoe, I mean to convert that thousand into cash—notes—portable property—and I shall keep it in my pocket. Don't think I am going to let the creditors have much of that! If the smash has to come off, I will then give you half, and keep the other half myself. Meantime, the possession of the money may stave off the smash. But if it comes, we will go away—different ways, you know—and own each other no more.'

'Not exactly, my dear Alec. You may go away, if you please, but I shall go with you. For the future, I mean to go the same way as you—with you—beside you.'

'Oh!' His face did not betray immoderate joy at this prospect. 'I suppose you have got something else to say. If that was all, I should ask how you propose to pay for your railway ticket and your hotel bill.'

'Of course, I have got something else to say.'

'It must be something substantial, then. Look here, Zoe: this is really no time for fooling. Everything, I tell you, has gone, and all at once. I can't explain. Credit—everything!'

'I have read,' said Zoe, taking the most comfortable chair and lying well back in it, 'that the wise man once discovered that everybody must be either a hammer or an anvil. I think it was Voltaire. He resolved on becoming the hammer. You, Alec, made the same useful discovery. You, also, became a hammer. So far, you have done pretty well, considering. But now there is a sudden check, and you are thrown out altogether.'

'Well?'

'That seems to show that your plans were incomplete. Your ideas were sound, but they were not fully developed.'

'I don't know you this morning, Zoe. I have never heard you talk like this before.'

'You have never known me, Alec,' she replied, perhaps a little sadly. 'You have never tried to know me. Well—I know all

Mr. Roland Lee, the painter, was one anvil—you played upon him very harmoniously. Effie Wilmot was another. Now, Alec, don't' —she knew the premonitory symptoms—'don't begin to deny, either with the "D" or without, because, I assure you, I know everything. You are like the ostrich, who buries his head in the sand and thinks himself invisible. Don't deny things, because it is quite useless. Before we go a step farther I am going to make you understand exactly. I know the whole story. I have suspected things for a long time, and now I have learned the truth. I learned it bit by bit through the fortunate accident of living with Armorel, who has been the real discoverer. First I saw the man's work, and I saw at once where you got your pictures from, and what was the meaning of certain words that had passed from Armorel. Why, Armorel was the model—your model, and you didn't know it. And the coast scenery is her scenery—the Scilly Isles, where you have never been. I won't tell you how I pieced things together till I had made a connected story and had no longer any doubt. But remember the night of the Reading. Why did Armorel hold that Reading? Why did she show the unfinished picture? Why did she sing that song? It was for you, Alec. It was to tell you a great deal more than it told the people. It was to let you know that everything was discovered. Do you deny it now?'

'I suppose that infernal girl—she is capable of everything——'

'Even of earthquakes? No, Alec, she has told me nothing. They've got into the habit of talking—she and Effie and the painter man—as if I was asleep. You see I lie about a good deal by the fireside, and I don't want to talk, and so I lie with my eyes shut and listen. Then Armorel leaves everything about—manuscript poems, sketches, letters—everything, and I read them. A companion, of course, must see that her ward is not getting into mischief. It is her duty to read private letters. When they talk in the evening, Effie, who worships Armorel, tells her everything, including your magnificent attempt to become a dramatic poet, my dear boy—wrong—wrong—you should not get more than one ghost from one family. You should not put all your ghosts into one basket. When the painter comes—Armorel is in love with him, and he is in love with her; but he has been a naughty boy, and has to show true repentance before . . . Oh! It's very pretty and sentimental: they play the fiddle and talk about Scilly and the old times, and Effie sighs with sympathy. It is really very pretty, especially as it all helped me to understand their ghostlinesses and to unravel the whole story. Fortunately, my dear Alec, you have had to do with a girl who is not of the ordinary society stamp, otherwise your story would have been given to the society papers long ago, and then even I could have done nothing for you. Armorel is a girl of quite extinct virtues—forbearing, unrevengeful, honourable, unselfish. You, my dear Alec, could never appreciate or understand such a girl.'

'The girl is—a girl. What is there to understand in one girl more than in another?'

'Nothing—nothing. O great Poet and greater Painter!—Nothing. O man of fine insight, and delicate fancy, and subtle intellect!—Nothing. Only a girl.'

'I know already that they are not going to say anything more about it. They are going to let the whole business be forgotten. If anything comes out through you——'

'Nothing will come out. I told you because it is well that we should perfectly understand each other. You will never again be able to parade before me in the disguise of genius. This is a great pity, because you have always enjoyed playing the part. Never again, Alec, because I have found you out. Should you ever find me out, I shall not be able to walk with you in the disguise of . . . but you must find out first.'

'What do you mean?'

'Oh! you must find out first. When you do find out, you will be able to hold out your arms and cry, "We are alike at last. You have come down to my level: we are now in the same depths. Come to my arms, sister in pretence! Come, my bride!"' She spread out her arms with an exaggerated gesture and laughed, but not mirthfully.

'What on earth do you mean, Zoe? I never saw you like this before.'

'No, we change sometimes, quite suddenly. It is very unaccountable. And now I shall never be anything else than what I am now—what you have made me.'

'What have you done, then?'

'Done? Nothing. To do something is polite for committing a crime. Could I have done something, do you think? Could I actually commit a crime? O Alec!—my dear Alec!—a crime? Well, the really important thing is that your troubles are over.'

'By Jove! They are only just beginning.'

'It is only money that troubles you. If it was conscience, or the sense of honour, I could not help you. As it is only money——how much, actually, will put a period to the trouble?'

'If I were to use Jagenal's promised thousand, I could really manage with two thousand more.'

'Oh! Then, my dear Alec, what do you think of this?'

She drew out of her pocket a new clean white bank-book, and handed it to him.

He opened it. 'Heavens, Zoe! What is the meaning of this?'

'You can read, Alec: it means what it says. Four thousand two hundred and twenty-five pounds standing to my credit. Observe the name—Mrs. Alexander Feilding—Mrs. Alexander Feilding—wife, that is, of Alec! Mrs. Elstree has vanished. She has gone to join the limbo of ghosts who never existed. Her adored Jerome is there, too.'

'What does it mean?'

'It means, again, that I have four thousand two hundred and twenty-five pounds of my own, who, the day before yesterday, had nothing. Where I got that money from is my own business. Perhaps Armorel relented and has advanced this money—perhaps some old friends of my father's—he had friends, though he was reputed so rich and died so miserably—have quietly subscribed this amount—perhaps my cousins, whom you forced me to abandon, have found me out and endowed me with this sum—a late but still acceptable act of generosity—perhaps my mother's sister, who swore she would never forgive me for going on the stage, has given way at last! In short, my dear Alec——'

'Four thousand pounds! Where could you raise that money?'

'Make any conjecture you please. I shall not tell you. The main point is that the money is here—safely deposited in my name and to my credit. It is mine, you see, my dear Alec; and it can only be used for your purposes with my consent—under my conditions.'

'How on earth,' he repeated slowly, 'did you get four thousand pounds?'

'It is difficult for you to find an answer to that question,' she replied, 'isn't it? Especially as I shall not answer it. About my conditions now.'

'What conditions?'

'The possession of this capital—I have thought it all out—will enable us, first of all, to pay off your creditors in full if you must—or at least to satisfy them. Next, it will restore your credit. Thirdly, it will enable you to live while I am laying the foundations of a new and more stable business.'

'You?'

'I, my dear boy. I mean in future to be the active working and contriving partner in the firm. I have the plans and method worked out already in my head. You struck out, I must say, a line of audacity. There is something novel about it. But your plan wanted elasticity. You kept a ghost. Well, I suppose other people have done this before. You kept three or four ghosts, each in his own line. Nobody thought of setting up as the Universal Genius before—at least, not to my knowledge. But, then, you placed your whole dependence upon your one single family of ghosts. Once deprived of him—whether your painter, your poet, your story-teller—and where were you? Lost! You are stranded. This has happened to you now. Your paper is to come out as usual, and you have got nothing to put into it. Your patrons will be flocking to your studio, and you have got nothing to show. You have made a grievous blunder. Now, Alec I am going to remedy all this.'

'You?'

'You shall see what I am capable of doing. You shall no longer waste your time and money in going about to great houses. Your wife shall have her *salon*, which shall be a centre of action far more useful and effective. You shall become, through her help, a far greater leader, with a far greater name, than you have ever dreamed of. And your paper shall be a bigger thing.'

'You, Zoe? You to talk like this?'

'You thought I was a helpless creature because I never succeeded on the stage, and could not even carry out your poor little schemes upon Armorel's purse, I suppose, and because I—— Well, you shall be undeceived.'

'If I could only believe this!'

'You will find, Alec, that my stage experiences will not go for nothing. Why, even if I was a poor actress, I did learn the whole business of stage management. I am going to transfer that business from the stage to the drawing-room, which shall be, at first, this room. We shall play our little comedy together, you and I.' She sprang to her feet, and began to act as if she was on the stage—'It will be a duologue. Your *rôle* will still be that of the Universal Genius; mine will be that of the supposed extinct Lady—the Lady of the Salon—I shall be at home one evening a week—say on Sunday. And it shall be an evening remembered and expected. We shall both take Art seriously: you as the Master, I as the sympathetic and intelligent worshipper of Art. We shall attract to our rooms artists of every kind and those who hang about artistic circles: our furniture shall show the latest artistic craze: foreigners shall come here as to the art centre of London—we will cultivate the foreign element: young people shall come for advice, for encouragement, for introduction: reputations shall be made and marred in this room: you shall be the Leader and Chief of the World of Art. If there is here and there one who knows that you are a humbug, what matters? Alec'—she struck a most effective attitude—'rise to the prospect! Have a little imagination! I see before me the most splendid future—oh! the most splendid future!'

'All very well. But there's the present staring us in the face. How and where are we to find the—the successors to Lady Frances and Effie and——'

'Where to find ghosts? Leave that to me. I know where there are plenty only too glad to be employed. They can be had very cheap, my dear Alec, I can assure you. Oh! I have not been so low down in the social levels for nothing. You paid a ridiculous price for your ghosts—quite ridiculous. I will find you ghosts enough, never fear.'

'Where are they?'

When one goes about the country with a travelling company one hears strange things. I have heard of painters—good painters—who once promised to become Royal Academicians, and anything you please, but took to ways—downward ways, you know—and now sit in public-houses and sell their work for fifteen shillings a picture. I will find you such a genius, and will make him take pains and produce a picture worthy of his better days, and you shall have it for a guinea and a pint of champagne.'

Alec Feilding gasped. The vista before him was too splendid.

'Or, if you want verses, I know of a poet who used to write little dainty pieces—*levers de rideau*, *libretti* for little operettas, and so forth. He carries the boards about the streets when he is very hard up. I can catch that creature and lock him up without drink till he has written a poem far better—more manly—than anything that girl of yours could ever produce, for half-a-crown. And he will never ask what becomes of it. If you want stories, I know a man—quite a young fellow—who gets about fifteen shillings a week in his travelling company. This fellow is wonderful at stories. For ten shillings a column he will reel you out as many as you want—good stuff mind—and the papers have never found him out: and he will never ask what has become of them, because he is never sober for more than an hour or two at a time in the middle of the day, and he will forget his own handiwork. Alec, I declare that I can find you as many ghosts as you like, and better—more popular—more interesting than your old lot.'

'If I could only believe——' he repeated.

'You say that because you have never even begun to believe that a woman can do anything. Well, I do not ask you to believe. I say that you shall see. I owe to you the idea. All the working out shall be my own. All the assistance you can give me will be your own big and important presence and your manner of authority. Yes; some men get rich by the labours of others: you, Alec, shall become famous—perhaps immortal—by the genius—the collected genius, of others.'

His imagination was not strong enough to understand the vision that she spread out before him. In a wooden way, he saw that she intended something big. He only half believed it: he only half understood it: but he did understand that ghosts were to be had.

'There's next week's paper, Zoe,' he said helplessly. 'Nothing for it yet! We mustn't have a breakdown—it would be fatal!'

'Breakdown! Of course not, even if I write it all myself. You don't believe that I can write even, I suppose?'

'Well, you shall do as you like.' He got up and stood over the fire again, sighing his relief. 'At all events, we have got this money. Good Heavens! What a chance! And what a day! I stood here this morning, Zoe, thinking all was lost. Then old

Jagenal comes in and tells me of a thousand pounds—said it would run to nearly a thousand. And then you come in with a bank-book of four thousand! Oh! it's Providential! It's enough to make a man humble. Zoe, I confess'—he took her hands in his, stooped, and kissed her tenderly—'I don't deserve such treatment from you. I do not, indeed. Are you sure about those ghosts? As for me, of course you are right. I can't paint a stroke. I can't make a rhyme. I can't write stories. I can do nothing—but live upon those who can do everything. You are quite sure about those ghosts?'

'Oh, yes! Quite sure. Of course I knew all along. But you must keep it up more religiously than ever, because the business is going to be so much—so very much—bigger. Now for my conditions.'

'Any conditions—any!'

'You will insert this advertisement for six days, beginning to-morrow, in the *Times*.'

'He read it aloud. He read it without the least change of countenance, so wooden was his face, so hard his heart.

'On Wednesday, April 21, 1887, at St. Leonard's, Worthing, Alexander Feilding, of the Grove Studio, Marlborough Road, to Zoe, only daughter of the late Peter Evelyn, formerly of Kensington Palace Gardens.'

'I believe,' he said, folding the paper, 'that was the date. It was three years ago, wasn't it? I say, Zoe, won't it be awkward having to explain things—long interval, you know—engagement as companion—wrong name?'

'I have thought of that. But it would be more awkward pretending that we were married to-day and being found out. No. There are not half-a-dozen people who will ever know that I was Armorel's companion. Then, a circumstance, which there is no need ever to explain, forbade the announcement of our marriage—hint at a near relation's will—I was compelled to assume another name. Cruel necessity!'

'You are a mighty clever woman, Zoe.'

'I am. If you are wise, now, you will assume a joyful air. You will go about rejoicing that the bar to this public announcement has been at length removed. Family reasons—you will say—no fault of yours or of mine. It is your business, of course, how you will look—but I recommend this line. Be the exultant bridegroom, not the downcast husband. Will you walk so?'—she assumed a buoyant dancing step with a smiling face—'or so?' she hung a dejected head and crawled sadly.

'By gad, it's wonderful!' he cried, looking at her with astonishment. And, indeed, who would recognise the quiet, sleepy, indolent woman of yesterday in the quick, restless, and alert woman of to-day?

'Henceforth I must work, Alec. I cannot sit down and go to sleep any longer. That time has gone. I think I have murdered sleep.'

'Work away, my girl. Nobody wants to prevent you. Are there any other conditions?'

'You will sell your riding-horses and buy a Victoria. Your wife must have something to drive about in. And you will lead, in many respects, an altered life. I must have, for the complete working out of my plans, an ideal domestic life. Turtle-doves we must be for affection, and angels incarnate for propriety. The highest Art in the home is the highest standard of manners that can be set up.'

'Very good. Any more conditions?'

'Only one more condition. *J'y suis. J'y reste.* You will call your servant and inform him that I am your wife, and the mistress of this establishment. I think there will be no more earthquakes and broken panels. Alec'—she laid her hand upon his arm—'you should have done this three years ago. I should have saved you. I should have saved myself. Now, whatever happens, we are on the same level—we cannot reproach each other. We shall walk hand in hand. It was done for you, Alec. And I would do it again. Yes—yes—yes. Again!' She repeated the words with flashing eyes. 'Fraud—sham—pretence—these are our servants. We command them. By them we live, and by them we climb. What matter—so we reach the top—by what ladders we have climbed?' She looked around with a gesture of defiance, fine and free. 'The world is all alike,' she said. 'There is no truth or honour anywhere. We are all in the same swim.'

The man dropped into his vacant chair. 'We are saved!' he cried.

'Saved!' she echoed. 'Saved! Did you ever see a Court of Justice, Alec? I have. Once, when our company was playing at Winchester, I went to see the Assizes. I remember then wondering how it would feel to be a prisoner. Henceforth I shall understand his sensations. There they stand, two prisoners, side by side—a man and a woman—a pair of them. Found out at last, and arrested and brought up for trial. There sits the Judge, stern and cold: there are the twelve men of the jury, grave and cold: there are the policemen, stony-hearted: there are the lawyers, laughing and talking: there are the people behind, all grave and cold. No pity in any single face—not a gleam of pity—for the poor prisoners. Some people go stealing and cheating because they are driven by poverty. These people did not: they were driven by vanity and greed. Look at them in the box: they are well dressed. See! they are curiously like you and me, Alec'—she was acting now better than she ever acted on the stage—

'The man is like you, and the woman—oh! you poor, unlucky wretch!—is like me—curiously, comically like me. They will be found guilty. What punishment will they get? As for her, it was for her husband's sake that she did it. But, I suppose, that will not help her. What will they get, Alec?'

He sat up in the chair and heaved a great sigh of relief.

'What are you talking about, my dear? I was not listening. Well; we are saved. It has been a mighty close shave. Another day, and I must have thrown up the sponge. We have a world of work before us; but if you are only half or quarter as clever as you think yourself, we shall do splendidly.' He laid his arm round her waist, and drew her gently and kissed her again. 'So—now you are sensible—what were you talking about prisoners for? No more separations now. Let me kiss away these tears. And now, Zoe—now—time presses. I am anxious to repair my losses. Where are we to find these ghosts? Sit down. To work! To work!'

CHAPTER XXIII

THE HOUR OF TRIUMPH

A MAN may do a great many things without receiving from the world the least sign of regard or interest. He may write the most lovely verses—and no one will read them. He may design and invent the most beautiful play—which no one will act: he may advocate a measure certain to bring about universal happiness—but no one will so much as read it. There is one thing, however, by which he may awaken a spirit of earnest curiosity and interest concerning himself: he may get married. Everybody will read the announcement of his marriage in the paper: everybody will immediately begin to talk about him. The bridegroom's present position and future prospects, his actual income and the style in which he will live: the question whether he has done well for himself, or whether he has thrown himself away: the bride's family, her age, her beauty, her *dot*, if she has got any: the question whether she had not a right to expect a better marriage—all these points are raised and debated when a man is married. Also, which is even more remarkable, whatever a man does shall be forgotten by the world, but the story of his marriage shall never be forgotten. A man may live down calumny; he may hold up his head though he has been the defendant in a disgraceful cause; he may survive the scandal of follies and profligacies; he may ride triumphant over misfortune: but he can never live down his own marriage. All those who have married 'beneath' them—whether beneath them in social rank, in manners, in morals, character, in spiritual or in mental elevation, will bear unwilling and grievous testimony to this great truth.

When, therefore, the *Times* announced the marriage of Mr. Alexander Feilding, together with the fact that the announcement was no less than three years late, great amazement fell upon all men and all women—yea, and dismay upon all those girls who knew this Universal Genius—and upon all who knew or remembered the lady, daughter of the financial City person who let in everybody to so frightful a tune, and then, like another treacherous person, went away and hanged himself. And as many questions were asked at the breakfast-tables of London as there were riddles asked at the famous dinner-party at the town of Mansoul. To these riddles there were answers, but to those none. For instance, why had Alec Feilding concealed his marriage? Where had he hidden his wife? And (among a very few) how could he permit her to go about the country in a provincial troupe? To these replies there have never been any answers. The lady herself, who certainly ought to know, sometimes among her intimate friends alludes to the cruelty of relations, and the power which one's own people have of making mischief. She also speaks of the hard necessity, owing to these cruelties, of concealing her marriage. This throws the glamour and magic of romance—the romance of money—over the story. But there are some who remain unconvinced.

The bridegroom wrote one letter, and only one, of explanation. It was to Mr. Jagenal, the family solicitor.

'To so old a friend,' he wrote, 'the fullest explanations are due concerning things which may appear strange. Until the day before yesterday there were still existing certain family reasons which rendered it absolutely necessary for us to conceal our marriage and to act with so much prudence that no one should so much as suspect the fact. This will explain to you why we lent ourselves to the little harmless—perfectly harmless—pretence by which my wife appeared in the character of a widow. It also explains why she was unwilling—while under false colours—to go into general society. The unexpected disappearance of these family reasons caused her to abandon her charge hurriedly. I had not learned the fact when you called yesterday. Now, I hope that we may receive, though late, the congratulations of our friends.—A. F.'

'This,' said Mr. Jagenal, 'is an explanation which explains nothing. Well, it is all very irregular; and there is something behind; and it is no concern of mine. Most things in the world are irregular. The little windfall of which I told him yesterday will be doubly welcome now that he has a wife to spend his money for him. And now we understand why he was always dangling after Armorel—because his wife was with her—and why he did not fall in love with that most beautiful creature.'

He folded up the note; put it, with a few words of his own, into an envelope, and sent it to Philippa. Then he went on with the cases in his hands. Among these were the materials for many other studies into the workings of the feminine heart and the masculine brain. The solicitor's tin boxes: the doctor's notebook: the priest's memory: should furnish full materials for that exhaustive psychological research which science will some day insist upon conducting.

In the afternoon of the same day was the Private View of the Grosvenor Gallery. There was the usual Private View crowd—so private now that everybody goes there. It would have been incomplete without the presence of Mr. Alec Feilding.

Now, at the very thickest and most crowded time, when the rooms were at their fullest, and when the talk was at its noisiest, he appeared, bearing on his arm a young, beautiful, and beautifully dressed woman. He calmly entered the room where half the people were talking of himself and of his marriage, concealed for three years, with as much coolness as if he had been about in public with his wife all that time: he spoke to his friends as if nothing had happened: and he introduced them to his wife as if it was by the merest accident that they had not already met. Nothing could exceed the unconsciousness of his manner, unless it was the simple and natural ease of his wife. No one could possibly guess that there was, or could be, the least awkwardness in the situation.

The thing itself, and the manner of carrying it through, constituted a *coup* of the most brilliant kind. This public appearance deprived the situation, in fact, of all its awkwardness. No one could ask them at the Grosvenor Gallery what it meant. There were one or two to whom the bridegroom whispered that it was a long and romantic story: that there had been a bar to the completion of his happiness, by a public avowal: that this bar—a purely private and family matter—had only yesterday been removed: nothing was really explained: but it was generally felt that the mystery added another to the eccentricities of genius. There was a something, they seemed to remember dimly, about the marriages and love-passages of Shelley, Coleridge, and Lord Byron.

Mrs. Feilding, clearly, was a woman born to be an artist's wife: herself, artistic in her dress, her manner, and her appearance: sympathetic in her caressing voice: gracious in her manners: and openly proud of a husband so richly endowed.

Alec presented a great many men to her. She had, it seemed, already made acquaintance with their works, which she knew by name: she betrayed involuntarily, by her gracious smile, and the interested, curious gaze of her large and limpid eyes, the genuine admiration which she felt for these works, and the very great pleasure with which she made the acquaintance of this very distinguished author. If any of them were on the walls, she bestowed upon them the flattery of measured and appreciative praise: she knew something of the technique.

'Alec is not exhibiting this year,' she said. 'I think he is right. He had but one picture: and that was in his old style. People will think he can do nothing but sea-coast, rock, and spray. So he is going to send his one picture away—if you want to see it you must make haste to the studio—and he is going—this is a profound secret—to break out in a new line—quite a new line. But you must not know anything about it.'

A paragraph in a column of personal news published the fact, the very next day, which shows how difficult it is to keep a secret.

Before Mrs. Feilding left the gallery she had made twenty friends for life, and had laid a solid foundation for her Sunday evenings.

In the evening there was a First Night. No First Nights are possible without the appearance of certain people, of whom Mr. Alec Feilding was one. He attended, bringing with him his wife. Some of the men who had been at the private view were also present at the performance, but not many, because the followers of one art do not—as they should—rally round any other. But all the dramatic critics were there, and all the regular first-nighters, including the wreckers—who go to pit and gallery—and the friends of the author and those of the actors. Between the acts there was a good deal of circulation and talking. Alec presented a good many more gentlemen to his wife. Before they went home Mrs. Feilding had made a dozen more friends for life, and placed her Sunday evenings on a firm and solid basis. Her social success—at least among the men—was assured from this first day.

CHAPTER XXIV

THE CUP AND THE LIP

Two days after the Private View Alec Feilding repaired, by special invitation, to Mr. Jagenal's office.

'I have sent for you, Alec,' said the solicitor, *ami de famille*, 'in continuance of our conversation of the other day—about that little windfall, you know.'

'I am not likely to forget it. Little windfalls of a thousand pounds do not come too often.'

'They do not. Meantime another very important event has happened. I saw the announcement in the paper, and I received your note——'

'You are the only person—believe me—to whom I have thought it right to explain the circumstances——'

'Yes? The explanation, at all events, is one that may be given in the same words—to all the world. I have no knowledge of Mrs. Feilding's friends, or of any obstacles that have been raised to her marriage! But I am rather sorry, Alec, that you sent her to me under a false name, because these things, if they get about, are apt to make mischief.'

'I assure you that this plan was only adopted in order the more effectually to divert suspicion. It was with the greatest reluctance that we consented to enter upon a path of deception. I knew, however, in whose hands I was. At any moment I was in readiness to confess the truth to you. In the case of a stranger the thing would have been impossible. You, however, I knew, would appreciate the motive of our action, and sympathise with the necessity.'

Mr. Jagenal laughed gently—behind the specious words he discerned—something—the shapeless spectre which suspicion calls up or creates. But he only laughed. 'Well, Alec,' he said, 'marriage is a perfectly personal matter. You are a married man. You had reasons of your own for concealing the fact. You are now enabled to proclaim the fact. That is all anybody need know. We condone the little pretence of the widowhood. Armorel Rosevean has lost her companion; whether she has also lost her friend I do not know. The rest concerns yourself alone. Very good. You are a married man. All the more reason that this little windfall should be acceptable.'

'It will be extremely acceptable, I assure you.'

'Whether it is money or money's worth?'

'To save trouble I should prefer money.'

'You must take it as it comes, my dear boy.'

'Well, what is it?'

'It is,' replied Mr. Jagenal solemnly, 'nothing short of the sea giving up its treasures, the dead giving up her secrets, and the restoration of what was never known to be lost.'

'You a maker of conundrums?'

'You shall hear. Before we come to the thing itself—the treasure, the windfall, the thing picked up on the beach—let me again recall to you two or three points in your own family history. Your mother's maiden name was Isabel Needham. She was the daughter of Henry Needham and Frances his wife. Frances was the daughter of Robert Fletcher.'

'Very good. I believe that is the case.'

'Your money came to you from this Robert Fletcher, your maternal great-grandfather. You should, therefore, remember him.'

'I recognise,' said Alec, sententiously, 'the respect that should be paid to the memory of every man who makes money for his children.'

'Very good. Now, this Robert Fletcher as a young man, went out to India in search of fortune. He was apparently an adventurous young man, not disposed to sit down at the desk after the usual fashion of young men who go out to India. We find him in

Burmah, for instance—then a country little known by Englishmen. While there he managed to attract the notice and the favour of the King, who employed him in some capacity—traded with him, perhaps; and, at all events, advanced his interests—so that, while still a young man, he found himself in the possession of a fortune ample enough for his wants——'

'Which he left to his daughters.'

'Don't be in a hurry. That was quite another fortune.'

'Oh! Another fortune? What became of the first?'

'Having enough, he resolved to return to his native country. But in Burmah there were then no banks, merchants, drafts, or cheques. He therefore converted his fortune into portable property, which he carried about his person, no one, I take it, knowing anything at all about it. Thus, carrying his treasure with him, he sailed for England. Have you heard anything of this?'

'Nothing at all. The beginning of the story, however, is interesting.'

'You will enjoy the end still better. The ship in which he sailed met with disaster. She was wrecked on the Isles of Scilly. It is said—but this I do not know—that the only man saved from the wreck was your great-grandfather: he was saved by one Emanuel Rosevean, great-great-grandfather to Armorel, the girl whose charge your own wife undertook.'

'Always that cursed girl!' murmured Alec.

'Robert Fletcher was clinging to a spar when he was picked up and dragged ashore. He recovered consciousness after a long illness, and then found that the leather case in which all his fortune lay had slipped from his neck and was lost. Therefore, he had to begin the world again. He went away, therefore. He went away——' Mr. Jagenal paused at this point, rattled his keys, and looked about him. He was not a story-teller by profession, but he knew instinctively that every story, in order to be dramatic—and he wished this to be a very dramatic history—should be cut up into paragraphs, illustrated by dialogue, and divided into sections. Dialogue being impossible, he stopped and rattled his keys. This meant the end of one chapter and the beginning of another.

'Do pray get along,' cried his client, now growing interested and impatient.

'He went away,' the narrator repeated, 'his treasure lost, to begin the world again. He came here, became a stockbroker, made money—and the rest you know. He appears never to have told his daughters of his loss. I have been in communication with the solicitors of the late Eleanor Fletcher, your great-aunt, and I cannot learn from them that she ever spoke of this calamity. Yet had she known of it she must have remembered it. To bring all your fortune—a considerable fortune—home in a bag tied round your neck, and to lose it in a shipwreck is a disaster which would, one thinks, be remembered to the third and fourth generations.'

'I should think so. But you said something about the sea giving up its treasure.'

'That we come to next. Five years ago, by the death of a very aged lady, her great-great-grandmother, Armorel Rosevean succeeded to an inheritance which turned out to be nothing less than the accumulated savings of many generations. Among other possessions she found in this old lady's room a sea-chest containing things apparently recovered from wrecks, or drowned men, or washed ashore by the sea—a very curious and interesting collection: there were snuff-boxes, watches, chains, rings, all kinds of things. Among these treasures she turned out, at the bottom of the chest, a case of shagreen with a leather thong. On opening this Armorel found it to contain a quantity of precious stones, and a scrap of paper which seemed to show that they had formerly been the property of one Robert Fletcher. We may suppose, if we please, that the case containing the jewels was cast up on the beach after the storm, and tossed into the chest without much knowledge of its contents or their value. We may suppose that Emanuel Rosevean found the case. We may suppose what we please, because we can prove nothing. For my own part, I think there is no reasonable doubt that the case actually contained the fortune of Robert Fletcher. The dates of the story seem to correspond: the handwriting appears to be his: we have letters of his speaking of his intention to return, and of his property being in convenient portable shape.'

'Well—then—this portable fortune belongs to Robert Fletcher's heirs.'

'Not so quick. How are you going to prove your claim? You have nothing to go by but a fragment of writing with part of his name on it. You cannot prove that he was shipwrecked, and if you could do that you could not prove that these jewels belonged to him.'

'If there is no doubt, she ought to give them up. She is bound in honour.'

'I said that in my mind there is no reasonable doubt. That is because I have heard a great deal more than could be admitted in evidence. But now—listen again without interrupting. When, five years ago, the young lady placed the management of her affairs in my hands through the Vicar of her parish, I had every part of her very miscellaneous fortune valued and a part of it sold. I had these rubies examined by a merchant in jewels.'

'And how much were they worth?'

'One with another—some being large and very valuable indeed, and others small—they were said, by my expert, to be worth thirty-five thousand pounds. They might, under favourable circumstances and if judiciously placed in the market realise much more. Thirty-five thousand pounds!'

'What?' He literally opened his mouth. 'How much do you say?'

'Thirty-five thousand pounds.'

'Oh! But the stones are not hers—they belong—they belong—to us—to the descendants of Robert Fletcher.' No one would have called that face wooden, now. It was full of excitement—the excitement of a newly awakened hope. 'Does she propose to buy me off with a thousand pounds? Does she think I am to be bought off at any price? The jewels are mine—mine—that is, I have a share in them.'

'Gently—gently—gently! What proof have you got of this story? Nothing. You never heard of it: your great-grandfather never spoke of it. Nothing would have been heard of it at all but for this old lady from whom Armorel inherited. The property is hers as much as anything else. If she gives up anything it is by her own free and uncompelled will. She need give nothing. Remember that.'

'Then she offers me a miserable thousand pounds for my share—which ought to be at least a third. Jagenal'—he turned purple and the veins stood out on his forehead—'That infernal girl hates me! She has done me—I cannot tell you how much mischief. She persecutes me. Now she offers to buy me out of my share of thirty-five thousand pounds—a third share—nay—a half, because my great-aunt left no children—for a thousand pounds down!'

'I did not say so.'

'You told me that the windfall would amount to a thousand pounds.'

'That was in joke, my boy. You are perfectly wrong about Armorel hating you. How can she hate you? You are so far wrong in this instance that she has instructed me to give you the whole of this fortune—actually to make you a free gift of the whole property—the whole, mind—thirty-five thousand pounds!'

'To me! Armorel gives me—me—the whole of this fortune?' Blank astonishment fell upon him. He stood staring—open-mouthed. 'To ME?' he repeated.

'To you. She does not, to be sure, know to whom she gives it. She is only desirous of restoring the jewels which she insists in believing to belong to Robert Fletcher's family. Therefore, as it would be obviously impossible to find out and to divide this fortune among all the descendants of Robert Fletcher, who are scattered about the globe, she was resolved to give them to the eldest descendant of the second daughter.'

'Oh!' Alec turned pale, and dropped into a chair, broken up. 'To the eldest descendant of the second—the second daughter. Then——'

'Then to you, as the only grandson of the second daughter—Frances.'

'The second daughter was——' He checked himself. He sighed. He sat up. His eyes, always small and too close together, grew smaller and closer together. 'The other branch of the family,' he said slowly, 'has vanished—as you say—it is scattered over the face of the globe. I do not know anything about my cousins—if I have any cousins. Perhaps when you have carried on the search a little further——'

'But I am not going to carry it on any further at all. Why should I? We have nothing more to learn. I am instructed by Armorel to give the rubies to you. It is a gift—not a right. It is not an inheritance, remember—it is a free gift. She says, "These rubies used to belong to Robert Fletcher. I will restore them to someone of his kin." You are that someone. Why should I inquire further?'

'Oh!' Alec sank back in his chair and closed his eyes as one who recovers from a sharp pang, and sighed deeply. 'If you are satisfied, then—— But if other cousins should turn up——'

'They will have nothing, because nobody is entitled to anything. Come Alec, my boy, you look a little overcome. It is natural. Pull yourself together, and look at the facts. You will have thirty-five thousand pounds—perhaps a little more. At four per cent.—I think I can put you in the way of getting so much with safety—you will have fourteen hundred a year. You will have that, apart from your literary and artistic income. It is not a gigantic fortune, it is true; but let me tell you that it is a very handsome addition indeed to any man's income. You will not be able to live in Kensington Palace Gardens, where your wife lived as a girl; but you can take a good house and see your friends, and have anything in reason. Well, that is all I have to say, except to congratulate you, which I do, my Alec'—he seized the fortunate young man's hand and shook it warmly—'most heartily. I do, indeed. You deserve your good luck—every bit of the good luck that has befallen you. Everybody who knows you will rejoice. And it comes just at the right moment—just when you have acknowledged your marriage and taken your wife home.'

'Really,' said Alec, now completely recovered, 'I am overwhelmed with this stroke of luck. It is the most unexpected thing in the world. I could never have dreamed of such a thing. To find out, on the same day, that one's great-grandfather once made a fortune and lost it, and that it has been recovered, and that it is all given to me—it naturally takes one's breath away at first.'

'You would like to gaze upon this fortune from the Ruby Mines of Burmah, would you not?' Mr. Jagenal threw open the door of a safe, and took out a parcel in brown paper. 'It is here.' He opened the parcel, and disclosed the shagreen case which we have already seen in the sea-chest. He laid it on the table, and unrolled the silk in which the stones were rolled. 'There they are—look common enough, don't they? One seems to have picked up stones twice as pretty on the sea-shore: here are two or three cut and polished—bits of red glass would look as pretty.'

'Thirty-five thousand pounds!' Alec cried, laying a hand, as if in episcopal benediction, upon the treasure. 'Is it possible that this little bundle of stones should be worth so much?'

'Quite possible. Now—they are yours—what will you do with them?'

'First, I will ask you to put them back in the safe.'

'I will send them to your bank if you please.'

'No—keep them here—I will consult you immediately about their disposition. Thirty-five thousand pounds! Thirty-five—— perhaps we may get more for them. What am I to say to this girl? Perhaps when she learns who has got the rubies she will refuse to let them go. I am sure she would never consent.'

'Nonsense—about persecution and annoyance! Armorel hate you? Why should she hate you? The sweetest girl in the world. You men of genius are too ready to take offence. The things are yours. I have given them to you by her instructions. I have written you a letter, formally conveying the jewels to you. Here it is. And now go home, my dear fellow, and when you feel like taking a holiday, do it with a tranquil mind, remembering that you've got fourteen hundred pounds a year given you for nothing at all by this young lady, who wasn't obliged to give you a penny. Why, in surrendering these jewels, she has surrendered a good half of her whole fortune. Find me another girl, anywhere, who would give up half her fortune for a scruple. And now go away, and tell your wife. Let her rejoice. Tell her it is Armorel's wedding present.'

Alec Feilding walked home. He was worth thirty-five thousand pounds—fourteen hundred pounds a year. When one comes to think of it, though we call ourselves such a very wealthy country, there are comparatively few, indeed, among us who can boast that they enjoy an income of fourteen hundred pounds a year, with no duties, responsibilities, or cares about their income—and with nothing to do for it. Fourteen hundred pounds a year is not great wealth; but it will enable a man to keep up a very respectable style of living: many people in society have got to live on a great deal less. He and his wife were going to live on nothing a year, except what they could get by their wits. Fourteen hundred a year! They could still exercise their wits: that is to say, he should expect his wife, now the thinking partner, to exercise her wits with zeal. But what a happiness for a man to feel that he does not live by his wits alone! Alas! It is a joy that is given to few indeed of us.

As for his late literary and artistic successes, how poor and paltry did they appear to this man, who had no touch of the artist nature, beside this solid lump of money, worth all the artistic or poetic fame that ever was achieved !

He went home dancing. He was at peace with all mankind. He found it in his heart to forgive everybody: Roland Lee, who had so basely deserted him: Effie, that snake in the grass: Lady Frances, the most treacherous of women: Armorel herself—— Oh! Heavens! what could not be forgiven to the girl who had made him such a gift? Even the revolt against his authority: even the broken panel, the shattered lock, and the earthquake.

In this mood he arrived home. His wife, the thinking partner, was hard at work in the interests of the new firm. In her hand was a manuscript volume of verse: on the table beside her lay an open portfolio of sketches and drawings.

'You see, Alec,' she looked up, smiling. 'Already the ghosts have begun to appear at my call. If you ask me where I found them, I reply, as before, that when one travels about with a country company one has opportunities. All kinds of queer people may be heard of. Your ghosts, in future, my dear boy, must be of the tribe which has broken down and given in, not of those who are still young and hopeful. I have found a man who can draw—here is a portfolio full of his things: in black and white: they can be reproduced by some photographic process: he is in an advanced stage of misery, and will never know or ask what becomes of his things. He ought to have made his fortune long ago. He hasn't, because he is always drunk and disreputable. It will do you good to illustrate the paper with your own drawings. There's a painter I have heard of. He drinks every afternoon and all the evening at a certain place, where you must go and find him. He has long since been turned out of every civilised kind of society, and you can get his pictures for anything you like; he can't draw much, I believe, but his colouring is wonderful. There is an elderly lady, too, of whom I have heard. She can draw, too, and she's got no friends, and can be got cheap. And this book is full of the verses of a poor wretch who was once a rising literary man, and now carries a banner at Drury-Lane Theatre whenever they want a super. As for your stories, I have got a broken-down actor—he writes better than he can act—to write stories of the boards. They will appear anonymously, and if people attribute them to you he will not be able to complain. Oh, I know what I am about, Alec! Your paper shall double its circulation in a month, and shall multiply its circulation by ten in six months, and without the least fear of such complications as have happened lately. They must be avoided for the future—proposals as well as earthquakes—my dear Alec.'

Alec sat down on the table and laughed carelessly. 'Zoe,' he said, 'you are the cleverest woman in the world. It was a lucky day for us both when you came here. I made a big mistake for three years. Now I've got some news for you—good news——'

'That can only mean—money.'

'It does mean—money, as you say. Money, my dear. Money that makes the mare to go.'

'How much, Alec?'

'More than your four thousand. Twenty times as much as that little balance in your book.'

'Oh, Alec! is it possible? Twenty times as much? Eighty thousand pounds?'

'About that sum,' he replied, exaggerating with the instincts of the City, inherited, no doubt, from Robert Fletcher. 'Perhaps quite that sum if I manage certain sales cleverly.'

'Is it a legacy?—or an inheritance?—how did you get it?'

'It is not exactly a legacy: it is a kind of restoration to an unknown person: a gift not made to me personally, but to me unknown.'

'You talk to me in riddles, Alec.'

'I would talk in blank verse if I could. It is, indeed, literally true. I have received an—estate—in portable property worth nearly forty thousand pounds.'

'Oh! Then we shall be really rich, and not have to pretend quite so much? A little pretence, Alec, I like. It makes me feel like returning to society: too much pretence reminds one of the policeman.'

'Don't you want to know how I have come into this money?'

'I am not curious, Alec. I like everything to be done for me. When I was a girl there were carriages and horses and everything that I wanted—all ready—all done for me, you know. Then I was stripped of all. I had nothing to do or to say in the matter. It was done for me. Now, you tell me you have got eighty thousand pounds. Oh! Heavens! It is done for me. The ways of fate are so wonderful. Things are given and things are taken away. Why should I inquire how things come? Perhaps this will be taken away in its turn.'

'Not quite, Zoe. I have got my hand over it. You can trust your husband, I think, to keep what he has got.' Indeed, he looked at this moment cunning enough to be trusted with keeping the National Debt itself.

'Eighty thousand pounds!' she said. 'Let me write it down. Eighty thousand pounds! Eight and one, two, three, four oughts.' She wrote them down, and clasped her hands, saying, 'Oh! the beauty—the incomparable beauty—of the last ought!'

'Perhaps not quite so much,' said her husband, thinking that the exaggeration was a little too much.

'Don't take off one of my oughts—not my fourth: not my Napoleon of oughts!'

'No—no. Keep your four oughts. Well, my dear, if it is

only sixty thousand or so, there is two thousand a year for us. Two thousand a year!'

'Don't, Alec; don't! Not all at once. Break it gently.'

'We will carry on the paper; and perhaps do something or other—carefully, you know—in Art. There is no need to knock things off. And if you can make the paper succeed, as you think, there will be so much the more. Well, we can use it all. For my part, Zoe, my dear, I don't care how big the income is. I am equal to ten thousand.'

'Of course, and you will still pronounce judgments and be a leader. Now let us talk of what we will do—where we will live—and all. Two thousand is pretty big to begin with, after three years' tight fit; but the paper will bring in another two thousand easily. I've been looking through the accounts—bills and returns—and I am sure it has been villanously managed. We will run it up: we will have ten thousand a year to spend. A vast deal may be done with ten thousand a year: we will have a big weekly dinner as well as an At Home. We will draw all the best people in London to the house: we will——'

She enlarged with great freedom on what could be done with this income: she displayed all the powers of a rich imagination: not even the milkmaid of the fable more largely anticipated the joys of the future.

'And, oh! Alec,' she cried. 'To be rich again! rich only to the limited extent of ten thousand a year, is too great happiness. When my father was ruined, I thought the world was ended. Well, it was ended for me, because you made me leave it and disappear. The last four years I should like to be clean forgotten and driven out of my mind—horrid years of failing and enduring and waiting! And now we are rich again! Oh! we are rich again! It is too much happiness!'

The tears rose to her eyes; her soft and murmuring voice broke.

'My poor Zoe,' her husband laid his hand on hers, 'I am rejoiced,' he said, 'as much for your sake as for my own.'

'How did you get this wonderful fortune, Alec?'

'Through Mr. Jagenal, the lawyer. It's a long story. A great-grandfather of mine was wrecked, and lost his property. That was eighty years ago. Now, his property was found. Who do you think found it? Armorel Rosevean. And she has restored it—to me.'

'What?' She sprang to her feet, her face suddenly turning white. 'What? Armorel?'

'Yes, certainly. Curious coincidence, isn't it? The very girl who has done me so much mischief. The man was wrecked on the island where her people lived.'

'Yes—yes—yes. The property—what was it? What was it! Quick!'

'It was a leather case filled with rubies—rubies worth at least thirty-five thousand pounds—— What's the matter?'

'Rubies! Her rubies! Oh! Armorel's rubies! No—no—no—not that! Anything—anything but that! Armorel's rubies-Armorel's rubies!'

'What is the matter, Zoe? What is it?'

She gasped. Her eyes were wild: her cheek was white. She was like one who is seized with some sudden horrible and unintelligible pain. Or she was like one who has suddenly heard the most dreadful and most terrible news possible.

'What is it, Zoe?' her husband asked again.

'You? Oh! you have brought me this news—you! I thought, perhaps, someone—Armorel—or some other might find me out. But you!—you!'

'Again, Zoe'—he tried to be calm, but a dreadful doubt seized him—'what does this mean?'

'I remember,' she laughed wildly, 'what I said when I gave you the bank-book. If you found me out, I said, we should be both on the same level. You would be able to hold out your arms, I said, and to cry, "You have come down to my level. Come to my heart, sister in wickedness." That is what I said. Oh! I little thought—it was a prophecy—my words have come true.'

She caught her head with her hand—it is a stagey gesture: she had learned it on the stage: yet at this moment of trouble it was simple and natural.

'What the Devil do you mean?' he cried with exasperation.

'They were *your* rubies all the time, and I did not know. Your rubies! If I had only known! Oh! what have I done? What have I done?

'Tell me quick, what you have done.' He caught her by the arm roughly. He actually shook her. His own face now was almost as white as hers. 'Quick—tell me—tell me—tell me!'

'You wanted money badly,' she gasped. Her words came with difficulty. 'You told me so every time I saw you. It was to get money that I went to live with Armorel. I could not get it in that way. But I found another way. She told me about the rubies. I knew where they were kept. In the bank. In a sealed packet. I had seen an inventory of the things in the bank. Armorel told me the story of the rubies, and I never believed it—I never thought that there would be any search for the man's heirs. I never thought the story was true. She told me, besides, all about her other things—her miniatures and snuff-boxes, and watches and rings. She showed me all her beautiful lace, worth thousands. And as for the gold things and the jewels, they were all in the bank, in separate sealed parcels, numbered. She showed me the bank receipts. Opposite each number was written the contents of each, and opposite Number Three was written "The case containing the rubies."'

'Well? Well?'

'Hush! What did I do? Let me think. I am going mad, I believe. It was for your sake—all for your sake, Alec! All for your sake that I have ruined you!'

'Ruined me? Quick! What have you done?'

'It was for your sake, Alec—all for your sake! Oh, for your own sake I have lost and ruined you!'

'You will drive me mad, I think!' he gasped.

'I wrote a letter, one day, to the manager of the bank. I wrote it in imitation of Armorel's hand. I signed her name at the end so that no one could have told it was a forgery. My letter told him to give the sealed packet numbered three to the bearer who was waiting. I sent the letter by a commissionaire. He returned bringing the packet with him.'

'And then?'

'Oh! Then—then—Alec, you will kill me—you will surely kill me when you know! You care for nothing in the world but for money—and I—I have stolen away your money! It is gone—it is gone!'

'You stole those rubies? But I have seen them. They are in Jagenal's safe. What do you mean?' he cried hoarsely.

'I have sold them. I stole them, and I sold them all—they were worth—how much did you say? Fifty—sixty—eighty thousand pounds? I sold them all, Alec, for four thousand two hundred and twenty-five pounds! I sold them to a Dutchman in Hatton Garden.'

'You are raving mad! You dream! I have seen them. I have handled them.'

'What you have seen were the worthless imitation jewels that I substituted. I found out where to get sham rubies made of paste, or something—some cut and some uncut. I bought them, and I substituted them in the case. Then I returned the packet to the bank. I had the packet in my possession no more than one morning. The man who bought the stones swore they were worth no more. He said he should lose money by them: he was going away to America immediately, and wanted to settle at once, otherwise he would not give so much. That is what I have done, Alec.'

'Oh!' he stood over her, his eyes glaring; he roared like a wild beast; he raised his hand as if to slay her with a single blow. But he could find no words. His hand remained raised—he was speechless—he was motionless—he was helpless with blind rage and madness.

His wife looked up, and waited. Now that she had told her tale she was calm.

'If you are going to kill me,' she said, 'you had better do it at once. I think I do not care about living any longer. Kill me, if you like.'

He dropped his arm: he straightened himself, and stood upright.

'You are a Thief!' he said hoarsely. 'You are a wretched, miserable THIEF!'

She pointed to the picture on the easel.

'And you—my husband?'

He threw himself into a chair. Then he got up and paced the room: he beat the air with his hands: his face was distorted: his eyes were wild: he abandoned himself to one of those magnificent rages of which we read in History. William the Conqueror—King Richard—King John—many mediæval kings used to fall into these rages. They are less common of late. But then such provocation as this is rare in any age.

When, at last, speech came to him, it was at first stuttering and broken: speech of the elementary kind: speech of primitive man in a rage: speech ejaculatory: speech interjectional: speech of railing and cursing. He walked—or, rather, tramped—about the room: he stamped with his foot: he banged the table with his fist: he roared: he threatened: he cleared the dictionary of its words of scorn, contempt, and loathing: he hurled all these words at his wife. As a tigress bereft of her young, so is such a man bereft of his money.

His wife, meantime, sat watching, silent. She waited for the storm to pass. As for what he said, it was no more than the rolling of thunder. She made no answer to his reproaches; but for her white face you would have thought she neither heard nor felt nor cared.

Outside the discreet man-servant heard every word. Once, when his master threatened violence, he thought it might be his duty to interfere. As the storm continued, he began to feel that this was no place for a man-servant who respected himself. He remembered the earthquake. He had then been called upon to remove from its hinges a door fractured in a row. That was a blow. He was now compelled to listen while a master, unworthy of such a servant, brutally swore at his wife. He perceived that his personal character and his dignity no longer allowed him to remain with such a person. He resigned, therefore, that very day.

When the bereaved sufferer could say no more—for there comes a time when even to shriek fails to bring relief—he threw himself into a chair and began to cry. Yes: he cried like a child: he wept and sobbed and lamented. The tears ran down his cheeks: his voice was choked with sobs. The discreet man-servant outside blushed with shame that such a thing should happen under his roof. The wife looked on without a sign or a word. We break down and cry when we have lost the thing which most we love—

it may be a wife; it may be a child: in the case of this young man the thing which most he loved and desired was money. It had been granted to him—in large and generous measure. And, lo! it was torn from his hands before his fingers had even closed around it. Oh! the pity—the pity of it!

This fit, too, passed away.

Half an hour later, when he was quite quiet, exhausted with his rage, his wife laid her hand upon his shoulder.

'Alec,' she said, 'I have always longed for one thing most of all. It was the only thing, I once thought, that made it worth the trouble to live. An hour ago it seemed that the thing had been granted to me. And I was happy even with this guilt upon my soul. I know you for what you are. Yet I desired your love. Henceforth, this dreadful thing stands between us. You can no longer love me—that is certain, because I have ruined you—any more than I can hold you in respect. Yet we will continue to walk together—hand in hand—I will work and you shall enjoy. If we do not love each other, we can continue in partnership, and show to the world faces full of affection. At least you cannot reproach me. I am a thief, it is true—most true! And you—Alec! you—oh! my husband!—what are you?'

CHAPTER XXV

TO FORGET IT ALL

When Philippa read the announcement in the *Times*, she held her breath for a space. It was at breakfast. Her father was reading the news; she was looking through that column which interests us all more than any other. Her eye fell upon her cousin's name. She read, she changed colour, she read again. Her self-control returned. She laid down the paper. 'Here,' she said, 'is a very astonishing announcement!' A very astonishing announcement indeed!

An hour later she called upon Armorel at her rooms.

'You are left quite alone in consequence of this—this amazing revelation?'

'Quite. Not that I mind being alone. And Effie Wilmot is coming.'

'Nothing in the world,' said Philippa, 'could have astonished me more. It is not so much the fact of the marriage—indeed, my cousin's name was mentioned at one time a good deal in connection with hers—but the dreadful duplicity. He sent her to you—she came to us—as a widow. And for three years they have been married! Is it possible?'

'Indeed,' said Armorel, 'I know nothing. She left me without a cause, and now I hear of her marriage. That is all.'

'My dear, the thing reflects upon us. It is my cousin who has brought this trouble upon you.'

'Oh! no, Philippa! As if you could be held responsible for his actions! And, indeed, you must not speak of trouble. I have had none. My companion was never my friend in any sense: we had nothing in common: we must have parted company very soon: she irritated me in many ways, especially in her blind praise of the man who now turns out to be her husband. I really feel much happier now that she has gone.'

'But you have no companion—no chaperon.'

'I don't want any chaperon, I assure you.'

'But you cannot go into society alone.'

'I never do go into society. You know that nobody ever called upon Mrs. Elstree—or Mrs. Feilding, as we must now call her. There are only two houses in the whole of this great London into which I have found an entrance—yours and Mr. Jagenal's.'

'Yes; I know now. And most disgraceful it is that you should have been so sacrificed. That also is my cousin's doing. He represented his wife—it seems difficult to believe that he has got a wife—as a person belonging to a wide and very desirable circle of friends. Not a soul called upon her! The world cannot continue to know a woman who has disappeared bodily for three long years, during which she was reported to have been seen on the stage of a country theatre. What has she been doing? Why has she been in hiding? It was culpable negligence in Mr. Jagenal not to make inquiries. What it must be called in my cousin others may determine. As for you, Armorel, you have been most disgracefully and shamefully treated.'

'I suppose I ought to have had a companion who was recognised by society. But it seems to matter very little. I have made one or two new friends, and I have found an old friend.'

'It is not too late, of course, even for this season. Now, my dear Armorel, I am charged with a mission. It is to bring you back with me—to get you to stay with us for the season and, at least, until the summer holidays. That is, if you would be satisfied with our friends.'

'Thank you, Philippa, a thousand times. I do not think I can accept your kindness, however, because I feel as if I must go away somewhere. I have had a great deal of anxiety and worry. It has been wretched to feel—as I have been made to feel—that I was in the midst of intrigues and designs, the nature of which I hardly understood. I must go away out of the atmosphere. I will return to London when I have forgotten this time. I cannot tell you all that has been going on, except that I have discovered one deception after another——'

'She is an abominable woman,' said Philippa.

'On the island of Samson, at least, there will be no wives who call themselves widows, and no men who call themselves'—painters and poets, she was going to say, but she checked herself—'call themselves,' she substituted, 'single men, when they are already married.'

'But, surely you will not go away now—just at the very beginning of the season?'

'The season is nothing at all to me.'

'Oh! But, Armorel—think. You ought to belong to society. You are wealthy: you are a most beautiful girl: you are quite young: and you have so many gifts and accomplishments. My dear cousin, you might do so well, so very well. There is no position to which you could not aspire.'

Armorel laughed. 'Not in that way,' she said. 'I have already told you, dear Philippa, that I am not able to think of things in that way.

'Always that dream of girlhood, dear? Well, then, come and show yourself, if only to make the men go mad with love and the women with envy. Stay with us. Or, if you prefer it, I will find you a companion who really does belong to the world.'

'No, no; for the present I have had enough of companions. I want nothing more than to go home and rest. I feel just a little battered. My first experience of London has not been, you see, quite what I expected. Let me go away, and come back when I feel more charitable towards my fellow-creatures.'

'You have had a most horrid experience,' said Philippa. 'I trembled for you when I learned who your companion was. I was at school with her, and—well, I do not love her. But what could I do? Mr. Jagenal said she had been most strongly recommended—I could not interfere: it was too late: and besides, after what had happened, years before, it would have looked vindictive. And then she has been rich and is now poor, and perhaps, I thought, she wanted money: and when one has quarrelled it is best to say nothing against your enemy. Besides, I knew nothing definite against her. She said she was a widow—my cousin Alec said that he had been an old friend of her husband: he spoke of having helped him. Oh! he made up quite a long and touching story about his dead friend. So, you see, I refrained, and if I could say nothing good, I would say nothing bad.'

'I am sure that no one can possibly blame you in the matter, Philippa.'

'Yet I blame myself. For if I had caused a few questions to be asked at first, all the lies about the widowhood might have been avoided.'

'Others would have been invented.'

'Perhaps. Well—she is married, and I don't suppose her stay here will have done you any real harm. As for her, to go masquerading as a widow and to tell a thousand lies daily can hardly do any woman much good. Have you made up your mind how you will treat her if you should meet?'

'She has settled that question. She wrote me a letter saying that she has behaved so badly that she wishes never to see me again. And if we should meet she begs that it will be as perfect strangers.'

'Really—after all that has been done—that is the very least——'

'So we are to meet as strangers. I suppose that will be best. It would be impossible to ask for explanations. Poor Zoe! One does not know all her history. She told me once that she had been very unhappy. I have heard her crying in her room at night. Perhaps, she is to be more pitied than blamed. It is her husband whom I find it difficult to forgive and to forget. He is like a nightmare: he cannot be put so easily out of my mind.'

'Unfortunately, no. I, who have thought of him all my life, must continue to think of him.'

'You will forgive him, Philippa. You must. Besides, you have less to forgive. He has never offered his hand and heart to you.'

Philippa blushed a rosy red, and confusion gathered to her eyes, because there had, in fact, been many occasions when things were said which—— Armorel was sorry that she had said this.

'You mean, Armorel, that he actually—did this—to you?'

'Yes. It was only the other day—the morning after we read the play. He came to the National Gallery, where I often go in the morning, and, in one of the rooms, he told me how much he loved me—words, however, go for nothing in such things—and kindly said that marriage with me would complete his happiness.'

'Oh! He is a villain—a villain indeed!' Her voice rose and her cheeks flushed. 'Forgive him, Armorel? Never!'

'Considering that it was only a day or two before he was going to announce in the paper the fact that he had been married for three years, it does seem pretty bad, doesn't it?'

'And you, Armorel?'

'Fortunately, I was able to dismiss him unmistakably.'

'Oh!' Philippa cried in exasperation. 'My cousin has been guilty of many treacherous and base actions; but this is quite the worst thing that I have heard of him—worse even than sending you his own wife, under a false name and disguised with a lying story on her lips. No, Armorel; I will never forgive him. Never!' Her eyes gleamed and her lips trembled. She meant what she said. 'Never! It is the worst, the most wicked thing he has ever done—because he might have succeeded.'

'I suppose he meant to get something by the pretence.'

'He wanted, I suppose, to have it reported that he was going to marry a rich girl. I had heard that he was continually seen with you. And I had also heard that he had confessed to an engagement which was not to be announced. My father has found out that his affairs are in great confusion.'

'But what good would an engagement of twenty-four hours do for him?'

'Indeed, I do not understand. Perhaps, after all, he had allowed himself to fall in love—but I do not know. Men sometimes seem to behave like mad creatures, with no reason or rule of self-control—as if there was no such thing as consequence and no such thing as the morrow. I do not understand anything about him. Why are his affairs in confusion? He had, to begin with, a fortune of more than twelve thousand pounds from his mother; his pictures latterly commanded a good price. And his paper is supposed to be doing well. To be sure he keeps horses and goes a great deal into society. And, perhaps, his wife has been a source of expense to him. But it is no use trying to explain or to find out things. Meantime, to you, his conduct has been simply outrageous. A man who sends his own wife as companion to a girl, and then makes love to her, is—my dear, there is no other word—he is a Wretch. I will never forgive him.' Armorel felt that she would keep her word. This pale, calm, self-contained Philippa could be moved to anger. And again she heard her companion's soft voice murmuring, 'My dear, the woman shows that she loves him still.'

'Fortunately for me,' said Armorel, 'my heart has remained untouched. I was never attracted by him; and latterly, when I had learned certain things, it became impossible for me to regard him with common kindliness. And, besides, his pretence and affectation of love were too transparent to deceive anybody. He was like the worst actor you ever saw on any stage—wooden, unreal—incapable of impressing anyone with the idea that he meant what he said.'

'I wonder how far Zoe—his wife—knew of this?'

'I would rather not consider the question, Philippa. But, indeed, one cannot help, just at first, thinking about it, and I am compelled to believe that she was his servant and his agent throughout. I believe she was instigated to get money from me if she could, and I believe she knew his intentions as regards me, and that she consented. She must have known, and she must have consented.'

'She would excuse herself on the ground of being his wife. For their husbands some women will do anything. Perhaps she worships him. His genius, very likely, overshadows and awes her.' Armorel smiled, but made no objection to this conjecture. 'Some women worship the genius in a man as if it was the man himself. Some women worship the man quite apart from his genius. I used to worship Alec long before he was discovered to be a genius at all. When I was a school-girl, Alec was my knight—my Galahad—purest-hearted and bravest of all the knights. There was no one in the world—no living man, and very few dead men—Bayard, Sidney, Charles the First, and two or three more only—who could stand beside him. He was so handsome, so brave, so great, and so good, that other men seemed small beside him. Well, my hero passed through Cambridge without the least distinction: I thought it was because he was too proud to show other men how easily he could beat them. Then he was called to the Bar, but he did not immediately show his eloquence and his abilities: that was because he wanted an opportunity. And then I went out into the world, and made the discovery that my hero was in reality quite an ordinary young man—rather big and good-looking, perhaps—with, as we all thought then, no very great abilities. And he certainly was always—and he is still—heavy in conversation. But he was still my cousin, though he ceased to be my hero. He was more than a cousin—he was almost my brother; and brothers, as you do not know, perhaps, Armorel, sometimes do things which require vast quantities of patience and forgiveness. I am sure no girl's brother ever wanted forgiveness more than my cousin Alec.'

Her face, cold and pale, had, in fact, the sisterly expression. Philippa's enemies always declared that in the composition and making of her the goddess Venus, who presumably takes a large personal interest in the feminine department, had no lot or part at all. Yet certain words—the late companion's words—kept ringing in Armorel's ears: 'My dear, the woman loves him still. She has never ceased to love him.'

'There was nothing to forgive at first,' she went on: 'on the contrary, everything to admire. Yet his career has been throughout so unexpected as to puzzle and bewilder us. Consider, Armorel. Here was a young man who had never in boyhood, or later, shown the least love or leaning towards Art or the least tinge of poetical feeling, or the smallest power as a *raconteur*, or any charm of writing—suddenly becoming a fine painter—a really fine painter—a respectable poet, and an admirable story-teller. When he began with the first picture there grew up in my head a very imaginative and certain set of ideas connecting the painter's mind with his Art. I saw a grave mind dwelling gravely and earnestly on the interpretation of nature. It seemed impossible that one who should so paint sea and shore should be otherwise than grave and serious.'

'Impossible,' said Armorel.

'What we had called, in our stupidity, dulness, now became only seriousness. He took his Art seriously. But then he began to write verses, and then I found that there was a new mind—not a part of the old mind, but a new mind altogether. It was a mind with a light vein of fancy and merriment: it was affectionate, sympathetic, and happy: and it seemed distinctly a feminine mind. I cannot tell you how difficult it was to fit that mind to my cousin Alec—it was like dressing him up in an ill-fitting woman's riding-habit. And then he began those stories of his—and, behold, another mind altogether!—this time a worldly mind—cynical, sarcastic, distrustful, epigrammatic, and heartless—not at all a pleasant mind. So that you see I had four different minds all going about in the same set of bones—the original Alec Feilding, handsome and commonplace, but a man of honour: the serious student of Art: the light and gay-hearted poet, sparkling in his verses like a glass of champagne: and the cynical man of the world, who does not believe that there are any men of honour or any good women. Why, how can one man be at the same time four men? It is impossible. And now we have a fifth development of Alec. He has become—at the same time—a creature who marries a wife secretly—no one knows why: and hides her away for three years and then suddenly produces her—no one knows why. What does he hide her away for? Why does she consent to be hidden away? Then, the very day before he has got to produce his wife for all the world to see—I am perfectly certain that she herself forced him to take that step—he makes love to a young lady, and formally asks her to marry him. Reconcile, if you can, all these contradictions.'

'They cannot possibly be reconciled.'

'We have heard of seven devils entering into one man; but never of angels and devils mixed, my dear. Such a man cannot be explained, any more than the Lady Melusina herself.'

'Do not let us try. As for me, I am going to forget the existence of Mr. Alec Feilding if I can. In order to do this the quicker I mean to go home and stay there. Come and see me on the island of Samson, Philippa. But you must not bring your father, or he may be disappointed at the loss of his ancestral hall. To you I shall not mind showing the little house where your ancestors lived.'

'I should like very much—above all things—to see the place.'

'I will bribe you to come. I have got a great silver punch-bowl—old silver, such as you love—for you. You shall have a choice of rings, a choice of snuff-boxes. There is a roll of lace put away in the cupboard that would make you a lovely dress. It will be like the receiving of presents which we read of in the old books.'

'I will try to come, Armorel, after the season.'

Armorel laughed.

'There is the difference between us, Philippa. You belong to the world, and I do not. Oh! I will come back again some day and look at it again. But it will always be a strange land to me. You will leave London after the season; I am leaving it before the season. Come, however, when you can. Scilly is never too hot in summer nor too cold in winter. Instead of a carriage you shall have a boat, and instead of a coachman you shall have my boy Peter. We will sail about and visit the Islands: we will carry our midday dinner with us: and in the evening we will play and sing. Nobody will call upon you there: there are no dinner-parties, and you need not bring an evening dress. The only audience to our music will be my old servants, Justinian and Dorcas his wife, and Chessun, and Peter the boy.'

There were no preparations to make: there was nothing to prevent Armorel from going away immediately. She asked Effie to go with her. She opened the subject in the evening, when she and her brother and Roland were all sitting together in her drawing-room by the light of the fire alone, which she loved. They were thoughtful and rather silent, conscious of recent events.

'While we were in Regent Street this afternoon, Effie,' said Armorel, 'I was thinking of the many happy faces that we met. The street seemed filled with happiness. I was wondering if it was all real. Are they all as happy as they seem? Is there no falsehood in their lives? The streets are filled with happy people. The theatres are filled with happy faces: society shows none but happy faces. It ought to be the happiest of worlds. Have we, alone, fallen among pretenders and intriguers?'

'They are gone from you, Armorel. Can you not forget them?' Effie murmured.

'I seem to hear the murmuring voice of my companion always. She whispers in her caressing voice, "Oh! my dear, he is so good and great! He is so full of truth and honour. Will you lend him a thousand pounds? He thinks so highly of you. A thousand pounds—two thousand pounds. If I had it to lay at the feet of so much genius!" And all the time she is his wife. And in my thoughts I am always hearing his voice, which I learned to hate, laying down a commonplace. And in my dreams I awake with a start, because he is making love to me while Zoe listens at the door.'

'You must go away somewhere,' said Roland.

'I shall go home—to my own place. Effie, will you come with me?'

'Go with you? Oh! To Scilly?'

'To the land of Lyonesse. I have arranged it all, dear. Archie shall have these rooms of mine to live in: you shall come with me. It is two years since you have been out of London: your cheeks are pale: you want our sea-breezes and our upland downs. Will you come with me, Effie?'

She held out her hand. 'I will go with you,' said the girl, 'round the whole world, if you order me.'

'Then that is settled. Archie, you must stay because your future demands it. I met Mr. Stephenson yesterday. He told me that he is in great hopes about the play, and that, meantime, he will be able to put some work into your hands.'

'You are always thinking about me,' said Archie.

'Come to us in the summer. Take your holiday on Samson. Oh! Effie, we will be perfectly happy. We will forget London, and everything that has happened. Thank Heaven, the rubies are gone! I will send a piano there: we will carry with us loads of books and music. We will have a perfectly lovely time, with no one but ourselves. Roland will tell you how we will live. You will do nothing for a time, while you are drinking in the fresh air and getting strong. Then—then—you shall have ideas—great and glorious ideas—and you shall write far, far better poetry than any you have attempted yet.'

'And, meantime—we who have to remain behind?' asked Roland. 'What shall we do when you are gone?'

It takes longer to get to Penzance than to Edinburgh, because the train ceases to run and begins to crawl as soon as it leaves Plymouth. The best way is to take the nine o'clock train and to travel all night. Then you will probably sleep from Reading to Bristol: from Bristol to Exeter: and from Exeter to Plymouth. After that you will keep awake.

In this way and by this train Armorel and Effie travelled to Penzance. Effie fell asleep very soon, and remained asleep all night long, waking up somewhere between Lostwithiel and Marazion. Armorel sat up wakeful the whole night through, yet was not tired in the morning. Partly, she was thinking of her stay in London, the crowning of her apprenticeship five years long. Nothing had happened as she had expected. Nothing, in this life, ever does. She had found the hero of her dreams defeated and fallen, a pitiable object. But he stood erect again, better armed and in better heart, his face turned upwards.

Partly, another thing filled her heart and made her wakeful.

Roland and Archie came with them to the station.

'Shall I ever be permitted to visit again the Land of Lyonesse?' whispered the former at the window just before the guard's whistle gave the signal for the train to start.

She gave him her hand. 'Good-bye, Roland. You will come to Scilly—when you please—as soon as you can.'

He held her hand.

'I live only in that hope,' he replied.

The train began to move. He bent and kissed her fingers.

She leaned forward. 'Roland,' she said, 'I also live only in that hope.'

CHAPTER XXVI

NOT THE HEIR, AFTER ALL

The storm expended itself. The gale cannot go on blowing: the injured man cannot go on raging, cursing, or weeping. Alec Feilding became calm. Yet a settled gloom rested like a dark cloud upon his front: he had lost something—a good part—of his pristine confidence. That enviable quality which so much impresses itself upon others—called swagger—had been knocked out of him. Indeed, he had sustained a blow from which he would never wholly recover: such a man could never get over the loss of such a fortune: his great-grandfather, so far as could be learned, lost his fortune and began again, with cheerful heart. Alec would begin again, because he must, but with rage and bitterness. It was like being struck down by an incurable disease: it might be alleviated, but it would never be driven out: from time to time, in spite of the physicians, the patient writhes and groans in the agony of this disease. So from time to time will this man, until the end of time, groan and lament over the wicked waste and loss of that superb inheritance.

Of course he disguised from himself—this is one of the things men always do hide away—the fact that he himself was part and parcel of the deed: he had destroyed himself by his own craft and cunning. Had he not placed his wife with Armorel under instructions to persuade and coax her into advancing money for his own purposes, the thing could never have happened.

Henceforth, though the pair should have the desire of their hearts: though they should march on to wealth and success: though the wife should invent and contrive with the cleverness of ten for the good of the firm: though the husband should grow more and more in the estimation of the outer world into the position of a Master and an Authority: between the two will lie the memory of fraud and crime, to divide them and keep them apart.

On the day after the revelation, a thought came into the mind of the inheritor of the rubies. The thing that had happened unto him—could he cause it to happen unto another? Perhaps one remembers how, on learning that the rubies were to be given to the eldest grandson of the second daughter, he had dropped, limp and pale, into a chair. One may also remember how, on learning that no further investigation would be made, he recovered again. The fact was, you see, that Mr. Jagenal had made a little mistake. His searchers had altered the order of the three sisters. Frances, Alec Feilding's grandmother, was not the second, but the third daughter. When the rubies were actually waiting and ready for him, it would have been foolish to mention that fact, especially as no further search was to be made, and the elder branch, wherever it was, would never know anything of the matter at all. Therefore, he then held his tongue.

Now, on the other hand, the jewels being worthless, he thought, first of all, that it would look extremely scrupulous to inform Mr. Jagenal of the discovery that his grandmother was really the third daughter: next, if the other branch should be discovered, the fortunate heir would, like himself, be raised to the heavens only to be dashed down again to earth. Let someone else, as well as himself, experience the agonies of that fall. He chuckled grimly as he considered the torments in store for this fortunate unknown cousin. As for danger to his wife, he considered rightly that there was none: the stones had been consigned to the bank by Armorel, and in her own name: she signed an order for their delivery to Mr. Jagenal: he had kept them in his safe. They would certainly lie there some time before he found the new heir. Nay. They had been in his custody for five years before he gave them over formally to Armorel. Who could say when the robbery had been effected? Who would think of asking the bank whether during the short time the parcel was held in the name of Armorel it had been taken out? Clearly the whole blame and responsibility lay with Mr. Jagenal himself. He would have a very curious problem to solve—namely, how the rubies had been changed in his own safe.

'Well, Alec, come to take away your rubies?' asked Mr. Jagenal, cheerily. 'There they are in that safe.'

'No,' he replied, sadly. 'I am grieved indeed to say that I have not come for the rubies. I shall never come for the rubies.'

'Why not?'

'Because they are not for me. According to your instructions, I have no claim to them.'

'No claim?'

'I understand that Miss Rosevean intends to give these jewels to the first representative of the family of Robert Fletcher. That is to say, to the eldest grandchild of the first, second, or third daughter, as the case may be?'

'That is so.'

'Very well. The eldest daughter left no children. You therefore sent for me as the eldest—and only—grandchild of the second daughter?'

'I did.'

'Then I have to tell you that you are wrong. My grandmother was the third daughter.'

'Is it possible?'

'Quite possible. She was the third daughter. I was not very accurately acquainted with that part of my genealogy, and the other day I could not have told you whether I came from the second or the third daughter. I have since ascertained the facts. It was the second daughter who went away to Australia or New Zealand, or somewhere. I do not know anything at all about my cousins, but I think it very unlikely that there are none in existence.'

'Very unlikely. What proof have you that your grandmother was the second daughter?'

'I have an old family Bible—I can show it you, if you like. In this has been entered the date of the birth, the place and date of baptism, the names of the sponsors of all three sisters. There is also a note on the second sister's marriage and on her emigration. I assure you there can be no doubt on the subject at all.'

'Oh! This is very disastrous, my dear boy. How could my people have made such a mistake? Alec, I feel for you—I do, indeed!'

'It is most disastrous!' Alec echoed with a groan. 'I have been in the unfortunate position of a man who is suddenly put into possession of a great fortune one day, and as suddenly deprived of it the next. Of course, as soon as I discovered the real facts, it became my duty to acquaint you with them.'

'By George!' cried Mr. Jagenal. 'If you had kept the facts to yourself, no one would ever have been any wiser. No one, because the transfer of the property is a sheer gift made by my client to you without any compulsion at all. It is a private transaction of which I should never have spoken to anyone. Well, Alec, I must not say that you are wrong. But many men—most men perhaps—with a less keen sense of honour than you—well—I say no more. Yet the loss and disappointment must be a bitter pill for you.'

'It is a bitter pill,' he replied truthfully. 'More bitter than you would suspect.'

'You will have the satisfaction of feeling that you have behaved in this matter as a man of the strictest honour.'

'I am very glad, considering all things, that I have not had the rubies in my own possession, even for a single hour.'

'That is nothing: of course they would have been safe in your hands. Well, Alec, I am sorry for you. But you are young: you are clever: you are succeeding hand over hand: pay a little more attention to your daily expenses, put down your horses and live for a few years quietly, and you will make your own fortune—ay, a fortune greater far than was contained in this unlucky case of precious stones.'

'I suppose you will renew your search, now, after the descendants of the second daughter?'

'I suppose we must. Do not forget that if there are no descendants—or, which is much the same thing, if we cannot find them in a reasonable time, I shall advise my client to transfer the jewels to the grandson of the third daughter. And I hope, my dear boy—I hope, I say, that we may never find those descendants.'

Alec departed, a little cheered by the consolation that he had passed on the disappointment to another.

He went home, and found his wife in the studio, apparently waiting for him. There were dark rings round her eyes. She had been weeping. Since the storm they had not spoken to each other.

He sat down at his table—it was perfectly bare of papers—no sign of any work at all upon it—and waited for her to begin.

'Is it not time,' she asked, 'that this should cease? You have reproached me enough, I think. Remember, we are on the same level. But, whatever I have done, it was done for your sake. Whatever you have done, was done for your own sake. Now, is there going to be an end to this situation?'

He made a gesture of impatience.

'Understand clearly—if I am to help you for the future: if I am going to pull you through this crisis: if I am to direct and invent and combine for you, I mean to be treated with the semblance of kindness—the show of politeness at least.'

He sat up, moved by this appeal, which, indeed, was to his purse—that is, to his heart.

'I say, my husband,' she repeated, 'you must understand me clearly. Again, what I have done was done for you—for you. Unless you agree to my conditions it shall have been done—for myself. I have four thousand pounds in the bank in my own name. You cannot touch it. I shall go away and live upon that money—apart from you. And you shall have nothing—nothing—unless——'

'Unless what?' He shook off his wrath with a mighty effort, as a sulky boy shakes off his sulks when he perceives that he must, and that instantly. He threw off his wrath and sat up with a wan semblance of a smile, a spectral smile, feebly painted on his lips 'Unless what, Zoe? My dear child, can you not make allowance for a man tried in this terrible fashion? I don't believe that any man was ever so mocked by Fortune. I have been crushed. Yes, any terms, any condition you please. Let us forget the past. Come, dear, let us forget what has happened.' He sprang to his feet and held out his arms.

She hesitated a moment. 'There is no other place for me now,' she murmured. 'We are on the same level. I am all yours—now.'

Then she drew herself away, and turned again to the table. 'Come, Alec,' she said, 'to business. Time presses. Sit down, and give me all your attention.'

CHAPTER XXVII

THE DESERT ISLAND

The train proceeded slowly along the head of Mount's-Bay, the waters of the high tide washing up almost to the sleepers on the line. Armorel let down the window and looked out across the bay—

> Where the great vision of the guarded Mount
> Looks towards Namancos and Bayona's hold.

'See, Effie!' she cried. 'There is Mount's Bay. There is the Lizard. There is Penzance. And there—oh! there is the Mount itself!'

St. Michael's Mount, always weird and mysterious, rose out of the waters wrapped in a thin white cloud, which the early sun had not yet been able to dissipate. I am told there is a very fine modern house upon the Mount. I prefer not to believe that story. The place should always remain lonely, awful, full of mystery and wonder. There is also said to be a battery with guns upon it.

Perhaps. But there are much more wonderful things than these to tell of the rock. Upon its highest point those gallant miners—Captain Caractac and Captain Caerleon, both of Boadicea Wheal—were wont to stand gazing out upon the stretch of waters expecting the white sails and flashing oars of the Phœnician fleet, come to buy their white and precious tin, with strong wines from Syria and spices from the far East, and purple robes and bronze swords and spearheads, far better than those made by Flint Jack of the Ordnance Department. Hither came white-robed priests with flowing beards and solemn faces—faces supernaturally solemn, till they were alone upon the rock. Then, perhaps, an eyelid trembled. What they did I know not, nor did the people, but it was something truly awful, with majestic rites and ineffable mysteries and mumbo-jumbo of the very noblest. Here St. Michael himself once, in the ages of Faith, condescended to appear. It was to a hermit. Such appearances were the prizes of the profession. Many went a-hermiting in hopes of getting a personal call from a Saint who would otherwise have fought and lived and died quite like the rest of the world. And, indeed, there were so many Cornish Saints—such as St. Buryan, St. Levan, St. Ives, St. Just, St. Keverne, St. Anthony, not to speak of St. Erth, St. Gulval, St. Austell, St. Wenn—all kindly disposed saints, anxious to encourage hermits, and pleased to extend their own sphere of usefulness, that few of these holy men were disappointed.

In the bay the blue water danced lightly in the morning breeze: the low, level sunlight shone upon Penzance on the western side: the fishing-boats, back from the night's cruise, lay at their moorings, their brown sails lowered: the merchant-men and trading craft were crowded in the port: beyond, the white curves chased each other across the water, and showed that, outside, the breeze was fresh and the water lively.

'We are almost at home,' said Armorel. 'There is our steamer lying off the quay—she looks very little, doesn't she? Only a short voyage of forty miles—oh! Effie, I do hope you are a good sailor—and we shall be at Hugh Town.'

'Are we really arrived? I believe I have slept the whole night through,' said Effie, sitting up and pulling herself straight. 'Oh! how lovely!'—as she too looked out of window. 'Have you slept well, Armorel?'

'I don't think I have been asleep much. But I am quite happy, Effie, dear—quite as happy as if I had been sound asleep all night. There are dreams, you know, which come to people in the night when they are awake as well as when they are asleep. I have been dreaming all night long—one dream which lasted all the night—one voice in my ears—one hand in mine. Oh! Effie, I have been quite happy!' She showed her happiness by kissing her companion. 'I am happier than I ever thought to be. Some day, perhaps, I shall be able to tell you why.'

And then the train rolled in to Penzance Station.

It was only half-past seven in the morning. The steamer would not start till half-past ten. The girls sent their luggage on board, and then went to one of the hotels which stand all in a row facing the Esplanade. Here they repaired the ravages of the night, which makes even a beautiful girl like Armorel show like Beauty neglected, and then they took breakfast, and, in due time, went on board.

Now behold! They had left in London a pitiless nor'-easter and a black sky. They found at Penzance a clear blue overhead, light and sunshine, and a glorious north-westerly breeze. That is not, certainly, the quarter whose winds allay the angry waves and soothe the heaving surge. Not at all. It is when the wind is from the north-west that the waves rise highest and heaviest. Then the boat bound to Scilly tosses and rolls like a round cork, yet persistently forces her way westward, diving, ploughing, climbing, slipping, sliding, and rolling, shipping great seas and shaking them off again, always getting ahead somehow. Then those who come forth at the start with elastic step and lofty looks lie low and wish that some friend would prod Father Time with a bradawl and make him run: and those who enjoy the sea, Sir, and are never sick, are fain to put down the pipe with which they proudly started and sink into nothingness. For taking the conceit out of a young man there is nothing better than the voyage from Penzance to Scilly, especially if it be a tripper's voyage—that is, back again the same day.

There is, on the Scilly boat, a cabin, or rather a roofed and walled apartment, within which is the companion to the saloon. Nobody ever goes into the saloon, though it is magnificent with red velvet, but round this roofed space there is a divan or sofa. And here lie the weak and fearful, and all those who give in and oppose no further resistance to the soft influences of ocean. Effie lay here, white of cheek and motionless. She had never been on the sea before, and she had a rough and tumbling day to begin with, and the sea in glory and grandeur—but all was lost and thrown away so far as she was concerned. Armorel stood outside, holding to the ropes with both hands. She was dressed in a waterproof: the spray flew over her: her cheek was wet with it: her eyes were bright with it: the heavy seas dashed over her: she laughed and shook her waterproof: as for wet boots, what Scillonian regardeth them? And the wind—how it blew through and through her! How friendly was its rough welcome! How splendid to be once more on rough water, the boat fighting against a head wind and rolling waves! How glorious to look out once more upon the wild ungoverned waves!

It was not until the boat had rounded the Point and was well out in the open that these things became really enjoyable. Away south stood the Wolf with its tall lighthouse: you could see the white waves boiling and fighting around it and climbing half-way up. Beyond the Wolf a great ocean steamer plunged through the water outward bound. Presently there came flying past them the most beautiful thing ever invented by the wit of man or made by his craft, a three-masted schooner under full sail—all sails spread—not forging slowly along under poverty-stricken stays which proclaim an insufficient crew, but flying over the water under all her canvas. She was a French boat, of Havre.

'There is Scilly, Miss,' said the steward, pointing out to sea.

Yes; low down the land lay, west by north. It looked like a cloud at first. Every moment it grew clearer; but always low down. What one sees at first are the eastern shores of St. Agnes and Gugh, St. Mary's, and the Eastern Islands. They are all massed together, so that the eye cannot distinguish one from the other, but all seem to form continuous land. By degrees they separated. Then one could discover the South Channel and the North Channel. When the tide is high and the weather fair the boat takes the former: at low tide, the latter. To-day the captain chose the South Channel. And now they were so near the land that Armorel could make out Porthellick Bay, and her heart beat, though she was going home to no kith or kin, and to nothing but her *familia*, her serving folk. Next she made out Giant's Castle, then the Old Town, then Peninnis Head, black and threatening. And now they were so near that every carn and every boulder upon it could be made out clearly: and one could see the water rising and falling at the foot of the rock, and hear it roaring as it was driven into the dark caves and the narrow places where the rocks opened out and made make-believe of a port or haven of refuge. And now Porthcressa Bay, and now the Garrison, and smooth water.

Then Armorel brought out Effie, pale and languid. 'Now, dear, the voyage is over: we are in smooth water, and shall be in port in ten minutes. Look round—it is all over: we are in the Road. And over there—see!—with his twin hills—is my dear old Samson.'

There was a little crowd on the quay waiting to see the boat arrive. All of them—boatmen, fishermen, and flower-farmers' men, to say nothing of those representing the interests of commerce—pressed forward to welcome Armorel. Everybody remembered her, but now she was a grand young lady who had left them a simple child. They shook hands with her and stepped aside. And then Peter came forward, looking no older but certainly no younger, and Armorel shook hands with him too. He had the boat alongside, and in five minutes more the luggage was on board, the mast was up, the sail set, and Armorel was sitting in her old place, the strings in her hand, while Peter held the rope and looked out ahead, shading his eyes with his right hand in the old familiar style.

'It is as if I never left home at all,' said Armorel. 'I sailed like this with Peter yesterday—and the day before.'

'You've growed,' said Peter, after an inquiring gaze, being for the moment satisfied that there was nothing ahead and that there was no immediate danger of shipwreck on the Nut Rock or Green Island.

'I am five years older,' Armorel replied.

'It's been a rare harvest this year,' he went on. 'I thought we should never come to the end of the daffodils.'

'Now I am at home indeed,' said Armorel, 'when I hear the old, old talk about the flowers. To-morrow, Effie, I will show you our little fields where we grow all the lovely flowers—the anemone and jonquil—the narcissus and the daffodil. This afternoon, when we have had dinner and rested a little, I will take you all round Samson and show you the glories of the place: they are principally views of other islands: but there is a headland and two bays, and there are the Tombs of the Kings—the Ancient Kings of Lyonesse—in one of them Roland Lee'—she blushed and turned away her head—henceforth, she understood, this was a name to be treated with more reverence—'found a golden torque, which you have seen me wear. And oh! my dear—you shall be so happy: the seabreeze shall fill your soul with music: the seabirds shall sing to you: the very waves shall lap on the shore in rhyme and rhythm for you: and the sun of Scilly, which is so warm and glowing, but never too warm, shall colour that pale cheek of yours, and fill out that spare form. And oh, Effie! I hope you will not get tired of Samson and of me! We are two maidens living on a desert island: there is nobody to talk to except each other: we shall wander about together as we list. Oh, I am so happy, Effie!—and oh, my dear, I am so hungry!'

The boat ran up over the white sand of the beach. They jumped out, and Armorel, leaving Peter to bring along the trunks by the assistance of the donkey, led the way over the southern hill to Holy Farm.

'Effie,' she said, 'I have been tormented this morning with the fear that everything would look small. I was afraid that my old memories—a child's memories—would seem distorted and exaggerated. Now I am not in the least afraid. Samson has got all his acres still: he looks quite as big and quite as homely as ever he did—the boulders are as huge, the rocks are as steep. I remember every boulder, Effie, and every bush, and every patch of brown fern, and almost every trailing branch of bramble. How glorious it is here! How the seabreeze sweeps across the hill—it comes all the way from America—across the Atlantic! Effie, I declare you are looking rosier already. I must sing—I must, indeed—I always used to sing!——' She threw up her arms in the old gesture, and sang a loud and clear and joyous burst of song—sang like the lark springing from the ground, because it cannot choose but sing. 'I used to jump, too; but I do not want, somehow, to jump any more. Ah, Effie, I was quite certain there would be some falling-off, but I could not tell in what direction. I can no longer jump. That comes of getting old. To be sure, I did not jump when I took Roland Lee about the islands. Sometimes I sang, but I was ashamed to jump. Here we are upon the top. It is not a mighty Alp, is it?—but it serves. Look round—but only for a moment, because Chessun will have dinner waiting for us, and you are exhausted by your bad passage—you poor thing. This is our way, down the narrow lanes. Here our fields begin: they are each about as big as a dinner-table. See the tall hedges to keep off the north wind: there is a field of narcissus, but there are no more flowers, and the leaves are dying away. This way: Ah! Here we are!'

The house did not look in the least mean, or any smaller than Armorel expected. She became even prouder of it. Where else could one find a row of palms, with great verbena-trees and prickly pear and aloes, not to speak of the creepers over the porch, the gilt figure-head, and the big ship's lantern hung in the porch? Within, the sunlight poured into the low rooms—all of them looking south—and made them bright: in the room where formerly the ancient lady passed her time in the hooded chair—the lady passed away and the chair gone—the cloth was spread for dinner. And in the porch were gathered the serving-folk—Justinian not a day older, Dorcas unchanged, and Chessun thin and worn, almost as old, to look at, as her mother. And as soon as the greetings were over, and the questions asked and answered, and the news told of the harvest and the prices, and the girls had run all over the house, Chessun brought in the dinner.

It is a blessed thing that we must eat, because upon this necessity we have woven so many pretty customs. We eat a welcome home: we eat a godspeed: we eat together because we love each other: we eat to celebrate anything and everything. Above all, upon such an event as the return of one who has long been parted from us we make a little banquet. Thought and pains had been bestowed upon the dinner which Chessun placed upon the table. Dorcas stood by the table, watching the effect of her cares. First there was a chicken roasted, with bread crumbs—a bird blessed with a delicacy of flavour and a tenderness of flesh and a willingness to separate at the joints unknown beyond the shores of Scilly: Dorcas said so, and the girls believed it—Effie, at least, willing to believe that nothing in the world was so good as in this happy realm of Queen Armorel. Dorcas also invited special attention to the home-cured ham, which was, she justly remarked, mild as a peach: the potatoes, served in their skins, were miracles of mealiness—had Armorel met with such potatoes out of Samson? had the young lady, her visitor, ever seen or dreamed of such potatoes? There was spinach grown on the farm, freshly cut, redolent of the earth, fragrant with the seabreeze. And there was home-made bread, sweet, wholesome, and firm. There was also placed upon the table a Brown George, filled with home-brewed, furnished with a head snow-white, venerable, and benevolent, such a head as not all the breweries of Burton—or even of the whole House of Lords combined—could furnish. Alas! that head smiled in vain upon this degenerate pair. They would not drink the nut-brown, sparkling beer. It was not wasted, however. Peter had it when he brought the pack-ass to the porch laden with the last trunk. Nor did they so much as remove the stopper from the decanter containing a bottle of the famous blackberry wine, the primest *crû* of Samson, opened expressly for this dinner. Yet this was not wasted either, for Justinian, who knew a glass of good wine, took it with three successive suppers. Is it beneath the dignity of history to mention pudding? Consider: pudding is festive: pudding contributes largely to the happiness of youth. Armorel and Effie tackled the pudding as only the young and hungry can. And this day, perhaps from the promptings of simple piety, being rejoiced that Armorel was back again; perhaps from some undeveloped touch of poetry in her nature, Chessun placed upon the table that delicacy seldom seen at the tables of the unfortunate Great—who really get so few of the good things—known as Grateful Pudding. You know the ingredients of this delightful dish? More. To mark the day, Chessun actually made it with cream instead of milk!

'To-morrow,' said Armorel, fired with emulation, 'I will show you, Effie, what I can do in the way of puddings and cakes. I always used to make them: and, unless my lightness of hand has left me, I think you will admire my teacakes, if not my puddings. Roland Lee praised them both. But, to be sure, he was so easily pleased. He liked everything on the island. He even liked—oh! Effie!—he liked me.'

'That was truly wonderful, Armorel.'

'Now, Effie, dear, lie down in this chair beside the window. You can look straight out to sea—that is Bishop's Rock, with its lighthouse. Lie down and rest, and I will talk to you about Scilly and Samson and my own people. Or I will play to you if you like. I am glad the new piano has arrived safely.'

'I like to look round this beautiful old room. How strange it is! I have never seen such a room—with things so odd.'

'They are all things from foreign lands, and things cast up by the sea. If you like odd things I will show you, presently, my punch-bowls and the snuff-boxes and watches and things. I did not give all of them to the care of Mr. Jagenal five years ago.'

'It is wonderful: it is lovely: as if one could ever tire of such a place!'

'Lie down, dear, and rest. You have had such a tossing about that you must rest after it, or you may be ill. It promises to be a fine and clear evening. If it is we will go out by-and-by and see the sun set behind the Western Rocks.'

'We are on a desert island,' Effie murmured obediently, lying down and closing her eyes. 'Nobody here but ourselves: we can do exactly what we please: think of it, Armorel! Nobody wants any money, here: nobody jostles his neighbour: nobody tramples upon his friend. It is like a dream of the primitive life.'

'With improvements, dear Effie. My ancestors used to lead the primitive life when Samson was a holy island and the cemetery of the Kings of Lyonesse: they went about barefooted and they were dressed in skins: they fought the wolves and bears, and if they did not kill the creatures, why, the creatures killed them: they were always fighting the nearest tribe. And they sucked the marrow-bones, Effie, think of that! Oh! we have made a wonderful advance in the civilisation of Samson Island.

CHAPTER XXVIII

AT HOME

'I AM so very pleased to see *you* here, Mr. Stephenson.' Mrs. Feilding welcomed him with her sweetest and most gracious smile. 'To attract our few really sincere critics—there are so many incompetent pretenders—as well as the leaders in all the Arts is my great ambition. And now you have come.'

'You are very kind,' said Dick, blushing. I dare say he is a really great critic at the hours when he is not a most superior clerk in the Admiralty. At the same time, one is not often told the whole, the naked, the gratifying truth.

'To have a *salon*, that is my desire: to fill it with men of light and leading. Now you have broken the ice, you will come often, will you not? Every Sunday evening, at least. My husband will be most pleased to find you here.'

'Again, you are very kind.'

'We saw you yesterday afternoon at that poor boy's *matinée*; did we not? The crush was too great for us to exchange a word with you. What do you think of the piece?'

'I always liked it. I was present, you know, at the reading that night.'

'Oh yes; the reading—Armorel Roseveau's Reading. Yes. Though that hardly gave one an idea of the play.'

'The piece went very well indeed. I should think it will catch on; but of course the public are very capricious. One never knows whether they will take to a thing or not. To my mind there is every prospect of success. In any case, young Wilmot has shown that he possesses poetical and dramatic powers of a very high order indeed. He seems the most promising of the men before us at present. That is, if he keeps up to the standard of this first effort.'

'Ye—es? Of course we must discount some of the promise. You have heard, for instance, that my husband lent his advice and assistance?'

'He said so, after the reading, did he not?'

'Nobody knows, Mr. Stephenson,' she clasped her hands and turned those eyes of limpid blue upon the young man, 'how many successes my husband has helped to make by his timely assistance! What he did to this particular play I do not know, of course. During the reading and during yesterday's performance, I seemed to hear his voice through all the acts. It haunted me. But Alec said nothing. He sat in silence, smiling, as if he had never heard the words before. Oh! It is wonderful! And now—not a word of recognition! You help people to climb up, and then they pretend—they pretend—to have got up by their own exertions! Not that Alec expects gratitude or troubles himself much about these things, but, naturally, I feel hurt. And oh! Mr. Stephenson, what must be the conscience of the man—how can he bear to live—who goes about the world pretending—pretending,' she shook her head sadly, 'pretending to have written other men's works!'

'Men will do anything, I suppose. This kind of assistance ought, however, to be recognised. I will make some allusion to it in my notice of the play. Meantime, if I can read the future at all, Master Archie Wilmot's fortune is made, and he will.'

'Mr. Roland Lee showed his picture that night. He had just come out of a madhouse, had he not?'

'Not quite that. He failed, and dropped out. But what he did with himself or how he lived for three years I do not exactly know. He has returned, and never alludes to that time.'

'And he exactly imitates my husband, I am told.'

'No, no—not exactly. The resemblance is close, only an experienced critic'—Oh! Dick Stephenson!—'could discern the real differences of treatment.' Mrs. Feilding smiled. 'But I knew him before he disappeared, and I assure you his method was then the same as it is now. Very much like your husband's style, yet with a difference.'

'I am glad there is a difference. An artist ought, at least, to have a style of his own. You know, I suppose, that Armorel has gone away?'

'I have heard so.'

'It became possible for us at last to acknowledge things. So I joined my husband. Armorel went home—to her own home in the Scilly Islands. She took Effie Wilmot with her. Indeed, the girl's flatteries have become necessary to her. I fear she was unhappy, poor child! I sometimes think, Mr. Stephenson, that she saw too much of Alec. Of course he was a good deal with us, and I could not tell her the whole truth, and—and—girls' heads are easily turned, you know, when genius seems to be attracted. Poor Armorel!' she sighed, playing with her fan. 'Time, I dare say, will help her to forget.'

'It is a pity,' said Dick Stephenson, changing the subject, because he did not quite believe this version, 'it is a pity that Mr.

Feilding, who can give such admirable advice to a young dramatist, does not write a play himself.'

'Hush!' she looked all round, 'nobody is listening. Alec *has* written a play, Mr. Stephenson. It is a three-act drama—a tragedy—strong—oh! so strong—so strong!' She clasped her hands again, letting the fan dangle from her wrist. 'So effective! I don't know when I have seen a play with more striking situations. It is accepted. But not a word has yet been said about it.'

'May I say something about it? Will you let me be the first to announce it, and to give some little account of it?'

'I will ask Alec. If he consents, I will tell you more about the play. And, my dear Mr. Stephenson, you, one of our old friends, really ought to do some work for the paper.'

'I have not been asked,' he replied, colouring, for he was still at that stage when the dramatic critic is flattered by being invited to write for a paper.

'You shall be. How do you like the paper?'

'It has so completely changed its character, one would think that the whole staff had been changed. Everybody reads it now, and everybody takes it, I believe.'

'The circulation has gone up by leaps and bounds. It is really wonderful. But, Mr. Stephenson, here is one of the reasons. Give me a little credit—poor me! I cannot write, but I can look on, and I have a pair of eyes, and I can see things. Now, I saw that Alec was killing himself with writing. Every week a story; also, every week, a poem; every week an original article; and then those notes. I made him stop. I said to him, "Stamp your own individuality on every line of the paper; but write it yourself no longer. Edit it.' You see, it is not as if Alec had to prove his powers: he has proved them already. So he can afford to let others do the hard work, while he adds the magic touch—the touch of genius—that touch that goes to the heart. And the result you see.'

'Yes; the brightest—cleverest—most varied paper that exists.

'With a large staff. Formerly Alec and one or two others formed the whole staff. Well, Mr. Stephenson, I know that Alec is going to ask you to do some of the dramatic criticism, and if you consent I shall be very pleased to have been the first to mention it.'

It will be understood from this conversation that the new methods of managing the business of the Firm were essentially different from the old. The paper had taken a new departure: it prospered. It was understood that the editor put less of his own work into it; but the articles, verses, and stories were all unsigned, and no one could tell exactly which were his papers: therefore, as all were clever, his reputation remained on the same level. Also, there was a thick and solid mass of advertisements each week, which represented public confidence widespread and deep. 'Give me,' cries the proprietor of a paper, 'the confidence of advertisers. That is proof enough of popularity.'

Mrs. Feilding moved to another part of the room, and began to talk with another man.

'My husband,' she said, 'has prepared a little surprise for us this evening. I say for us, because I have not seen what he has to show—since it came back from the frame-maker.'

'It is a picture, then?'

'A picture in a new style. He has abandoned for a time his coast and seashore studies. This is in quite a new style. I think —I hope—that it will be liked as well as his old.'

'He is indeed a wonderful man!'

'Is he not?' She laughed—a low and musical—a contented and a happy laugh. 'Is he not? You never know what Alec may be going to do next.'

Mrs. Feilding's Sundays have already become a great success: such a success as a woman of the world may desire, and a clever woman can achieve. There is once more, as she says proudly, a *salon* in London. If it does not quite take the lead that she pretends in Art and Letters, it is always full. Men who go there once, go again: they find the kind of entertainment that they like: plenty of people for talk, to begin with. Then, every man is made, by the hostess, to feel that his own position in the literary and artistic world is above even his own estimate: that is soothing: in fact, the note of the *salon* is appreciation—not mutual admiration, as the envious do enviously affirm. Moreover, everybody in the *salon* has done something—perhaps not much, but something. And then the place is one where the talk is delightfully free, almost as free as in a club smoking-room. Every evening, again, there is some kind of entertainment, but not too much, because the *salon* has to keep up its reputation for conversation, and music destroys conversation. 'Let us,' said Mrs. Feilding, 'revive the dead art of conversation. Let the men in this room make their reputation as they did a hundred years ago, for brilliant talk.' I have not heard that Mrs. Feilding has yet developed a talker like the mighty men of old: perhaps one will come along later: those, however, who have looked into the subject with an ambition in that line, and have ascertained the nature of the epigrams, repartees, retorts, quips, jokes, and personal observations attributed to Messrs. Douglas Jerrold and his brilliant circle are doubtful of reviving that Art except in a modified and a greatly chastened, even an effeminate form.

The entertainments provided by Mrs. Feilding consisted of a little music or a little singing—always by a young and little-known professional: there was generally something in the fashion—young lady with a banjo or a tum-tum, or anything which was popular: young gentleman to whistle: young actor or actress to give a character sketch: sometimes a picture sent in for private exhibition: sometimes a little poem printed for the evening and handed about—one never knew what would be done.

But always the hostess would be gracious, winning, caressing, smiling, and talking incessantly: always she would be gliding about the room, making her friends talk: the happy wife of the most accomplished and most versatile man in London. And always that illustrious genius himself, calm and grave, taking Art seriously, laying down with authority the opinion that should be held to a circle who surrounded him. The circle consisted chiefly of women and of young men. Older men, with that reluctance to listen to the voice of Authority which distinguishes many after thirty, held aloof and talked with each other. 'Alec Feilding,' said one of them, expressing the general opinion, 'may be a mighty clever fellow, but he talks like a dull book. You've heard it all before. And you've heard it better put. It's wonderful that such a clever dog should be such a dull dog.

They came, however, in spite of the dulness: the wife would have carried off a hundred dull dogs.

As in certain earlier and better-known circles, the men greatly outnumbered the women. 'I am not in love with my own sex,' said Mrs. Feilding, quite openly. 'I prefer the society of men.' But some women came of their own accord, and some were brought by their fathers, husbands, lovers, and brothers. No one could say that ladies kept away from Mrs. Feilding's Sunday evenings.

This evening, the principal thing was the uncovering of a new picture—Mr. Feilding's new picture.

At ten o'clock the painter-poet, in obedience to a whisper from his wife, moved slowly, followed by his ring of disciples—male and female—all young—a callow brood—to the upper end of the room, where was an easel. A picture stood upon it, but a large green cloth was thrown over it.

'I thought,' said Mr. Alec Feilding, in his most dignified manner, 'that you would like to see this picture before anyone else. It is one of the little privileges of our Sunday evenings to show things to each other. Some of you may remember,' he said, with the true humility of genius, 'that I have exhibited, hitherto, chiefly pictures of coast scenery. I have always been of opinion that a man should not confine himself to one class of subjects. His purchasing public may demand it, but the true artist should disregard all and any considerations connected with money.'

'Your true artist hasn't always got a weekly journal to fall back upon,' growled a young A.R.A. who did stick to one class of subjects. He had been brought there. As a rule, artists are not found at Mrs. Feilding's, nor do they rally round the cleverest man in London.

'I say,' repeated the really great man, 'that the wishes of buyers must not be weighed for an instant in comparison with the true interests of Art.'

'Like a copy-book,' murmured the Associate.

'Therefore, I have attempted a new line altogether. I have made new studies. They have cost a great deal of time and trouble and anxious thought. It is quite a new departure. I anticipate, beforehand, what you will say at first. But—Eccolo!'

He lifted the green cloth. At the same moment his wife turned up a light that stood beside the painting. He disclosed a really very beautiful painting: a group of trees beside a shallow pool of water: the trees were leafless: a little snow lay at their roots: the pool was frozen over: there was a little mist over the ground, and between the trunks one saw the setting sun.

'By Jove! It's a Belgian picture!' cried the Associate. And, indeed, you may see hundreds of pictures exactly in this style in the Brussels galleries, where the artists are never tired of painting the flat country and the trees, at every season and under every light.

'Precisely,' said the painter. 'That is the remark which I anticipated. Let us call it—if you like—a Belgian picture. The subject is English: the treatment, perhaps, Belgian. For my part, I am not too proud to learn something from the Belgians.'

The Associate touched the man nearest him—an artist, not yet an Associate—by the arm.

'Ghosts!' he murmured. 'Spooks and ghosts!'

'Spectres!' replied the other. 'Phantoms and bogies!'

'A Haunted Studio!' said the Associate. 'My knees totter My hair stands on end!'

'I tremble—I have goose-flesh!' replied his friend.

'Let us—let us run to the Society of Psychical Research! whispered the Associate.

'Let us swiftly run!' said the other.

They fled, swiftly and softly. Only Mrs. Feilding observed their flight. She also gathered from their looks the subject of their talk. And she resolved that she would not, henceforth, encourage artists at her Sunday evenings. She turned to Dick Stephenson.

'You, Mr. Stephenson,' she said, 'who are a true critic and understand work, tell me what *you* think of the picture.'

The great critic—he was not really a humbug. he was very fond of looking at pictures; only, you see, he was not an artist—advanced to the front, bent forward, considered a few moments, and then spoke.

'A dexterous piece of work—truly dexterous in the highest sense: full of observation intelligently and poetically rendered: careful: truthful: with intense feeling. I could hardly have believed that any English painter was capable of work in this *genre*.'

The people all gazed upon the canvas with rapt admiration: they murmured that it was wonderful and beautiful. Then

Alec covered up the picture, and somebody began to play something.

'Alec,' said Mr. Jagenal, who seldom came to these gatherings, 'I congratulate you. Your picture is very good. And in a new style. When will you be content to settle down in the jog-trot that the British public love?'

'Let me change my subject sometimes. When I am tired of trees I will go back, perhaps, to the coast and seapieces.'

'Ah! But take care. There's a fellow coming along—— By the way, Alec, I have made a discovery lately.'

'What is it?'

'About those rubies. Why, man'—for Alec turned suddenly pale—'you remember that business still?'

'Indeed I do,' he replied. 'And I am not likely to forget it in a hurry.'

'My dear boy, to paint such pictures is worth many such bags of precious stones, if you will only think so.'

'What's your discovery?' Alec asked hoarsely.

'Well; I have found, quite accidentally, the eldest grandchild of the second daughter—your great-aunt.'

'Oh!' Again he changed colour. 'Then you will, I suppose, hand him over the things.'

'Yes, certainly. I have sent for him. He does not yet know what I want him for. And I shall give him the jewels in obedience to Armorel's instructions. Alec, I have always been desperately sorry for your unfortunate discovery.'

'It caused a pang, certainly. And who is my cousin?'

'Well, Alec, I will not tell you until I have made quite sure. Not that there is any doubt. But I had better not. You will perhaps like to make his acquaintance. Perhaps you know him already. I don't say, mind.'

'Well, Sir,' said Alec, 'when he realises the extent and value of this windfall, I expect he will show a depth of gratitude which will astonish you. I do, indeed.'

'Zoe,' he said, when everybody was gone, 'are you quite sure that in the matter of those rubies your action can never be discovered?'

'Anything may be discovered. But I think—I believe—that it will be difficult. Why?'

'Because my cousin, the grandson of Robert Fletcher's second daughter, has been found, and he will receive the jewels tomorrow. And when he finds out what they are worth——'

'Then, Alec, it will be asked who had the jewels. They were taken to the bank by Mr. Jagenal and taken thence to Mr. Jagenal. What have you—what have I—to do with them? Don't think about it, Alec. It has nothing to do with us. No suspicion can possibly attach to us. Forget the whole business. The evening went off very well. The picture struck everybody very much. And I've laid the foundation for curiosity about the play. And as for the paper, I was going into the accounts this morning: it is paying at the rate of three thousand a year. Alec, you have never until now been really and truly the cleverest man in London.'

CHAPTER XXIX

THE TRESPASS OFFERING

It was a day in midwinter. Over the adjacent island of Great Britain there was either a yellow fog, or a white fog, or a black fog. Perhaps there was no fog at all, but a black east wind, or there was melting snow, or there was cold sleet and rain: whatever there was, to be out of doors brought no joy, and the early darkness was tolerable because it closed and hid and put away the day. In the archipelago of Scilly, the sky was bright and clear: the sea was blue, except in the shallow places, where it was a light transparent green: the waves danced and sparkled: round the ledges of the rocks the white foam rolled and leaped: the sunshine was warm: the air was fresh. The girls stood on the northern carn of Samson. They had been on the island now for eight months. For the greater part of that time they were alone. Only in the summer Archie came to pay them a visit. His play was accepted: it would probably be brought out in January, perhaps not till later, according to the success of the piece then running. Meantime, he had got introductions, thanks to Armorel's evening, and now found work enough to keep him going on one or two journals, where his occasional papers—the papers of a young and clever man feeling his way to style—were taken and published. And he was, of course, writing another play: he was in love with another heroine—happy, if he knew his own happiness, in starting on that rare career in which a man is always in love, and blamelessly, even with the knowledge of his wife, with a succession of the loveliest and most delightful damsels—country girls and princesses—lasses of the city and of the milking path—Dolly and Molly and stately Kate, and the Duchess of Dainty Device. As yet, he had only lost his heart to two and was now raving over the second of his sweethearts. One such youth I have known and followed as he passed from the Twenties to the Thirties—to the Forties—even to the Fifties. He has always loved one girl after the other. He knows not how life can exist unless a man is in love: he is a mere slave and votary of Love: yet never with a goddess of the earth. He loves an image—a simulacrum—a phantom: and he looks on with joy and satisfaction—yea! the tears of happiness rise to his eyes when he sees that phantom at the last, after many cruel delays, fondly embraced—not by himself—but by another phantom. Happy lover! so to have lost the substance, yet to be satisfied with the shadow!

Except for Archie's visit they had no guests all through the summer. The holiday visitors mostly arrive at Hugh Town, sail across to Tresco Gardens and back, some the same day, some the next day, thinking they have seen Scilly. None of them land on Samson. Few there are who sail about the Outer Islands where Armorel mostly loved to steer her boat. The two girls spent the whole time alone with each other for company. I do not know whether the literature of the country will be enriched by Effie's sojourn in Lyonesse, but one hopes. At least, she lost her pale cheeks and thin form: she put on roses, and she filled out: she became almost as strong as Armorel, almost as dexterous with the sheet, and almost as handy with the oar. But of verses I fear that few came to her. With the best intentions, with piles of books, these two maidens idled away the summer, basking on the headlands, lying among the fern, walking over the downs of Bryher and St. Martin's, sailing in and out among the channels, bathing in Porth Bay, or off the lonely beach of Ganilly in the Eastern group. Always something to see or something to do. Once they ventured to sail by themselves—a parlous voyage, but the day was calm—all the way round Bishop's Rock and back: another time they sailed—but this time they took Peter—among the Dogs of Scilly, climbed up on Black Rosevean, and stood on Gorregan with the cruel teeth. Once, on a very calm day in July, they even threaded the narrow channel between the twin rocks known together as the Scilly. Always there was something new to do or to see. So the morning and the afternoon passed away, and there was nothing left but tea and a little music, and a stroll in the moonlight or beneath the stars, and a talk together, and so to bed: and if there came a rainy day, the cakes to make and the puddings to compose! A happy, lazy, idle, profitable time!

'We have been six months here and more, Effie,' said Armorel. They were sitting in the sunshine in the sheltered orchard, among the wrinkled and twisted old apple-trees. 'What next? When shall we think of going back to London? We must not stay here altogether, lest we rust. We will go back—shall we?—as soon as the short, dark days are over, and we will make a new departure somehow, but in what direction I do not quite know. Shall we travel? Shall we cultivate society? What shall we do?'

'We will go back to London as soon as Archie's play is produced. Dear Armorel, I do not want ever to go away. I should like to stay here with you always and always. It has been a time of peace and quiet. Never before have I known such peace and such quiet. But we must go. We must go while the spell of the place is still upon us. Perhaps if we were to stay too long—Nature does not expect us to outstay her welcome—not that her welcome is exhausted yet—but if we go away, shall we ever come back? And, if so, will it be quite the same?'

'Nothing ever returns,' said Armorel the sage. 'We shall go

away and we shall come back again, and there will be changes. Everything changes daily. The very music of the sea changes from day to day; but it is always music. My old grandmother in the great chair used to hold her hand to her ear—so—to catch the lapping of the waves and the washing of the tide among the rocks. It was the music that she had known all her life. But the tune was different—the words of the song in her head were different—the key was changed—but always the music. Oh, my dear! I never tire of this music. We will go away, Effie; we must not stay too long here, lest we fall in love with solitude and renounce the world. But we will come back and hear the same music again, with a new song. We must go back.' She sighed. 'Eight months. We must go and see Archie's play. Archie! It will be a proud and glorious day for him, if it succeeds. It must succeed. And not a word or a sign all this time from Roland! What is he doing? Why——' She stopped.

Effie laid a hand on hers.

'You have been restless for some days, Armorel,' she said.

'Yes—yes. I do not doubt him. No—no—he has returned to himself. He can never—never again—I do not doubt him.' She sprang to her feet. 'Oh, Effie! I do not doubt, but sometimes I fear. What do I fear? Why, I know there may be failure, but there can never again be disgrace.'

'You think of him so much, Armorel,' said Effie, with a touch of jealousy.

'I cannot think of him too much.' She looked out upon the sunlit sea at their feet, talking as one who talks to herself. 'How can I think of him too much? I have thought of him every day for five years—every day. I love him, Effie. How can you think too much of the man you love? Suppose I were to hear that he had failed again. That would make no difference. Suppose he were to sink low—low—deep down among the worst of men—that would make no difference. I love the man as he may be—as he shall be—by the help of God, if not in this world, then in the world to come! I love him, Effie!'

She stopped because her voice choked with a sob. The strength of her passion—not for nothing was the Castilian invader wrecked upon Scilly!—frightened the other girl. She had never dreamed of such a passion; yet she knew that Armorel thought continually of this man. She did not dare to speak. She looked on with clasped hands, in silence.

Armorel softened again. The tumult of her heart subsided. She turned to Effie and kissed her.

'Forgive me, dear: you know now—but you have guessed already. Let us say no more. But I must see him soon. I must go to see him if he cannot come to see me. Let us go over the hill. This little orchard is like a hothouse this morning.'

When they reached the top of the hill they saw the steamer

from Penzance rounding Bar Point on St. Mary's and coming through the North Channel.

'They have had a fine passage,' said Armorel. 'The boat must have done it in three hours. I wonder if she brings anything for us. It is too early for the magazines. I wrote for those books, but I doubt if there has been time. And I wrote to Philippa, but I do not expect a letter in reply by this post.'

'And I wrote to Archie, but I do not know whether I shall get a letter to-day. Suppose there should come a visitor?'

'Few visitors come to Scilly in the winter—and none to Samson. We are alone on our desert island, Effie. See, the steamer is entering the port: the tide is low: she cannot get alongside the quay. It is such a fine day that it is a pity we did not sail over this morning and meet the steamer. There goes the steam-launch from Tresco.'

It is quite a mile from Samson to the quay of Hugh Town; but the air was so clear that Armorel, whose eyes were as good as any ordinary field-glass, could plainly make out the agitation and bustle on the quay caused by the arrival of the steamer.

'The boat always carries my thoughts back to London,' said Armorel. 'And we have been talking about London, have we not? When I was a child the boat came into the Road out of the Unknown, and next day went back to the Unknown. What was the other side like? I filled it up with the vague splendour of a child's imagination. The Unknown to me was like the sunrise or the sunset. Well . . . now I know. The poets say that knowledge makes us no happier. I think they are quite wrong. It is always better to know everything, even though it's little joy—

> To feel that Heaven is farther off
> Than when one was a boy.

'There is a boat,' she went on, after a while. 'She is putting out from the port. I wonder what boat it is. Perhaps she is going to Bryher—or to St. Martin's—or to St. Agnes. It is not the lighthouse boat. She is sailing as if for Samson; but she cannot be coming here. What a lovely breeze! She would be here in a quarter of an hour. I suppose she must be going to Tresco. See what comes of living on a desert island. We are actually speculating about the voyage of a sailing-boat across the Road! Effie, we are little better than village gossips. You shall marry Mr. Paul Pry.'

'She looks very pretty,' said Effie, 'heeling over with the wind, wherever she is going.'

'They are steering south of Green Island,' said Armorel. 'That is very odd. If she had been making for Bryher or Tresco she would leave Green Island on the lee and steer up the channel past Puffin. I really believe that she is coming to Samson. I expect there is a parcel for us. Let us run down to the beach, Effie. We shall get there just in time.'

They ran down the hill. As the boatman lowered the sail and the boat grounded on the firm white sand of the beach, the girls arrived. The boat brought, however, no packet——

'Oh!' cried Effie. 'It is Roland Lee!'

It was none other than that young man of whom they had been speaking. Armorel changed colour: she blushed a rosy red: then she recovered quickly and stepped forward, as Roland leaped out upon the sand. 'Welcome back to Samson!' she said, giving him her hand with her old frankness. 'We expected you to come, but we did not know when.'

'May I stay?' he murmured, taking her hand and looking into her face.

'You know—yourself,' she replied.

He made answer by shouldering his portmanteau. 'No new road has been made, I suppose,' he said. 'Shall I go first? How well I remember the way over the hill! Samson has changed little since I was here last.'

He led the way, all laughing and chatting as if his visit was expected, and as if it were the most natural thing in the world and the most common thing to run down to the beach and meet a morning caller from London Town. But Effie, who was as observant as a poet ought to be, saw how Roland kept looking round as he led, as if he would be still catching sight of Armorel.

'Come, Dorcas,' cried Armorel, when they arrived at the house. 'Come, Chessun—here is Mr. Roland Lee. You have not forgotten Mr. Lee. He has come to stay with us again.' The serving-women came out and shook hands with him in friendly fashion. Forgotten Mr. Lee? Why, he was the only young man who had been seen at Holy Farm since Armorel's brothers were drowned—victims to the relentless wrath of those execrable rubies.

'You shall have your old room,' said Dorcas. 'Chessun will air the bed for you and light a fire to warm the room. Well, Mr. Lee, you are not much altered. Your beard is grown, and you're a bit stouter. Not much changed. You're married yet?'

'Not yet, Dorcas.'

'Armorel, she's a woman now. When you left her she was little better than a child. I say she's improved, but perhaps you wish she was a child again?'

'Indeed, no,' said Roland.

Everything was quite commonplace. There was not the least romance about the return of the wanderer. It was half-past two. He had had nothing to eat since breakfast, and after three hours and more upon the sea one is naturally hungry. Chessun laid the cloth and put the cold beef—cold boiled beef—upon the table. Pickles were also produced—a pickled walnut is not a romantic object. The young man was madly in love: he had come all the way from town on purpose to explain and dilate upon that wonderful accident: yet he took a pickled walnut. Nay, he was in a famishing condition, and he tackled the beef and beer—that old Brown George full of the home-brewed with a head of foam like the head of a venerable bishop—as if he was not in love at all. And Armorel sat opposite to him at the table talking to him about the voyage and his studio and whether he had furnished it, and all kinds of things, and Chessun hovered over him suggesting more pickles. And he laughed, and Armorel laughed—why not? They were both as happy as they could be. But Effie wondered how Armorel, whose heart was so full, whose soul was so charged and heavy with love, could laugh thus gaily and talk thus idly.

After luncheon, which of course was, in Samson fashion, dinner, Roland got up and stood in the square window, looking out to sea. Armorel stood beside him.

'I remember standing here,' he said, 'one morning five years ago. A great deal has happened since then.'

'A great deal. We are older—we know more of the world.'

'We are stronger, Armorel'—their eyes met—'else I should not be here.'

It was quite natural that Armorel should put on her jacket and take her hat, and that they should go out together. Effie took her seat in the window and lay in the sunshine, a book neglected in her lap. Armorel had got her lover back. She loved him. Oh! she loved him. So heavenly is the contemplation of human love that Effie found it more soothing than the words of wisdom in her book, more full of comfort than any printed page. Human love, she knew well, would never fall to her lot: all the more should she meditate on love in others. Well, she has her compensations: while others act she looks on: while others feel, she will tell the world, in her verse, what and how they feel: to be loved is the chief and crowning blessing for a woman, but such as Effie have their consolations.

She looked up, and saw old Dorcas standing in the door.

'They have gone out in the boat,' she said. 'When I saw him coming over the hill I said to Chessun, "He's come again. He's come for Armorel at last." I always knew he would. And now they've gone out in the boat to be quite alone. Is he worth her, Miss Effie? Is he worth my girl?'

'If he is not she will make him worth her. But nobody could be worth Armorel. Are you sure you are not mistaken, Dorcas?'

'No—no—no, I am not mistaken. The love-light is in his eyes, and the answering love in hers. I know the child. She loved him six years ago. She is as steadfast as the compass. She can never change. Once love always love, and no other love. She has thought about him ever since. Why did she go away and leave us alone without her for five long years? She wanted to learn things so as to make herself fit for him. As if he would care what things she knew if only he loved her! 'Twas the beautiful maid he would love, with her soft heart and her tender voice and her steadfast ways—not what she knew.'

'Oh! but, Dorcas, perhaps—you are not quite sure—we do not know—one may be mistaken.'

'*You* may be mistaken, Miss Effie. As for me, I've been married for five-and-fifty years. A woman of my age is never mistaken. I saw the love-light in his eyes, and I saw the answering love in hers. And I know my own girl that I've nursed and brought up since the cruel sea swallowed up her father and her mother and her brothers. No, Miss Effie, I know what I can see.'

One does not, as a rule, go in a small open boat upon the water in December, even in Scilly, whose winter hath nor frost nor snow. But these two young people quite naturally, and without so much as asking whether it was summer or winter, got into the boat. Roland took the oars—Armorel sat in the stern. They put out from Samson what time the midwinter sun was sinking low. The tide was rising fast, and the wind was from the south-east. When they were clear of Green Island, Roland hoisted the sail.

'I have a fancy,' he said, 'to sail out to Round Island and to see Camber Rock again, this first day of my return. Shall we have time? We can let the sun go down: there will be light enough yet for an hour. You can steer the craft in the dark, Armorel. You are captain of this boat, and I am your crew. You can steer me safely home, even on the darkest night—in the blackest time,' he added, with a deeper meaning than lay in his simple words.

The sail caught the breeze, and the boat heeled over. Roland sat holding the rope while Armorel steered. Neither spoke. They sailed up New Grinsey Channel between Tresco and Bryher, past Hangman's Island, past Cromwell's Castle. They sailed right through beyond the rocks and ledges outlying Tresco, outside Menovawr, the great triple rock, with his two narrow channels, and so to the north of Round Island. The sky was aflame: the waters were splendid with the colours of the west. They rounded the island. Then Roland lowered the sail and put out the oars. 'We must row now,' he said. 'How glorious it all is! I am back again. Nine short months ago—you remember, Armorel?—how could I have hoped to come here again—to sail with you in your boat?'

'Yet you are here,' she said simply.

'I have so much to say, and I could not say it, except in the boat.'

'Yes, Roland.'

'First of all, I have sold that picture. It is not a great price that I have taken. But I have sold it. You will be pleased to hear that. Next, I have two commissions, at a better price. Don't believe, Armorel, that I am thinking about nothing but money. The first step towards success, remember, is to be self-supporting. Well—I have taken that first step. I have also obtained some work on an illustrated paper. That keeps me going. I have regained my lost position—and more—more, Armorel. The way is open to me at last: everything is open to me now if I can force myself to the front.'

'No man can ask for more, can he?'

'No. He cannot. As for the time, Armorel, the horrible, shameful time——'

'Roland, you said you would not come here until the shame of that time belonged altogether to the past.'

'It does: it does: yet the memory lingers—sometimes, at night, I think of it—and I am abased.'

'We cannot forget—I suppose we can never forget. That is the burden which we lay upon ourselves. Oh! we must all walk humbly, because we have all fallen so far short of the best, and because we cannot forget.'

'But—to be forgiven. That also is so hard.'

'Oh! Roland, you mistake. We can always forgive those we love—yes—everything—everything—until seventy times seven. How can we love if we cannot forgive? The difficulty is to forgive ourselves. We shall do that when we have risen high enough to understand how great a thing is the soul—I don't know how to put what I wish to say. Once I read in a book that there was a soul who wished—who would not?—to enter into heaven. The doors were wide open: the hands of the angels were held out in love and welcome: but the soul shrank back. "I cannot enter," he said, "I cannot forgive myself." You must learn to forgive yourself, Roland. As for those who love you, they ask for nothing more than to see your foot upon the upward slope.'

'It is there, Armorel. Twice you have saved me: once from death by drowning: once from a worse death still—the second death. Twice your arms have been stretched out to save me from destruction.'

They were silent again. The boat rocked gently in the water: the setting sun upon Armorel's face lent her cheek a warmer, softer glow, and lit her eyes, which were suffused with tears. Roland, sitting in his place, started up and dipped the oars again.

'It is nearly half-tide now,' he said. 'Let us row through the Camber Pass. I want to see that dark ravine again. It is the place I painted with you—you of the present, not of the past—in it. I have sold the picture, but I have a copy. Now I have two paintings, with you in each. One hangs in the studio, and the other in my own room, so that by night as well as by day I feel that my guardian angel is always with me.'

Through the narrow ravine between Camber Rock and Round

Island the water races and boils and roars when the tide runs strongly. Now, it was flowing gently—almost still. The sun was so low that the rock on the east side was obscured by the great mass of Round Island: the channel was quite dark. The dipping of the oars echoed along the black walls of rock; but overhead there was the soft and glowing sky, and in the light blue already appeared two or three stars.

'A strange thing has happened to me, Armorel,' Roland said, speaking low, as if in a church—'a very strange and wonderful thing. It is a thing which connects me with you and with your people and with the Island of Samson. You remember the story told us one evening—the evening before I left you—by the Ancient Lady?'

'Of course. She told that story so often, and I used to suffer such agonies of shame that my ancestor should act so basely, and such terrors in thinking of the fate of his soul, that I am not likely to forget the story.'

'You remember that she mistook me for Robert Fletcher?'

'Yes; I remember.'

'She was not so very far wrong, Armorel; because, you see, I am Robert Fletcher's great-grandson.'

'Oh! Roland! Is it possible?'

'I suppose that there may have been some resemblance. She forgot the present, and was carried back in imagination to the past, eighty years ago.'

'Oh! And you did not know?'

'If you think of it, Armorel, very few middle-class people are able to tell the maiden name of their grandmother. We do not keep our genealogies, as we should.'

'Then how did you find it out?'

'Mr. Jagenal, your lawyer, found it out. He sent for me and proved it quite clearly. Robert Fletcher left three daughters. The eldest died unmarried: the second and third married. I am the grandson of the second daughter who went to Australia. Now, which is very odd, the only grandson of the third daughter is a man whose name you may remember. They call him Alec Feilding. He is at once a painter, a poet, a novelist, and is about to become, I hear, a dramatist. He is my own cousin. This is strange, is it not?'

'Oh! It is wonderful.'

'Mr. Jagenal, at the same time, made me a communication. He was instructed, he said, by you. Therefore, you know the nature of the communication.'

'He gave you the rubies.'

'Yes. He gave them to me. I have brought them back. They are in my pocket. I restore them to you, Armorel.' He drew forth the packet—the case of shagreen—and laid it in Armorel's lap.

'Keep them. I will not have them. Let me never see them.' She gave them back to him quickly. 'Keep them out of my sight, Roland. They are horrible things. They bring disaster and destruction.'

'You will not have them? You positively refuse to have them? Then I can keep them to myself. Why—that is brave!' He opened the case and unrolled the silken wrapper.

'See, Armorel, the pretty things! They sparkle in the dying light. Do you know that they are worth many thousands? You have given me a fortune. I am rich at last. What is there in the word to compare with being rich? Now I can buy anything I want. The Way of Wealth is the Way of Pleasure. What did I tell you? My feet were dragged into that way as if with ropes: now they can go dancing of their own accord—no need to drag them. They fly—they trip—they have wings. What is art?—what is work?—what is the soul?—nothing! Here'—he took up a handful of the stones and dropped them back again—'here, Armorel, is what will purchase pleasure—solid comfort! I shall live in ease and sloth: I shall do nothing: I shall feast every day: everybody will call me a great painter because I am rich. Oh, I have a splendid vision of the days to come, when I have turned these glittering things into cash! Farewell drudgery—I am rich! Farewell disappointment—I am rich! Farewell servitude—I am rich! Farewell work and struggle—I am rich! Why should I care any more for Art? I am rich, Armorel! I am rich!'

'That is not all you are going to say about the rubies, Roland. Come to the conclusion.'

'Not quite all. In the old days I flung away everything for the Way of Wealth and the Way of Pleasure—as I thought. Good Heavens! What Wealth came to me? What Pleasure? Well, Armorel, in your presence I now throw away the wealth. Since you will not have it, I will not.'

He seized the case as if he would throw it overboard. She leaned forward eagerly and stopped him.

'Will you really do this, Roland? Stop a moment. Think. It is a great sacrifice. You might use that wealth for all kinds of good and useful things. You could command the making of beautiful things: you could help yourself in your Art: you could travel and study—you could do a great deal, you know, with all this money. Think, before you do what can never be undone.'

Roland, for reply, laid the rubies again in her lap. It was as if one should bring a Trespass offering and lay it upon the altar. The case was open, and the light was still strong enough overhead for the rubies to be seen in a glittering heap.

He took them up again. 'Do you consent, Armorel?'

She bowed her head.

He took a handful of the stones and dropped them in the water. There was a little splash, and the precious stones, the fortune of

Robert Fletcher, the gems of the Burmah mines, dropped like a shower upon the surface. They were, as we know, nothing but bits of paste and glass, but this he did not know. And therefore the Trespass offering was rich and precious. Then he took the silken kerchief which had wrapped them and threw the rest away, as one throws into the sea a handful of pebbles picked up on the beach.

'So,' he said, 'that is done. And now I am poor again. You shall keep the empty case, Armorel, if you like.'

'No—no. I do not want even the case. I want never to be reminded again of the rubies and the story of Robert Fletcher.' Roland dipped the oars again, and with two or three vigorous strokes pulled the boat out of the dark channel—the tomb of his wealth—into the open water beyond. There in the dying light the puffins swam and dived, and the seagulls screamed as they flew overhead, and on the edge of the rocks the shags stood in meditative rows.

Far away in the studio of the poet-painter—the cleverest man in London—sat two who were uneasy with the same gnawing anxiety. Roland Lee—they knew by this time—had the rubies. When would the discovery be made? When would there be an inquiry? What would come out? As the time goes on this anxiety will grow less, but it will never wholly vanish. It will change perhaps into curiosity as to what has been done with those bits of glass and paste. Why has not Roland found out? He must have given them to his wife, and she must have kept them locked up. Some day it will be discovered that they are valueless. But then it will be far too late for any inquiry. As yet they do not speak to each other of the thing. It is too recent. Roland Lee has but just acquired his fortune: he is still gloating over the stones: he is building castles in the air: he is planning his future. When he finds out the truth about them—what will happen then?

'I have had a bad dream of temptation with rubies, Armorel. Temptation harder than you would believe. How calm is the sea to-night! How warm the air! The last light of the west lies on your cheek, and—Armorel! Oh! Armorel!'

It was nearly six o'clock, long after dark, when the two came home. They walked over the hill hand in hand. They entered the room hand in hand, their faces grave and solemn. I know not what things had been said between them, but they were things quite sacred. Only the lighter things—the things of the surface—the things that everybody expects—can be set down concerning love. The tears stood in Armorel's eyes. And, as if Effie had not been in the room at all, she held out both her hands for her lover to take, and when he bent his head she raised her face to meet his lips.

'You have come back to me, Roland,' she said. 'You have grown so tall—so tall—grown to your full height. Welcome home!'

At seven the door opened and the serving-folk came in. First marched Justinian, bowed and bent, but still active. Then Dorcas, also bowed and bent, but active. Then Chessun. Effie turned down the lamp.

Dorcas stood for a moment, while Chessun placed the chairs, gazing upon Roland, who stood erect as a soldier surveyed by his captain.

'You have got a good face,' she said, 'if a loving face is a good face. If you love her you will make her happy. If she loves you your lot is happy. If you deserve her, you are not far from the Kingdom of Heaven.'

'Your words, Dorcas,' he replied, 'are of good omen.'

'Chessun shall make a posset to-night,' she said. 'If ever a posset was made, one shall be made to-night—a sherry posset! I remember the posset for your mother, Armorel, and for your grandmother, the first day she came here with her sweetheart. A sherry posset you shall have—hot and strong!'

The old man sat down and threw small lumps of coal upon the fire. Then the flames leaped up, and the red light played about the room and showed the golden torque round Armorel's neck and played upon her glowing face as she took her fiddle and stood up in the old place to play to them in the old fashion.

Dorcas sat opposite her husband. At her left hand, Chessun with her spinning-wheel. It was all—except for the Ancient Lady and the hooded chair—all exactly as Roland remembered it nearly six years before. Yet, as Armorel said, though outside there was the music of the waves and within the music of her violin—the music was set to other words and arranged for another key. Between himself of that time and of the present, how great a gulf!

Armorel finished tuning, and looked towards her master.

'"Dissembling Love"!' he commanded. ''Tis a moving piece, and you play it rarely. "Dissembling Love"!'

Also published by Llanerch:

SCILLY AND ITS LEGENDS
by H. J. Whitfeld.

POPULAR ROMANCES
OF THE WEST OF ENGLAND:
THE TRADITIONS OF
OLD CORNWALL
by Robert Hunt.

HEARTHSIDE STORIES OF
WEST CORNWALL
by W. Bottrell.

From booksellers. For a
complete list of our facsimile
reprints and small-press
editions, write to:
LLANERCH PUBLISHERS,
FELINFACH, LAMPETER,
DYFED, SA48 8PJ.